I0715527

That's LIFE

ANZLEY LUKEHART

To Uncle Thomas. You have been my biggest supporter since I mentioned I wanted to write at a young age. You convinced me to not give up, you listened to all my outlandish ideas, and always gave real feedback. I wouldn't have gotten this far if it weren't for you and your constant pestering. Thank you for being the best.

Note from the Author

Before jumping into the book, I want to take note of a few things. I understand everyone's sensitivities and triggers are unique, and I want to ensure you approach this book with full awareness. This book includes a few triggers, including:

Drug/alcohol abuse

Explicit sexual content

Depressive states

Attempted suicide

Abuse

If you believe that any of these topics may be triggering for you, I encourage you to take care of yourself while reading. It's okay to pause, take breaks, or skip certain sections if needed. However you decide to read, I hope you enjoy the journey!

–Anzley Lukehart

Chapter 1

Life hasn't been bad. It hasn't been great, but it hasn't been bad. I think I have all of you to thank for that.

I always expected more out of life. More happiness, more love, more comfort. More support and laughter. More of all things I could ever want or need. What I didn't expect was more death and tears. More leaving. More drugs, more booze, more heartbreak. More of feeling like I had nothing and no one. Most of all, I never expected to want—more than anything—to have nothing. To end it all. To be gone from where I am. Knowing what I know now, I'd give anything to have less.

*   *   *

The head laying in my lap stirs, distracting me from my thoughts and mindless phone scrolling. Smiling, I run my hand over her long brown hair. Her eyes flutter, signaling she's close to waking up.

Said head belongs to my little sister, Suzie, the most important thing in my life. Even now as I look at her, I have no idea how something so pure and perfect could have come from such a fucked-up and dysfunctional family. But Suzie is exactly that. Perfect. The pink tint on her cheeks from sleeping against my leg makes the grin grow bigger on my face. She never changes, this teenager who only yesterday was a six-year-old, always wearing the same innocent look, the same sweet and loving heart.

"Hey, Bug. I was just going to wake you up. It's ten, so you should probably go to bed." I grab her shoulder and shake her a little, getting her to fully wake up.

After rubbing her eyes, she squints at me and sits up. Her eyes dart around the room, confused about where she is. It makes me laugh; she's always been such a heavy sleeper.

"Alright. Night, Jace." She stands up, holding onto my shoulder for support before steadying herself. "Don't you dare watch any more of the show without me!"

She pats my back before she leaves. I glance at the TV and chuckle. I know how she feels about missing her shows. Once I know she's asleep, I turn it off and resume scrolling on my phone. Like I'd ever watch that dumb show on purpose anyway. It's some paranormal show she's into, no doubt because the two main characters aren't bad to look at.

I know Suzie asked me to watch that show with her to get me out of my room. Usually, she's out with friends or doing homework. I've been spending a lot of time alone. I've been going through a…thing, I guess. But Suzie's been trying to keep me in check. It's cute that she thinks I don't know what's going on.

My family is always scattered around the house at this time of night. Mom, when she chooses to be here, is in her chair reading some book I'm almost positive its erotica. Dad, of course, is in the bedroom he never leaves. My two brothers are in the kitchen arguing about some online video game.

Mom was the type of person who wasn't going to be done having babies until she had a girl. Tyson, my oldest brother, is twenty-six. He's a rough one. He dropped out of high school pretty much before he even started, though it wasn't because he was lazy. He had his reasons. My other brother, Will, just turned twenty-four. He's a normal kid. Goes to community college and gets pretty good grades. He takes it seriously. Then he comes home to clean or torture whoever he sees first. He has a huge, goofy personality, but also the worst anger.

I'm the next in line. I'm twenty-one. I honestly don't know if there's anything special to talk about. I'm a closet drug addict. I attend and get good grades at the local community college, the one Will pressured me to go to. He thinks going to school and getting a degree can set your life up for success, so he got me to enroll in some core classes. What am I majoring in? No fucking clue. I'd love to argue that our asshole dad has a degree and is less than successful, but I don't because Will genuinely likes school and I don't want to ruin that for him.

Next, we have our sweet Suzie. The golden child. The one person in this family that's quite literally perfect. She's everyone's favorite. I know my brothers and I would kill for her, no second thought to it. She's seventeen and a stellar student. She's involved in all the extracurricular things. Never has an attitude. Never sneaks out at night (or back in in the mornings). Most importantly, she's naïve to the family drama and everyone else's imperfections. Maybe that's what keeps her going, keeps her motivated. Whatever it is, we all have an unspoken agreement to not ruin it for her. Still, I find it a tad hard to believe that she doesn't see or hear half the shit that goes on around here.

"Wow, you're out of your cave this late at night?" Will plops onto the couch, spilling his popcorn all over the both of us. "Should I be concerned?"

"Nah, man, it just looks like it. I'm actually still in my room." I flick the popcorn he spilled on me back at him.

"Don't be an ass. It's been a while since I've seen you out in the open. Ya know, communicating and stuff." He tries to make it a joke but I can see the concern on his face. "What have you been up to these past few months?"

This would be why I'm always hiding. I hate it when everyone starts asking me about where I am or what I'm doing. I'm 100 percent an introvert, and I prefer being an introvert alone and locked away.

I throw some of his popcorn in my mouth and chew it before answering. I'm not sure what kind of answer he's looking for, so I pull one out of my ass. "Homework. I've been trying to catch up for these damn midterms." I rub my palms on my thighs, looking away to avoid eye contact.

"What, studying for weeks at a time?" a new voice chimes in as Tyson walks into the room.

Fuck, I hate being around everyone. It always turns into some type of interrogation and all I can think about is how long I have to endure this shit before I can go back to my room. It's the worst when they both gang up on me.

"Yeah, these midterms are no joke. I hardly have time for myself." I make eye contact with Tyson, then turn to look back at Will. Neither shows any indication that they do or don't believe me.

Will laughs. "Jace, if you had time for yourself, you wouldn't even do anything. What do you do for fun?"

I glare at him. I hate that I don't have an answer. Well, I do. But I don't think "drink until I pass out" or "pop pills with my friends until we forget we exist" is going to go over well with them. So I say, "Umm…read." It's not a lie. I used to read an insane number of books.

Tyson's eyes narrow at me and he tilts his head as if he can smell my bullshit from across the room. "I don't think midterms are coming up soon, and I also don't think it takes that much time out of your day to study for them," he says, leaning on the doorframe between the kitchen and the living room.

"They're coming up, but also still kind of far away. You're really studying for them now?" Will leans onto his elbows to look at me. You can almost see the panic in his eyes, probably wondering if he should be studying too.

I decide to ignore Will and leave him to his internal panic. "Come on, Tyson, let's not bring school into the mix. I know that's a hard subject for you to comprehend, and we wouldn't want you to hurt yourself thinking about it." I let out a half laugh.

"Hey, fuck you!" he yells and storms over to the couch. Before I can duck out of the way, his balled-up fist hits me hard on the shoulder. Defensively, my arm swings up and my elbow hits Will on the chin.

Okay, so we all have a temper. And for some reason, we all really enjoy pissing each other off. Usually, it's Will pissing Tyson off while I listen from my bedroom.

"What the hell? I didn't say anything, why did I get hit?" Will's hand comes dramatically up under his chin as if it's about to start bleeding.

Tyson lunges toward me again but I lean back and push my foot into his chest to keep him off. His arms are swinging, either trying to hit me or grab my shirt—I'm not sure which—but my foot slides off and his fist connects with my jaw.

Finally, Will grabs the back of his shirt and pulls him off of me. "Dude, chill out! It's not that deep!"

I can still feel the impact on my jaw and it's for sure going to bruise. "Fuck, you, Tyson, that hurt!" I rub my jaw and flip him off.

Tyson isn't usually the one to get that upset about something. He's usually calm and collected. I must have hit on something a bit touchy.

"Don't talk shit on me. You don't know anything." He shrugs Will off and takes a deep breath.

Ah, absolutely a touchy subject, then. That will be fun later.

"Boys, *please!*" Mom yells from her chair, breaking us all from our fight to turn toward her. She doesn't even look up from her book—not that any of us expected her to. I think just hearing her voice is surprising enough. Usually, she isn't around. And when she is, she never parents.

We all brush her off, ignoring how off her voice sounds in the house. Now calm, Tyson sits down on the couch with Will between us. "All I'm saying is that you've been MIA for a long time. You act weird, and I want to know why you're using school as an obvious excuse." Tyson is shaking his hand, which he probably hurt against my face. Pussy.

Will nudges me with his elbow. "Seriously, man, if you ever need any help, let us know. It's been weird having you lock yourself away so often. We could even turn off the TV and just chill in here with you while you work. No talking, no questions. Just being together."

"Thanks, man." I give him a halfhearted smile and nod in appreciation. I know they want to help, and I wish I was interested in accepting it. "I'm going to bed."

I stand and give them a slight nod before leaving them to sit silently on the couch with each other. Before I'm out of the room, I turn back to Tyson. "Tys, I'm sorry. That was a low blow. I shouldn't have said it." I don't mean it, but I know he's expecting an apology. I leave without waiting for a response.

Our house is one story with five bedrooms and two

bathrooms—one in our parents' room, the other in the hallway that all four of us kids get to share. When we moved in, it was a four-bedroom house, but Dad didn't like that someone would have to share a room. As the years went on, he got more creative. First one of us was sleeping in the living room, or in our parents' big walk-in closet. Later, he decided to just throw up some sheet rock in the bigger room to create another. The boys got that room. They enjoy it because they can play video games together and yell through the wall at each other.

My room is the farthest from everyone. I like it that way. They can't hear the bottles or cans I open, no fear of the sound of rattling pills being heard. Best of all, they can't hear my creaky window being opened and closed at all hours of the night. The house is in a pretty run-down neighborhood, but after growing up here it's become less scary and more welcoming. It's comfortable being here, the atmosphere and the people. We all just keep to ourselves.

The door to my room swings swiftly shut behind me. The only sound present is the beep of my phone connecting to my speaker. I turn on Frank Sinatra's "That's Life" and toss my phone onto the bed. The window is open, letting in a nice cool breeze. I keep reminding myself to close it when I'm not here, but it's nice to be welcomed into a cold room.

I'm not known for being a clean person. Notebooks are scattered on my floor, I've got a shelf of books that are worn out from how often I read them, and there's a pile of dirty clothes on my corner chair. You know, the chair that accents the room well but in the end becomes a hamper. The red LED lights across the top of my wall and the blue around the baseboards are the only lights this room sees. I honestly can't remember the last time I used the light switch.

I look at the book on my shelf that Suzie got for my birthday last year: *High Achiever* by Tiffany Jenkins. I haven't gotten around to reading it. I pull it off the shelf and open it up to reveal the pages I carved out. Yes, I use my sister's thoughtful gift as a stash box. In the box is a bag with one Oxy and four Xanax. Next to that is a pre-rolled joint, a lighter, and a bottle opener. I always try to keep my stash light but full.

My poison of choice for tonight is the Xanax. I already took a few earlier, so one more should hold me off for the night. I wash it down with the water bottle I keep on my dresser and lie on the bed, listening to the melody playing. God, I love Frank. This is the only song I have in my "liked songs" playlist.

I sit up and pull the joint out of the stash box, then sit on the open window with my feet hanging out. The lighter clicks as I hold the fire up to the rolled paper and inhale deeply. The smoke is carried with the wind, pulling it away from the house and down the street.

I like the silence, the way you can't hear any life happening. Just the wind through the trees, the bugs, the faint music coming from inside my room, and the burning sound the paper makes when I take a drag from it. All day every day, it's like radio static playing through my head. The only things that break through are my negative thoughts. I assume that's because they're louder than my few positive thoughts. The silence combined with the drugs keeps me calm, makes me feel less crazy than I do throughout the day.

Still, I hate the nighttime. Every single one of those negative thoughts are always so much louder when it's dark. Keeping my room unlit and cold is my way of training my mind to never know when it's night or day—some sort of mind manipulation to throw myself off whenever I can. I'd rather manipulate my mind than break myself trying to fix it. Or maybe I've been in this state of mind for so long that I find comfort in the empty feeling I get at night. Maybe I've grown accustomed to being alone and empty. I've done it for so long it's bound to become a habit at some point. Comfortable in my own pain…or lack thereof, I guess. I'm not sure which it is.

One thing I do know is that I've gotten to a point where I'm terrified of anything that causes me to have feelings. Not that there's a whole lot that would do that, but I do know it's the same reason I've been pushing myself away from my family.

"The past few months…" I whisper to myself and laugh before taking another hit.

That's what Will said. *The past few months.* I don't know if it makes me feel better or worse that they have no idea how much I'm going through, and that it's been years and not just months.

I pull myself back into my room and take one last drag from the joint before throwing it out the window. After scouring my floor, I find a notebook and a pen and hop back onto my bed. I feel the Xanax kicking in. It warms my arms and legs and finally brings a sense of relaxation to my body. I sit up against the headboard with the notebook on my lap and pen in my hands.

The best part of the drugs is the numbness. It makes you feel like you're sitting behind a screen, watching someone else live your life. If I'm honest, that's what it's like most of the time anyway. Most of the things I do, the stuff I go through day by day, are robotic. Things I assume people expect me to do.

Masking my depression and my drug use is easy but tiring. The house is always so busy, so chaotic that no one ever notices the small changes in your mood or personality. I'm not sure how they don't notice the fact I'm a complete zombie most of the time. I don't care either way; it makes hiding it easier.

I let out a deep breath and chew the skin on my cheek. I stare at the blank notebook, trying to figure out what I want to write, and if I have any feelings to express.

I don't even know what to write. I've never written anything in my life. I slide down the bed and turn toward the wall. Sleep seems to be the best option at this point.

Chapter 2

You guys have always helped me be the best that you could. I feel bad that school always came so easy to me while Tyson couldn't even make it past third grade. Sorry, Tyson.

The notebook rolled out of my arms onto the floor with a loud thud as it hit the other books, scaring me awake. After realizing the sound was from the notebook, I let out a long breath and roll onto my back. Waking up is always the worst part of my day. Honestly, I could go without it happening. I rub my head and sit up, glancing at the clock. Cold air fills the room, causing goosebumps to spread across my chest and arms. Leave it to me to keep my room a solid sixty-four degrees and still sleep in shorts and no shirt. I look around in search of a hoodie clean enough to warrant wearing.

I guess I should go to class today. The boys will literally beat my ass if I miss another day. Finally, I find a gray hoodie on the floor and deem it acceptable. I pull it over my head and grab some jeans to wear over my shorts.

For the past three days, I've been rocking the basketball shorts and no-shirt look. I hate putting on jeans after I've been comfortable in only shorts for such a long time. The best part of my wardrobe of choice? The less I wear, the less laundry I have to do.

Of course, the occasional times I do leave my room, I'll throw on a T-shirt or one of my many hoodies so I can keep the fact that I'm losing weight hidden from everyone. It's become increasingly apparent lately. I've got almost no fat on me, and my ribs are starting to show.

I look into the mirror to make sure I'm decent enough to leave my bubble and enter the real world. My hair is getting so long. Jesus Christ. At this point, I'm going to have to figure out how to style it. For now, I brush out all the tangles and push it back out of my face. The natural curls have a mind of their own and curve around my face and ears. Usually, they fall in front of my face and annoy me all day, so I've developed a habit of pushing it back constantly.

When I get to the kitchen, Will is dressed in his nice school clothes and Tyson is asleep on the couch. I'm sure Suzie is already at school or on her way there now. Will is the "dress to impress" type, probably the most civilized of us all. I see him going places in life. It doesn't surprise me to find Tyson asleep. He wakes up early to be there for Suzie and make sure she gets out of the house on time with breakfast, but he almost always passes out after.

"Ah, he lives!" The amusement is clear in Will's voice as he pushes something into the toaster, and his eyebrows furrow with surprise. "Are you actually going to school today?"

It's not that I actively try to skip school. Sometimes I just sleep through it or mistake my days and assume it's Saturday when it's actually Tuesday. My favorite reason for missing school is when I wake up at 2 a.m. and can't get back to sleep, so instead I stay up drinking or crushing up pills, and in the morning I'm too intoxicated to go. It may not sound pleasant, but some of those nights are my favorites.

"Uh, yeah," I say and nod lazily, pouring coffee into a thermos. "Think you could give me a ride?"

"Hell yeah!" he says. "I didn't make any breakfast for you, and Tyson devoured whatever it was he made today, so make sure you eat." He looks me up and down before continuing, obviously noting my attire. "Also, I'm leaving in a few minutes, so get ready."

I look down at my clothes and back up at him. "What's wrong with this?" I smile and take a sip of coffee. Will is very stylish, so I know my dressing like this physically hurts him.

"Uh…nothing's wrong with it. It's just that the hobo down the road is getting cold because you keep taking his clothes." He crosses his arms and leans against the counter with a dumb grin on his face.

"Ah, come on, that's all you got?" I tease. "Besides, if there's a hobo down the road, I think he has bigger problems than being cold."

As I briefly mentioned earlier, our neighborhood isn't the nicest. The people here don't offer a warm welcome to anyone, especially those who hang outside too much. Any hobo out there would probably be beaten to a pulp or thrown into a lake.

After realizing I'm right, Will chuckles softly. "Yeah. I guess the closest thing to a hobo this city has *is* you."

The toaster pops with what I'm assuming are Will's Pop-Tarts. I lean around him and see I'm right, and before he can stop me, I grab one of them, and my coffee, then leave the kitchen for my room.

"Hey, dick. That's mine!" he yells down the hallway.

"Let me grab my shit, I'll be right back!"

Once in my room, I shut my door and fill the rest of the thermos with the remaining whiskey I have. This, of course, will cure whatever type of hangover I have—hair of the dog or whatever. I smile down at my hands: Pop-Tarts and spiked coffee, breakfast of champions. I screw the thermos lid on and take a bite of the Pop-

Tart. I find my phone, my bag, and my shoes and yell, "Alright, let's go!"

In the car, Will plays it cool and doesn't ask any further questions about where I've been or what I've been up to. I can't tell if he knows there's something deeper happening and doesn't want to know, or if maybe our conversation last night on the couch was good enough for him.

I like driving with Will. He's got a very comforting vibe. It might be the fact that he literally burns incense in his car because he doesn't believe in air fresheners, whatever that means. It's a simple black 2013 Honda Civic, nothing special. I like the simplicity; I also like that it reminds me that Will is human too. He spent three summers doing nothing but working to get enough money to buy this piece of shit.

"You still listening to that old-ass music?" he asks me, turning up the volume on the classical radio station.

Everyone in my family hates my musical choices, though I'm not sure what they consider "good music." I listen to the oldies because they have good stuff to say, and I love that the story is deep, but the instrumentation sounds happy. It's why Frank Sinatra is my favorite. He sounds like he just *gets* it.

"It's not that old," is all I say before reclining the seat and closing my eyes.

*   *   *

When I get to my class, I make my way to the desk in the back. I don't necessarily have to participate, just show up. Although I hate being pulled out of the comfort of my room, I do like getting away from the people in my house. Between Tyson and Dad, I don't know if I'd survive being there all day. I definitely wouldn't survive with Dad. Who knows what might happen if I were to breathe wrong around him.

I take a seat, pull my hood up over my head, and pull the strings to close it over my face—leaving just enough room to keep drinking my coffee. School honestly isn't that bad. I know a lot of this stuff already, so it makes turning in homework easier. It's impossible to fail if you turn stuff in, regardless of how good or bad it is. I swear, you get a C just for showing up. Still, I hate that I have to risk getting called on during a lecture I'm quite obviously not paying attention to.

About an hour into class, I'm buzzing pretty good, and I have no idea what the professor's talking about. In fact, I'm not even sure what class I'm in. My phone buzzes on my desk and I try to stop it before anyone notices, but I end up knocking it off the desk and onto the floor, causing an even louder commotion.

"Excuse me, phones off, please!" the professor yells, never turning around.

I take a deep breath and read the text.

Ian: *Hey dude, Caden and I are headed to the bathroom in 10. Meet you there?*

I unlock my phone and respond. *Sure thing.*

The best part about college is you don't have to ask for permission to go to the bathroom. Well, I don't know that for sure, but I never get into trouble when I leave, and I tend to leave a lot.

I pretend to pay attention for as long as I possibly can, which is about three minutes, and then I stand and head for the door, leaving my bag and my coffee behind. I manage to trip over a chair, someone's backpack, and my own foot on the way. Safe to say, I have a few eyes on me when I get to the door. I ignore everyone and step out into the hallway.

When I get to the bathroom, its empty, which is typical for Ian.

He's always exactly on time, and I'm early. I go to the sink and wash my hands, then use the water to try and manage my hair. With my hood on, it's no big problem, but once I take it off, this sorry excuse for hair has more attitude than I'd like. It sticks up all over the place. It's now about shoulder length and curled in layers. I'd get it cut, but I fucking hate people touching me.

Caden's loud entrance makes me jump.

"I did not say that!" he says, regarding something he and Ian are talking about.

Seeing me already standing here, Ian's eyes light up and he pulls his hand out of his jacket. "Yo, Jace! Long time, bro!" He slaps me on the shoulder. "This class I'm in is kicking my ass. I'm pretty sure I'll fail it, so I needed a break. Thanks for meeting us here. What are we in for today, friends? Uppers or downers?" He smiles and reaches back into his pocket.

"What kind of uppers you got?" I ask, leaning against the wall. I enjoy uppers. They give me a temporary false sense of not being depressed.

"Uh, let me see." He rummages through his stash, picking out different pills. "Looks like I have some Addy and half a Ritalin. I haven't been getting many recently because we've all been pretty heavy on the Xanax instead. I can start packing more if you want."

Ian is the worst type of drug dealer. I'm not sure if it's obvious by that last sentence he just spoke, but it's true. What kind of drug dealer offers you half a Ritalin? I guess he isn't really a dealer. We're just a few friends who hang out and share whatever drugs we have on hand.

I don't say anything, but I nod at his offer. I scrunch my nose at both options. I've been trying to keep off the downers since they seem to make my mood worse and make me sleepy as hell. School isn't the best place to get doped up and pass out, though I do indulge in the appropriate settings. I'm responsible, what can I say?

"Tree?" I ask.

He nods and reaches behind his ear where he has an already rolled joint. He used to keep a packed pipe in his bag that he'd pull out and pass around. The more we hung out, the more he noticed I was only smoking joints. After that, it's all he keeps on him. "Fresh joint, rolled it just for you. I figured you'd ask about it when I offered you half a pill."

"Thanks." I grab it from his hand and put it between my lips, then pull the lighter out of my pocket.

The damn thing takes longer than I like to spark up an actual flame, but once it's lit, it burns nicely. When the smoke hits my lungs, it causes a feeling of familiar comfort to run across my body. The exhale only makes that feeling more intense. Pot's a good "hold me over," but it's never really been my thing. It makes me think too much about everything. Almost gives me anxiety how much it makes me think, so I try my hardest to keep away from it, but sometimes it's exactly what you need.

"I thought you were quitting?" Ian grabs the joint out of my hand and takes a hit. He leans up against the wall next to me, holding our eye contact. "Didn't you start getting that weed anxiety or whatever?"

I'd mentioned to him that I don't want to smoke because it's bad for my mental health and my lungs. Like I gave a shit about what it's doing to my lungs.

"Yeah, well, I'll quit. But when your dealer offers only stupid shit, this is the next best thing." I drop my gaze from Ian and look at Caden, who's oblivious to everything, crushing something up.

"Dealer, huh? That's cold, Jace." Ian waits for me to respond. After realizing I'm not going to, he rudely continues. "How are things at home?"

Is he really asking me about my home life right now? Does he really think this is the best time to get deep and personal?

"Fine." It comes out colder than I'm trying to be. But I'm hoping to get the point across that I don't want to talk to him about things like that.

"I haven't seen you around much, you doing okay?" He leans over and looks at the bruise on my jaw from Tyson's punch last night.

Once upon a time, I came to school with a black eye from my douchebag dad. It was the only time I'd ever opened up about anything. I told Ian what happened. It was a moment of weakness. But now, he always acts like he gives a shit.

I turn my head to glare at him. "What is this, some kind of therapy session?"

I wonder if he's been talking to my brothers. I hate this. I hate that everywhere I go, someone wants to have a heart-to-heart. I mean, fuck, my drug dealer is trying to get me to open up to him? What is this shit? It was one time, two years ago that I opened up to him for *one* minute.

"I just want you to know, we got you if you need anything, man. It doesn't always have to be about drugs." He hands the joint back to me. "We're friends too, you know. I know we aren't as close as we used to be, but I still notice things."

Caden walks toward us and takes a hit of the joint before adding, "Yeah, Jace, seriously. You have been kind of MIA lately. And when you are around, you're an entirely different person. We've tried to ignore it, but we're a little worried."

Ian gives Caden a look as if to tell him, "Shut the fuck up."

I roll my eyes and take another hit, trying to ignore the looks on their faces. "Fuck off, yeah?"

"Dude, we aren't attacking you. I just want you to know that if you don't have anyone at home to talk to, we're here, and we're your friends."

I push up off the wall. "I'm fine." I flick the joint onto the floor, smash it with my shoe, and walk out.

Great. Now I've got nowhere to go where people aren't bombarding me with stupid questions. Can't stay home. Can't go to school. What the hell am I going to do to get out of my head?

When I get back to class, I slam down in my seat, causing several heads to turn my way. I do the universal eyes wide, shoulder shrug, headshake way of saying, "What?"

My thermos is still there, thank God. I'm going to need some booze after whatever the fuck just happened in the bathroom. I pick it up and take a big drink to find that it's not booze or coffee, but just water.

What the hell. I swallow hard, forcing myself not to spit it out in surprise. I swear to God this wasn't water when I left. It was also placed back onto the desk exactly where I left it.

After getting over the shock of drinking ice-cold water instead of warm whiskey, I look around the room trying to scope out who would have switched out my drink. The room has over thirty students in it, all different types of people.

I check my backpack to make sure nothing's missing from it. I don't have anything that would be worth anything to anyone anyway, but I do have my notebook, which contains some pretty personal stuff. After loudly rummaging through the pack and finding nothing missing, I look around to see if anyone's acting strangely.

Not one person looks suspicious. No one even glances in my direction. Why would anyone want to switch out my drink? There's no one in here I know, no one who knows I was drinking, and no one who would even give a fuck.

I drink the rest of it anyway because honestly, it's refreshing, and I can't remember the last time I had water. I lean back in my chair, pull my hoodie closed again, and shut my eyes.

Chapter 3

You know, it's kind of crazy how we used to always be so against spending time together because now we prefer it. Sucks that Mom's enthusiasm to get us to bond ended before Suzie could really enjoy it.

Once I get home, I run to my room and take the first pill I can find. Between my booze being switched out for water and my drug dealer being a fucking pussy, I have less than the ideal amount of substance in my body. I can feel my hands start to shake, and the TV static sound is slowly starting to turn into the thoughts and voices I hate. If I don't get this under control and fast, I'm going to fall into a full-blown panic attack.

Without thinking, I fall backwards onto my bed, staring at the ceiling, questioning everything in life. So many thoughts are running through my head that I don't even know how to stop and make sense of them. School, drugs, family, beliefs, goals, ambitions, friends, home life, fucking everything. Everything is running through my head like buzzing bees. I can't figure out how to get ahold of myself. I feel myself starting to hyperventilate, which kicks in a small amount of panic I've been running from for years.

I stay on my back but glance over at my stash book. As much as I was thinking maybe I don't need to take anything else, I've been laying here for the past thirty minutes wondering when the next acceptable time would be to take something, anything.

Fuck it.

The contents of the book rattle as I pull it out of the shelf and grab two and a half Xanax out of it. I throw them back with some water and keep the book lingering in my hand. I twist and turn it around, looking at all the words, then look up at my bookshelf. Sometimes, in brief moments like these, I realize I'm not who I used to be at all. I don't laugh, or read, or smile, or joke.

I used to be the outgoing one. The one who would force all of us siblings to hang out. I told jokes and made fun of Tyson and Will for dying in their video games. I'd come into my room and read a whole book while eating an entire box of cereal. Now I do nothing. Well, I'd like to do nothing. Not even the thought of a good book pulling me out of this world and putting me into an entirely new body in a new place is tempting enough. I'd like to leave this world and enter blackness. Not another world where people have different types of problems.

"Jace?" a voice calls from the hallway.

I jump, slamming the book shut and turning toward my bedroom door. I try to play it off without seeming suspicious and fail. "Oh, shit, you scared me!" I half-whisper.

Suzie is leaning against the doorframe with a hollow, unimpressed look on her face. She looks down at the book in my hand, now hung to my side. "Sorry." She moves her long hair out of her face. "Will you come watch *Supernatural* with me?"

They say karma has a way of coming around and biting you in the ass. Well, this must be a part of my karma. I'm two Xanax in, which means in about an hour I'll be in full zombie mode. There's no denying that the best part of a nice downer is how it makes you sleep for hours, sometimes days. But it's only nice when you're not interrupted.

I swallow hard and hesitate a bit too long before answering. Did she see what I was doing? How long has she been standing there, and why did I leave my door open? I try to move, to talk, to do anything. She saw the book in my hand, I know she did. Would she believe I was reading it?

My breathing is getting heavier and I'm sure the hollow look on her face is reflecting off mine. She sighs and looks down at her feet before turning to leave without saying a word.

"Bug!" I yell.

She turns around, not even a sliver of hope visible. I can't tell if it's because she saw me take those pills or if it's because of all the recent times I've blown her off to stay in my room. I should tell her sorry. I should tell her I have homework and can't watch TV with her. I should make her leave and lock myself in my room so I can Xan out in peace. But as much as I hate and hurt myself, I can't hurt her. Not anymore.

"Of course I will," I say, forcing a smile. "Think you could make some coffee?"

The smallest smile spreads across her face, relieved that she's getting me out of my room. She nods and walks away.

Oh, God, please, please don't make me regret this.

I leave my room, unsure of how I'm going to deal with this. Normally I take my pills under the assumption I won't have to hide it, so this kind of kills my vibe. I usually don't take more than one if I'm planning on leaving my room. My family has this weird way of sniffing out things that are wrong, or different. That's why Dad's closet alcoholism was only closeted for two months. If you're going to get blackout drunk every morning, at least try to hide it. That's why I hide mine by hiding myself.

This is fine, I'll be fine. One time last year, I was pretty damn fucked up with a mix of pills and booze when Will walked into my room. We talked for a good hour. I doubt he suspected anything. This is no different.

I got this. I can do this. Do this for her. For Suzie.

*   *   *

"Do you think I'll meet someone as handsome as Dean?" Suzie asks from the opposite end of the couch.

I sit up more to look at her, but it feels like I'm moving wrong, or too slow. "If Dean was real, he would be asking if he would meet someone as beautiful as you."

Am I slurring?

She narrows her eyes at me. "Hmm, that your way of telling me no?"

"Of course not! It's just that I for one hope no Dean-looking dude finds you. We don't want any handsome, rugged, dumbass guys stealing our sister. Do we, Tyson?" I shout.

Genius idea Jace, let's bring another person into this conversation.

"Absolutely not!" he yells back from the kitchen.

I can see his brown hair by the doorway as he moves around in the kitchen. I look at Suzie, whose green eyes are looking back at mine, full of amusement. You can tell she's holding back a laugh. She says she hates it when we get all "older brother" on her, but I know she loves it. I just hope she never grows out of it. Not that she's going to need us around much. She holds her own perfectly. I just wish she could stay young forever.

All of us kids look the same: brown hair, green eyes, olive skin. Our mom has brown hair and brown eyes; our dad has blond hair and brown eyes. None of us are insanely good-looking, but we sure as hell aren't ugly—not really the type you'd take a second glance at, but also not someone you'd shoot down if we came up to you.

Except for Suzie. She's beautiful. Tyson always jokes that he's going to lock her up when she turns eighteen. We assume he's joking, but honestly, there isn't much humor in his eyes anytime he mentions it. Suzie's the kind of beautiful that doesn't need makeup. She never wears it. Her hair is always curled and draped down her back. She has the best outfits and the purest heart. Dean from *Supernatural* would be lucky to have her, even if he'd have to live through three older brothers beating the shit out of him first.

Suzie rolls her eyes. "I'll probably be single forever. Not that I mind. Love looks pretty fucked up." She leans back into the couch and folds her arms over her chest.

I know she's referring to our parents, and it's not like any of us have had any lasting relationships. "Yeah, it is. I suggest just never leaving your room. That way, you don't meet yourself a nice young Dean-looking kid who's going to whisp you away and carry you into the sunset." I tap her on the nose.

What in the actual fuck did I just do that for?

Luckily, no one notices except for Suzie, who just gives me a weird look.

"Ah, is that why you never leave *your* room, Jace?" Will says from the chair across from us. "Scared you're going to meet a nice lady out there?"

"Ha-ha." I lean back and flip him off. My chest feels heavy, and lord, could I use a nap. It's a struggle to keep my eyes open through the few episodes she's made me watch. There's no way I'm coherent enough to sit through this conversation.

"Honestly, though, looks like it's working. Jace hasn't been laid in years," Tyson says as he walks in from the kitchen carrying a few different types of snacks. "Or at all, maybe?" He raises his eyebrows and tilts his head in question.

I hate when they start talking about this shit. Don't people ever have anything better to talk about than other people having sex? It's so weird, especially for us. I don't want to hear about the things my brothers do in the bedroom.

I push off the couch and go to the kitchen to grab a drink and get out of this conversation. The good news is I've managed to stay awake for four episodes. The bad news is I'm drowning in my own weight's worth of coffee. Somehow, I'm ready to go to bed and run a marathon all at the same time.

As I pour another mug, Tyson walks up behind me. "Damn, brother, you're bound to have an anxiety attack with how much coffee you're downing. What's going on?" He leans against the counter, an obvious indication he's not dropping the conversation.

"Just tired," I say as I add in my desired amount of cream.

"Tired from what?" he asks with a bit of an edge to his voice.

I turn and look into his eyes. "I told you. Homework." Without breaking eye contact, I take a sip of coffee.

He furrows his brows at me. "Uh-huh. See, I'm not buying that anymore."

I shrug my shoulders and push past him. "Then don't."

"Jace." He grabs my shoulder and turns me around. "What are you doing? You haven't been right in a long time. Don't give me that homework excuse, either. I just want to make sure you're alright. You can talk to me and Will about anything, you know that, right?"

"Yeah, Tyson. Thanks."

"Seriously. Is this about Dad?" He pauses for a second, looking me up and down. "You might have the others fooled, but not me." He grabs my shirt and pulls it up, but I immediately shove his hand away. "You've lost so much weight. Usually, you're running around with no shirt on, and now it's nothing but baggy T-shirts and sweaters. You say you have so much homework, but I'm constantly covering for your ass with Dad when you skip school. I'm not buying it. I want to make sure you aren't doing anything…"

"Stupid? Idiotic? Dumb? Fucking up my life?" I finish for him. "Don't worry about me." I shove him in the chest and walk around him.

I had no idea Tyson was keeping such close tabs on me.

"I have to head out," I tell Suzie. "Don't watch anymore of that show without me!" I force a smile, but before I leave, I make eye contact with Tyson again. A flash of disappointment appears on his face. It does nothing to me. I don't care how they feel about me or what I'm doing to them right now.

Between the conversation with Tyson and the one with Will, I'm not about to stay there. Once they break the "Jace doesn't get laid" or "You can talk to us" seal, you have to get out or they never close the fucker back up.

I go to my room for my shoes and swallow two more pills. I decide I need to get out of the house altogether. While pulling on my black Vans, I half-hop half-walk to the front door just in time to see Dad leaving his room.

"Going somewhere?" he asks, slamming his bedroom door shut behind him.

You have got to be kidding me. I cannot fucking deal with this right now.

"Just going outside." My heart rate picks up and I start thinking of exits. If he starts coming at me, I should have enough time to get out the front door and run before he catches up. If not, the bathroom to my right has a lock. It can be unlocked from the outside with a butter knife, but it also has a drawer you can pull out to prevent it from opening. I can always jump out the window in my room.

"Dad. You're drunk," Tyson says. "Don't start shit you don't need to start. Especially with Suzie right here." He stands in front of Dad, blocking his view of me.

It's usually me he targets. Sometimes Will or Tyson get hit or screamed at, but if I'm around, it's me. He'd never lay a hand on Suzie. He knows the shit that would start, and it would end with all three of us boys in jail.

"I was just hoping he was leaving for good this time," Dad says. "Fucking useless-ass kids. If that one left," he says and points a finger at me, stumbling into Tyson, "this family could get back on its feet."

My chest and my fists tighten. I feel the heat of the anger boiling up from my stomach into my face. "Oh, yeah. Because the kid who stays in their room and doesn't do anything is the reason the family is so fucked."

I want to laugh, but I'm too worried about what I just said. I never talk back, but this one came without warning.

"That's right, you do *nothing!*" Dad's attention switches to Tys. "You either! Find a fucking job, be a goddamn adult. I'm tired of being embarrassed by you kids."

He pushes Tyson aside and comes toward me. I jump to the door and grab the handle, but he walks past me into the kitchen.

"What, are you scared?" Dad says. "I'm just grabbing myself a beer." A sinister smile spreads across his face. He hates me. He would probably pay money to see me be afraid of him. I'm pissed that I just gave him that power.

I open the door and sprint out of the house. Running off the steam, the anger, the fear, the sadness. I don't know what else to do at this point.

When I get to the end of the block, I stop to catch my breath. Tyson was right. I shouldn't have drunk all that coffee. My body is fighting itself between having an anxiety attack, running seven miles, and passing out right here right now. My head spins and I lean over to throw up into a bush.

After throwing up a few times, I lie down on the sidewalk to rest my head against the cold pavement. I take pills—a lot—and I drink a lot, too. To be taken out by some coffee is insane.

I want to scream. I want to punch something or slam my head into the concrete. I knew this was happening. I knew my tolerance was getting higher and my cravings getting worse, but I didn't expect the anxiety to seep through so quickly. I need to go home. I need to get home right now.

Dad fills my brain, drowning me in his face and his words. It's always me. Why is it always me he targets? I went to school. I graduated. I clean, I cook, I go to college. There must be some reason he doesn't beat the shit out of Tyson or Will. My body is shaking and my eyes burning. Every breath feels like it's being sucked through a tiny straw. I sit up and try to stand but before I do, I lean back into the bush and throw up again. This can't be good for me.

Fuck.

Chapter 4

As close as we've been, we never had conversations about feelings or thoughts with each other. We're such a "deal with it on your own" type of family. Then again, I guess we had to be.

When I finally make it home, it's almost like no one has moved. No one worried about where I was going or what was happening. Tyson's in the kitchen, Will in the chair, and Suzie on the couch. Dad's probably passed out in his bed, and Mom's in one of her things where she disappears. Who knows where she is.

It's weird to come home feeling the way I do and seeing everyone acting so normal. I guess It's expected. It's not like I talk to anyone about the shit I'm going through, about how I can't stop the thoughts from swirling around my head and screaming at me. Even when they do ask, I just shake it off, so I'm not sure why I expect any different tonight.

"Will, I need a ride to school tomorrow," I half-yell as I walk to my room. I don't stop to hear his answer. I just wanted a casual way to enter the house without people following me.

Today's been one of the longest days of my life, and it's only 8 p.m. There's no way I'm going to be able to continue on today, so I crawl into bed and lie on my side and stare down the vodka resting against my dresser. This is the ongoing battle in my head. Use up a good high just to fall asleep, or stay awake so I can have a day of intoxicated bliss. Okay, so I do have a problem. But it's much better than the other problems I'd have if drugs weren't there to numb myself and my brain.

I breathe heavily for a moment, thinking about life and my family. So much is always on my mind, and I wish there was a way to turn it off. My heart beats in my chest too hard. A heart attack, maybe? I turn onto my back and focus on my breathing. I swear my arm hurts…it has to be a heart attack.

It didn't used to be like this. I remember waking up and being excited to see my family. Now the first thing on my mind is what can get me numb the quickest, or how I can manage going the whole day without seeing someone.

I get up and take two shots of vodka. This way maybe I'll have a chance at staying asleep longer than two hours. After swallowing the burning liquid, I lean against my dresser with my hand on my chest. My heart is *pounding*. It feels like my chest is being crushed like a can.

Holy shit, this has to be a heart attack.

The room is closing in on me and the air is getting thicker. My body feels weird, and my chest hurts. The smallest sounds are flooding my ears: a clock, the wind, leaves tapping on my window, the sound of the air flowing through the vents. It's all too much. I drop the bottle on the floor and sit down with my head between my knees.

Within moments, my arms are numb and my stomach is turning. I'm almost positive this is exactly what a heart attack feels like. My breath slowly grows shallower, and my chest gets tighter and tighter.

I can't take it any longer. I stand up and bolt to my bedroom door. I run to the bathroom, knocking over a vase, and the sound of shattering glass fills the hallway. The hall feels more narrow than normal. It feels fake, like it's from a dream or a video game. It's like watching myself through someone else's eyes. I'm going through the movements but I'm not the one making the choices.

My arm hits the toilet seat right as I vomit again. Beads of sweat drip down my forehead but I'm freezing cold and shivering. The booze burning its way up my throat is a lot less pleasant than it was going down. Every time I think I'm done, I vomit again. I'm not sure how. All I had to eat today was a Pop-Tart, and that had to have come out in the bushes earlier.

"Oh, shit, Jace! Are you okay?" Tyson closes and locks the door.

I don't answer but continue puking my guts out, which turns into a painful dry heaving. Tyson kneels next to me and rests his hand on my back. He looks into my eyes. "Jace?"

I use the back of my sleeve to wipe my mouth and pull myself away from the toilet. The room is still spinning, so I hold my position just in case I'm not done yet.

Once I'm sure there's nothing left in me to come back up, I fall onto my butt and lean up against the wall, slamming my head back. I close my eyes but the lights are still too bright. Everything is too quiet. It feels like I can hear the thoughts in Tyson's head as he kneels beside me. I don't know how long he lets me sit here silently, but it feels like days. That's when I really notice how quiet it is. There's no TV on in the living room. Will isn't laughing. Suzie isn't talking.

The house hasn't been this quiet since the day Dad beat the shit out of his brother a few years ago. We all silently hid in Will's room listening to the chaos in the living room. There's always so much shit going on in this house, but for some reason, none of us have ever left. I guess we all secretly worry about one another. We won't admit it, but each of us hangs around to keep an eye on everyone else.

Will and Suzie are probably within earshot of the bathroom, trying to hear what's going on. Old habits die hard, but I'm not sure I have anything to give them. I'm still not really sure what Tyson is expecting to happen next.

The look on Tyson's face is the same one Mom used to give Dad. Scared, worried, angry, sad—a look that can only truly be described as love. Because when you love someone, they make you scared, worried, angry, and sad. The look also makes me wonder if he knows what's going on and why I threw up. Maybe he really has known all along.

He gets blurrier, but I never look away. I can feel the water pooling in my eyes. I'm tired of holding it back. Tired of pretending I don't have feelings; tired of acting like nothing gets to me. I'm so tired of being so angry, and sad. I tell myself I feel numb, that the drugs and the alcohol make me numb, but truly, they just cloak the anger and sadness. It's all I feel. It overwhelms me and controls me. The drugs just allow me to keep it to myself, to not go off on the people around me.

That same angry want-to-scream-and-punch-something feeling floods back into me. My head is pounding. Angry is all I can feel. Like I want to rip out my teeth. This is it, the breakdown I've feared. After six years of pent-up emotion, anger, and substance abuse, I knew it was bound to happen.

I throw my head back against the wall again and again and again. I want the feeling of being crazy to stop. The anger and emotion feel like they're going to make my head explode. I just don't want to fucking be here anymore. Not here on the bathroom floor or in this house or in the fucking world.

My fists are closed so tight that I'm sure I'm bleeding from my fingernails digging into my palms. Maybe the anger will escape through the open wounds. That's what I'm looking for, right? A way to let all the emotion escape me. Maybe I do need to rip myself open, or scream and hope it takes the feelings with it.

Harder and harder, I bash my head into the wall. I feel the tears falling down my face. It's not working. The feelings are somehow still building. One more hard bash into the wall, this time leaving a hole in the drywall. I can't bring myself to care about it. I'm too busy thinking of how to free myself of this shit feeling.

"Jace, stop it! Now!" Tyson stands and grabs my arm to pull me away from the wall. I pull out of his hands immediately.

"Get off of me!" I jump to my feet and throw my fist at the wall, but Tyson catches it before I can do any more damage. I bring my other hand up and punch myself in the side of the face. "I hate myself! I fucking hate myself!"

Tears are now streaming down my face. I know this outburst is a product of the vodka and nothing else. It did what it needed to do to calm the panic attack, but in its place, it left me exploding.

"Stop it, you're hurting yourself!" Tyson grabs my wrists and tries to pin them down, but he can't hold onto everything flailing at the same time.

"I don't want to be here anymore! I don't want to be here!" My sobs turn into silent screams and pleas. I'm not sure what I'm begging for.

I realize I'm lying on the ground with Tyson above me, pinning me down. "Calm down, take some deep breaths. God, you smell like alcohol…what did you do, Jace?"

Still on top of me, Tyson looks from the hole in the wall to the toilet. He's trying to piece things together, figure out where all of this is coming from. I'm the calm brother, the one who stays in his room, goes to school, and watches TV.

His grip on my wrists loosens when I stop thrashing. "Okay," he says, "we're going to stand up now."

I lie motionless, no plans on moving or going anywhere with him.

"Jace, get up."

I can tell his worry is turning into anger. Good, he should be mad at me.

"Just leave me here, let me rot." I close my eyes, letting more tears fall.

"Let's go!" he yells in my face then yanks me to my feet.

Slowly, he leads me to the door, trying to get me out of the bathroom, probably so he can clean it up and make sure I'm okay. He handles me carefully, and it pisses me off that this is what I am now—the one who has to be carried out of the bathroom after a violent fit of rage.

"It's okay. We're just going to go to the couch. Can you make it to the couch?"

I look down at both of my hands in his. "Why do you care?"

He sighs then drops one of my hands, letting it fall to my side. "Why wouldn't I care? You were throwing up, then hurting yourself and telling me you don't want to be here. Am I supposed to ignore that? You want me to just walk away from you after all that? What's going on? This isn't like you."

I'm not going to answer him. How can I tell him this is exactly me, the shit that goes through my head every day that I don't act on? That the only thing containing it are pills and alcohol, which obviously aren't working for me anymore? I don't want to have to rely on the pills to keep me from feeling things. But most of all, I want to stop anger and sadness from being my only feelings. I just want to be normal. I don't want to hate myself anymore or have to hide from everyone including myself.

I catch my reflection in the mirror as he walks me out. My regular numb expression has transformed into red puffy eyes, tears, sadness, and something I threw up stuck to the side of my face. I hate being vulnerable in front of Tyson. I know now that there's no going back to when everyone was naive about what I was doing with myself. Tonight, everything's going to change.

"FUCK!" My fist slams against the mirror, causing it to shatter the broken boy who looks back at me. My fist, now bleeding and aching, comes up to my hair and I slide back down the wall to the floor. Tears are steadily flowing down my face now, and I'm not holding anything back. "I need help," I whispered from behind my hands.

Chapter 5

Tyson, you are going to be the best dad. I think you've seen so much shit that it's impossible for you to judge anyone. I look up to that a lot.

You know that feeling when you're sitting in your shower, the water is running down on top of you while you stare into nothingness, and you just feel…gone? Like, physically you're here but your mind is gone; you aren't experiencing the real world. It's just you sitting blankly on the cold shower floor with the warm water falling against you as a subtle reminder that you're still there. That's how I feel right now. Like nothing around me is real. Like I'm going to wake up in a few hours and shake off this horrible nightmare and everyone will go on not knowing that I'm an emotional bomb.

After watching me smash the shit out of the mirror, Tyson says nothing. He isn't mad or disappointed. He just opens the door and calls for Will to come help him.

"What the hell happened?" Will looks at me, then at Tys.

"Don't worry about it. Can you help me clean this up? Jace is bleeding. We need to clean that up and make sure he doesn't need stitches. There's puke on and around the toilet, and glass every-where."

"Yeah, of course," Will says, his voice even and quiet. "Are you okay?" I feel him look at me, but I don't move from the floor. My face is still in my palms. "Is he okay?" he asks Tyson when I don't respond.

I don't hear anyone talk, but I do hear the glass being moved from the counter. Will grabs my hand and pulls it away from my face before flipping it over to look at my knuckles. "Damn. You busted this up pretty good. I imagine you feel better now." He grabs my other hand and pulls me up. "Let me help you wash it. We have to make sure there's no glass in it."

They don't talk as they clean up the blood on me, the counter, and the floor. I can't believe I did that. It still feels like tunnel vision. I have no idea how we're going to get away from this and honestly, I just want to go to bed.

Gently, they carry me to the couch, sit me down, and walk away. I hear them cleaning up the bathroom, whispering my name occasionally when talking about me. But I just sit here, still letting a tear escape every few minutes, looking at nothing more than a hole in the wall that Dad left once upon a time.

Why didn't we fix that? Why is Dad such a fuckup, and why doesn't Mom care? Leaves her kids to raise each other while Dad stays home drunk as shit, whales on us, then passes out like nothing happened. I wanted to black it out like he does, see if maybe I could understand why the fuck he does it. All their kids are fucked up and they don't seem to care about us. They're not worried about anything going on here.

From the outside, Dad cares—enough to hope he finds you doing something wrong so he has an excuse to fuck you up. The hole in the wall is a reminder of that. Or maybe the hole is a reminder to all of us about what we're trying so hard not to become. If that's it, then I've failed, because the hole I put in the bathroom looks identical to the one right there in the living room.

It's so quiet that it feels like Tyson and Will are in the bathroom pulling straws, and whoever gets the short straw has to come in here to talk to me. I'm just like Dad. I don't blame them for not wanting to be the one. Hell, I wouldn't blame them if they left me here without ever talking to me again.

Light footsteps come from the direction of the kitchen, but I don't move to see who it is. I don't need to. Not to mention, I don't want to see the terrified look in her helpless eyes.

"Water?" Suzie asks, holding a glass out to me. She isn't scared like I thought she'd be. She doesn't even hesitate to approach me. I probably need the water after everything that happened. My mouth still tastes like Pop-Tart-flavored vodka.

Moving feels impossible, even the small motion of shaking my head. I want to tell her I'm sorry, and that I feel better, and I'll never do anything like this again. I want to tell her she has nothing to do with the way I acted. Yet, I stay silent.

She sets the water on the end table next to the arm of the couch and sits down next to me. After a few minutes, I can feel her move closer to me and lay her head on my shoulder without saying any-thing else. This is her way of telling me it's okay, her way of com-forting me, and damn does it work. I mimic her and lay my head on hers. Her shoulders bounce with what I'm guessing are sobs. She shouldn't be comforting me. I should be hugging her, telling her it's okay.

She lets us sit in silence, not making me talk, and not asking questions or giving me words of encouragement. Suzie always got me better than anyone else. This is exactly what I need. Just her being here, letting me know I'm not alone.

I hate being touched, not because of the touch itself but because of the physical intimacy it creates. Once someone touches you, they assume they can continue, and then they want to know all about you and all your darkest secrets. Not Suzie right now. She's just here to be here in the way she knows best. For the first time in who knows how long, the touch is soothing and comforting.

I hate that I can still do nothing but stare at that damn hole in the wall. It's like I can hear it whispering to me the things that everyone in the house wants to say to me. "I knew it would be you"… "You're no better than your piece of shit dad"… "What, you wanna hit your family, too? I bet you do."

"Hey Suzie, can we talk to Jace for a minute?" Tyson sounds like an echo, like he's standing in a different room, but he's standing right next to us.

Suzie nods and walks out after turning her head and kissing my shoulder. I feel Tyson and Will sit down on opposite sides of me. It seems no one knows what to say because no one says anything, but the tension in the room is thick. We sit in silence for about fifteen minutes, all of us trying to figure out who should start, or what the hell we would even say.

I'm surprised they both came to me. I wish I could be the first to speak but I still feel numb, and I don't really deserve to explain myself, nor do I really have anything to explain. I'm just a piece of shit, that's really all there is to it.

"Jace…I, uh…I'm not really sure what I'm supposed to say right now," Tyson starts, his voice filled with worry, concern, and sadness. He's rubbing his hands together as he looks for the words, his eyes never leaving his lap.

When people say "on the edge of their seat," I always assumed it was a metaphor, but it turns out it's a real thing. If I wasn't so caught up in myself and all that just happened, I'd be very impressed by how much of Tyson's body isn't actually on the couch.

Will lightly grabs my hand and removes the paper towels on the bleeding wound. Then he lets out a defeated sigh. I wonder how bad it is, what it looks like to them. After we washed it, he couldn't tell how bad it was so he wrapped it up and let me know we'd look at it later. I don't give a shit about it at the moment. There are bigger things to deal with tonight. Things I'll never be ready for.

"Tys, we're going to have to take him in to get stitches," Will says and softly wraps the towel back around my hand, putting it back in my lap.

His voice is next to me, but it sounds like he's yelling down a tunnel. Maybe he isn't even speaking at all? That can't be right because I see Tyson's mouth moving from the corner of my eye. I don't hear anything else that's exchanged between them until Tyson speaks to me directly.

"No one is mad at you, it's just…it's a bit of a surprise. I wish you'd talked to us about whatever happened before it got that bad." I can tell Tyson is a little lost. Fuck, I would be too if my seemingly calm brother freaked out one day. "I didn't know you'd been holding so much in, you're always so…calm, I guess. I know we aren't the best, but I wish you would have felt like you could come to us." Clearly still at a loss for words, he clears his throat. "Is it depression, or anxiety? How are you feeling? What's going on? Is it just the way you're feeling, or… You said you needed help."

"Are you using anything?" Will blurts. He seems a little more upset than Tyson is, as he should be. I know his fears are the same as mine. Who would want another person like Dad in the house? I need to tell him that's what I'm scared of too, that we have the same fear. "You've been acting out of character for a while, are you on drugs? Tyson won't just come out and ask, but I'm not going to beat around the bush here."

Without taking my eyes off the hole, I nod my head just enough for them to see. I feel Will stiffen next to me, and Tyson drops his head, nodding. Admitting that is like a load off my back. They know I'm on drugs. They know I'm using, and that I'm depressed, and who the hell knows what else. But now I don't have to hide it or sneak around. It's odd that with the load off my back, I feel like my entire personality just flew out the door. Without the sneaking and hiding, I don't know who or what I am. How am I supposed to act in the future?

"How long?" Will asks. "And don't give me some bullshit answer like a few days or something, because you've been off for longer than that."

Thank you, Will, yes, please continue telling me how I've been a piece of shit for a long time. This is exactly what I need to hear right now.

Regardless, I finally tear my eyes away from the wall to meet his. I lick my lips before answering, "Six years." My voice comes out cracked and broken. A lot like the mirror I just destroyed and the way the inside of my soul feels.

Will's eyes widen in surprise. I'm sure beside me, Tyson has the same look. I know they were expecting me to say something like "two months" or something because surely, they would have noticed their baby brother acting differently for six years. Luckily, at that point, they had puberty to blame, so maybe they weren't complete assholes.

"Holy shit, what are you using?" Will's fuming words blow over me as he crosses his arms in front of him. A power play to show me he's mad and now closed off too. "Six fucking years? That's a long time. What. Are. You. Using?"

"William, stop." Tyson gives him a stern look. "What can we do to help…"

"No! I want to know what he's using!" Will is yelling now. I can see water in his eyes threatening to fall. Is this good cop, bad cop? Did they plan this? I assume not because Will is genuinely boiling over with anger, and Tys just wants to make sure I'm okay.

"I think it's more important that we get him help right now—" Tyson starts, but I interrupt after I decide to throw Will a bone. I'd be the same way if I found this out about anyone, and I'd rather push them to the point of hating me rather than trying to deep-dive into my heart.

I take a deep breath and spit it out. "Xanax, Klonopin, Adderall, alcohol, Ritalin, pot, codeine. Anything I can find, really," I say, pulling at the strings on my basketball shorts. "I'm a non-discriminatory drug user." I give them a soft smile, trying to lighten the mood. Not sure how I went from not being able to talk to making fucking jokes.

"You think it's funny?" Tyson snaps. "This is serious, Jace. I had no idea. I assumed it was a pain pill that you'd been taking for a few weeks. Six years, and all of those?! How did we not notice this? How have you survived this long?" He's getting upset now.

"My family isn't very observant when it comes to the younger people in the house, I guess," I say. "I never had any problems hiding anything until recently, when for some reason you two decided to give a crap."

I have no idea where that came from, or why I said it. Sure, it's true, but it isn't something I'd ever imagine saying out loud, especially at a time like this.

Silence. Silence from the both of them. Silence is never good in this house.

Chapter 6

Will, no one is angrier than you are. You handle it well, though, always letting it out in jokes about Tyson being dumb.

Will starts laughing. Like, laughing a lot. It throws Tyson and me off as we shoot our heads in his direction.

"I mean, I get it," Will says. "I do. But what…Dad looks like a good role model? You want to follow in that direction? Are you fucking *kidding* me?" He stands up and lets a few tears fall through the laughter. "I shouldn't be surprised. You always have acted the most like him."

The statement hurts more than I would have expected. He's right. They all are. I always have been the most like Dad. Mom used to tell me that all the time; how I reminded her of him when he was younger. Back then, it was meant as a compliment; that it was only a matter of time before I grew up to act just like an adult version of him.

"Will, that's enough!" Tyson stands and takes a step toward Will. "You think this is going to fucking help? He feels like shit. I don't know about you, but to me this doesn't seem like the best time to be knocking down his confidence."

To be fair, I'd be concerned if someone wasn't upset. I know Will isn't really mad at me. He's just worried about me. But his words still hurt, and I wish I wasn't feeling so numb so I could fight him.

"No, seriously. He thinks life hasn't been shitty for us too?" Will says. "Like we've just been fine and dandy and he's the only one going through shit? Just because we wear it well doesn't mean we aren't hurting too." He turns back to me. "You gonna start hitting us? Huh? Telling us we're the problem and the reason you do what you do? Fuck you, Jace."

Defensively, I stand and rush at Will, our chests almost touching. I want to tell him off. I didn't see anyone calling Tyson "Dad" when he punched me in the face the other day. "Fuck *me*? Dad doesn't hit you! He hits me, he comes after *me*. Don't ever throw that in my face again because you hardly know how it feels to be a victim of Dad."

"Jace, he's just worried!" Tyson says, pulling on my arm. I wouldn't believe him if it wasn't for the tears in Will's eyes.

I sit back down, never taking my eyes off Will. "What I meant was, 'Yes, William, that's exactly what I'm going to start doing.'" I roll my eyes.

"No? Then what? You named off a lot of drugs, and I assume because you're self-medicating that you're just throwing them down left and right. You're gonna end up fucking killing yourself!" Will yells, finally letting himself full-on cry.

I can feel the boiling again, the rage under my skin. "Maybe that's the fucking goal!" I swat the glass of water off the table. It flies to the wall and hits the floor with a thud, but it doesn't break. I don't want to say anything else or make them feel worse than they already do, so I storm to my room.

This isn't me. I'm usually very well-tempered and calm. I mind my own business. For as long as I can remember, I've never really yelled at anyone. But the moment I let my guard down and ask for help, I get treated like this? Fuck that. I'm not even sure I meant it anyway. Maybe I just said it as a way to get Tyson off my back. I don't know what I'm doing. I don't know what I want.

Maybe I *am* Dad. Maybe someday I'm going to blame all my problems on someone else, and maybe I'll lay hands on them. If you have a parent who's addicted to something, you can either learn from them or do as they do. How did they expect four kids to be the kind to learn from the experience, anyway?

Right now, the biggest question is: What's Tyson going to make me do? I'm not even sure what my asking for help meant. A therapist? Rehab? Being grounded forever? Maybe they'll take the door off my bedroom so they can always see what I'm doing.

Fuuuccckkk.

I run my hands through my hair and look down at the hand I used to punch the mirror. The glass got me pretty damn good up to my wrist, and as I figured, I have eight bloody fingernail indents in my palms. I guess I can mark *Have a panic attack so big you'll never be able to come back from it* off my bucket list. I wondered when I'd accomplish that one.

I get to my room and throw myself onto my bed. More thoughts are stirring through my head than ever before. What am I going to do? How am I supposed to act around everyone now? Do things just go back to normal, or will they always be on my ass?

The bedroom door creaks open, and when I look up, Suzie is walking in, her head hung low.

"Hey, Bug." My words seemed forced.

"Are you going to kill yourself?" she asks.

The look on her face breaks my heart. How the hell do I answer that? I don't want to lie and tell her I haven't thought about it, or that I don't care if I do. But maybe, with whatever Tyson is planning…maybe I'll change. Maybe things will get better.

I pat the bed beside me, signaling for her to come sit. Now it's my turn to comfort her. I know she heard everything I said to Will and Tyson. She sits, and I lay back and pull her into me so her head is lying on my chest and my arm is wrapped around her.

"I was mad," I tell her. "Will was pushing my buttons. Don't worry about me." I kiss the top of her head.

"So, you aren't?" I feel her head move so she can look up at me.

I take a breath. "Can't get rid of me that easy." I smile and poke her cheek. She doesn't smile back. I can tell she isn't convinced. But what else can I say? "I'll work on it. It's been exhausting feeling the way I've been feeling for so long. I think I'm ready to actually try to work on whatever fucked-up shit is going on in my head."

She nods slightly. "I'm sorry you've been feeling that way. I wish I would have known the extent of it. I could have found ways to…help, or something."

I pull her away so I can look at her face. "Hey, there's nothing you could have done to help. This is a personal situation. No one could have done anything, no one but me."

We stay silent, just enjoying each other being here, both of us focused on our breathing, thinking about everything that happened.

Suzie's voice breaks the silence. "Can I sleep in here tonight?"

Nodding, I reach across the bed to grab another pillow, then pull the blankets over us. "Of course you can."

"Are you going to stop doing drugs?" she asks.

I take a deep breath but don't answer. Am I going to stop? I've never tried to. I assume it won't be easy, and that it will probably be more trouble than it's worth. I've seen movies of people going through detox and withdrawal and shit. I wonder if any of that will happen to me.

"I don't think it's as easy as just stopping," I say, letting out the breath slowly, worried about the truth behind that statement.

"What are you going to do?"

I shrug. "No fucking clue. Take it step by step, day by day. Maybe even just hour by hour. I have no idea what this process is like."

"First hour, huh? What's first on the list?"

"I don't know. I should probably start by apologizing to Will and Tyson. I'm sorry, Bug, for everything tonight. I'm a damn mess and I have no excuse. I shouldn't have acted like that." I pause before asking, "Should I apologize to them tonight, or would it be better to wait until tomorrow?"

Suzie throws the blankets off us. "Don't let them go to bed like this. I know they would appreciate it more if you were to go talk to them now. A lot happened tonight, a lot of new stuff, and everyone's anger came out. They're going to be worried about you, and if you don't talk to them tonight, no one's going to get any sleep. Then tomorrow is going to be awkward as hell."

She's right. I may be a piece of shit, but I'm not an ass. I don't want them going to bed like this. They don't deserve that. I'm not going to act like anything that happened tonight was their fault. I was way out of line fighting back like that. I just put them through an insane thing and then tried to hurt their feelings. No one does that. I'm not sure what compelled me to say anything to them at all. I should have just said what I needed to say about my depression and the drugs and let it go.

No time to redeem yourself like the present. I nod and get up, glancing at the half-empty vodka bottle on my dresser. I pick it up and carry it with me to the living room to repair everything I managed to destroy. I hope they understand it's not me acting like this. It's not like me at all.

Chapter 7

All jokes aside, Tyson, I'm sorry for all the school and stupid jokes. I know the only reason you dropped out was because Dad was getting psychotic and Mom was completely checking out. You had no choice. Suzie and I were still young, and you stepped up to take care of us. Thank you for that. I'm sorry it cost you your life and education.

I pop open the vodka and, against my better judgment and the shitty feeling in my stomach, take a drink. I figure if this is all ending tonight, I might as well go out with a bang and enjoy myself. I already threw up everything that was in my stomach, which cost me a good amount of my buzz.

I down a good amount and then toss the bottle in the trash on my way to the living room, where Tyson and Will are still arguing on the couch.

"Hey… guys."

Wow, this is awkward. I silently curse Suzie for encouraging me to do this. I should have waited longer or maybe just ignored it until it went away. I'm not entirely sure what's expected of me right now.

They both look at me. Will is still crying, and Tyson is still lost over what to do. Not only do they have me to deal with, but also the emotional weight of my drug problems. Tyson doesn't know how to talk to Will right now. We've never had to comfort one another. I figure I'll just hop right on into it.

"I'm really sorry. I didn't mean to blow up like that and tell you that killing myself was the goal of everything I've been doing these past few years." I look down at my feet, trying to figure out exactly what I'm apologizing for. "Honestly, I'm so sorry that all of this happened. I don't really have an excuse for any of it, but you guys and Suzie have nothing to do with it. I'm just…I'm a wreck. I guess tonight was my breaking point."

It's quiet for three seconds too long.

"Oh," I add, "and…it hasn't been six years straight. It's never been anything heavy or hardcore. I went through some times where I'd be sober for a few weeks at a time, sometimes a month. Not that it matters. I just wanted to let you know."

I bite my lip and wait for a reaction or more yelling. I never considered my drug use a problem, not until about a year and a half ago. I wasn't doing stuff every day and didn't obsess about when the next time I'd get my hands on something would be. I'm not sure what happened to turn me into that person, but when I did, the drug use turned into every day, usually all day long.

Will stood and came toward me. I braced myself for another fight or for his words to come out and break me all over again. Instead, his arms flew around my neck and he pulled me into his chest.

"You aren't like Dad," he says. "I'm sorry that even came out of my mouth. I've never thought that, ever. The whole drinking thing just kind of triggered me. You're an amazing person and I wish I could take all of that back" He sniffed a few times "I really am so sorry. I know we're brothers and we get into fights, and we hit each other and yell, but I promise you I've never had the thought about you and Dad being the same in my head, ever."

I pat his back a few times in appreciation before he starts again

"I don't think I've ever hugged you like this before, but now I know I need to more often." His arms tighten around me.

Softly, I push against his ribs to get him off of me "Yeah, let's not hug or make a habit of hugging. This is kind of weird."

We both let out light chuckles.

"Well, I'm glad we know there's a problem now with both your emotions and the drug thing," Tyson says. "I'm glad I now know why you do so much 'homework.' I wasn't sure what to do with the information you were giving us. But I knew you were acting different. So knowing there's something wrong…that's a good step. What do you think the best course of action is to get you the help you need?"

I think about it for a moment. Is this what I want? We don't have the money for actual help, not even if I wanted it. I'm not sure what I was expecting when I told Tyson I needed help. I just wanted support, or to not be stuck in my own head all the time. Somewhere safe that I could unload all my pent-up emotions. But I know I can't ever have that with them. There's too much going on. It'll get too personal. God knows I'm not going to start talking to Ian or Caden. They can both go suck a bag of dicks for all I care.

Baby steps, hour by hour. I can do that.

"Well, for one, you should probably take this." I hand Tyson my phone. It's not like I use it for anything but getting pills anyway. "And I don't know. Therapy, maybe?"

I absolutely don't want to go to rehab. And the therapy suggestion is a bluff, but it's what they want to hear.

Tyson nods and puts my phone into his back pocket. "You sure you don't need it? What about texting your friends? I mean, I don't want to be the guy who's taking things away from you, especially because I'm not your parent." He shakes his head. "I guess what

I'm trying to say is, when you want this and you're mad that you don't have it, you gave it to me. I didn't take it. I don't want you holding this over me later."

"Yeah, I only use it to get pills and listen to music. I don't really have any friends that would text or call me anyway." This seems so easy now, but I know it will get harder. "I just need you guys to know, this isn't going to be easy. It's been a really long time…I'm expecting it'll be ugly before it gets anywhere near pretty. I just need you to be patient with me and any attitude I have or whatever."

"We know," Will nods. "We're ready to be here for you, but you need to talk to us. Don't close yourself out. I don't want you to feel like you need to do this on your own."

"Yeah, you aren't alone," Tyson says. "We might not understand, but we're more than happy to try." This time, he pulls me into a hug.

I push Tyson away and take a step back. "Okay, if I knew using drugs would lead to all the hugging, I wouldn't have ever started them. So…we're cool for now, then?"

"Yes, you're forgiven for the shit that happened tonight. But expect us all to be on your ass constantly."

"Yeah, dude, but I don't do puke," Will adds. "So if you throw up and Tyson's gone, you're on your own. I don't care if you're about to choke and die in there, I'm not doing it." He throws his hands up and makes a face full of disgust.

"Noted," I say with a huff. "Well, if that's all taken care of, I'm going to go to bed. I'll need a ride to school tomorrow, Will, so don't leave without me."

"Are you sure?" he says. "Don't feel pressured to go after all this. You seemed pretty messed up tonight. Take a break if you need it. Going through all this at school would suck. Of course I'll drive you if you really do want to go… But wouldn't you rather take a break?"

I shake my head. "Nah, I've, uh… Gone to school in much worse condition," I admit. I laugh to try to hide the seriousness behind my voice. I'd rather they not know the depths of my habits. One time, Ian and I were so high that we went outside behind the building and lay on the grass for three hours straight. I thought I was going to die that day.

I walk to my room, but before I get there, Tyson says, "Wait, Jace!" He jogs down the hall to me. "What about the throwing up? Were you on something then? Do we need to go to the hospital?"

I shake my head. "No, I think it was just the panic attack mixed with the running and stuff. I feel fine. Honestly, Tyson. I know you aren't the smartest, but it's been almost two hours, I think I'd already be dead if it was something worth going to the hospital for."

He gives me the smallest smile possible then looks down at my hand. "What about for your hand?"

My hand looks rough. The paper towels Will wrapped around it are covered in blood, but I don't want to go to the hospital and have to explain anything.

"I think I'll be alright for now."

I can do the old-fashioned "super glue it together" thing tomorrow if I need to.

Tyson makes a face like he thinks I'm insane but doesn't say any more about it. I'm sure he understands why I don't want to go.

When I get to my room, Suzie is asleep. I'm guessing the excessive crying I put everyone through got us all exhausted. I crawl into the bed next to her and lie on my back looking at the ceiling.

I want this to be a fresh start. I hope now that everyone knows about everything, things can be different and I can start to feel better. But I can't shake this feeling that tonight might just be the beginning of more hard and shitty days ahead. It doesn't exactly fill me with warm feelings.

My mind goes back to the hole in the bathroom wall I made with my head. I should probably patch that up tomorrow. That and the hole in the living room wall Dad made the day he beat the shit out of his own brother; my favorite uncle, and probably everybody's favorite, Lennon.

Uncle Lennon had come over that day to tell Dad he was gay and to introduce him to his new boyfriend. We'd just had an amazing dinner that Mom made and watched a movie. But when Lennon announced that the man he'd brought wasn't just a friend from work but his boyfriend, shit got bad.

Turned out Dad was a raging homophobe who didn't take too kindly to the news. He beat the fuck out of Uncle Lennon and put him in the hospital for a week. I know for a fact he wanted to kill him.

We haven't heard from him since. I think about him a lot. I miss him. That whole night Dad kept mumbling about his faggot brother tainting the Carter blood with his demonic practices. There were a lot of words passed around that night. Words I didn't know. I ended up asking Tyson about them, and although he was extremely awkward, he answered every question as best as he could. He told me what all the slang was that Dad had used. He told me what made Uncle Lennon happy and how it was different from other people. Tyson gave me the birds and the bees that night— the bees and the bees, the birds and the birds, two birds and one bee, everything. But when I asked him why Dad hated Uncle Lennon for doing what made him happy, he didn't have an answer.

"I've known for a while," Suzie whispers, pulling me out of the memory.

"Hm?"

"The drugs. I knew you were getting high and drunk all the time. I've known for three or four years. I'm just a shitty person and never said anything about it. I thought maybe if I made you spend time with us you wouldn't have time to do it, or you'd remember how much we love you. I thought it was just an occasional thing, though, until you really started changing and hiding away. You weren't you anymore, and the small flashes of time that you were, I could tell it was forced."

That explains why she chose the longest show in all of history to make me watch with her. I mean, how many seasons are there, like twenty? *Supernatural* isn't even good after the first season or two. But she looked forward to it every day, so I continued to watch it with her.

"No, Bug, you aren't a bad person. That isn't easy to bring up to someone. How did you know?"

"Please," she scoffs. "I'm not sure how everyone else *didn't* know. You lost like fifty pounds super fast. You stopped eating and started acting like you had no emotions, stopped being sarcastic and funny, and started spending all your time either in your room or out of the house. The life drained from your eyes…it's still gone. I was hoping I could help you bring it back or something. After a while, I knew it wasn't going to come back." She pauses for a moment then continues. "I saw the book. One day, I came in to see if you'd started reading it and saw it was carved out with some pills in there."

My heart drops as soon as the words are out of her mouth. I thought back to the day she came into my room looking upset. She had already known by that point.

"I had hoped I got to you before you used anything tonight. I thought maybe you'd choose me instead of drugs…"

"Suz, I always choose you. Always. It's just… It's a lot harder to explain than that. It's like…" I struggle for words. "It's like two different worlds. When I'm using something, the real world doesn't exist. I can finally breathe, and my head is silent. When I'm not using, it feels like…like I'm scared to be alive. Everything feels too real." I shake my head. I sound like a psycho. "I don't know."

"Well, personally, I'm glad you had a freakout tonight. I hope you can get through this. I need you here."

"Hmm," I say. It's all I can get out. I'm starting to feel nauseous again, and the cold sweats are already starting up, probably because I know how real this is now. Already, I'm panicking about how I'm going to survive this. Am I going to follow through with it? It's been a long time of living in my little fucked-up fantasy. Honestly, I just want to sleep. Too much talking about feelings for one day.

Instead of dwelling on the day or trying to solve every single one of my problems right this second, I close my eyes and drift away with Suzie lying in a ball next to me. Tomorrow, we give this new life a shot. What's the worst that can happen?

Chapter 8

Waking up sucks, but waking up to reality isn't that bad. I guess I've spent so much time being high and drunk that I forgot how it feels to be real. I can't say I don't resent all three of you for forcing me back into real life, but I'm also grateful.

Waking up in the morning is even harder than I imagined it would be. My head is pounding, and my brain is trying to jump out and scream at me for my overindulgence last night. I'm also not 100 percent convinced I won't throw up.

Suzie was already gone when I woke up. I assumed she would be, and honestly, I'm glad she was. It's too early to have an awkward conversation with her about last night. I don't think I'm ready to have any type of conversation on that yet. I should have taken Will's advice and avoided school today. Then I'd be able to stay in my room all day without anyone expecting to have a conversation with me.

When I finally decide to leave my room and head into the kitchen, the boys are oddly super chill about everything. We all woke up and pretended nothing had happened. There's coffee made, bacon on the counter, and the usual morning arguments between Will and Tyson.

Once we get to the campus, Will mentions having to miss his first class because he has something to do. What? I don't know; I don't listen. I'm too busy trying to figure out how I'm going to get through today without dying. After he drops me off at the front of the building, he drives away, leaving the parking. The ride here wasn't awkward at all, either. We both stayed silent and just enjoyed the drive and the music.

For the first time in history, I'm ten minutes early to class. This means I get the pick of the seats. I choose my regular spot at the back, sit down, and pull my hood over my head. Just because I'm here and not on drugs doesn't automatically mean I have to participate.

My head is still pounding and of course, my stomach is still turning. I'm sure this is due to the inevitable withdrawals I'm going to have to go through. That and not eating anything. As more students come in, my leg shakes rapidly in an attempt to get my mind off of the twisting feeling in my gut. I know that if I can take just one pill, or maybe even a shot, it'll calm my body down. It would be so easy to just text Ian and have him meet me. But I can't fail on this whole "sobriety" journey five minutes after it starts. So I stick to trying to ignore the nausea and the cravings.

A few minutes later, the professor comes in, and I realize I'm not going to make it without throwing up. I run to the bathroom and into a stall, leaning against the toilet as I empty myself into it. Sitting on the nasty floor with my head in the dirtiest toilet I've ever seen, I realize this may be my lowest moment. Nice.

I should have listened to my brothers and stayed home today. But having Tyson watch every single move I make would drive me insane. I remain sitting on the bathroom floor with my head against the stall. I'm not worried about how dirty everything is. I have better things to worry about. Maybe I should go home. I know Will won't hesitate to pick me up.

This definitely isn't my last day feeling like this. I have a lot to look forward to. If I were to miss school every time I felt sick, I'd probably end up missing so many days I'd never come back. Anyway, I probably look like a goddamn zombie.

I wash my hands and rinse my mouth in the sink. When I look in the mirror, I realize how bad I look. Somehow, it's worse than I've ever looked while on drugs. I'm pale and clammy, and there are purple bags under my eyes. I look like I'm dying. I splash water on my face and return to class. When I get there, I stop in my tracks. There's a full water bottle sitting on my desk. Now I *know* I didn't put that there.

"Mr. Carter, your seat, please?" the professor says, annoyed.

"Oh, yeah. Sorry." Moving again, I never take my eyes off the water.

I sit down and look around to see if anyone shows signs of guilt. The bottle hasn't yet been opened, so I screw the lid off and take a sip. It helps my stomach a bit. I just wish this mystery water came with a mystery Tylenol for this fucking headache.

After a few moments, I notice a blonde a few seats away who's softly smiling in my direction. I've seen her before. She's had a few classes with me, but we've never talked or had any type of interaction.

I point at the water bottle with a raised brow, silently asking if she's the one who put it there. She nods and mouths the words, "Drink it."

Now, I'm no professional, but that sounds a bit serial killer-like to me. I'm pretty sure this is how people get drugged. Still, I keep drinking the water—perhaps just a bit hopeful there are drugs in it. I'll have to ask her which of my siblings put her up to babysitting me because there's no way she just decided to take an interest in me. Out of everyone here, she saw me and thought, *That one's a good one?* Doubtful.

The class drags on and on, stuff about how art and creative works can keep emotion trailing on through the generations. And just like class drags on, so does the horrible feeling in my body. I hate this. The only thing on my mind right now is texting Ian and telling him to meet me in the bathroom. All I need is one pill. Hell, I'll even take weed at this point. Instead, I distract myself by focusing on the mystery blonde.

I watch the way she moves. When she writes, I can tell she isn't taking the teacher's notes. Maybe writing a letter to someone? Or maybe she writes for fun. Occasionally, she spaces out and looks past the walls, deep in thought. I wonder what she's thinking about. What has her face scrunching like that? It's a pretty face, and she's got an athletic body, but the way she sits tells me she probably doesn't play many sports. Her shoulder-length blond hair glides swiftly with every movement she makes. She has pronounced cheekbones, and from the small glimpses I get, I bet there are dimples to go with that smile.

Now, I know what you're thinking. *Get at it, Jace.* It's not like that at all. I've always been observant of other people. I'm more curious than anything. No one's ever been interested in me, so I can't help but wonder why she is. She's got a water bottle on her desk that matches mine. She had to have thought about me this morning and brought an extra. She had to be the one who dumped my coffee out yesterday and replaced it with water. What an asshole.

Even through the distraction of picking apart this girl's every movement, I can't fathom how long this class is. God damn, I swear. No wonder I always ditch it to get high in the bathroom. Sitting here for this long should be illegal. Finally, everyone starts packing up. I grab my stuff, drink the rest of the water, and approach the blonde.

"Hey, thanks for the water." My attempt at a friendly smile probably falls flat with how sick I look.

She raises her head to greet me, and her dazzling blue eyes look at mine. With just that short look, I can feel that she understands. I'm not sure what it is she understands, but it's a comforting look that says, *I get it.*

"Yeah," she says, a small smile appearing on her face, "no problem."

She seems nice enough, although maybe a little shy. I decide to use that against her and ask her if my brothers put her up to this, and if so, which one.

"You don't happen to know any of my siblings, do you?" I ask a little accusingly.

Her eyes widen with surprise. "Um, no. But you know one of mine." She steps past me and walks out of the classroom. I follow her.

"Woah, woah, wait. Who is it?" I grab her arm, and she stops and faces me.

"Ian," is all she says with a slight eyebrow raise.

Oh, shit. I did *not* see that coming. I guess I should have. Ian is the only person I know, and they both have the same hair and similar features.

"Fuck. Really? Ian? Damn, I didn't even know he had a sister."

She nods. "Twins. I'm shocked he hasn't mentioned me." The sarcasm in her voice tugs the corner of my mouth. That's a language I understand very well, and if she isn't surprised that we don't talk about our families together, I assume it means she knows of Ian's habits. Which means she knows of mine. Well, obviously she does. She dumped out my alcohol just twenty-four hours ago.

"Yeah, very weird. Did he put you up to babysitting me?"

Her face wrinkles in confusion. "No. Why? Do you need to be babysat?" She pulls her bag over her shoulder with a curious look.

"Uh, no." Maybe she doesn't know? What's going on? "It's a long story…I guess." I run my hand through my hair, pushing it back nervously. There's no way Ian knows what happened at my house last night, or that I'm working on getting sober, so there'd be no reason to ask his sister to keep an eye on me.

"He talks about you sometimes at home. He doesn't know we're in the same class. I've just heard so much about you, I thought I'd introduce myself." She holds her hand out for me to shake. "I'm Katie."

"Jace." I give her hand a few shakes. "He talks about me? Why? What the hell would he have to say about me?" I wonder what would cause him to bring me up in conversation with his sister. Unless she's asked him about me?

She pulls her lips into her mouth, obviously not willing to talk about it, and I sigh with the smallest eye roll. "Well, Katie, thanks for the water." I take a step back. "Unfortunately, I'm not currently in the best place to make friends."

I decide to leave it at that, simple yet effective, because I'm sure something along the lines of, "Sorry, I'm battling some really bad depression and a little bit of detox so friend-making isn't really in my favor right now" would be a bit much for someone I just met.

"I didn't ask to be your friend," Katie says, then winks and turns and walks away.

Scratch "might be shy" off the list. She's a little fiery.

A smile spread across my face. I like her. I decide to throw my very recent "no friends" rule out the window and see if I can get to know her more.

"Don't you want to know why?" I ask, continuing to follow her.

Scoffing, she says, "I'm sure I have a pretty good idea."

She pushes open the front door of the school, leading us out into the parking lot, and pulls her keys from her pocket. Damn, I forgot I'd have to either sit here and wait for Will or walk home.

"Well, have a good rest of your day, Katie. I'll see you in class." I sit on the bench in front of the school to twiddle my thumbs and wait for my ride.

"You don't drive?" she asks, brow raised.

"Great question. I'd love to answer it. However, I would assume that if you are in fact Ian's sister, and you know I'm friends with Ian, you may already know the answer to that question." I nod and narrow my eyes at her.

From what I've heard, in Ian's household, it's no secret how much he abuses any type of substance. That kid is the definition of addiction; when someone says they're addicted to pills or alcohol, he's exactly what you imagine. It's kind of hard to hide a problem that big from the people you live with.

Katie thinks about it for a moment. "I guess you're right. It would seem that way. How very responsible of you. Have a good rest of your day, Jace."

Jace. The way it sounds coming from her is very menacing, like maybe she doesn't like me at all. I wonder why she's been force-feeding me water if she isn't interested in my friendship. I wave at her car as it leaves then look at my watch. Will is already ten minutes late. Where the hell could he be?

Another ten minutes later, he pulls up. "I'm so sorry. I had to take the biggest dump, and you don't have a phone for me to text."

I roll my eyes before getting into the car. "What did you do, drive to a bathroom ten miles away?"

"Maybe I did. When duty calls, it calls." He shifts the car into drive and we leave the parking lot.

Chapter 9

Our friends always loved coming to our house to sleep over. Until Dad got the way he is. The one time Will brought home a friend, and Dad thought it was me... That almost turned out very bad.

"How was today?" Tyson asks before I'm even able to close the front door behind me.

"Horrible. My head hurts, I threw up, some girl at school was weird to me, and Will here was twenty minutes late picking me up." I flip Will off for the seventh time since he picked me up.

"Hey, now, I had to take a shit!" Will throws his hands up defensively. "I told him that."

He shakes his head and goes to his room. Will is a child, and he still believes in "school clothes" and "play clothes," so usually after school he changes into more casual attire. He's trying his best to be supportive, I know that, but I think it would be best if he assumed this was easy for me. The whole drug thing makes him uncomfortable, and I can already tell he's going to get upset anytime I bring it up. I'd love to make him feel like he's helping me without actually leaning on him for help.

Once Will is gone, I turn to Tyson. "I can't stop thinking about how easy it would be to make myself feel better."

"I know, I'm sorry man. If it helps, you look like shit." He shrugs.

I don't doubt it. Last night was the worst sleep I ever got, and school was one big clusterfuck of sickness.

"Thanks, yeah, that helps a lot." I flip him off and turn to the fridge. I'm not hungry. I assume that's a drug thing. A lot of the pills I took make you never feel hungry, and that's something I still have. No appetite at all. I should probably force myself to eat before I get sick for lack of eating.

"We already knew it wouldn't be easy," Tyson says. "I'm not really sure what we can do to help you, either. I keep wishing I had the answer for you, but I don't. Other than that, are you feeling okay? Still planning on going through with it?" He's leaning against the counter watching me as I look blankly into the fridge.

I find a small piece of leftover pizza and take a bite. "I think so. It's kind of a weird situation. I'm sick because I'm not using. But because I'm sick, the drugs and alcohol don't even sound good. The high sounds great, but the actual act of consuming either, no thank you." Just the thought of any type of alcohol makes my stomach tighten.

"Hmm. I guess that makes sense. Make sure you come to me if things get bad, alright?"

"I will. I think I just have to keep myself busy."

I take two more bites of the pizza and leave it on the counter. I'd throw it away, but I know how money is around here, and I'm positive Will won't have a problem devouring it.

"For now, I'm going to go sulk and be sick in my room," I say. Tyson is silent as he watches me leave.

I'm glad to know the darkness of my room still feels like home. It pulls me in and gives me the space to feel numb. Maybe the dark, cold, depressing atmosphere puts my brain into a place of comfort since it's where I've always gone to get high.

I throw the clothes off my chair and sit down. It's too quiet with no music, and it's bound to drive me crazy. I'm not a fan of TV, so I don't have one in my room. I'm more of a music person. But without my phone, there's no music. I wish I had a computer or an iPod or something.

I need to find something to turn off or drown out my brain. I know the longer I sit here thinking the more insane I'm going to get. Finally, I remember something that could work. It's way out of character for me, and I'd never do this any other time, but right now I need an escape. I change into a pair of basketball shorts and a clean dark-green hoodie. Then I snatch up my bag with my homework in it and run out to the living room.

"Hey, I'm going over to a friend's house," I announce. "I'll be back for dinner."

Will stops me before I can get the front door open. "No you're not. You don't have friends." He puts his hands on his hips. The honesty in his voice is humorous and doesn't sting at all. He's right, but I'm trying to fix that problem.

"Oooh, is little Jacey going to get laid?" Suzie says and makes a kissy face.

I slouch my shoulders in defeat. "Come on, Bug, not you too."

"If you can't beat 'em, join 'em." She chuckles and then looks back down to her phone.

I give Will a smile. "You are correct. I don't have friends. But I'm working on convincing someone to be one. Don't worry about me. I don't go to my drug dealers, they come to me."

"Ah, nice, Jace. Good to know," Will says. "Thanks for that. Good luck with tricking people into being your friends."

I roll my eyes and pull the door open to start my walk down the street to Ian's house. He doesn't live too far, and the walk is nice.

When I knock on his door, a woman opens it and greets me. "Oh, hi, Jace! Ian just left, I'm sorry."

It makes me feel weird that she knows who I am. Ian and I aren't friends like that. "Oh, it's okay. I, uh. I'm actually here for Katie. Is she home?"

"Oh, Katie?" She tries to contain the surprise on her face that her deviant son's equally deviant friend is here asking for her only daughter. "Yes, come on in."

Confused, she opens the door for me to step in. She calls out for Katie and then shoots me another questioning look. All I can do is give her a fake smile in response.

I enjoy the fact that she doesn't treat me like some kind of outsider and doesn't linger around to make sure I'm not doing anything bad or plotting. It's nice to be looked at as a real person. That's something I don't get too often. Especially being the "bad child."

I hear the loud thud of Katie's footsteps as she runs down the stairs and stops at the bottom. "Jace?" she says, surprised.

"Hey!" I smile. "Wanna go on a walk?" I shift my weight as I wait for her to answer.

"Not really," she says.

"Oh, alright." I think for a moment. "What about food? Or a movie? I could use some help on the homework for our Humanities class?" I'm determined to figure out why she decided to talk to me. That, and it *would* be kind of nice to have a friend who doesn't do drugs. I used to be good at meeting people and making friends. Until I stopped caring.

She thinks about it for a second. "I could get some food."

"Yeah? Cool, let's go somewhere! But…you have to drive." I take a few steps back out the door and onto the porch.

With a small smile, she replies, "Oh, I remember. Don't think I let that get past me. Let me grab my keys and I'll meet you back out here."

"Okay, I'll just—" Before I can finish, she slams the door in my face. "Wait here," I mumble to myself.

Honestly, this Katie girl reminds me of myself. The me of six years ago before drugs scrambled what personality I had. As I wait on the porch, I can't help but be excited to get to know her, and maybe get to know myself again. The garage door starts opening, making me jump. I walk around the flower bed in front of the house to where the sound is coming from.

She backs the car out of the driveway and stops. "I get to choose where we go," she calls out the window.

"Fine by me. There's not a lot of women in the world who know what they want," I laugh as I climb into the car and buckle up.

"We know what we want," she counters. "We just want to feel like the men in our lives know us better than they do. You'd be surprised at how much you learn when you pay attention to people. It seems men just don't have that going for them."

I don't know how to respond to that, so I don't. I sit back in my seat and stare out the window. Once we're on the road and driving to who knows where, Katie finally breaks the awkward silence.

"So, why exactly do you not drive?" she asks, never turning her head away from the road.

"It never seemed important, I guess. Also, who says I don't drive?" I pull my eyes from the window and look at her.

"So, you do drive?" she asks, eyebrows raised.

I shrug. "Not legally."

She rolls her eyes and turns them back to the road. "Not legally as in 'without a license,' or not legally as in 'high or drunk'?"

There's a little sting in her voice, but mostly she's just curious. I don't have a license, and I've only driven a handful of times. Back when I first started drugs, I convinced Will it would be fun to take Tyson's car and go to the movies in the middle of the night. We got there to find the theater closed. Most of my driving experience comes from taking other people's cars to do stupid shit.

"Where are we going, anyway?" I ask, changing the subject. It's not my responsibility to mold her impression of me. She's going to see me how she wants to see me.

"Ah, nope, I'm a pro at this game. You answer mine, I'll answer yours. You can't manipulate a manipulator."

"I don't think those are equal," I shoot back. "Mine was a lot less of a question than yours. Besides, it's 'you can't bullshit a bull-shitter,' and I'm not manipulative."

She licks her lips. "It depends on your answer to my question. It could be a simple answer, like 'without a license,' or it could be a deeper answer like the high or drunk option. How many DUIs do you have, Mr. Bullshitter?"

Hmm, does she have a point? Sure, the few times I took cars I was probably a little high, but I've never gotten a DUI. I'd never drive if I was feeling fucked up. Instead, I decide to keep the mood playful. "I'm not sure I want to hang out with you anymore," I joke.

"I'm not the one that showed up to your house and demanded to hang out. I can drop you off at home if you'd like. I can find some food on my own if needed."

I think about the comfort my room could offer me, which oddly enough makes me think about being like my dad. Suddenly, my brain is flowing with fears and anxiety, all of the "what if?" questions you can think of. But most of all, what if I end up having a breakdown with her here? I know I have a hell of a withdrawal coming up, but how long until that happens? Could it randomly start while I'm in her car?

"I'm alright. Maybe if I wasn't so hungry, I'd take you up on that. I don't know why I thought you'd be good company." I turn the volume to her radio up to drown out my anxiety and Queen fills the car.

Though she was trying to push me away, she can't hide the sliver of a smile on her face. "I'm sorry. I don't know how to talk to new people. I hope I'm not being an ass." She glances at me out of the corner of her eye.

"Nothing I can't handle. Besides, you're the one who started watering me, so you can hardly act like I decided to start this. It was bound to happen." I'm not sure what it is about her, but she makes me want to talk and participate. I can't remember the last time I contributed this much to a conversation.

"True," she says. "I'll give you that one. What made you decide to invade on my day?"

I take a deep breath and put my feet up on the dashboard. "Acting on impulse, I guess. I needed to get out of my house, out of my usual daily routine. It's a big day for me." I do believe that to get my mind off the shit I usually do, I had to get out of my routine. I wasn't going to do myself any good going back to my room and doing the same thing I always do, only this time without drugs.

"You're lucky you caught me on a good day," Katie says. "But don't make it a habit, persistence is a turn-off."

An actual laugh escapes me—a real laugh, one I haven't had in a while. "Persistence? What do you think my motives are here?"

"The same motives every other guy has?" She smirks and taps the steering wheel with her thumb. "What, should I honestly believe you came over only due to a momentary lapse in judgment?"

I rub my face to get rid of my smug look. Her words couldn't be further from the truth. I have no other motives here, nor was it a momentary lapse in judgment. It was exactly what I said it was, just acting on impulse. "I thought you said you were good at reading people?"

Her lip twitches. "Get your feet off my dash." She pushes my legs down with one hand.

Chapter 10

Grandma used to always tell us "If you want to know, ask the question. You may not get another chance." Will, you and Suzie never pass up the moment to ask some really fucking weird or awkward questions. You two kill me...too soon?

"I didn't take you as a Denny's type of person." I look around the diner as the waiter brings us to our table.

"I didn't take you as the *eating* type of person," Katie shoots back.

"What's that supposed to mean?" It comes out sounding more amused than I feel.

"You weigh like what, a hundred pounds?" She looks me up and down before sliding into her side of the booth.

I bite the inside of my cheek. I hate myself quite a bit, if I'm honest. But the one thing I hate more than anything is the way I look these days. The constant throwing up hasn't been doing me any favors either.

"Guess so." My eyes drop to the table; the playful mood I've worked to keep going is shifting, leaving in its place an awkward, uncomfortable feeling. Maybe this was a mistake. She clearly thinks very lowly of me, or anyone who does drugs, I suppose. I don't blame her. I'm sure she sees what it does to her brother every day.

I wouldn't be very happy if someone who encouraged my brother to do things like that suddenly wanted to be my friend.

After we order our food and the waiter goes to get it started, I decide that there's no use in waiting anymore, especially if my friendship goal is being thrown out the window. I cut right into it. "So, why the sudden fascination with me?"

She swirls her straw around her Coke and meets my eyes. "I wouldn't call it a fascination."

"Interest, then. Whatever." My eyes roll almost as far as they can.

"I don't know. Call it intuition."

"Intuition?" One single eyebrow raises. "To what, exactly?"

"I've just seen some things, heard others. I guess you could say I'm pretty observant."

I pull my head back a bit. "What is that supposed to mean?" I'm not even going to humor the fact that she took my comment about her being observant and turned it around on me.

"Jesus, why do you keep saying that? I hate that question." She shakes her head and leans forward on the table. "I hear a lot about you from Ian and I always thought wow, this guy could use a real friend. The more I heard about you, the more I thought maybe I could…help, or something. I don't know. I just know Ian isn't a great friend and you don't ever seem to be around anyone else except that one guy who drives you around. But you guys look similar. I assume it's your brother."

"Help me? You told me you didn't want to be my friend. And what does Ian have to say about me? I'm not sure why he's even bringing me up in conversation."

I lean back in the booth a little harder than expected. Ian and I aren't what normal people would call friends. We just get together, do drugs, and go our separate ways. Really, it's the only kind of friendship I've been interested in until now. Still, It's surprising to me that he assumes he has enough information about me to bring me up in casual conversation. I'm almost positive I've never mentioned him or Caden to anyone. Why would I?

I can feel the anger rising. I have to remember I'm not mad at Katie, or Ian. I'm just mad, and that's okay. I take a few slow and silent deep breaths. I can't let any type of emotion out while I'm here with her. I'm making a friend, not scaring the shit out of someone.

Still, I can't help but think I should have sat in my room alone for the rest of the night. The silence would be better than this. I'm not sure why I'm getting so worked up about it anyway. People talk. It's not out of the ordinary. I have to remember that just because I don't talk to anyone doesn't mean normal people don't.

"Hey, now. Don't shoot the messenger. He just worries about you. Says you haven't seemed 'human' for a while. He's been your friend for a long time, I'm sure he can see when there's a difference in you, and it's just something he mentioned recently. I guess I just kind of get where you're coming from. So I thought it might be nice to have a friend who understands. Nice for both you and me. Someone we don't have to pretend around. I figured I'd make a move and see what you thought. If you told me to fuck off, it would be no sweat off my back and we'd just go back to how we were before. Which is not knowing each other." She shrugs like it's the simplest plan and I should have already known about it.

I put my elbows on the table and lean into them. "Do you, though?" I ask. "Get it?" I'm not entirely sure what she meant or what she was talking about when she said she *understands*. But something tells me she's telling the truth. Whether it's about drugs, depression, the feeling of being alone, being beaten by her dad, or wanting to die. Who knows? But whatever it is, she truly feels it.

"Jace, the only difference between the two of us is that you hide everything behind drugs and booze, and I let mine marinate and eat me alive." She looks down at my folded arms and smirks. "That, and you have a dick. I don't."

I'm not sure about the look she just threw me with that comment, but I truly hope she knows I'm a hundred percent serious when I said there aren't any further motives beyond friendship.

I shake my head and pull back. "Then we aren't that different." My words come out almost as a whisper. "Well, not about the dick thing, that's true. I just… I'm creating a bit of a cell for myself inside my head as well."

The straw wrapper I've been messing with rips, so I toss it aside and meet her eyes. That's when I notice that her eyes are reflecting mine. Little to no emotion. It's like what Suzie described in me. As If maybe the life has been drained from Katie. It seems as if she too would rather be in her room with the lights off where no one could bother her or ask her dumb questions.

"Wait, are you sober?" Katie's eyes grow wide and she looks proud, shocked, and impressed. As much as I hate to admit it, the praise makes me feel good. Like I've got a reason to put myself through all this shit. She leans in and inspects my face as if my eyes can answer her question. She might be trying to steal my soul, for all I know. I haven't been this close to someone else's face in a long time.

I answer her quickly in the hope of getting her to back off. "Yeah, I'm sober. A whole twenty-four hours or something." The words leave my mouth but they don't sound as proud as I thought they would. How embarrassing to admit to someone you haven't done any drugs in twenty-four hours yet fail to admit that you think about them every second. It's only been a day and I'm already having to force myself to be out with some strange girl to keep my mind off of them. It's pathetic, and I guarantee I'll get home and immediately come up with at least ten different excuses to tell myself why it wouldn't be bad to take something, just this once.

"I'm sorry," she says, "I know how hard that is. I wish I could tell you it gets better. It doesn't. But it does get easier with time. It gets easier to ignore the cravings. They're always there, screaming at you, but sometimes it's like they're coming from the end of a long tunnel. It's easy to push them away then. But other times, it's just as hard as it is the first day when it's standing in front of you, yelling."

My head shoots up and my face is probably filled with confusion. How does she know all that? From watching others go through it, or from personal experience?

"When I told you I get it, I get it," she continues. "Believe it or not, I'm eighteen months sober myself. I'd tell you my secret, but I'm sure it would make me a bad influence."

"What about the depression?" Since we're being open and honest, I feel no shame in asking. At this point, I'll take all the advice I can get. I don't think the drugs are going to get me, but I don't doubt the depression will. I've been in a deep, dark abyss of depression for a while. I absolutely hate trying to live life manually, reminding myself to have every emotion.

The waiter drops off Katie's pancakes and my chicken sandwich. I force myself to take a bite. It feels like sand in my mouth and I wonder if that will ever change.

Katie grabs one of my fries and shrugs. "What about it?"

"Did you get it…bad? How do you manage it, or does it go away?" I turn my plate so the fries are facing her. I'm not a huge fan of them anyway. I know everyone is different, and it's possible she doesn't experience depression at all. But I'd rather just throw out all my questions at one time.

"That depends on you, I think. It comes and goes for me. Some days are harder than others. When it does pop up, though, it's usually pretty bad without the pills masking it. It started happening to me after I got sober. I never had any of those feelings before. I was never sad or upset or anything. I started on coke because it was fun. Then it led to worse things, probably because all I had around me was whatever I could get from Ian." She takes a bite of her pancakes. "I'm not sure why I said that. The moral of the story is, the lows are low, and the highs are high."

"Yeah, I don't doubt it." I pick up my sandwich and put it right back down. "What about right now?"

She waits until she's done chewing to ask, "What *about* right now?"

I half-smile. "Is it coming or going?"

Looking down at her plate, she whispers, "It's been here. You?"

"Well, I'm not sure. I've been depressed and feeling like shit for basically my whole life. It's been bad, but since the whole sobering up thing, it seems like all I can think about is the withdrawal." I lick my lips and take a sip of water. "I feel so bad, and down, and it's the first day. It's scary to say, but I don't even think this is the worst of it. I think it's coming."

"Damn…I'm sorry. The first day was easy for me. It's all the shit that comes after. It's like the longer you go without it, the easier it is for you mentally but the harder it is for your body." She thinks for a moment. "I asked Ian about you. I saw you with him at school one day and asked him about who you were. After that, I sorta just continued keeping tabs on you. You looked broken and empty every time I saw you. You looked the way I felt, and the more he talked about you the more I felt we were already friends. I eventually started worrying about you. So here we are." She shakes her head. "That's why Ian was talking about you. It was mostly against his will."

I'll admit, it's nice to have an actual conversation with her instead of her just pushing back on everything I say.

Her words make me smile. "That's sweet, thank you. It's weird, though. I'm glad you decided to stop stalking me." I let out a small chuckle. "Well, how about we help each other? Let's be there for each other through all the depressive states, boring moments, or any time we just need a friend. For me, when I'm feeling low, I like sitting in my dark bedroom, making no noise, and pretending I'm not there. You could do that with me when I need you. Then whenever you need me, you can let me know and we can do whatever you enjoy."

"Okay, Harry Potter," she says and smirks, taking a few more fries from my plate. "So we can just sit silently with each other and that way we aren't alone? Okay, deal. But we also have to try and pull each other out of it. Go on walks or just get out of the house, stuff like that. It's one thing to be there for each other, but we can't let ourselves sit in sadness, either. We have to get out, go places, breathe in fresh air."

I bring my hand up to my chin like I'm deep in thought. "Deal. But I have one more task for you, as my friend. Anytime you're around me, you have to hold my hair while I throw up until I'm done with this bitch of a detox." I wink and take a drink of water.

"Really? That's one of your conditions?" She hides her smile behind her fork. "Lucky for you I'm good with puke, so I think this is something I can agree to."

"Good, because my brother might make a newspaper bed out on the front lawn for me if I leave the task up to him." Will's rant on hating puke was a fun one.

"We wouldn't want that, now, would we? Do you plan on continuing to go to school through the whole thing?"

Slowly, I nod. "That would be a lot of school to miss. Not that I really care, but my brothers put a lot of work into getting the money for both Will and me to go. I don't know how they do it, but I'm not going to put them in a position where it bites them in the ass." I pull the bread off my sandwich and throw a pickle into my mouth. I can't eat much of this, but I never say no to pickles.

"That makes sense. I'm sorry to hear that, though. I know how it is to be stressed about shit like that."

"Oh, don't get me wrong. I don't really give a shit about the overall money situation. I'm too worried about whether I'm going to make it to the next day. I just don't want them throwing it at me for no reason." I run my hands through my hair.

"Well, alright, then. I guess that means we're friends."

"I guess it does." I chew the inside of my cheek nervously. I haven't had a friend in so long. This feels weird.

"Are you two doing okay?" The waiter's voice pulls me out of my thoughts.

"Yeah, thanks," I say, and it comes out overly rude, which I don't intend. There's just so much going on.

He turns to Katie, his cheeks heating up as he gives her his best "fuck me" eyes. "And you?"

She smiles at him, looking up through long eyelashes. "It's wonderful." She gestures to the menu at the end of the table. "I see you have a deal on this breakfast here. I thought that was the one I ordered, but it looks like it wasn't. Could I maybe get that deal on it anyway?"

"Maybe if you throw in your number," the waiter says with a smile. It isn't as sexy as he thinks it is. I scoff and go back to picking apart my sandwich.

Katie looks down at her food, up at me, then back at him. "Does the number come with a name?" The look on her face is pure manipulation. How he isn't seeing that, I don't know. He's probably some shy, nerdy video game boy pretending to be some big bad player. Pathetic.

"Mason," he says. "Nice to meet you. I'll go ring that up with the discount. When you leave, there better be a phone number somewhere on this table." He winks with a playful smile.

"Sure thing, Mason." Katie looks down as he walks away, and I realize she's writing her number on a napkin.

"You're actually going to give it to him?" I ask, the disbelief clear in my voice.

She shrugs. "He was cute. Why not?"

I look back over my shoulder to where Mason is standing by the register. "He isn't that cute…kind of a dick, if you ask me."

"You think?" Katie pushes the napkin to the end of the table before signaling for me to stand up so we can leave.

Chapter 11

I'm starting to think it's true that your parents know you better than anyone else, even if you don't think they do. Maybe they really did know our burning secrets the whole time.

A few years pass. Okay, more like a month and a half—but it feels like forever with all the shit I've gone through. In that time, Katie and I have hung out almost every day, mostly at school, but sometimes we get food after class or coffee before. We decided to keep our friendship to ourselves while I go through the worst of my detox. Ian doesn't know we're friends, and my family doesn't either. It's nice to have a friend and not feel pressure from everyone. It's also made it easier for us to get to know each other.

Katie stayed with me after that day at the diner, and as she promised, she held my hair through every single puking moment. She never made me feel bad, never made me feel like I was less than worth it. In fact, I think my throwing up made her proud. It was a sign that I was following through with getting clean, which has been the hardest thing I've ever done. Like she said, the cravings got worse with each passing day. It's been a wild ride, these past weeks.

The withdrawal and the detox have been straight-up shit. There hasn't been a single day that I've felt good about myself or my decision to go through this.

One day when I was sweating to death, shivering and fighting a fever, I broke down. I just started bawling right there in the hallway of the school, another moment in life when I wished I was dead instead of dealing with whatever I was going through.

I begged Katie to call Ian, to tell him to bring me something, just one Xanax, or anything he had. I told her it wouldn't be a problem or a relapse. I just needed it to stop the pain. She didn't.

Another breakdown I had at school happened outside. I just didn't feel good, about myself or anything. The coffee from that morning made me sick, and every thought I had about booze or pills made me dry heave. Katie held me and didn't ask any questions, practically carrying me to the bathroom whenever I felt sick. Most of the time, I was able to wait until a break between classes or after school altogether, thank God. After, we'd walk to class together and not talk about it again for the rest of the day.

Katie is doing okay. I can tell she's sliding into something but doesn't want to bring it up because of how bad I've been feeling. I want to push her to talk to me about it, but I hardly have enough energy to keep myself above water. I know there's no way I can help her right now.

The siblings are great. Will has a new job, so he leaves school earlier than I do now, which works out perfectly now that I have Katie for rides home. Suzie makes me hang out with her every day after school and never lets me out of her sight. At this point, I should probably be paying her to babysit me.

Mom came back and then left again. Who the fuck knows what that's all about. Dad's been coming out of his cave a bit. The last time I saw him, he demanded I buy him more beer, which of course Tyson handled for me. Recovering addicts going into a liquor store is *highly* frowned upon, and I guess in a weird way, I'm grateful for that.

Personally, I'm not doing great. Some days, I don't even care anymore and I just want to down some shots, take some pills, sleep all day, and dig myself a hole to die in. I'm pathetic, I know.

After I asked Katie to get something from Ian and she didn't, I know it's insanely irresponsible and stupid of me, but I started an emergency stash of Oxy just in case one day I really can't take it anymore, in case one day I really need to take the edge off. Katie tells me there are going to be lots of those days, the kind where you feel like you can't live anymore or don't want to. Days when it feels like it isn't worth it. I keep those pills mostly to feel some sense of control, to know I have them but don't have to use them.

"Want to come to my house today?" I pull the strings on my hoodie and it tightens around my head. Kate and I are sitting on the floor in the hallway outside our Humanities class, waiting for the door to open. She somehow convinced me to come to school way too early today instead of stopping for coffee.

She's busy writing again. She writes a lot in that little notebook of hers. I never ask her what. If she wants me to know, she'll tell me. I like the way her nose wrinkles when she's thinking or writing intensely like she's really feeling what she's putting down.

She stops and looks up at me. "Like what, inside your house?" Her pen hits the table dramatically "I've never been inside your house. What if there's, like, monsters?"

She's only half kidding. She's dropped me off at home a few times, but it's never more than pulling up to the curb and waiting for me to get out. Usually, she drives to her house and I walk home from there.

"No monsters." I smile. "Although we do have a few skeletons in our closet."

"Don't we all. Sure, I can hang out. What were you planning?"

I make a face while trying to decide if I want to just flat-out say it or sugarcoat it. "I was hoping we could maybe sit in my bedroom, making no noise and pretending we don't exist." I know that by saying this, she'll know what I mean. That I'm not doing well and I just want her to be alone with me, the two of us in our own worlds, but together.

She nods. "Oh, yeah, of course we can." There's a slight smile on her face that tells me she's feeling the same way.

"I do have to warn you, though, my brothers and sister will be home, so I'm not sure how quiet it's going to be."

"Damn, how many siblings do you have?" She closes her book and sits up, facing me.

"Two older brothers and a younger sister. They're really the only ones you need to worry about. My dad's a fuckup and he never leaves his room. My mom may or may not be there. Sometimes she disappears for months at a time. Normal family stuff."

"Oh, wow, and you're sure you're the only one doing drugs? Because from the little bits and pieces you give me, I'm surprised your whole family isn't."

I laugh. "Yeah, just me. I'm the minority for a lot in my family." I press my head against the wall. "Try living among five other people and being the oddest of them all. I don't think I have one single thing in common with any of them." Besides being an angry asshole like my dad, but I decide to leave that one out for now.

"That feels like it has a deeper meaning," she says, "and I don't have the energy for that right now, so I'll take your word for it. I'll drive you home after class and we can hang out there for a bit. As long as those skeletons don't bite."

I roll my head against the wall to look at her. "Honestly, they might." I blow a huff of air out of my nose in a shitty attempt at a laugh so she knows I'm not kidding.

"Scandalous. Can't wait." She looks at my backpack and kicks it. "Do you ever do your homework? I feel like I always see you with your backpack but I've never seen you open it or take anything out."

I glance over at it, then back at her. "I do enough to pass."

"C's get degrees, right?"

"I'm actually getting all A's except for one B that I can't be bothered to fix."

"How?!" Her eyes widen. "I work my ass off doing homework and studying, and I'm scraping by most of my classes with C's or B+'s. I hate you."

"One of the things that make me different from my family is that I'm naturally, ridiculously smart. I've never had to stress over grades or school."

*   *   *

After class, Katie drives us to my house and parks in the driveway. "I'm really sorry in advance if things are weird," I warn her. "They're super protective, and with the sober thing being so new…they might ask you a lot of questions."

Katie laughs. "So did you when I first met you."

Very true. "So nothing new, then. Awesome. Well, you can come in, make yourself at home, and if Tyson looks like he could use a good punch in the face, go on ahead and give him one."

"Damn, Jace, I said I could take some questions, not conquer the world. Jesus." She gets out of the car laughing. "But just in case, Tyson is the older one, right?" She winks as she waits for me on her side of the car. Once I get there, we walk up to the house together.

"Also," I add, "we aren't the calmest or cleanest family, so I apologize if the house is a mess. I've never really brought anyone here, so I don't know what you're expecting or what I should be apologizing for."

"Don't apologize about anything. I'm a no-judgment zone, and I don't have any expectations except for getting out of the cold, so please open the door," she demands with a slight shiver.

We walk inside, and even though I try my hardest to creep us both into my bedroom without being noticed, Will spots us as he walks out of the kitchen with a mouthful of food. When his eyes meet us, he almost drops his sandwich.

"Oh shit, what's this? A girl?" His eyebrows are raised, and his eyes are wide. "William J. Curtis the third," he announces, holding his hand out. "But you can call me Will." He glances at me and then back to Katie. "Or you can just call me later."

I roll my eyes as Katie laughs and shakes his hand. "Your middle name is Ben," I remind him. Then, turning to Katie, I add, "And he's the only William in our family, so I have no idea how he could possibly be the third."

"Does that 'call me later' line usually work on people?" Katie asks Will, but before he can answer, Tyson comes running around the corner.

"Hi, I'm Tyson," he says, standing behind Will.

"Will and Tyson, I'm Katie." She smiles politely and looks at me for direction. All I have time for is a quick "I'm sorry" look before the boys start talking again.

"Nice to meet you," they say at the same time, which is quite creepy.

I widen my eyes at them and mouth "stop" hoping that they'll just let us go. I should have known better.

"Jacey-boy here has never brought home a friend," Will says, spitting a bit of sandwich in our direction.

"Gross, Will, keep it in your mouth!" I groan. "And Jacey-boy? I've never heard that nickname in my life." I take Katie's arm to pull her away. "Well, we're going to my room."

"Whoa, whoa, whoa," Tyson says, "not so fast! Why not stay? Let's get to know one another. Bug will be home soon. Hang out until she gets home."

"If we wait for her to get here, she'll never let us go do our own thing," I argue.

"Not our problem," Will says with a smile.

I look at Katie for her input. "Oh, come on, Jacey-boy," she says. "We can wait."

"Great," I say, "you too now?"

She smiles and shrugs, and the four of us go into the living room to sit. I guess we're hanging out like old people. I try to guide Katie to the chair so she can sit by herself, but Will practically herds her to the couch and sits next to her.

"So, Katie, what do you do for fun?" Tyson asks, no sort of accusation behind his voice.

Okay, innocent enough…

"I'm sorry, what my brother meant to ask was, do you do drugs? Or drink?" Will asks bluntly. His face is curious, while Tyson looks like a disappointed dad as he sits in the chair, pressing his elbows into his knees.

I almost choke on my saliva. "Easy, Will, you can't just ask someone that." I turn to Katie. "I'm so sorry. I told you…"

She shakes her head and holds her hand up. "No, no! It's okay. If I was in their situation, I'd ask the same. No, I don't drink or do drugs. I paint…sometimes. Um…I also like to write."

"You're just about as interesting as Jace here, then, aren't you?" Tyson jokes. "How did you guys meet?"

Katie looks at me before she replies. "Sometimes, life has a way of taking away the things that create dopamine in your body. For reasons you can't control. Trauma, for example, can force your body to remove anything that brings you joy. That way, you don't feel like you will have that joy forcibly removed. Like Jace, I've been through some stuff that changed me."

Wait… Did she just stand up for me? Also, how did she know that? I've never mentioned going through any type of trauma. Was that real? Is that why I can't seem to find anything that remotely brings me joy?

Everyone is silent. The boys look at each other and back to me and Katie, unsure of what to say or do.

"As for how we met," Katie continues, "we have a class together. I started replacing Jacey-boy's booze-laced coffee with water when went to the bathroom. He hated it. I thought of it as my part of bettering the world. Then he started stalking me and showed up at my house to demand we hang out. Almost two months later, here we are."

"Booze-laced coffee?" Tys asks, but his expression reads "Really? That's what you were doing?" I realize that I failed to mention to him or Will that I was taking stuff to school. Oops.

"I also helped him through his withdrawal. When we met, he made a joke about me holding his hair while he threw up. Turns out it wasn't a joke, and I did that a lot. He thought that one of you two was going to put him outside if he threw up because you don't like puke."

"Okay!" I stand up and walk toward her. "Enough story time, Katie. We can go to my room now."

"No!" Tyson insists. "Suzie isn't here yet and you guys said you would wait. Besides, we don't want you in your dark depressing room with a girl, it might ruin her!" He and Will laugh.

"I for one," Will jumps in, "don't want you in your room with a girl because it puts a bad image in my head." He contorts his face. "Then again, maybe it would fix your mood and attitude. Hell, go to your room, close the door, and lock it!"

Oh, God. I had assumed this was going to get awkward fast, but not this fucking awkward.

While everyone's laughing at Will's stupid joke, I hear a very specific door open.

"Jace?" a voice says, emerging from behind the door. "In his room with a woman? Now, why would he do that?"

We all turned our heads to see my dad standing in the living room holding a beer.

"He's a fucking faggot," he says. "He'd be no good with a woman in his room." He swallows the rest of his beer, never breaking eye contact with me.

Motherfucker.

Chapter 12

I've always wondered what happened with Mom and Dad. It felt like a switch, like one day we were all okay, and the next we weren't. What could have caused that? Let me know if you ever find out.

"Fuck, Dad! Back off!" Tyson stands quickly, his hand raised.

Maybe this is luck or just good timing because I've been holding back so much pent-up anger since the day I stopped using that I've been looking for a way to let it all out. There have been many times I've almost snapped at Will or Tyson for no reason. Fortunately, I realize it isn't their fault I'm feeling the way I do before I can lash out.

"No," I say, "he clearly has something on his mind. Say it, Dad. Say what you feel you need to say." I stand up and move closer.

"I already did!" He laughs and swirls the last few drops of beer around the bottle. "You. Are. A. Fucking. Faggot." His hot, beer-laced breath fans past my face, fueling my anger.

I bite my lip and nod slowly. "That right?"

His laughter gets louder. "Ask anyone in this house! We all know it! Fuck, I'm sure *she* knows it." He points at Katie with the tip of the bottle. "You think you're tough shit, but you're weak. You aren't hiding anything from anyone," he tells me, then looks at Katie. "Is he good at hiding things? Huh?"

"Don't talk to her," I say and step even closer to him.

There's a look of fear on Katie's face. Will steps closer to her in an attempt to make her feel safer. Tyson is standing nearby but not interfering. I'm sure he knows I need this, to feel in control of something. But I don't doubt he'll step in if needed.

"Sucks, too." Dad pushes the tip of the bottle into my side. "Such a pretty girl, wasting her time on such a…well…waste of space."

I squint my eyes and ball up my fists, waiting for him to say something, anything, to warrant my knocking his teeth out. Instead, he steps around me and makes his way to the kitchen. I follow him with my eyes, my body still. Tyson and Will do the same, but Katie's eyes are fixed on me.

"Come on, *Jacey-boy*," Dad says, "it's a joke. Pull the stick out of your ass." He takes another beer from the fridge, pops it open, and turns around, spilling a mouthful. "Or don't, I guess, if that's what you like."

He downs almost half the bottle before pointing his finger at me. "I've kept my damn mouth shut for years about you and who you are. But you are the problem. You ruined this fucking family, you and your piece of shit uncle tainting us, cursing us. It was bad enough that you were born, but then you spent your whole life disappointing everyone around you too."

In one swift motion, he takes another sip and then throws the bottle at me. I duck and it sails past, shattering against the wall. The burning within turns to fire—a fire I'm not going to be able to keep inside. I'm ready to fight back this time.

Will comes up behind me to grab my arm and hold me back, but I'm faster. I walk right up to that pile of shit and punch him as hard as I fucking can, square in the face. Probably due to his excessive drinking and the fact he's skinny and never eats, Dad drops to the floor.

"Fuck, Jace, you hit like a girl, you pussy!" he howls, spitting blood at me, which only pisses me off more. I throw hit after hit until my hand's throbbing, not caring where my blows land.

I feel Tyson behind me, pulling me off of Dad, holding his arms around me until I calm down.

"You better watch yourself, boy," Dad snaps. "I'll make you wish you were never alive. I run this house. *I* run this family. I suggest you clean up your act before I put you out on your ass. You're lucky I haven't done it already just for who you are!"

He gets to his feet, wipes his mouth with the back of his fist, and comes toward me. He's got blood smeared on his face, his hand, and the top of his shirt. The closer he gets, the more I can see how drunk he is, and he smells like he hasn't changed or showered in days.

What could Mom have ever seen in him? Has he always been like this? I have only a few good memories with him. I can't imagine someone just decides to change that much. It has to have always been there, right?

Will stands on one side of me holding my arm, Tyson on the other.

"Fuck you," I spit.

Dad chuckles and turns toward his room. He takes two steps, stops, and whips around as fast as he can, connecting his fist to the side of my face and forcing me to the ground. "You made me spill my beer."

Tyson and Will drop to the floor with me, watching as Dad takes another beer and goes to his room. I cup my nose and my jaw, not sure where he made contact. All I know is my whole face hurts. For someone who weighs ten pounds and is so drunk he can't stand up, Dad has a wicked right hook.

"Hey! I'm home!" Suzie walks in to see the three of us on the floor. "Oh, my God, what happened?!"

"Dad," is all I hear from Tyson. The rest of the conversation is a blur. There's blood on the floor but I can't tell if it's mine. My hand's probably broken, my face hurts, and I feel worse than I did before, which is crazy because I've been wanting to do that for a long time.

Will, Tyson, and Suzie are all talking and shouting. I can't tell what they're saying, though. It's like I have tunnel vision All I can focus on is my pain, the blood that seemed to keep dripping, the words he said to me, and the look on Katie's face.

Fuck, Katie.

My head snaps toward her and I get up, ignoring whatever it is that Will is telling me. She's hardly moved at all this whole time, but now she grabs my arm. "Where's your bathroom?" I hear her ask my siblings, and in a few moments, she's walking me down the hall.

She sits me down on the toilet and gets a wet rag. As she cleans my face and my fists, she talks softly, most of which I don't hear until she tells me, "My dad beat us kids and my mom, too. My mom got tired of it. She was always standing up for us and getting in the middle of his spats with us. Eventually, she got fed up with it and ended up… Well, she killed him."

My head shoots up. "What? Didn't she answer the door the first time I came to your house?"

She shakes her head. "That's my aunt. She took us in after my mom went to prison. Mom's still there. The justice system is fucked up. She prevented three deaths by causing one that honestly bettered the world and got a life sentence."

"Wow, I'm so sorry." I don't know what else to say. What else can you say to something like that?

"Don't be. If she didn't do what she did, Ian and I wouldn't be here anymore. Our dad came after Ian when he was eight with a knife. If Ian hadn't locked himself in the bathroom, he would have died that night. No doubt about it. Luckily, Aunt Grace took us in and gave us a half-decent life. We don't talk to our mom anymore, though. I figured since she wasn't getting out anyway and she knew we were safe, there was no reason to keep forcing a relationship. I didn't know your dad did that, I'm so sorry."

I sit silently processing her words. She really does understand a lot more about me than I thought. It's quiet for a good five minutes while she continues cleaning the blood off my hand and arm.

"Did you know?" I ask quietly.

She stops cleaning my hand and moves to my face. Dabbing the wet rag under my nose, she takes a deep breath and shrugs. "I assumed, but I wasn't sure." I'm glad she knows what I'm talking about. "You should probably get this checked out. Your hand doesn't look great. Other than that, you'll probably get out with just a black eye." She runs her thumb under my left eye and then drops her hands to her side. "Did *you* know?" she asks with a slight smile.

"Did I know?" I repeat, just to be sure I heard her right and that she's actually asking me if I know I'm gay. "Well, I…uh…I assumed." I chuckle. "Thank you for cleaning me up. I'm so sorry again about all this."

She just shakes her head. "Don't apologize for someone else's mistakes, Jace."

"I didn't expect anything like this to happen. This is why I don't normally bring people over. He's just been so…mellow lately. I figured one day with a friend over wouldn't kill me." I stand and lean against the counter. "So, what gave me away? Not that I want to keep bringing it up. I'm just curious."

She gives me a sympathetic smile. "Nothing insane," she jokes. "Not to sound cocky or anything, but when you chased me down after I gave you the water bottle, I assumed you were trying to…get at me, or whatever. Most guys only want one thing from me because of the way I look. It's why I was so standoffish with you. I was making assumptions before I knew you. It wasn't until the car ride to the diner that I realized maybe you weren't. But then the whole waiter thing happened, and I thought you were acting jealous."

"Oh, my God, I'm rambling. I'm sorry. You never hit on me or even tried to make a move, which is something that's never happened before with a guy. After a while, I saw you checking out the same guys I was checking out. You think you're sly, but you practically had a sign hung over your head."

"I don't check people out." Then again, I guess I could have been. Our school is full of some nice-looking men that I notice, but I never thought I was looking at them like that.

"Oh, yes. You do." She laughs.

"Do you think they knew?" I nod toward the bathroom door.

"You never told them?" The surprise is evident in her voice.

Is that something people usually tell their siblings? It's never really come up in conversation, I guess. "No…? I've never even said it out loud to myself."

Katie looks at the door and then back to me. "I bet they know. I've only known you for a few months and I figured it out."

"I don't think you understand how…much of a hermit I am. I've probably seen you more these last two months than I've seen them in the past five years."

"Shit. That's rough, dude." She matches my posture and leans against the counter.

I look over my shoulder to check out my face in the mirror. The left side of my face is tender. Seems he got a good spot to hit my cheek, eye, and nose all at the same time. I should have hit him harder than I did. I wish the boys hadn't pulled him off me.

"This was a fun way to end a shit day," I huff, lightly touching my cheek and nose. I open the cabinet and find an ACE bandage. "Will you help me put this on?"

"You don't want to get it checked?"

I tilt my head and hand her the bandage. "Do I look like the kind of person who should be going anywhere right now?"

"I guess not."

Katie holds my hand and wraps the bandage around it. It won't do much in the way of stability, but it should help it stop hurting so much. Everything hurts. My head and face and hand are throbbing, my heart breaking even more. It's all becoming too much for me to handle today. I let a few silent tears escape as she wraps my hand but wipe them away before she can see.

Chapter 13

The summer after my first year in junior high was when I started spiraling down. I was twelve and people at school weren't very nice, especially when I was going to school covered in bruises and blood. I always wondered why Dad chose me so often. Why he would sit down with Will and watch a movie then the second I got home find some reason to beat the hell out of me. He was a strong man. I have never and will never blame any of you for not getting between it.

I'll decide tomorrow if I need to get my hand checked out. Besides, I'm too frustrated to deal with going anywhere right now. Everyone strongly suggested I don't wait it out, but I figure the bandage will hold me over. Okay fine, I'm probably not going to the hospital at all. Hospitals cost too much and are filled with sadness. Not to mention that freaky "too clean" smell. Plus, what kind of story am I going to give them about the hand and the face? I'll get to choose between an abusive dad and the fact I'm a recovering addict. I'd probably have to tell them both. I'm not really in the mood for more judgment tonight.

Katie and I choose to follow through with our original plan of hanging out in my room. All I want right now is to curl up in a ball and fade to black. Instead, I settle for being alone with Katie and away from everyone else.

When we get to my room, I turn to Katie. "Do you think you

could get my phone from Tyson? Just so we can listen to some music. I'll clean up in here a little."

I glance around my room at the books and clothes all over my floor. I guess I should have thought about this before I invited her over.

"No problem," she says and leaves the room, closing the door behind her.

The first book I pick up is the one with the carved-out pages, the one I keep my emergency stash in. They'll never suspect I'd leave it in there again, especially since I leave it out with the rest of the mess. I pop it open and see the five pills in a Ziplock bag.

My mouth waters and my heart rate picks up. I deserve it tonight, right? After everything that's happened…

Fuck. Fuck. Fuck, why? Why am I like this? Don't do this, Jace, don't do it. You're better than this.

Before I can change my mind, I pop two Oxys in my mouth and dry swallow them. Guilt immediately hits me, but I take the time to convince myself it's for my hand, which really does hurt like a bitch.

The book slams shut as I shove it into the shelf with the others. I run around the room and throw my clothes back onto the laundry chair and pick up all my notebooks. By the time Katie gets back, I'm sitting on my bed pushing the hair back out of my face.

She's scrolling through my phone when she comes in. "Can I choose a song?"

"Yeah, of course. I just wanted to say again that I'm so sorry about all of this. I haven't had a solid conversation with my dad for months. I didn't expect all my family drama to come out tonight, the only night I bring someone home. I know I sound like a broken record. I'm just shocked by how much happened tonight."

She smiles dismissively and continues flipping through my

music until she finds what she wants. I knew she doesn't want to hear my sad sorry anymore, but fuck, what are you supposed to say to someone when shit like this happens? Frank Sinatra's voice plays through the Bluetooth speaker. It's a song I know very well.

The dumbest smile spread across my face. If there's anyone who can make me feel better, it's Frank Sinatra. Katie sings along word for word, the perfect distraction from what I just did and hid from her.

"Sing with me I know you know the words." She takes my hand and pulls me up.

I shake my head. "Why do you assume I know the words?"

She turns my phone to my face. "Because it's the only song in your 'liked songs' folder."

That's embarrassing. I really need to fix that by either removing it or adding more. If anything screams "I'm depressed" more, it's "That's Life" being your most listened-to song.

"That'll do it." I smile and start dancing with her. This has always been my song; it always fits the mood. Whether I want to die or I feel invincible. With Katie, it has a whole new meaning. It's fun, and it's her way of telling me she gets it.

We scream out the chorus together while moving in a way that hardly counts as dancing. She keeps tripping over my foot and laughing. This is how I imagined life feels for normal people. Care-free, fun, energetic. When was the last time I danced? I used to love it—not real dancing but just moving to music that made me feel something.

We flop onto my bed, out of breath and laughing. "What's your secret to sobriety?" I ask her.

She stops moving, still breathing heavily. "What?"

"At the diner, you told me you'd tell me your secret, but it would be a bad influence. What's the secret?"

She sits up to look at me. "Pot," she answers without hesitating.

"You smoke weed? How? Doesn't it heighten the craving for other things?"

"Yeah, it did at first, but if you push past that, it honestly helps a lot with the depression and it doesn't fuck with your body. Believe it or not, when you're a recovering addict, doctors are hesitant to give you anything for the depression." She laughs. "Weed helps a little when I feel nothing else will."

"Maybe I'll try it sometime, although usually it makes my anxiety a lot worse than it already is. That's one of the reasons I started the pills. I was tired of having anxiety attacks every day all day. I couldn't leave my house without crumbling to the ground. I couldn't sleep or focus on anything. The anxiety kicked in the depression, I think. I just hated being alive. Living every day in a constant state of anxiety sucks. If I wasn't having anxiety, I was constantly wondering when it would come or worried that I'd have an attack. I just wanted it all to stop. And the pills helped. For a bit, anyway."

I doubt I'll be giving weed a try anytime soon. I don't think I'm anywhere near the right state of mind to do something that would make me want the stronger stuff. The stronger stuff like Oxy…fuck. I took something. I took pills.

Quickly, I stand up and walk to my window, rubbing my palms on my jeans. For some reason, up until now, it didn't fully process that I'd just relapsed. A fucking relapse. I can't do that. I've been working my ass off. I have so many people around me who I could have talked to, literally like five fucking people in the same house as me. A whole month and a half of excruciating cravings and I give in that easy? Because of some shit my fuckup dad said? Shit.

"I have to go get some water. Want anything?" I try to hide it, but the panic is evident in my voice.

"No, I'll wait here." Her tone is a little questioning as she watches me pace and rub my hands on my pants.

"Alright, I…uh…I'll be right back." I run to the bathroom, shut the door, and turn the sink on. "Shit, shit, shit, shit…"

I bend over the toilet and shove my fingers down my throat. My nonexistent gag reflex is no help. It seems like nothing's going to make me puke. Sighing, I pick up my toothbrush and try again. It causes me to hurl everywhere, and much more loudly than I expected.

The two pills float in the toilet water and I flush them down. Thank the lord for capsules. If those had been the nasty chalky fucking things, they'd have been long gone and I'd be having a wonderful time.

The guilt feels almost worse than the withdrawals. Scratch that—nothing is worse than withdrawal. I refuse to go through that again. Still, I can't believe I took those fucking pills without even a second's thought. And while everyone's here, too. I know for a fact I'm going to have worse days than this, and I gave in because I was feeling…what? Like I had an excuse that would warrant getting high? I'm such a piece of shit person.

"Jace?" It's Suzie's voice. "Are you okay, can I come in?" I unlock the door for her. "Were you just throwing up?" she asks, slightly worried. The look in her eyes makes me realize she isn't as naïve as I've always assumed. She might be the only person in this household that nothing gets past. She already knows I took something. I'm not going to lie to her.

I hold up the toothbrush and throw it up onto the bathroom counter. Suzie's face falls, and she slides down the wall to sit next to me. She lets out a dramatic sigh—a little too dramatic if you ask me—and looks me over. "Was this the first time?"

I nod. "I guess the whole dad thing was just too much or

something. I don't know, I'm pissed off that I did it. I don't even have a real excuse. It just made sense in my head. I convinced myself that if it was a good enough reason, it wouldn't count as a relapse. I'm sorry. I know I keep saying I'm sorry, but it really isn't easy on me, Suzie. It really fucking isn't. I've gone a whole month and a half thinking about everything I could do and how easy it would be to hide it."

"I know. Well, I don't *know*, but I can tell you're battling with yourself all the time. I didn't expect you to go through this and just stop everything, be happy, and go back to normal. You were fifteen when you started…there's a lot of empty space between then and now, and I know you won't ever be the old you again. But that's okay. I'm excited to meet the new you, the adult you. We all know you're going to go over bumps, and it's not going to be pretty, but we're here to support you in any way you need. Hard part first, then the fun part, where you get to rebuild yourself. Day by day…"

Softly nodding, I raise one side of my mouth into a half-smile. "…hour by hour," I finish. I hate myself more than she can understand right now. Honestly, she probably hates me more than I hate myself. How could I have done that? Yeah, I threw it up, but I still did it.

"I'm proud of you," she says. "You could have gone the rest of the night with no one knowing, but you chose to throw it up. All on your own, you chose that." Her fingers start running through my hair, massaging my scalp.

She doesn't hate me? My eyes begin to fill up and try to blink it away. Instead, I blink the tears right out. She's proud of me, and she's right. I did choose that. No one knew I took anything, but I chose on my own to do what I could to take it back.

"Whoa, bathroom party!?" Will asks, amused. His face changes when he sees I'm crying. He sits down on the other side of me and pats my leg.

I wipe a tear from my face and laugh. "Damn, okay, why don't we invite the whole neighborhood over to watch Jace cry in the tiny bathroom?"

"That is a wonderful idea," Will says, then shouts, "KATIE, TYSON, BATHROOM NOW!"

Tyson runs in like a fucking tornado with the most horrified look I've ever seen. I can tell he thought I'd died or overdosed or something. It makes my chest ache knowing this is what people assume now about me. Katie follows shortly behind him, still worried but a lot less chaotic.

Here I am, after a partial relapse, lying in my sister's lap in the bathroom surrounded by people who love me. I wish that were enough. But it's more than I've ever had, so for now I let it fill my heart.

"What exactly is going on here?" Tyson asks, even though he's already accepted his fate is to sit on the floor with us.

"Jace relapsed," Suzie says with no sign of emotion.

More tears start falling down my cheeks. I hate hearing such technical terms with my name next to them.

"Aww. Oh, no! I'm so sorry. Why didn't you talk to us? Are you okay?" Tyson puts his hand on my foot and pats me.

"No, I'm okay. I had convinced myself in my head that I was taking them for my hand. It's hard to explain, but I had a whole argument with myself, and before I knew it, I was swallowing them. It wasn't until later that I realized what I'd done and what it meant. I came in here and threw them up immediately."

Will shakes his head. "So, it doesn't count?"

I squeeze his hand and look up to Katie, who gives me a sympathetic smile.

"No. Unfortunately, it still counts. But I feel okay. I'm okay."

I'm not okay, and right now, I'm not sure I'll ever be okay. I don't want to create a whole new Jace. Suzie is right. I missed my whole teenage life and skipped right to adult. I don't know anything about this life, and I'm starting it by trying to not do drugs. Sounds real fucking promising, doesn't it?

Chapter 14

Mom always told us that the word "danger" had "anger" in it for a reason. I never got that. Again, the angriest person I know is Will. I'm sorry life has been so unfair. It has to suck to have a heart so pure in a world so fucked up.

A few more weeks pass. It's the last day in April, which is pretty good considering my whole breakdown on the bathroom floor took place in February. I've made no mistakes. Well…no mistakes that are general public knowledge. I've been collecting pills from Ian again. Flushing those two pills caused me some small anxiety attacks. It put me on edge to know I didn't have anything because that made me feel I controlled them instead of the other way around. I need to feel the power of knowing even though I have them, I'm the one deciding not to take them. The good news is that Ian apparently doesn't know his sister and I are close friends. She hasn't mentioned anything about me getting pills from him, so hopefully it stays that way.

It sounds bad, I know. But I haven't been taking them. Just holding onto them for a rainy day. I've been trying to get at least two of anything every time I see him at school. I've got a good collection of about thirty different kinds. Anyway, I figure I can't just drop off the face of the earth and ghost Ian.

Suzie started seeing a boy. Nobody acted like was a big deal.

They had more of a reaction to me bringing home Katie. Tyson is still grumpy like an old man, and when Will isn't busy pestering us, he's spending a lot of time working.

Katie is still great. She's been super supportive, no surprise there. It's crazy how life happens. Your little sister gets a boyfriend, your brother gets a job, and things in the world keep going—but when you have a brother who's addicted to drugs and recovering from it, it's like nothing else matters.

"Hey," Katie whispers once our professor turns his back to the class. "Can I come over tonight? Ian's being a fucking ass and Will still owes me a pizza."

Will and Katie have been getting close. They're actually pretty good friends now. It's weird, and I'd be concerned about it, but I really don't give a shit about whatever's going on there. As long as Katie keeps being my friend, she can commit murder for all I care.

"Yeah, I don't see why not." I force a brief smile then go back to chewing on my cheek.

My siblings have always been very welcoming, especially Tyson. He's worried they'll all scare Katie away; he thinks she's really good for me. Suzie's been warming up to her as well. Even in the times when I've wanted to be alone in my room, I can hear all four of them in the living room laughing or playing some dumb video game. I found myself a best friend and turned her into another sister.

I pull the strings on my hood a little tighter. Today's a rough day. If I had my choice, I'd be hiding in my room, never leaving my bed. But between Will and Katie, I lost that fight before it even started. My phone buzzes in my back pocket. It's Ian.

Bathroom?

I side-eye Katie. She saw me check my phone, but I'm not sure if she read what the message said.

Coming, I text back.

"I have to take a shit," I whisper to Katie. "Be right back." I get up and half run to the bathroom.

When I get there, it's just Ian. Caden decided to drop out a week or two ago, and despite how close he and Ian were, Ian didn't seem too upset about it. I didn't ask questions; I don't really care.

"Hey, dude," Ian says to me. "Two of whatever?"

I nod and hand him $45, which I found in my dad's room after he last disappeared. The best part about having parents who disappear is being able to loot their rooms when they're gone.

"How's it going?" he asks. "You really using this heavy?" He tilts his head as he hands me the pills like he's trying to find the emotion in my face.

I scoff and put the pills in my pocket. "Nah, not really. Just stocking up. Hey, do you have any cigs?"

"Really? Yeah, sure." He looks surprised by my request. I'm not usually one to smoke.

I take the cigarette and lighter and hold them to my mouth. The lighter flicks a few times, still not sparking a flame. Oh, for fuck's sake, this damn lighter again.

"You need to get a new lighter." My voice comes out stern and demanding. I flick it a few more times, the frustration making its way to my head. I keep thinking about how this felt oddly like the night I confessed all my sins.

flick…flick…flick…

"Fuck!" I throw the lighter at the wall. "Fuck this. Get a new goddamn lighter." I drop the cigarette and it rolls into a puddle by the sink.

I storm out of the bathroom, now full-blown angry. It feels like the blood in my arms and neck is boiling. I throw my phone down the hall and hear it shatter. I shove open the doors leading outside and sit down on a bench.

Why do I feel so angry? Nothing happened. I was fine ten minutes ago. My leg is bouncing up and down, almost making the anger worse. I swing my legs around and lie on my back, the bench pushing into my shoulder blades. The clouds are moving swiftly and the sky is a nice color of blue today. I hear birds around me, and the sound of cars on the freeway. The breeze grazes my body, causing my hair to softly brush my face. After a few calming deep breaths, I sit up and put my head into my hands.

I'm such a shitty person, but honestly, I don't mind anymore. No harm, no foul. I'm not using, so it doesn't even matter. I'm not even sure I care what anyone thinks of me anymore, either. I know how disappointed they'd be if they found the pills in my room, but I can't bring myself to give a fuck. Maybe I'm just a bad person and I was always meant to be, regardless of who my dad is.

"You okay?" I lift my head and see Ian walking toward me.

My leg is now shaking so hard I'm surprised the ground isn't shaking with it. "I wish people would stop asking me that." I scoot over so he can sit down. He's obviously not going to leave me alone.

"I know, I'm sorry." There's pity in his voice, like he's worried he might break me with one wrong word. "Is there anything I can help you with?" He rests his elbows on his knees so he can meet my eyes.

I mean to say, "No thanks," but what comes out instead is a very fake laugh.

"Dude," Ian says, "I know we aren't anything but drug friends, but I also see you as a human. I wish you saw me the same way… Anyway, I know you haven't been right since you started buying again, and I just want you to know I can talk about more than just drugs."

I run my hands through my hair in an attempt to calm myself down. "Sorry, I know I've been a piece of shit. I mean, it's been what? Like five years?" I put my head back into my hands and shake my head. "I don't even know your birthday or your favorite color. Damn, I don't even know what color eyes you have, and I've had seven hundred conversations with you."

He laughs and puts his hand on my back, trying to make me feel better. "Birthday's March 8th, and I don't have a favorite color. They're are all good. As for my eyes…weird observation, by the way. You tell me."

He lifts my chin and I look at him confusedly. Did he just…? He leans in a little closer and widens his eyes playfully so I can see better.

"Blue," I whisper.

They're blue like Katie's. He's got a gold ring around his pupils and stripes of darker blue coming out of the gold. They're pretty eyes. I finally realize that Ian is a person, and he's Katie's brother. Not just some guy I buy drugs from, but someone who actually has a life.

"Blue," he agrees, then smiles and sits back up. "Looked like you were having an anxiety attack. Feeling better now?"

"I'm…" I lean back against the bench. "I'm sober. It's been taking a bit of a toll on me. So honestly, I'm never feeling better."

"No shit? Congrats, man! That's awesome! But if you're sober, why are you still buying from me?"

I laugh and shake my head. "It's complicated."

"Well, if you ever want to talk," he says and knocks his knee into mine, "I'm good at complicated. And just to be a good sport, I'm not going to sell to you anymore."

I glance down at my leg, then at his. He hasn't moved his knee away from mine and it's making me feel all types of awkward.

"Fair enough," I say.

"Jace?!" Katie yells from the doors behind us.

We turn toward her and I stand up, walking quickly toward Katie and glancing back at Ian, who's still sitting on the bench. The confusion is clear on his face.

"Hey, sorry, I had a moment," I tell Katie. "I just needed some fresh air. I didn't mean to just leave."

"You scared the hell out of me," she says, lightly punching my shoulder. "I see you get a text from Ian, you tell me you have to go to the *bathroom*, and then you don't come back! I went into the disgusting-ass men's room to look for you. When you weren't there, I just…I got scared." She stops talking and hugs me.

"I know, I'm sorry." I hug her back. I know she feels a lot of pressure to babysit me and keep me in check since the relapse, especially now that she's close with my family. She doesn't want anything to happen and have it be her fault.

"Uh…Katie? What the hell?"

She pushes away from me and looks at her brother. "Ian."

The way she's acting would make you think we'd just got caught raw dogging in the back of a pickup truck. She brushes her hands down her shirt and flips her hair. I just stand there, not doing whatever weird thing it is that she's doing.

"This is why you've been asking about him so much?" Ian says. "You guys are…fucking? Oh, hell no! What are you guys doing?"

"She's my friend," I tell him. "She's the strongest support system I have. She helped me through my detox. She's always there when I need her. She's…she's my best friend."

Ian nods his head. "As long as there's no funny business going on."

Katie laughs and grabs my hand, causing me to wince. "The funniest of business."

"No funny business," I say. "I don't…uh, I don't like her like that. Strictly friendship. Although my brother may be trying to get her into some funny business." I smile at Katie.

"Who, Will?" she says. "Yeah, not going to happen."

I find it telling that she didn't ask which brother I was talking about.

Chapter 15

There are not a lot of great people in this world. I'm so lucky and grateful for Katie. With her, everything just kind of clicks and feels right. I'm sorry, Katie.

May fucking sucks. I cannot believe how much May sucks, it's only the fourth day. I haven't been this low since I was lying face-down in the toilet at school.

I've been skipping school again, which is weird because I've been really wanting to talk to Katie. I can't explain how hard it's been to leave my bed, and I'm at a point where I don't really care for help, either. I don't even care if she's mad at me or doesn't want to be my friend anymore.

I lie on my side staring at the wall. Lately, I can't stop thinking about the things Dad said to me, or the fact no one has talked about it since. I've been trying hard to push everything down, to forget about it or ignore it, but I can't. Why hasn't anyone mentioned it or asked me about it?

I should have treated everyone better growing up. What if I really am the reason everyone is the way they are in this family? Dad is a shit person, but he's never been a liar. I'm the only one fucking up this badly. Even Suzie is better, so I must be where things fucked up.

I don't know how long I've been lying here or how many days

it's been since I laid down. I hear the front door open and assume it's Tyson. Will and Suzie are at school. Tyson disappeared shortly after they left, so it's just been me and Dad in the house. The energy in the house is so weird. No one's even mentioned me missing school or resorting to never leaving my room. I could be on drugs again and no one would know. Tempting.

Everything aside, I figure I should go say hi and make it known I'm still alive even, if it is just Tyson. I drag myself up and put on one of my black T-shirts. It's not even clean, but it doesn't smell bad, so I'll call it a win. When I turn the corner in the hallway, I'm met by Mom standing in the living room.

"Mom?"

"Oh! You scared me. I thought everyone would be gone." She never looks at me, just walks past me to the chair in the living room. She sits down and takes her shoes off.

"I don't feel well," I tell her, "so I stayed home today." I sit on the couch next to the chair. "Can I ask you something?" My hands instinctually come up to my hair and push it out of my face.

She makes a face like she really doesn't want to have a conversation but nods anyway. It's like she's thinking *I hate when my children inconvenience me by wanting to talk, especially when I've been missing for months*. How dare I intrude on her peace.

I ignore the dismissive feeling and jump right in. "Did I fuck the family up?"

She turns to me, her eyes wide with surprise. "Why would you think that?"

I shrug. "You're always gone. Dad beats the shit out of me. Everyone's better than I am. They say I act like Dad." I know Will denied believing that, but I know he does. They all do. "Where do you go when you leave?"

She thinks about it for a moment, probably trying to decide

whether she wants to lie or not. "Just out. Sometimes I need to get away. All of you boys remind me of your dad, and sleeping on the couch gets old."

Her answer is filled with hate, but it also serves to distract from the first part of my question. She doesn't tell me I'm not the reason our family is so screwed up.

"So you leave, only because you want to get away from your family? For months at a time?"

She shrugs. "Suzie's okay. But you have to understand, there's a lot of pressure in raising you boys."

"*Raising* us? You did no such thing. Ever. I can't remember a moment in time when you were raising anyone."

I came to her for some advice, and now I'm fucking mad. I should have known to just turn around and go back to my room when I saw her. Then she tells me the reason she's never here is because of her sons. That's bullshit. "Do you even know what's going on here?" I ask. "What's been going on here?"

"Is something going on? Is everyone okay?"

I scoff, my eyes already gathering water. "You're a piece of work, you know that?" I laugh.

"Jace…"

I cut her off by standing up and turning around. Before walking to my room, I turn back toward her. I can't help myself. I want to make her hurt. "Why don't you just stay out forever? We don't need you. Hell, I don't even think Suzie knows you're her mom. Dad's a better parent than you. At least he shows the fuck up. I'm fed up that all your kids think there's something wrong with *them* because you and Dad fucked everyone out of a life. Fuck off, and don't come back. No one will even notice, I promise."

I wish I had real parents. I wish we'd been taken away and given to new families when we had CPS called on us. I think we'd have had a fighting chance, even if it meant splitting us up.

My door slams shut behind me and I lie back in my bed. I can feel an indent in the mattress from where I've been lying for the past few days. I'm getting to a mental state where I don't give a shit if I piss myself. I'm not leaving this spot ever again.

A few hours later, I open my eyes. I hear a few different voices in the living room. One sounds like Katie. Instead of getting up I just turn over. I really don't care who's here right now. I just want to disappear into a black hole. Footsteps are getting closer to my room. I groan and pull the blanket over my head in the hope no one sees me.

It's Katie. "Hey! We're all going to get food if you want to go…" She stops before finishing the sentence. She's silent for a while, making me think she's gone. Then she says, "Actually, hold on."

I hear her walk away, back into the living room, I assume. I pull the blanket back down and look at the door to be sure she left. When I don't see her, I stay like that, looking at the door. She comes back a few minutes later with a cup of water and half a peanut butter and jelly sandwich.

"I didn't know it was this bad," she whispers and sits down next to my bed, offering me the water and the sandwich. "What can I do to help?"

You can leave me alone and take everyone else with you too, that's how you can help.

I shake my head. "I'm fine." I sit up enough to drink the water without drowning and turn down the sandwich.

"Jace, your room is a disaster. I haven't seen you in days, and you have a…smell. When was the last time you ate or took a shower?"

I smile at her, putting no effort or emotion into the gesture. I don't have answers for her because I have no idea. I eat occasionally. Will has been keeping a steady flow of crackers in the house for me. I think he knows it's the only food that interests me. I meet Katie's eyes. They're the same as Ian's. Both have that beautiful gold ring around their pupils. I've never noticed how alike they are.

How could I have let her into my life, this pure wonderful soul who wanted nothing more than to help a boy she didn't even know? How could I have let her get so close to me, brought her into not only my life but my family's? My fucking dad met her. How could I have let that happen? I might need her, but she doesn't need this. She doesn't need a selfish friend in her life when she's been fighting for her own mental sanity for so long.

My smile morphs into a frown, and I let out a few tears. How could I let myself become her best friend and keep her in such a shit environment? How would I feel if someone like me took Suzie into their life?

With tears in my eyes, I whisper, "I'm so sorry, Katie. I fucking hate myself. I hate that I let you get so close to me, to my life."

"Jace, no, no! No, don't be sorry. Come here." She pulls me off the bed into a hug.

I hate how good it feels to be comforted. I imagine this is how you always feel when you have a normal family.

"Come with me." She walks me to the bathroom, and after locking the door and sitting me down on the toilet lid, she kneels in front of me. "Never apologize for being a friend, Jace. I've been where you are. I know what you're thinking and how you feel. You aren't using me for anything, you aren't a bad friend, and you aren't going anywhere. You do, however, stink." She pulls her oversized sweater over her head, leaving her in just her sports bra and her volleyball-looking shorts.

I lift an eyebrow, confused. I hope she remembers the

conversation about me not having an interest in women.

"Shirt. Off," she demands.

I'm in no position to care or question what's going on, so I obey and remove my shirt and shorts. It's weird to be a gay man standing in my boxers with a straight woman in her bra. I'm slightly disappointed that seeing her like this doesn't make me feel anything.

She pulls the shower curtain open and turns on the water, adjusting it until it's the right temperature. Once the water is perfect, she steps in and gestures for me to follow. "Come sit."

This is pathetic.

After pointing to the shower floor, she demanded more sternly, "Sit."

That small lazy smile fills my face again, but I sit down in front of her on the floor of the tub. She holds the shower head and runs hot water over my head. God, it feels good.

Without talking, she washes my hair, and her fingers massage my scalp for longer than she needs. The smell of shampoo fills the bathroom, the clean scent making me feel a little better already.

"You need a haircut," she says, and I can hear the smile in her voice.

"Don't even think about it."

She grabs one of the luffas that are hanging on the bathtub wall and drags it across my back. I close my eyes and let her take care of me. I've never had someone care so much. As pathetic as it is to have a girl shower me, I'm grateful for it.

"Okay," she says, "I'm going to go get your bed stuff and throw it in the wash. Use this." She hands me the luffa. "Wash the rest of yourself. I'll give you privacy to do that, and I'll bring you new clothes. You smell better already." With a wink, she climbs out of the tub and leaves.

After I finish my shower, I wrap myself in a towel and sit on the toilet, waiting for Katie to bring me the clothes she promised. This is a new type of low. Maybe I'm the pathetic one.

"You have no clean clothes! None!" She shakes her head. "I stole some from Will. I hope you aren't against underwear sharing."

"Not today I'm not." I give her my best smile.

"Alright, well, here you go." The clothes fall onto the floor in front of me. "Once you're dressed, we're leaving the house. You need to eat."

I decide not to fight her on it. The woman just gave me a shower and stole clothes from my brother. Who knows what she had to see in his room to get them? "Thank you for showering me and taking care of me."

"Don't worry about it. Sometimes we all need a friend to get our asses up and in the shower. Plus, I've been trying to get at you since I first saw you. I figured this was the closest I'd get to seeing you naked."

"No, you haven't." I smile when she turns around so I can pull on Will's underwear and pants.

"Not true," Katie says. "When I first started asking Ian about you, it was because I was totally interested. Have you seen yourself? You and your family are practically olive-skinned, green-eyed gods. Seriously, not one of you has an imperfection."

I raise an eyebrow at her as if she forgot what she had to do for me.

"Well, no physical imperfections…from what I've seen so far." Her gaze drops to the zipper of my jeans.

"Katie!" I furrow my brows and shake my head at her.

"Hey, you can't blame a girl for trying."

Sometimes I think Katie can't get any weirder, and then she does. You can't just ask people about their dick size, especially after you just gave them a shower.

I pull the T-shirt over my head. "Jesus, let's go get food or whatever you wanted to do so I can forget this happened."

Katie laughs as she links her arm to mine and leads me out of the bathroom.

Chapter 16

I'm sorry I was never a great brother. I know I didn't bond well like everyone else did. I guess I wasn't sure how. I've always been so different. I wasn't sure what things to talk about that you would understand. Suzie, on the other hand, Bug, you kept me going through all of life. You have always been so relatable, and I am so selfishly glad Mom and Dad had just one more kid to neglect so I could have my best friend.

Finally, the fucking weekend. Not that it really mattered to me. Last night was really nice with Katie. It felt good to feel cared about. After the shower, she tried her hardest to get me to agree to her cutting my hair. I probably should have just let her, but I had been over-touched at that moment and didn't feel like sitting through a haircut.

I haven't done laundry in so long that I still don't have any clean shirts, so I go to the kitchen in just my shorts. Everyone knows about the weight loss now anyway.

"Hey! Good morning, are you feeling any better today?" Tyson asks, genuine concern spread across his face. He glances at my chest for a moment. This is his first time seeing me without my shirt. I know how bad it must look.

I nod, knowing it's a lie, but it's probably one he needs to hear. "Yeah, just need some toast or something."

"Do you need me to make you something?" he asks as he finishes doing the few dishes in the sink.

"No, but thank you. I'm not really feeling up to eating a whole lot."

I know there's more he wants to say, and he isn't fully impressed with my answer, but he lets it go anyway. "Hey, Jace. Um…I just wanted to talk to you about what happened…with Dad."

I freeze, my arm still holding the fridge open and my back toward him. I figured he had more to say but I didn't think it would be about that specific subject. Squeezing my eyes shut, I ask, "What about it?"

He gestures to the table. "Can we sit?"

I let out a deep breath. This conversation could go very well, or very bad. "Yeah, sure." I close the fridge and sit in the chair across from him.

"I wanted to let you know," Tyson begins, "that I'm so sorry about all of that. I know how that must have felt, and I would never have put you through that ever. We all knew Dad was a dick, but I never expected that from him honestly. I should have never doubted it. Anyway, I wanted to let you know I love you, dude. I know it's super overused advice and doesn't mean anything, but don't listen to anything he says." He wraps both his hands around his coffee mug. "He just wants a reaction. I doubt he even believes half the shit that comes out of his own mouth."

"It's fine." I smile. I wish I had more to say. I wish I had the energy in me to have a real-life intellectual conversation.

"Also, you've been back to never leaving your room. I'm worried about you. I'm worried you think we all hate you."

Ah, so they *have* noticed I've been running off to my room again. "I don't think you guys hate me. It's been…weird since the Dad thing." I chew on my cheek, trying to figure out what I want to say. "It's just…we never really talked about any of the stuff that was thrown around that night. I'm assuming Dad was right when he mentioned that everyone already knows, but I still can't help but wonder if you guys do. Did you know? About the gay thing?"

Tyson raises one side of his mouth. I'm guessing he didn't think he was going to hear so much come from me during this conversation. It makes him happy to know I'm participating.

"I practically raised you," he says, "of course I knew. There was never really anything big that said 'Oh, yeah, he's gay as fuck,' but I could just tell. I didn't really think it was a big deal, that you would either tell us at some point or end up bringing home a dude and introducing him as your boyfriend. Although I will say, say most gay men have way better hair than you. I mean, come on. What's going on with that? Why do you always look so homeless?"

We both laugh.

"Ah, yeah" I push my hair over my head and smile. "Long and messy hair comes in the 'doing drugs' contract I signed."

"That's funny. What else was on that contract? Anything I should know about?"

I shake my head. "Nope. Just the hair thing, really. And that I continuously disappoint my family in any way I can."

"Well, you haven't really met that last requirement. You're a good kid. It makes me sad to see where you've been going. I hope you're actually feeling better, and that you understand how proud we all are of you."

"I don't know. I've been pretty disappointing. I pissed off Dad and Mom. Scared the hell out of you guys more than once. I brought Katie into all this shit as if she doesn't have enough of her own to deal with."

"That's just life, Jace. No one can be perfect, and no one expects anyone else to be. You just have to take a deep breath and step back sometimes to look at yourself. As long as you aren't disappointed, most of the time no one else is either."

It sounds easy enough. But I'm disappointed with myself at least 98 percent of the time. I just wish he could tell me exactly what I need to do to fix myself. I don't want to feel this way anymore, and I don't know what to do about it. My previous methods aren't working out for me.

"You're probably right. Thanks for being such a great stand-in dad for me."

I can tell that made him feel good. His cheeks gain a light blush, and he looks down at the table with a smile. "So, you're okay, then?"

"Want the truth?" I ask, raising an eyebrow.

There's a worried look in his eyes as he nods. I have nothing to lose by telling the truth anymore. But how much of the truth can I give him? I could come clean about the pills I've been hoarding for no real reason at all, or tell him that I truly have been wanting to just end myself, end everything I've been doing to everyone else, too.

"I'm a gay 21-year-old man who cried in a shower with a straight 20-year-old woman as she washed my hair. I've been better," I say and laugh.

"It's so weird how different we are." Tyson chuckles and shakes his head. "I wish I was crying in the shower with a straight woman."

Just then, Will walks into the kitchen. "Who's different?" he asks.

How is he always eating? I wonder.

"We were just talking about how Jace had the worst day in his life yesterday because he had to shower with a 20-year-old straight girl," Tyson says. He stands, pats Will on the back, and leaves the kitchen as a very confused-looking Will chokes on his cereal. Tyson likes to be here for me, to be there to help. But he knows I close myself off whenever it's more than just me and him, so he doesn't waste any time even trying.

"Good morning," I laugh.

Despite Tyson knowing I'm pretty closed off to Will, I also know he's trying to get everyone to "express themselves" to me. I know the pat on the back was a hint to Will that it's his turn.

I should have stayed in bed. What is this, some kind of feelings intervention?

I jump right into it before Will has a chance to talk. "Will, I love you too, dude. Dad didn't hurt me at all, and I'm not doing drugs." Hopefully, that covers all the questions he was going to ask. "Also, were you aware of my queerness?" I'm honestly very interested to know who knew and who didn't. I thought I was doing the whole closet thing well, but I guess not.

His smile fades a bit. He looks like he's almost as uncomfortable as I am over what's about to happen. "I wasn't going to tell you I loved you, but alright." He smiles. "I just really want to make sure you're okay, not just from that, but in general. That relapse could have been bad. But I'm glad you told us about it. As for the gay thing…um, no, I didn't." He sits awkwardly in the chair Tyson just left. "I thought Dad was just trying to be a dick to you when he said that. After the whole thing, Tyson let me know you really are gay, and that's why you hated my getting-laid jokes. Now that I know, it does explain a whole lot."

I roll my eyes. "That's not why I hate your sex jokes. I hate them because they aren't funny. And oh, yeah, I'm sure it explains *so* much."

"No, seriously. I kept finding really weird websites on the computer when we shared a room. I assumed Mom was getting…"

I reach across the table and smack my hand over his mouth. "Okay! Okay, I get it. Oh, my God, I can't believe you found that stuff." I drop my head into my hands, grinning. I know Tyson is right in the other room, and this is already embarrassing enough without mention of whatever gay porn-type stuff was about to come out of Will's mouth.

"I mean, come on, Jace. You didn't even close the tab! It also explains how you never bring home women or talk about them. Then, of course, it explains the bad things…like why Dad is such a dick to you. But I don't see you any differently, and I love you. Plus, you just became my new wingman. Now I get to tell women that my little brother is gay. They love that shit!"

"I thought closing the computer *would* close the tab. Overall, I guess you're right. It does explain some stuff. Your point has been proven. Let's end the topic there. Also, I am *not* a wingman, but feel free to use the gay brother thing anytime if you think it'll help your case."

"Can I ask one more question?"

"No. No more questions. I'm banning you from asking any more."

He winks but asks anyway. "So…are you a top, or a bottom?"

"Will!" I bring my hand up to pinch the bridge of my nose. I can't believe he just asked that. "I'm done now. Thanks for the chat." I stand up feeling quite traumatized.

"No, seriously. I want to know!" he yells as I leave the kitchen. "JACE!"

Tyson's sitting on the couch and I glare at him. "Now I'm mad at you. That was terrifying."

He smiles, shrugs, and turns back to his video game.

When I get back to my room, nothing feels right. How is it that I'm closer than ever to my family yet I still don't have a single grain of happiness running through me? It's much more than just the family life. As much as I try to explain how I feel, it's just a never-ending circle. I always—*always*—come back to this exact spot by the end of the day. It's affecting everyone around me, too. They feel like they can't live normal lives because someone always has to be around babysitting me. I'm not sure how much more I can take before my brain explodes.

I decide to take a quick walk to the gas station to pick up a lighter and a pack of cigs. If I'm going to stop one habit, I suppose I could start another. Besides, no one bats an eye at a cigarette, but heaven forbid you hold a Xanax in your hand.

After pulling on a hoodie, I walk into the living room and call over to the boys, "Hey, I'm running to the gas station, I'll be back."

The air outside isn't necessarily cold, but it's not warm either. The spring air always makes it cooler at night and in the morning, and a lot warmer mid-day. Once I get to the gas station, I ask for a pack of cigs I've heard of before and grab one of the lighters from the stand.

I go outside and don't walk five feet before pulling one out and lighting it. The smoke entering my lungs is dry and scratchy. It tastes dirty, which is why I've never been a fan of these. But within a few seconds, my body's tingling and my brain is filled with fog. I close my eyes and bask in the thirty seconds of silence. I bring the cigarette back up to my lips and take another drag before starting my walk back home. I've never had nicotine calm me down like this before. I can't believe I didn't try this sooner. I shove the pack and lighter into the pocket of my hoodie and head home.

Chapter 17

You know when you wake up and have to pee really bad but your alarm goes off in an hour so you try to hold it in? But doing that just keeps you up thinking about it constantly, so you don't get that hour of sleep anyway? That's a horrible example, but imagine doing that for six-and-a-half years. Well, not every night for six years but like holding it in for the whole six years—never mind. Forget I wrote that.

I wake up. *Yay.*

I hear thunder and rain pattering against my window as the wind blows it in my direction.

The time on my clock reads 2:30 a.m. This is probably one of the only times I've ever been happy to be up. It's quiet, and the streets stand still. Almost like I'm the only person on earth. For a bit, nothing else matters.

Slowly, I slide out of bed and dig through the pile of clothes strung all over my room to find the blue hoodie with the pack of cigarettes in it. It became a new habit faster than I expected; sue me. I also make a mental note to do some damn laundry.

"Fuck, where's the lighter?" I whisper to myself as I continue throwing my shit all over my room.

It's hard to dig through all my stuff quietly so I don't wake anyone up. After giving up on looking for the lighter, I slowly open my door and tiptoe to the kitchen. With no other logical options available to me, I light my cigarette on the stove and walk quickly out the front door to sit outside on the porch.

It's a little cold with the rain, so with every drag I take I hear the sizzle of the paper surrounding the tobacco. I take in a deep breath and slowly let it out. It's humid out. I love springtime thunderstorms. They bring out the best smells in everything, and the air gets humid and thick.

I take a deep drag and hold it in until it makes my head swirl. I close my eyes and smile. I wish someone had told me how nice cigarettes were when I was first getting clean. This could have saved us a lot of time, and maybe even one relapse.

I look toward the dark street. The only source of light comes from the shitty streetlamp that emits an orange glow and flickers every five minutes. Everything out here is so still and clear. The streetlight flickers off and lightning lights up the sky, illuminating the street. Something about being outside at night by yourself makes you really think.

I feel like these streets know me so well. Things like the neighbor's grass, where I've thrown up a few times, and the sidewalks where I'd stumble or trip on my way back inside. Most of all, my own front yard. The yard that saw me growing up, from running through the sprinklers with friends, playing tag with the family, learning to catch with Tyson, and learning to wrestle with Will. From that to sitting on the stairs talking and hanging out, then onto other things like the first time I got drunk or the first time I snorted a pill on the side of the house. This house, this yard—they saw me change and grow up to become this version of me I didn't expect.

How long has it been since I was outside? I notice the grass is green again, and the trees have filled in with their leaves, flowers growing in people's yards. The world really does keep going even when you aren't in it, or at least not mentally.

The days have been getting harder, presenting me with thoughts I've never had before. Things are getting serious and I'm not sure what I'm supposed to be doing at this point. They say it takes loss to know love; it's in the shattered pieces of our hearts that we learn to appreciate the beauty of what once made it whole. But what does it mean for us if we're born with our hearts already shattered? I don't know loss, so how am I supposed to know any type of love?

I don't know love, not toward life, people, or even things. If I knew love, I wouldn't think about ending it, ending myself knowing, the effect it will have on the people around me, the people I'm supposed to love. I look down at the puddle of water at my feet and take another drag.

Maybe I should have followed through with therapy. I know we don't have the money for it, and I don't think it's my siblings' responsibility to find a way to pay for me to do anything, especially if it means putting them in debt. I couldn't do that to them. There is no guarantee therapy would help anyway. It's just what everyone expects you to do when you're in a negative mental position.

It sucks to see everything around me still going strong while I seem to be stuck, feeling nothing. I used to love doing so many things: journaling, writing, drawing, dancing, laughing. Now I can't even bring myself to shower. Not only is it pulling me into the deep, dark depths of depression, but it's holding everyone else back. It's not even like I'm drowning anymore. It's more like someone is holding my leg, pulling me down, and all I can do is kick and scream but my lungs are filling up with water and I'm running out of energy to fight.

I pull my phone out of my pocket as I stand, turning on my boy, Frank. Are you surprised? Then I lie in the grass looking up at the rain. I hear water droplets splashing into puddles, and thunder rumbles all around me. After taking one more drag, I close my eyes and flick the cigarette off to the side.

Would I be different if I was able to be openly gay my whole life? Would I maybe be normal if my dad wasn't such a piece of shit and my mom a dismissive fuck?

My eyes slowly open, and I look up to the sky. The parts of the sky not covered by clouds have bright stars peeking through. I wish I could fly away, start over or something, just to see what I would have done differently if I'd been given a different environment to grow up in.

My head rolls to the side and for the first time, I allow myself to imagine it, imagine what it would be like to have another man lying next to me. Someone I love and care about to lie beside me and watch the stars as the rain falls on both our faces. I can see us laughing at some dumb joke. The atmosphere between us would feel like home, and it would be just us here. I'd slide my hand over to his and tangle our fingers together while he made up constellations that were obviously wrong. Unfortunately, even that isn't good enough to make me feel life is worth living.

No, life *is* worth living. There are so many great opportunities and places to see that you can only do and see while living. Life is a wonderful gift if your cards are dealt right. You can have everything you ever wanted and more. Life is beautiful. The truth is, I don't think *I* am worth living. I've offered the world nothing but another drug addict, alcoholic, angry fuckup who can't keep their hands to themselves.

It's not my dad's or my mom's fault. I choose this. I do this to myself. I could have had a perfect family, one that spends Christmas together cooking and baking, watching movies together, going to the fucking store like normal people. Maybe we wouldn't eat so much pizza. I swear to God, we live off that shit. We wouldn't hurt each other, or ourselves. Most of all, we wouldn't be so scared of the world hurting *us*.

I will always choose the drug life, a hundred times over, because when you can't feel anything or you get that perfect high, it's like someone has their arms wrapped around you in the most comforting hug. You could have the worst day of your life, and they're always there, no questions asked. You're warm and alone; the world is quiet and peaceful. You aren't worried about who's talking about you or what anyone else is doing. It's truly just you. Nothing else exists or matters at all.

I sit up, my clothes dripping and my hair pressed to my face. The ground beneath me is muddy, which means I'm muddy now. Usually I would hate it, but right now I don't mind.

I wish I had more time to imagine a life where I had someone who loved me. I'd love to get lost in a dream like that and feel genuinely happy for the first time.

I stand and brush some of the wet dirt off my pants before glancing around the yard. I can't believe how much this place has seen. Better yet, I can't believe how much I've been through and how much I've changed. I'm not a confused, wandering 15-year-old anymore. I'm a lost and empty 21-year-old who has no solid grasp on the world. I wonder what 15-year-old me would have to say about who I am now.

As I walk back to the door, mud tracks follow. Before going into the house, I turn off Frank's voice. There's no need to wake everyone up. I might explode if I have to talk to anyone tonight. I'm not in the mood to exist.

Maybe someday soon, a tall blue-eyed dude will come around and it will be like all the books portray it. We'll fall in love and everything will be fixed. All the problems I've had will be cured by just one look at him. One touch will cure every bad part of me, and

I'll be happy, and funny. Love at first sight. We'll move to somewhere far away where depression and drugs will be a distant memory. Maybe in an even better world, we can both be huge druggies and do drugs together without the fear of ever being judged. I've always wanted to try shrooms.

Whatever it is, it needs to happen quickly because I'm losing this fight. I'm about to tap out. I wish I could fix myself.

Back in my room, I strip off the wet clothes and throw them into the corner, leaving me standing in just my boxers. Just for tonight, I'll let myself feel. I need a break from shoving it down and forcing it to remain hidden. I go to my window and turn around to sit under it.

I pull my knees up to my chest. I wrap my arms around them, and already I can feel the tears coming. After the first tear falls, the rest keep coming. There's no stopping them or the sobs that leave my chest.

I'm surrounded by so many people who say they love me, yet I feel so alone. I wonder if they've ever felt loss.

Do they really love me? I know that without me there would be a lot less for people to stress about. It might hurt for a while, but pain is temporary, along with the echoes of laughter and the warmth of shared moments.

As the tears blur my vision, I cling to the memories of our past, knowing they're all I have left. But even memories fade, and as they do, I hope someone will remember me not for the sadness that consumes me now but for the love I tried so desperately to give. I wish I was able to rewrite my own story and change who I am or the jokes I make. I wish I could have something more to be remembered by. I give myself a good hour to wallow in self-pity. Then I wipe my eyes, fix my hair, and climb into bed to go to sleep, wake up, and do it all again tomorrow.

Chapter 18

I'm woken by the sound of clattering in the kitchen. The sun is hardly out, and I know it has to be earlier than 7 a.m. I groan before rolling over and practically fall out of bed. I pull on shorts and a T-shirt and walk into the hallway. I find Suzie singing some dumb song while putting away the dishes.

"Morning!" I yell to her before going into the bathroom. I don't bother closing the door. After being in a place with one bathroom, you find it pretty easy to tell when someone's taking a piss.

"Hey, do you know why there's mud everywhere?" she calls back to me.

"Why do you assume I'd know about there being mud everywhere?"

"Because it leads to your room."

After washing my hands, I step out of the bathroom and see that she's right. There's mud everywhere, and it all leads right to my room. "Oh, yeah. I had a rough night. I couldn't sleep, so I went outside for a bit to think…but it was raining. Anyway, sorry about the mud. I'll clean it up."

"You went outside in the middle of the night while it was raining?" she asks. "Wow, that sounds like a very eventful night. I was just worried that some ax murderer came into the house and stole you or something." She laughs. "Coffee?"

"I'd love some coffee. I'm glad to know that you woke up and thought I'd been kidnapped and didn't even come check on me. You must have been so worried!"

"Hey. I've learned that it's better to wait and see if you ever come out. It's never a good idea to just walk into a boy's room. I've seen some *shit* from doing that."

"Eww." I rub my face, attempting to get rid of the tired feeling. "That's fair though. You want some breakfast?'

"You have dirt in your hair. I'm not sure I want to eat anything you're offering if it's going to come with an entire garden. I'll make breakfast while you go shower? Or should I call Katie to force you into it again?" she teases.

Katie showering me is something I'll never live down. I know they're all very grateful to have had someone that cared so much for me. But it doesn't stop them from bringing it up every chance they get.

I kiss Suzie on the head and turn toward the bathroom. "I guess I can shower, but only for you."

She laughs as I walk down the hall. In the bathroom, I stare blankly at myself in the mirror. The weird thing is that for me, the longer I look at myself or my siblings, the more beauty I see. We really are a good-looking family, and green eyes are always a crowd-pleaser. Self-confidence isn't something any of us lack. We all know how we look, but it doesn't fix the fact that I still hate every other thing about me.

The hot water fills the room with steam and makes me feel

better, especially after being outside in the cold last night. I sit down on the tub floor and let the water fall over me. A few minutes later, I stand up and wash the dirt from my hair. Though we all joke about it, it totally felt so much better when Katie was doing it.

After the five-minute shower, I leave the bathroom and head out to the living room where I sit down on the floor in front of the couch and lay my head back on it.

Suzie comes back in a moment later with two cups of coffee. "Did you use soap?" She scrunches her nose like she can smell something nasty.

"Very funny." I take a sip of coffee. Suzie always adds way too much sugar. I'm not sure how she isn't just constantly hyperactive. Of course, I wouldn't have it any other way. "Sorry I haven't been hanging out with you too much. I know you're just dying to watch more of that Dean guy, or whatever his name is."

She puts her hand over her heart and flops down onto the couch. "Yes, it's been a very rough time for me, so many Dean withdrawals. But I think I'll survive."

I smile. I know how much she loves that show. She's been begging me to watch it with her for years, but I'm a horrible person and only watch a few episodes a month before I go MIA. We're still on Season 10.

"You can watch it without me, you know that, right?"

Suzie puts her mug down on the coffee table and scrunches up her face again. "Yeah, but it's our thing! I don't want to watch it without you. There would be no fun, and I wouldn't have anyone to talk about it with. It wouldn't be the same. Besides, I know you have the hots for Sam too. You act like you don't, but I can always see right through you, as you know."

My mouth falls open and I scoff. "*What?* Where did you come up with that idea? I do not!"

"Oh, please. 'Did Sam work out?' 'Has Sam always had abs like that?' 'Do you think Sam is that tall, or is Dean just that short?' And my absolute favorite: 'Sam's hair looks so soft.' "

"Um, okay. Those are innocent questions!" I throw my hands up. "Anyone would ask them. Have you seen that dude's hair? It's where I get my inspiration, though I come off more crackhead than I do sexy demon slayer."

"Innocent questions. Funny. You literally just called him a sexy demon slayer."

"What demon slayer *isn't* sexy? That doesn't mean anything. Have you seen Buffy?"

"She's a vampire slayer." She smirks and hits my head with a couch pillow. "Admit it, you're hot for Sam."

She might be right, but I'm not going to admit that to her. "I love you, Bug. Thanks for always spending time with me even when I've been a dick. It's always meant a lot to me." I look down at my hands in my lap.

Suzie hesitates before asking, "Does it mean a lot to you now? You're different again, and it's a little scary."

I frown and tilt my head to the side. "What do you mean?"

She bites the skin on her lip. "Like, you've been acting like you're better. But it's not in an 'I'm better' type of way. It's almost like you have to remind yourself to act certain ways or do certain things. It just doesn't seem very genuine, and I feel like if you were actually better or wanting to work on yourself, you'd let us know something was up instead of faking it. Every time you hang out with us, it feels like you're apologizing for something."

"Apologizing for something?" I shake my head. "I haven't done anything."

She shrugs. "Maybe it's something you're going to do, or

something you assume is going to happen…I don't know. Something's off."

My face drops and my breathing gets a tad heavier. I lick my lips and turn my head toward the TV. Does this girl read my notebooks, or is she really just that observant? If she's that observant, do the others see right through me too? It's not that I'm planning or assuming that something is going to happen. But I do know what goes through my head every single second of every day.

"Yeah," she says. "I keep telling you, I always see right through you. You need to talk to someone. It doesn't have to be the boys, or even me. Just…I don't know, go to the doctor or a therapist or something. There's so much we can do to help."

I shake my head more insistently this time. "Are you going to pay for that, Bug? Huh? Or I guess we could all just starve and not pay the house payment so that Will and Tyson can help, right?" I take a deep breath. "You think I haven't thought of every situation already? You don't think I'd like to stop feeling like this every damn day? Every. Damn. Day. Not only do I feel as bad as I could possibly feel every day, but I'm a burden on everyone. My friend had to give me a shower because I couldn't even find the energy or motivation to do that. Tyson won't leave the house when I'm here because he's scared of leaving me alone. No one wants to bring friends over or have their own life because everyone is so concerned about me. I'm trying, I'm trying so fucking hard, so please don't act like that or say things like that because it doesn't help. I am trying. Everyone keeps saying 'There's so much we can do,' but there isn't. There's nothing we can do. I just have to endure this shit and hope I don't fall into a relapse or do something to disappoint everyone."

It sounds rude, I know, but it's the calmest and most real conversation I've had in a long time. I think they deserve to know the truth. It's not that I'm trying to fool everyone into thinking I'm fine. It's just not their problem to carry.

"I'm sorry. I know, it's just a lot for us, too," Suzie says. "The boys walk on eggshells around you because they're worried they'll say the wrong thing, which is weird for me because now it's like…well, it's like instead of just you being weird and different, all three of my brothers are different now. I don't feel like that with you. I feel like I can be more open, and that we're closer than we have been. So I ask all the questions and it just gets jumbled in my head, and I don't know if I should be relieved and thankful that we're talking about it or if I should be holding everything back so I don't send you off into a downhill spiral when I can see you're already at the bottom of one."

She shakes her head like she's trying to get rid of the conversation, the image—and me, I'm sure. I'm clearly not in the right headspace to have this conversation. I can feel the anger building up again, and I don't want to take it out on her.

"Are you in the mood for *Supernatural* right now?" she asks. "I'd rather we spend our time doing that."

My eyes are wide and my face is blank. When did she grow up? How did I miss her growing up so much? I can't believe the conversation I'm having with my sister, who apparently isn't ten anymore. I nod and turn away. The pain and confusion in her eyes scare me. They almost look like mine, like they're losing the life in them. Did I do that to her?

It's weird how after you stop doing drugs, everything else comes to light. All the lives you've changed and missed, the people you've broken, and all the things you can never get back. I didn't just miss my teenage years. I missed watching Suzie grow up. Those are years I won't ever fucking get back, and I didn't get to see my sister become this…woman. Drugs really do change you and every single thing around you. I miss how we used to be. How we used to joke with each other and fight on the ground. No one held back. No one talked about feelings or emotions. I miss that, and I know I can never get it back.

"What was your first day of high school like?" I may not have been there mentally for it, but I'd like to know more.

Confusion fills her face, but she answers anyway. "Scary. But good. Tyson wouldn't leave me alone. He convinced me he was going to drop me off but ended up staying and showing me where all my classes were before he left. I hated it, but once he was gone and I was alone, I was so glad he did that so I didn't look stupid and lost. He said he did the same thing for you and Will."

I do remember having the same feelings that Suz did. I was so embarrassed and couldn't wait for Tyson to leave. But when I was the only one getting to each class with ease, I was grateful he'd taken the time to do that for me.

"I remember that." Smiling slightly, I let out a small laugh. "And you graduate next year?"

A proud smile spreads across her face "I do. I've been working my ass off. I can't wait until it's over."

"Yeah, goodbye school, hello working a shit job the rest of your life." When I look back at her, she's wearing an annoyed face. "I'm sorry. Of course, it's amazing to graduate, I'm so proud of you. Are you planning on going to college after?"

She shrugs and pulls her lips to the side deep, in thought. "I don't know. It kind of sucks being the youngest. The praise and money for going to college is kind of all used up." That amused smile reappears on her face. "I'm undecided. I thought about just doing core classes like you until I figure out what I want to do, but I don't know. I'd rather just wait until I have an idea to start."

I nod in understanding. I wish I would have done the same.

"Well, just know that we're all so proud of you, with or without college. I'm proud of you, Bug. You've done amazing things, and I know nothing was handed out to you, so I'm surprised it hasn't kicked your ass."

"Who says it hasn't?" She lifts an eyebrow in accusation. "As Will once said, just because I wear it well doesn't mean I'm not feeling the same as you."

"Fair. I'm sorry, it isn't easy growing up in this family. I'm assuming being the last born doesn't help that at all."

She sits up and slides off the couch onto the floor next to me. "Honestly, Jace, the hand you're given doesn't matter. It's the way you deal with it that shapes you."

My eyes meet hers as what she says shoots through me like a bullet. Maybe I've been wrong this whole time; maybe they do judge me for the way I am. I spent so much of my time blaming my parents for making me the way I am, but I know that I created myself. It's just rough hearing that from Suzie because I do wonder now if she judges me for everything. She clearly judges me for the way I'm handling it.

I look away from her and back to the TV. "I guess you're right."

Chapter 19

You have all known this for a while… Not the gay thing. Well, that too. But this. Eventually, I was going to relieve the piss I've been holding in for six years. Being a drug addict isn't fun, and it isn't a life I'd ask for or wish upon anyone. The way I see it, I've always had two options, but as life went on, I found that both options led to the same destination, so why take the long way?

Our morning is mostly silent and *Supernatural*. We don't talk much after the energy in the room changed. I didn't mean to take the comment so personally, but come on. How could I not? About two hours into the show, Tyson comes in, sits down, and watches with us. Will follows shortly after. No one asks why we're all awake and watching the show so early in the morning. I can't remember one time when we all woke up early and just hung out. Honestly, for such a dysfunctional family, it's weird how close we all are.

We watch the show for hours. Tyson teases Suzie occasionally for drooling over Dean, and Will…well, Will is just being himself, so you know how that goes. It's the worst experience you could imagine.

"Dude, okay, so Sam walks into your bedroom and he's naked. What do you do?" Will asks me.

This is not what I meant when I mentioned that no one had

commented on the whole "gay" thing that happened with Dad. I was just curious to hear what everyone thought, or if anyone hated me for it. I didn't invite an interrogation about what I'd do if a naked man appeared in my room. But I mean I guess it's something. I'm just not sure why everyone is so obsessed over me thinking Sam is an attractive man.

"Why is he naked?" I ask, my face contorted.

"I don't know! Needs, or desires, or maybe his clothes got burned off. Who knows? Anyway, do you top him, or are you more of a bottom?"

Oh, my God, this again? Why he's so interested in this I'll never know, but I just sigh heavily in response.

This family could feel complete. I'm sure it could. But I don't feel like I belong. I know I don't. I'm the "trial" or whatever, the person in your life you feel you have to love, but if it was some random person or a friend, you'd turn your back on them. I shoot Suzie an apologetic look.

"Come on," Will insists, "I'll tell you mine if you tell me yours!"

"Dude?" Tyson shakes his head in confusion.

Nodding in agreement with Tyson, I add, "Yeah, I'm not sure I want to know your answer."

"Fine, I'll go first, then. I'd bottom for Sam, no questions asked."

I huff and look at the wall, wishing it would suck me in and away from this conversation. "Will, you wouldn't know what to do if some naked man walked into your room. You'd probably run away screaming."

"Aha! And what would *you* do?!"

"I don't know! I'd probably question why there's a stranger in my bedroom with his wang out." I throw my arms up.

Tyson nods. "Yeah, kind of gay to walk into a sleeping dude's room naked," he jokes. He thinks for a few seconds then looks back over at Will. "Is he hard, or soft?"

"Oh, my God, come on!" I bury my head in my hands.

With no hesitation, Will answers. "Hard."

"Alright! That's enough for me."

I get up from the couch, but before I can go anywhere, Suzie hits me with eye daggers, begging me not to leave her with them. After waving the cigarette pack in the air, I continue toward the front door.

Will and Tyson argue about why Sam would be hard and what they'd each do if it happened to them. Poor Suzie really is getting the shit end of the stick in that conversation. In fact, I've never been more excited to leave a debate between the two.

I sit on the front step and light the cig. As always, the first inhale makes my body and hands tingle. I hold it in as long as I can before blowing it out. I've never really enjoyed living. Drugs made it bearable, but let's face it: they'll eventually end up killing me. The hardest thing is trying to figure out what options I have that won't hurt me or my family. I get that I'm being selfish. But isn't the world being selfish about me? People always say, "If you aren't happy in a relationship, just leave. Don't worry about hurting the other person." Why should I make myself miserable to keep everyone else happy?

I live by two simple words. They also happen to be the answer to everything: that's life. Inspired by the only person who's ever gotten me.

Recently, cigarettes have been holding me over quite a bit. They provide their own little sense of security. Once a nasty way to get an escape, they're now a welcomed taste in my mouth, one I find myself craving. Ian always had cigs on him, but I'd only smoked them once in a while when we had nothing better to do. Back then

I hated the stale tobacco taste that stayed in my mouth the rest of the day. I wonder if 15-year-old Jace had picked these up instead, would I still have jumped into the pills? Probably. I'm pretty predictable.

After finishing and smashing the smoke, I roll my shoulders and get ready to put myself back into the interesting conversations that are waiting for me. I go back inside and sit between Tyson and Will.

The smoke break did nothing to calm my nerves like it usually did. I'm not sure why the anxiety, panic, and depression are all hitting at the same time. Hanging out with them like this isn't making me feel any better. I was hoping that maybe being around everyone would pull me out of the hole I've fallen into. But this whole thing is just horrible, sitting here like this is what I planned on doing for the rest of my life. Like this is how it will always be.

Everything is moving too fast—my head, my heart, my leg, the show, and the time of day. I've been thinking about Xanax a lot. It's always had a way of slowing down the crazy in life. Instead of five million things running through your head and screaming at you at the same time, it dulls it down to three distant voices. I needed a break from all the screaming. No wonder I've been so on edge and irritable. I can't even hear myself fucking think.

The TV is still on. Will's voice rings through the room, followed by Suzie's laugh. I'm pretty sure I can hear a drip in the kitchen sink and every car that passes the house. Has the traffic always been this busy around here? Everyone's living, living, and not fighting themselves for the way they feel. No one else in this room has to remind themselves to smile at the right time, or that they can't just disappear to have a drink. No one else here has to count five things they can hear, smell, touch, and taste every ten minutes. No one here has to give themselves three reasons to live every five minutes. They just live, talk, and laugh.

The heater kicks on, causing another sound to whirl into my brain. The faint squeaking noise the vent above the coffee table makes is going to drive me insane.

I'm done. I cannot do this anymore. I don't want to be in a constant war with myself on not doing drugs and feeling like a complete ass, having to look my family in the eye every day. This isn't normal. I'm not normal. Life shouldn't be like this; I shouldn't have to remind myself to be human every three seconds.

"I have to piss." I stand up quickly, pushing Will over at the same time and almost sprinting to the bathroom.

When I get there, the bathroom's too hot. It's always been like this. If you leave the door shut, the hot air from the vent gets trapped and makes it a sauna. I splash my face with cold water. I look at the hole in the wall that's still there from when I smashed my head into it. That seems so long ago now.

After flushing the toilet and looking into the living room to make sure everything's clear, I sneak off to my room. I pull the stash book off the shelf and take a deep breath before opening it. I count twenty-five random pills. Then I dig through all the shit on my floor to find my notebook.

With the notebook and pills in hand, I pace the room, counting my steps. Everything that seemed to be moving so fast now feels like slow motion. The voices from the living room are still fogging my brain. The rain continues falling, tapping against the roof and my window. I sit on the floor. This is too much, too much too fast, I want it to stop. I want the feeling to stop, and the noise and the pity and the babysitting. I want it to stop.

I wish I could go back to that night; the night everything changed. I wish I could tell Tyson I had a stomach flu. I wish I'd never met Katie, and that she didn't give a shit about what was in my cup. I wish I was still living my perfect laid-back drug-using life. Fuck, if I could go back those three months, I would. I'd go back to February so fast.

I pop a handful of pills into my mouth and wash them down with water before I can change my mind. I've already made my decision, and I don't want to be here. I've had years to think about this. If I was going to change my mind, I would have already.

I think about Suzie and let a tear spill over. I wish I had been better for her, stronger. I wish I could have been the brother to her that Will and Tyson have been to me.

I hope she forgives me. I hope they all do.

Chapter 20

You have all known this for a while… Not the gay thing. Well, that too. But this. Eventually, I was going to relieve the piss I've been holding in for six years. Being a drug addict isn't fun, and it isn't a life I'd ask for or wish upon anyone. The way I see it, I've always had two options, but as life went on, I found that both options led to the same destination, so why take the long way?

Life hasn't been bad. It hasn't been great, but it hasn't been bad. I think I have all of you to thank for that. You guys have always helped me be the best that you could. I feel bad that school always came so easy to me while Tyson couldn't even make it past third grade. Sorry, Tyson.

You know, it's kind of crazy how we used to always be so against spending time together because now we prefer it. Sucks that Mom's enthusiasm to get us to bond ended before Suzie could really enjoy it. As close as we've been, we never had conversations about feelings or thoughts with each other. We're such a "deal with it on your own" type of family. Then again, I guess we had to be. But, Tyson, you are going to be the best dad. I think you've seen so much shit that it's impossible for you to judge anyone. I look up to that a lot.

Will, no one is angrier than you are. You handle it well, though, always letting it out in jokes about Tyson being dumb. All jokes aside, Tyson, I'm sorry for all the school and stupid jokes. I know the only reason you dropped out was because Dad was getting psychotic and Mom was completely checking out. You had no choice. Suzie and I were still young, and you stepped up to take care of us. Thank you for that. I'm sorry it cost you your life and education.

Waking up sucks, but waking up to reality isn't that bad. I guess I've spent so much time being high and drunk that I forgot how it feels to be real. I can't say I don't resent all three of you for forcing me back into real life, but I'm also grateful.

Our friends always loved coming to our house to sleep over. Until Dad got the way he is. The one time Will brought home a friend, and Dad thought it was me... That almost turned out very bad. After that day, Grandma used to always tell us "If you want to know, ask the question. You may not get another chance." Will, you and Suzie never pass up the moment to ask some really fucking weird or awkward questions. You two kill me...too soon?

I'm starting to think it's true that your parents know you better than any-one else, even if you don't think they do. Maybe they really did know our burning secrets the whole time. I've always wondered what happened with Mom and Dad. It felt like a switch, like one day we were all okay, and the next we weren't. What could have caused that? Let me know if you ever find out.

I'm sure you're curious. The summer after my first year in junior high was when I started spiraling down. I was twelve and people at school weren't very nice, especially when I was going to school covered in bruises and blood. I always wondered why Dad chose me so often. Why he would sit down with Will and watch a movie then the second I got home find some reason to beat the hell out of me. He was a strong man. I have never and will never blame any of you for not getting between it. Mom always told us that the word "danger" had "anger" in it for a reason. I never got that. Again, the angriest person I know is Will. I'm sorry life has been so unfair. It has to suck to have a heart so pure in a world so fucked up. There are not a lot of great people in this world. I'm so lucky and grateful for Katie. With her, everything just kind of clicks and feels right. I'm sorry, Katie.

I'm sorry I was never a great brother. I know I didn't bond well like eve-ryone else did. I guess I wasn't sure how. I've always been so different. I wasn't sure what things to talk about that you would understand. Suzie, on the other hand, Bug, you kept me going through all of life. You have always been so relatable, and I am so selfishly glad Mom and Dad had just one more kid to neglect so I could have my best friend.

I wish I could explain how it feels… You know when you wake up and have to pee really bad but your alarm goes off in an hour so you try to hold it in? But doing that just keeps you up thinking about it constantly, so you don't get that hour of sleep anyway? That's a horrible example, but imagine doing that for six-and-a-half years. Well, not every night for six years but like holding it in for the whole six years—never mind. Forget I wrote that.

Suzie, I'll admit it. You are and always will be my favorite sibling. You have always gotten me without my even having to talk, and seriously, you aren't scared of anything! You're going to be so crazy smart and loving. Dean would be lucky to have you.

William, one last thing for you—and I can't believe I'm going to say it. I would absolutely be a top, no doubt about it. I hate you for making me admit that.

Tyson, thanks for being the best dad I could have ever wished for.
I'm sorry, I'm so sorry. I love you all. Tell Dad I said fuck you for me.

Chapter 21: Tyson

We were watching that stupid *Supernatural* show when Suzie stood up and walked quickly to the bathroom. I could have sworn Jace went back there a while ago. I turned my back to the TV and watched her open the bathroom door then slam it shut and walk toward Jace's room. I wondered where he went off to. If he went back to bed, I was going to be so mad. The only reason I got up was because I heard he and Suzie were awake. No normal person should have been up at that time.

The front door squeaked, signaling someone was coming in. I pulled my eyes away from Suzie to see Katie walking through the door.

"Hey, Tyson!" Katie seemed as happy as ever. She always had the best attitude. I really thought she was making a difference in Jace's life. I absolutely loved having her around. It was a little weird having another girl around. It felt like I had another sister. It was exhausting trying to keep up with how many people I was supposed to be protecting. Katie, though, was an amazing addition to the family.

"Hey, Kat—" I began but was cut off.

"OH, MY GOD!"

The scream came from Jace's room. I immediately jumped up and ran to Suzie's voice.

"TYSON!" her panicked scream cried out. My heart dropped

before I even got to her.

No, I thought, *this can't be happening, it can't be what I think it is.*

The beating in my chest turned heavy, pounding in slow motion.

I braced myself for what I assumed I'd see and pushed the door open. Jace was lying on the floor with a notebook, a water bottle, and a Ziplock bag with ten or more pills.

"Fuck. NO!"

I knelt beside him and shoved my fingers down his throat. He was still breathing but unresponsive. Tears flowed down my face as I screamed, "Get up! Jace, open your fucking eyes!"

I shook him and shook him with no luck. I turned around as Katie appeared at the door, trying to stay calm.

I turned Jace onto his side and continued shoving my fingers down his throat. "Come on, buddy," I whispered. "Come on, Jace, throw up, man. Come on, please. You can't do this, don't do this, Jace."

The fact that I couldn't get him to throw up was stirring panic within the deepest parts of me. How long had it been since he'd taken those?!

"Will called 911, they're three minutes away." The voice came from Katie—I thought.

I didn't know what else to do. Should I keep trying to make him puke? I placed my hand on his chest and felt a slow and soft heartbeat.

"The police mentioned Narcan, do we have any?" Will yelled as he rammed himself into the room. "DO WE HAVE ANY?!"

All I could do was shake my head. We never needed that in the house. Why would we have needed that in the house? I brought my fist to my head, hitting my forehead four times. *How could I not have that in the house?*

I stared into Jace's face as I held him in my arms. I looked up to Suzie, who was holding onto her legs on the far end of Jace's bed with the notebook in her hand. She was in shock, I was sure.

I tried to steady my voice before speaking, but it still came out panicked and shaky. "Katie, get Suzie out of here." Katie hesitated by the door for two seconds too long and I bellowed, "NOW!"

I should have known this was going to happen. He had become so distant that past week. I knew there was something wrong but I never asked him about it or brought it up.

I'm a horrible brother, I thought. *I could have prevented this!*

*　　　　　*　　　　　*

Suzie refused to get off the floor, so Katie pretty much carried her out and sat her on the floor in my room. I could hear her crying from Jace's room but I couldn't do anything about it, couldn't do anything for her.

When the cops and paramedics got there, Jace was still lying across my lap, my hands in his hair and my head pressed against his. My tears slid down my face onto his. I can't explain how I felt. Hollow. Like this wasn't actually happening I kept waiting to wake up from this recurring dream. Only this time I didn't wake up. This time, it was real.

I stood back with my hand over my face as I watched the paramedics pull Jace up into the ambulance.

"Name and age?" one of the paramedics asked me.

I couldn't peel my eyes away from Jace. He hadn't moved at all since we'd found him. No muscle movement, no half-assed fake smile, no sarcastic remarks.

"Sir, I understand this is hard, but I need his name and age."

"Jace, he's, um…" I paused to swallow. "He's 21." So young,

still so much life to live.

"Okay, and what did he take?" she asked, and my face tore from Jace to her.

"What?"

"What did he take? We need to know so we don't give him anything that will counteract with it, and so we know how to help." She held a pen and notebook in her hands, acting as if this was just another day on the job. She didn't know Jace; didn't know anything about him. She didn't know how funny he was, how full of life he used to be, the way he used to dream of being a dancer. She didn't know our dad beat him or called him names. Nothing. She knew nothing. She was just doing her job. To her, he was just another kid who took too many pills on accident trying to get high.

The panic and the tears came back to me as I tried to find the answers to her question. "I-I don't know. I don't know what he took, the bag was full of different things. I don't even know how many were originally in there. He's a recovering addict…anything he could find."

"That's fine. We're going to take him down. You're free to follow us down there, but once at the hospital, we'll ask you to stay in the waiting room until we have more information." She finished taking her notes and hopped into the back of the ambulance. I turned to Katie and Will, who were both standing outside.

"Let's go, I can drive." Will pulled the keys out of his pocket, and Katie ran back inside to get Suzie. A few moments later, we were all in Will's car speeding down the road behind the ambulance.

"Is he going to be okay?" Will asked me.

"I don't know," I said and wiped my eyes.

"Tyson, please, tell me he's okay," Will pleaded.

"I said I don't KNOW!" I threw my hands up to my head.

I was supposed to be the big brother, I was supposed to keep everyone from this type of stuff. I couldn't fix this; I couldn't reassure Will. I knew he was feeling the same way I was, like we wanted someone to tell us right now "he's fine" or "this was a joke." Anything but this.

I reached over and turned on the radio. It was on the oldies station, and if we were in any other position, I would have teased Will for it. But the music reminded me of Jace. He was always listening to old music.

"Oh, my God," Suzie said, leaning into the front seat and turning up the music. "Oh, fuck." I couldn't tell if she was laughing or crying.

"What?" I asked frantically.

"This song! This is his song." She covered her mouth. Definitely crying.

It was silent in the car as we all listened to the music coming out of the speakers.

"It's called "That's Life" by Frank Sinatra," Suzie said. "I don't know what this means."

She shook her head, tears still falling from her face. I gave her a confused look.

"If it's a sign from the universe, it could be telling us he's going to be okay. If it's a sign from Jace…" She stopped.

Suzie was always into that spiritual energy stuff, whatever you want to call it. I hoped she didn't know what she was talking about, but I couldn't bring myself to tease her for this, not this time.

I slowly turned to face the road just as the ambulance sirens started going off and the lights turned on.

Fuck, Jace.

*　　　　　*　　　　　*

The waiting room was small. There was a coffee bar, a few vending machines, the front desk, and about twenty chairs. Every once in a while you could hear the receptionist typing away on her computer. Suzie was lying on Katie's lap, her eyes empty and sad. I was worried about her. She hadn't really said anything or shown any type of emotion after Katie pulled her out of Jace's room.

Katie was running her hands through Suzie's hair in a soothing fashion. I was glad she was there to help because I was in no position to be comforting anyone.

Will had disappeared a while ago, yelling and kicking a chair over before storming out of the waiting room, slamming the door behind him. Usually, I'd follow him to make sure he was okay, but not today. Today it was everyone for themselves because we all had way more important things to think about.

The ticking clock was louder than I remembered clocks being, and slower too. It had been an hour and a half with no news. Every time someone came through the doors leading to the emergency room, we all shot our heads in that direction, hoping it was for us. The hospital smelled bad, and the intercom was annoying. I heard all these code colors that I didn't know the meaning of and just hoped they weren't about the person we were here for.

The receptionist wouldn't tell us anything about Jace, not even the condition he was in. I was really not fond of the fact we were sitting there waiting for information and for all we knew, he could have been gone before they got here.

Another hour passed in this way. No one spoke. Just the clicking of the keyboard and the ticking of the clock. The door to the waiting room whipped open and Will walked toward us, slamming himself into the chair beside me. Pure anger was flowing out of him, so thick you could almost see it. I'd seen him mad plenty of times. But I'd never seen him so worried that it turned into anger. This was a side of him I hadn't seen before.

"If Jace isn't dead, I'm going to fucking kill him," Will yelled. Other people in the room glanced over at us, and the receptionist even stopped her typing to glance at who had said such a thing.

"Will, please, there are other people here." I rested my hand on his shoulder before he shoved it off of him.

Suzie started laughing from her position on Katie's lap. We all looked at her. Katie stopped messing with her hair and leaned over to see Suzie's face. The laughter increased and she sat up to hold her stomach.

"Care to share with the class?" Will said in one of the harshest tones I'd ever heard from him.

"If he isn't dead, you're going to kill him," Suzie said and laughed again. "If he isn't dead." She took a deep breath and stood up with her hands on her hips.

"And that's funny to you?" Will said. "You think Jace being dead is funny?" He stood and took a few steps in Suzie's direction.

I felt like I should stop him, but for the first time, I was kind of on the same page. What was she talking about? None of us even worried about how the room had stopped what they were doing to look over at us, very interested in the conversation we were about to have.

"It's just that I never thought I'd hear that sentence." Suzie licked her lips and looked up at the ceiling lights. "If Jace isn't *dead.*" She laughed once more and then looked down at the floor. We all knew how Jace was feeling, and that he was having some problems. But none of us expected this to happen. Then again, you never do. We all knew he just had to push through it, endure for a little longer. Maybe we didn't know the extent of it, but the one thing I did know was that this was something I'd only have to go through in my dreams.

Suzie's head shot in Will's direction after a dramatic pause. "And what if he is, Will? What if Jace *is* dead, huh? Then what?" She threw her arms out before letting them fall back to her sides. She didn't move her gaze from his eyes, staring at him, demanding an answer I wasn't sure she wanted.

"Guys, no news is good news, right?" Katie said, moving between Suzie and Will. "Do you think they would have him back there for this long if he wasn't either alive or still fighting to be alive?"

Will pushed Katie to the side and stepped closer to Suzie. "If Jace is dead, then I guess we don't have anyone to babysit anymore. Maybe we can start living life again like a normal fucking family."

Finally, this made me stand up. "William. Shut the fuck up. You don't mean that. Jace already hurt her, why are you trying to make it worse? That was a fucked-up thing to say. I don't give a shit if you're mad or upset. Bring it down a notch."

Will shrugged. "That's what you want to hear, right, Suz? That I don't care if Jace is dead, that I prefer it that way?"

Suzie walked up to him and shoved his shoulders back. "You had no problem telling him he was the problem a few months ago. Looked to me like you were pushing for this exact thing. He was doing better! He was trying to get better for us!" She pushed him again and pounded her fists into his chest.

They had gained an audience. Everyone in the waiting room was watching them, and I was sure the receptionist was calling security. I shook my head and sat back down in the chair. We were already all screwed up, couldn't get much worse than the Jace situation.

"Tyson? You going to stop this?" Katie asked, rushing over to me. She wasn't going to get anywhere near trying to stop him on her own.

I felt my eyes fill up with tears. What was happening to us? One minute we were home watching TV. The next minute Jace was back in a room by himself in who knew what kind of condition. Will and Suzie were biting each other's heads off, and I was just sitting there ignoring it.

"I didn't want him to fucking *die*, Suzie. I wanted him to understand that he was scaring us! Scaring me. He wasn't trying, he wasn't trying for anyone. If he was, he would have talked to us about this before he decided to be ignorant." His hands dropped to his side. "Don't try to blame this on me. Jace did what he did, and it wasn't my fault."

Suzie shook her head. "No, you didn't even try to let him know you were scared, you showed him you were angry. That you were mad at him. That doesn't exactly shout "Hey, I'm here for support." He did come to us. He came to me, he went to Tyson. Fuck, he even went to Katie!"

She pointed at Katie, who like me had decided it was best for them to get it out and had sat back down.

"He didn't go to you because you're so goddamn angry, he thinks you hate him. He was probably scared of how you'd react if he had talked to you about anything." Her arms crossed in front of her as my head dropped down to the floor. I knew Jace was a little standoffish to Will, but I didn't know he wasn't talking to him about this at all. Did Will think Jace was just a new person and completely healed?

Will dropped his shoulders and turned toward me. "He went to you? He was talking to you?"

My heart dropped. I didn't know how to answer, but I looked back up at him and took a deep breath. "I mean, kind of… He told me he was having a hard time with the drug thing." That was true. He did feel comfortable enough to tell me he was having a hard time and couldn't stop thinking about doing them. Which I guess for Jace was opening up quite a bit.

Will looked at Katie. "And you?"

She just gave him a shrug that said, "What do you want me to say?"

Will stepped back and sat softly down on the chair. His face turned red and he held back tears. "Jace is going to die thinking I hate him."

No one answered. No one could. We didn't know if Jace was alive, if he was going to stay alive, or if maybe he was already gone. Just like earlier, Will yelled, kicked a chair, and stormed out the door.

One single tear fell down my face. I quickly wiped it away with the sleeve of my shirt and leaned back in the chair with my arms crossed.

"That went well," Katie breathed.

"Did you know Jace wasn't talking to Will about stuff?" Suzie asked me.

"No. But honestly, he was talking to all three of us, so why would he need to bring it up to a fourth person, you know? But you aren't wrong. If I was Jace, I would have been worried about how Will would have reacted too."

"You shouldn't have thrown it in his face," Katie said to Suzie as she crossed one leg over the other and leaned back in her chair, resting her head on the wall.

I was leaning on my elbows on my knees, my hands interlocked. I didn't get it. Why would Jace have been talking to us so openly if he was planning on doing this?

"What was he talking to you about?" I asked Suzie.

"This." She looked around the waiting room. "I mean, not that he was planning on it or anything, but there were some red flags. Especially this morning. It's why I went to check on him in the bathroom after he'd been in there for so long. I had this really weird feeling all night. I woke up to get water and saw him outside lying on the grass in the rain at like two in the morning. This morning I asked him about it. He didn't really say much, just that he had a rough night."

"He talked to you about the way he was feeling?" I looked back at the ground, trying to figure out what had caused this or led him to this point. I was trying to find a way to link it back to me, to make it my fault. "He never talked to me about feelings. Just the drug thing, the cravings. What did he talk to you about, Katie?"

"Everything. Anything. I don't know. I don't really understand why it matters."

I slapped my hands on my knees and stood up, running a hand down my face. "There has to be something. Something we weren't doing. This feels like my fault, and I just want to connect the dots. See if we can figure out where he snapped."

"Tyson." Suzie places her hand on my arm. "We can't always walk on eggshells around him. It wasn't your fault. We all feel that way. We could have done more, we should have known, we should have been there for him. We have been doing everything we can."

Katie sat up in her chair nodding. "He was going to do this regardless. I know he's been fighting himself for years. Back in February when I first met him, he was already struggling every day. He held on for a long time, but he's going to pull through this. He isn't dead, and he isn't going to die. Okay?"

It felt like false positivity, but it helped calm me down. Hearing those words, even if they weren't true, relieved so much weight. I sat back down. All we could do now was wait.

I didn't know how much time passed. It could have been five minutes, could have been four hours. I sat and reminisced on everything from our childhood to now. Looking back, I could pinpoint exactly where Jace changed, exactly when things started. How could we not have seen it?

I guess we put it off as puberty. We could have stopped it. We could have stopped it before it got so bad. We should have put him in therapy like we talked about. Hell, we should all have been in therapy.

The door to the emergency room opened and a short woman stepped out. She didn't hold any emotion at the front of her face to give away the news that followed. "Jace Carter's family?"

*　　　　*　　　　*

I could have sworn time stood still. The clock didn't tick, the receptionist didn't type, the vending machines even stopped their humming.

"We can only have two come back at a time," the woman said when we all stood up. I turned around and gave Katie an apologetic look.

"Go," Katie nodded.

"Suzie," I said and held my hand out to her. She pushed past and followed the nurse, who was now walking away. After silently thanking Katie, I turned around and followed Suzie and the nurse back.

"Is he okay?" I asked.

"He's stable," she said. "The doctor will give you more information."

"So, he's alive?" Suzie asked.

"He is alive, but he isn't awake," was all the nurse said before opening the door to Jace's room and moving aside so we could walk in.

Jace lay on the bed looking peaceful, as if he were asleep. As horrible as it was to see him here, it was nice to know he was in the safest place he could be. The knowledge of this eased a pain in my chest that had been there for the past few months. The constant worry and watching and thinking. Now there were people around who could help, and it wasn't my responsibility.

Suzie started crying and ran to him. She pulled a chair up and sat down with her head on his bed next to him. She grabbed his hand and sobbed.

"The doctor will be in shortly," the nurse said and left, closing the door behind her.

"Look at him," Suzie cried.

I did, and then I quickly looked at the wall. I hated how he looked. He had a heart monitor on, an oxygen mask, a few IVs were connected to him, and there was a blood pressure cuff on his right arm. He was laid back to look like he was sleeping. His hospital gown was slid down to his shoulders, and his hair was in his face.

There was a steady beep in the room coming from one of the machines. The overhead lights were bright, too bright. He wouldn't have liked it. I walked over to the light switches and turned them off. The light from the window and the small reading light behind the bed lit up the room just enough for us to be able to see.

"Thank you," Suzie said for Jace.

If Jace were an animal, he would be a bat. Just hanging out in cold dark caves, sleeping and eating.

The door flung open and Will stepped in. "Those bastards were trying to keep me out of here." He swung the door closed behind him. "Like I'm going to wait any fucking longer to see my own damn family." His voice carried across the empty room. Hospitals are not a place for people like Will.

"Oh, my God…" Will approached Jace and moved the hair out of his face. "They did you dirty, my brother."

"What do you mean?" I asked, facing my fears and looking back at Jace. I didn't like how not real he looked, almost like he might already be dead but the doctor felt bad and put him here to tell us he was alive.

"Look at this gown, it is not his color," Will said. He grabbed the sleeve of the pale blue-and-white gown and tugged on it. "Do you think he has clothes on under this?" The smile on Will's face was a red flag.

"What the hell is your problem?" Suzie said.

"What? If he did, I'd help him out and take this god-awful thing off him. I know he would thank me for it."

"Will…" Suzie leaned into Will and sniffed. "Oh, my God, are you drunk?"

Will shrugged. "No, but I had, like, two beers. I just didn't want to come in here angry if Jace was…you know…if he was dead, or awake. Either way, I didn't want to take it out on you anymore, and I didn't want to risk yelling at him."

Drinking for me and Will wasn't like it was for Jace and Dad. We could drink and have fun then not even think about it for months.

"I wasn't sure you were coming back," I whispered.

Will nodded. "Neither was I." He chuckled lightly. "He looks like shit." He used the back of his sleeve to wipe his nose and a tear that had escaped. "Good, I was worried he was going to take my place as best-looking Carter."

"So how are you going to do it?" Suzie asked, looking at Will.

"Do what?"

"Kill him."

They both started laughing through their tears.

"Oh, yeah, that." Will sat on the bed by Jace's feet. "Kindness."

"Kill him with kindness?" I remarked. "That doesn't really sound like your type of thing. I'm not sure I can imagine it."

He shrugged. "It's better than strangulation, which is a very close runner-up."

This time a smile broke from me. "That it is."

The doctor came into the room and pulled out a clipboard. "Good morning. You must be the family?"

"We are," I said. "How is he?"

The doctor read over the chart. "Well, he seems to be okay. He had a few touch-and-go moments, so we—"

"He died!?" Will half-yelled, interrupting the doctor.

"In the ambulance," the doctor clarified. "He didn't die, but he did have an irregular heart rhythm. The paramedics had to shock him. Luckily, you guys found him very quickly and called us right on time. They were able to get him to throw up most of what he took in the ambulance."

"So, is he like, in a coma, just sleeping, or what?" Will asked.

"He's been through a lot. We did give him a bit of a sedative. Many times when someone comes out of a drug overdose, they're violent or get a little upset. The Xanax he took was slowing down his heart rate and his breathing pattern. We didn't want him to wake up and lash out while we were watching his vitals. The pills aren't really the problem, it's what they do to your body and how it reacts. Since he's been taking them for so long, his body has already built a bit of tolerance for the effects."

So…his drug problem *saved* him? I wasn't sure what I was hearing, but it sounded like in any other scenario, we wouldn't have had such a good outcome.

"So, is he in the clear?" Will asked. "When will he wake up?"

"He seems to be stable," the doctor said. "We want to watch him for a few days and make sure we don't see anything funky pop up. We did an intense inspection on him and didn't find any swelling or bleeding anywhere, so that's good. His hand seems to be a little injured, but other than that, it's just the breathing, heart rate, and blood pressure we're looking at."

"But he looks…alright?" I asked.

"He'll survive. But often when a suicide doesn't go through successfully, it changes the person. Sometimes in a good way, and sometimes in a bad way. I suggest looking into state-assisted therapy and maybe transferring him up to our mental ward for a few weeks to be observed."

"State-assisted therapy?" I asked. "What does that mean?"

He put the clipboard down and placed his hands behind his back. "It's an application you can fill out that will ask the state to pay for therapy. They can approve or deny, of course, and it can be paid in full, or they could agree to pay for a portion of it."

I didn't know that was a thing. I thought maybe we should look into that.

The doctor took our silence as an indication we had some thinking to do. "Well, you don't need to make any decisions now, but someone from the psychiatric floor will be down to speak with you sometime today." He said goodbye, shook my hand, and walked out the door. We all looked at each other, relieved Jace was going to be okay. But now there were other things to worry about.

"He could be different?" Suzie asked. "I don't know if he could get much worse than he has been. What happens if he wakes up and he's just…gone, more zombie than he has been?"

"Well, let's take it one step at a time," Will whispered. He looked over to me and asked, "Can we qualify for it? The therapy?"

I shrugged. "I have no idea. I would think so, but I think Jace would have to sign up for it himself. I don't know how we would convince him to do that." I sat down on the couch against the wall. "Maybe he'll be better and not worse? I mean, you guys saw how he acted when he relapsed. He could have gone through with it and no one would have known. But he didn't. He threw it up for himself and not for us. I think we have to think positively here. Will, don't be a dick to him when he wakes up. Forget about everything else, just be happy that he's still here."

I never thought I'd be having this conversation with my family. Especially not about Jace. I felt so lost and had no idea how to fix this. Usually, I would offer up some pussy or beer, but I didn't think either of those would work for Jacey-boy.

"What about the loony bin?" Will asked.

"Will!" Suzie exclaimed.

"I don't know…" I dropped my head back onto the couch. "I don't think he would want that, but it might be a good idea. I just doubt we're going to get much assistance from the state for both, and the hospital trip itself is going to take us out." I had no idea how this state assistance thing worked, but I really hoped it was as simple as it sounded.

"Fuck. America, man. Do we want money or stable mental health? Because you can't have both!" Will shook his head. "Should we ask him what he wants?"

I doubted Jace was going to want anything that would be good for him. "I think the best bet is to make him feel as included as possible, so yeah. Let's ask him what he wants to do but also put a persuasive spin on it so he knows what way we're leaning."

"And we're leaning…?" Suzie asked, still unsure of what it was we should want.

"He should do it. Right?" Will asked.

"Mm-hmm." I couldn't help but try and play out the scenario in my head. How he would react, what we were going to say, and the argument that could break out.

"Well, might as well start making him feel included now." Suzie reached into her bag, pulled out some pink nail polish, and took Jace's hand.

"What are you doing?!" Will asked.

"What? We're going to need some type of proof that we were sitting here with him the whole time. I just want to show him we care. Plus, he'll think this is hilarious. Maybe he won't be so grumpy that his stupid plan fell through."

"Damn, I wish I had a Sharpie," Will said. "I'd give him a mustache. I know he's always wanted one of those."

I hope I wake up and find this is a dream, I thought. *Let this be a dream, and I'll be there for him more, I'll walk right into his room when I wake up and force him to go to therapy, or talk to me, or something.*

Lying on the hospital bed, Jace never looked so calm. I was terrified of the storm that would follow when he woke up. I was terrified for him, for what we were going to do after. Eventually, we had to take him home, right? Then what? How would any of us sleep, how would we not treat him differently?

God damn it, Jace, you bastard.

Chapter 22

eep. Beep. Beep.

My ears focus on a sound I haven't heard before. Everything in my head is swirling around, and I can't think clearly, move, or even open my eyes. Everything feels heavy. Why am I so heavy and tired?

"Why would you put them there?" A feminine voice fills my room.

"Why *wouldn't* I put them there?" Now a male.

Why are there people in my room so early in the morning? What the hell are they doing? I manage to pry one of my eyes open just to immediately shut it again when a blinding light flashes over me. Did I fall asleep on my floor? Why is the window so bright?

I open one eye again and see Suzie and Tyson standing on a couch under a window; a couch and a window that aren't in my room. I open the other eye and try to sit up, but my body is still too heavy.

Beep. Beep. Beep.

I look up and see a machine, which is the source of the odd beeping. It's the kind they have in hospitals. Oh, shit...

That night comes flooding back to me. I should be dead. I shouldn't be in a hospital bed connected to some annoying machine while my siblings stand on a couch and argue. Maybe I'm dead. I don't think that's a normal thing to see in a hospital.

I lay my head back down slowly and stayed silent. My throat is so dry, there's no way I could talk even if I wanted to. As I watch them, it looks like they're hanging up LED lights around the room. When they stop arguing for a moment, I hear the faint sound of Frank Sinatra playing on someone's phone. It's the song "The World We Knew." You'd expect to wake up from a suicide attempt with happier music. It's one of my favorites, but I'd bet money none of my siblings have heard it before, nor are they paying attention to it now.

I break my gaze from them and look at the ceiling. I can't believe I woke up, that I'm still here. I let myself cry. I don't know yet if I'm happy it didn't work or if I'm really pissed at myself for failing at even that. God, is there anything I *can* do right? Not only that but how embarrassing that they're all here because of what I did. Now I have to face them and the situation.

"This hospital food is literal shit." The room door opens and Will and I make eye contact before I can pretend to be asleep. "*Jace!* What the hell, why is no one freaking out or talking to you?" He drops whatever is in his hands and runs over to me. Leave it to Will to rip you right out of your peace.

"Oh, my God!" Suzie and Tyson drop the lights they were arguing over. Suzie runs right to my side, and Tyson runs out the door into the hall.

"The nurse told us to grab her when you woke up so she could come check you out," Will tells me. "They wanted to make sure you could be awake and breathe okay before taking off this ugly-ass mask."

Suzie smacks Will's arm. "He just woke up! Do not call him ugly."

He throws his hands up defensively. "I didn't! I called the *mask* ugly. Jace, you look great. Well, not really…you look like shit."

If I could laugh I would. My family is unique, that's for sure.

"William!" The look on Suzie's face could kill if she really wanted it to.

Can we go back to ten minutes ago when I was asleep and not in a hospital bed hating myself?

"Have a nice nap, Mr. Carter?" the nurse says as she enters the room with a smile on her face. I'm sure she works with people in situations like mine all the time. I hope she doesn't ask everyone that stupid question.

She takes all my vitals. Then she takes off my oxygen mask and one of the IVs in my arm. She waits a few minutes and then takes my vitals again.

"Everything looks good, Jace!" she announces. "Do you want some ice chips? I know the oxygen can dry out your throat, but I can't let you drink anything until the doctor comes in to check on you."

I don't answer. I just stare ahead at the TV that isn't on. I'm not very happy to be here, and the medical bill I'm racking up… I don't even want to think about it.

"Yes, please bring the ice chips," Tyson says and smiles at her before she leaves.

Will leans into me and whispers, "I will force-feed you these ice chips. You have no option."

Our eyes meet, mine probably full of doubt, his leaking the satisfaction of a challenge presenting itself. I don't doubt he'd pry my mouth open and shove them down my throat. I do want them; my throat is killing me. But the idea of giving into something Will wants isn't going to happen. Even after trying to die and waking up in a hospital bed, the fact that we still act like siblings is somewhat comforting.

"Will, seriously, stop it!" Suzie says. Then, to Tyson, she adds,

"He called Jace ugly when you went to get the nurse."

"I did not! I told him the mask was ugly. Well…then yeah, I guess I told him he looked like shit. But he does! Look at him." Will points over to me, his finger inches from my face.

This is unbelievable. Do they not remember why we're here? Are they not mad at me? Why is no one yelling? I lick my lips to try and make them stop burning. They've never been so dry.

"You told him he looks like shit," Suzie argues. "The first thing you tell him when he wakes up is that he looks like shit."

Tyson shakes his head, and I can see the amusement on his face. It is kind of funny. The lightness of the room makes me feel not so heavy or scared. I feel surrounded by love, and God am I glad no one's yelling at me. It's weird, and don't get me wrong, but it's exactly what I needed. I can still feel wetness on my cheek. I'm not sure if it's from earlier when I was crying or maybe I haven't stopped.

"Here are those ice chips," the nurse says, returning to the room and handing them to Tyson.

Of course, Will immediately snatches the cup from his hand. He holds the spoon up and gives me a sideways look with his eyebrows raised. "You heard me," he whispers.

I raise my eyebrows at him. What is he going to do? Would he *actually* pry my mouth open and shove ice chips into my mouth with the nurse right there? Not even a crazy person would do that. I do want the ice chips. I need them. But knowing how badly he wants me to eat them makes me not want to.

Will shrugs, and before giving me a moment to tell him to stop, he grabs a handful and shoves it into my mouth, completely ignoring the spoon that was in the cup as well.

"Ahh!" is all I get out as I try to pull my head away.

"Oh! Umm, maybe don't do that?" the nurse says, looking like she wants to intervene but not knowing how.

"They're fine, thank you," Suzie smiles, dismissing her. The nurse makes a face but leaves us to it anyway.

"Fuck!" I finally break free of Will's hand on my face.

Currently, he is on top of me, cup in one hand, his other dripping with melted ice. "Hey, you said a word!"

Suzie takes the cup and signals for Will to get down. Then she holds up the spoon with a scoop of ice on top of it. I open my mouth while staring at Will. Suzie softly places the spoonful of ice into my mouth. It feels amazing. I let the ice melt and turn into water so I can swish it around before swallowing. I reach up to grab the cup from Suzie, mostly to test my strength, and notice I've got hot-pink fingernails. My hand drops back down onto the bed.

I groan and whisper, "Why are my nails pink?"

Suzie smiles. "You like it?"

I give her a half-smile in response. My body still feels weak, and I'd love to go back to sleep for a bit. But if I know my family, that's not happening.

"I love you, man," Tyson says, moving to the other side of my bed. "I'm so sorry, so sorry for everything. I just…I love you and I'm so glad you're here and that you're alive and breathing and talking."

He wraps his arm around me and rests his head on my chest. His shoulders shake with sobs.

"Nice," Will remarks. "So much for no emotional outbursts." Suzie only nods her head in agreement.

"I was so worried he wouldn't wake up, I didn't know what I was saying," Tyson says into my chest. Then he lifts his head and looks into my eyes. "We have a lot to talk about, but I know you probably don't want to right now, which is absolutely understandable. Right now, I just really want to know…how are you feeling?

If it's too early to know, that's okay. In fact, we don't have to talk about it at all. I just…fuck. I'm so glad you're okay."

"I feel tired," I say. "I just want to take a nap."

"Seriously? Didn't you just sleep for like three weeks?" Will asks, looking at his watch.

With an annoyed tone, Tyson says, "It hasn't been three weeks." He stands upright and puts a hand on my chest. "Do you need anything?"

I shake my head and take another spoonful of ice, my bright-pink nails making me smile. "I think I'm alright." I look up at Tyson and his dark-green eyes meet with mine. I know he understands the double meaning without me having to say anything more.

I do, too. I feel alright. Nowhere near a healthy mental spot, but I feel like I could go to bed right now thinking of what I'm going to do when I wake up. If you don't know what the opposite of that is like, good for you. It's a rough life going to bed every day hoping you don't wake up, but for the first time in a long time, I want to sleep for the rest, and I'm somewhat relieved that I'll get to wake up to my annoying family.

Chapter 23

One week later. It's finally June. I'm so happy the month of May is done and over with. Hopefully, the warm weather can start bringing in happier moments or whatever…but fuck May. Maybe June will offer a clean slate.

Throughout the time I was in the hospital, I always had someone by my side. Katie stopped by a few times. I couldn't help but feel that either she was mad at me or was uncomfortable being in the hospital. She seemed relieved that I was okay but didn't talk much. Even she and Will didn't have their usual pointless arguments. As for everyone else, they took shifts being with me. Since we're too broke to afford to miss work, Suzie took some time off of school to keep me company. I'll admit, it was nice to not be alone.

On top of all that, when I first got home I heard Tyson telling Will that Dad had left the house when everyone was at the hospital. He hasn't been back since. Of course, this has done wonders at keeping me on edge constantly.

Currently, Dean Martin is playing through the speaker in my room while I pick up and clean out absolutely everything. My room is to be completely empty by the end of the day: furniture, clothes, books, shoes, trash. Everything. The therapist at the hospital told the boys that a fresh clean start would be best for me. That I should remove myself from my old life and accept a new beginning. I think it's bullshit because the only thing that cleaning my room is making me feel is irritated and exhausted. I don't have the body strength for this shit.

The therapist came to the hospital room to talk to us and give us some tips and tricks before basically telling me I should spend some time in the psych ward, a week to a month. Which we all know ends up being the longest possible time. I politely declined. If anything was going to make me feel worse, I was positive that going to a glorified group home was it.

I know they think they have me fooled. That I believe they just want me to refresh everything. But I know they want to make sure I don't have anything hidden in here. It's why Will shakes out every book and pulls out every pocket of my clothing. The reason every piece of furniture is flipped upside down and thoroughly searched. Not sure why they think they're getting away with it, but I don't say anything about it. I don't have the energy to.

"Can't we listen to good music?" Tyson asks.

I drop the trash bag and plop onto the floor with my legs thrown out in front of me. "We can listen to good music if I can take a nap," I counter.

"You already took a nap."

We got home two days ago. I'm still trying to figure out exactly how I feel about being back. But I do know the depression is different. In a way, I'm oddly relieved the attempt didn't work. I don't know how to explain it. I just remember being so scared from the moment I took them. I started rethinking everything. But it was too late by the time I started feeling funky.

I can't say the depression is gone. It's just different. I'm so tired all the time. I don't want to do anything. The good news is, I haven't thought about drugs too much since being back. I think all the puking in the ambulance really put me off for a while. I won't ever forget that ride. It was the worst feeling in my life. I looked down and saw black everywhere. In my fog, I thought it was blood, which caused me to throw up even more. I later found it was some type of black charcoal they used to force me to throw up. Still disgusting, though.

"I'm going to go outside for a second, then. I need some air." I walk out of my room and grab the cigarettes from my pocket before turning back around. Tyson is already holding the lighter up for me. "Thanks," I say and take the lighter.

Tyson is positive that keeping all the lighters will help me with…something. What will it help with? I have no clue, but again, it makes him feel better, so why the hell not just go along with it? I got my phone back so I could fill my gloomy days with music, but most of the time it's dead or lost since I don't really use it.

I sit down on the front porch and light the tip of the cigarette. I watch as the paper continues to burn down. I blow out the smoke and lean back against the front door. At least I'm still allowed to smoke. I thought I was going to get my head chewed off yesterday when I first pulled out the pack in front of them. No one said anything. They just looked at me and then at each other like they weren't sure if this was "allowed." It's the weirdest thing to be twenty-one and still feel like I'm not able to make my own decisions.

"Hey, Zombie!" a familiar voice sounds from the sidewalk. I look to the corner of our lawn and see Ian standing there awkwardly.

"Ian?" I stand up and walk over to him. "What are you doing here?" I flick some of the ash off the cigarette and take another drag. Zombie is an odd nickname to give someone. Although he probably knows what happened. Still, it isn't a nickname I would have chosen for myself.

"Katie told me what happened," he says. "I just wanted to stop by, mostly to make sure you're doing okay, but also to tell you I'm not selling to you anymore."

I smile like he's making a joke, but I'm not sure he is. "Well, I'm not really in the market anymore. Your last batch almost killed me." If you can't cry or lash out, you might as well laugh and make jokes, right? I've been put in so many uncomfortable situations since the hospital. I found if you joke about the most uncomfortable parts, people seem to ease up a little.

"Hey now," Ian says, "I…" but I cut him off with a soft laugh. "You're kidding. Jesus." He lets out a relieved sigh. "I've been worried that maybe you and everyone else had been blaming me for what happened."

I raise an eyebrow at him. "You think it's your fault I tried to kill myself?"

"Well, no. I guess not when you put it that way." He leans back on his heels. "But I was the reason you had all of it."

"No one blames you, Ian. You can chill. I don't know if you came over here to apologize or whatever, but there's no need." I pat his shoulder once then take another drag of the cigarette before holding it out to him.

Halfheartedly, he smiles before taking it. "You're really into the hard stuff now, aren't you?" he jokes.

He takes a drag and then looks at me. His blue eyes are just as striking today as they were the first time I looked into them. I could have been convinced I was talking to Katie instead of Ian just from those eyes.

"No one knows where I was getting anything. I don't really talk to anyone."

He takes a deep inhale before handing the cig back to me. Although I've bummed cigs from him in the past, I realize I've never actually seen him smoke them before. I'm glad he accepted. It's the closest thing to a "truce" blunt I have.

"Katie blames me," he adds.

I tilt my head in disbelief. "No, she doesn't."

Ian nods slowly. "We had a big fight. She found out I was still giving you shit even though you weren't doing them. It got pretty rough. I wasn't sure what to tell her because I didn't know why I was doing it either. You and I are friends. I should have known something was going on. Anyway, we aren't on good terms right now."

"I'm sorry to hear that."

I have no idea what to say. Now I really am wondering if Katie was mad at me when I was in the hospital since she knew I was still getting pills the whole time I was sober. These are the things I wish I'd thought about before trying to off myself. Now I have to face all the problems I had assumed would fix themselves.

"I think she was just scared," I say. "She walked into a pretty bad scene at my house. You can't really blame her for lashing out. Honestly, I'm still waiting for my siblings to blow up on me."

"I guess so. But anyway, you inspired me, so I'm getting sober. Though I'll probably need more intense help than you, so my aunt's going to look into either drug therapy or rehab."

"No shit? Damn… Good for you, man!" I can't imagine Ian being sober. "It's a really rough road, but you'll get through it. Keep Katie close to you. She's the only thing that held me together those three months."

"I'm hoping I can go away for a bit and come back a changed man. But…I don't know. With school and stuff, I assume it'll be hard."

"Yeah, that was hard for me too. I'm proud of you, though." His blond hair looks almost white in the sun; freckles pepper his face. Summer weather looks good on Ian. It heightens all the high-lights in his features. "Hopefully you can get out without the de-pression."

He smirks. "I'm a pretty happy guy. I don't think I'll have any problem with that."

"That's true," I say. "You've always been too happy for my lik-ing." I kick a rock off the sidewalk into the road. "There's never any reason to be that happy," I huff.

Before Ian can say another word, the front door opens. "Jace!" I turn around to see Will in the doorway.

Oh, God, anyone but him. I attempt to lean in front of Ian so Will can't see I'm with someone, but I guess that only works in the movies.

"Sorry, just making sure you weren't snorting shit out here." Will leans out farther and notices there's another person with me. "Oh! Uh, who's your friend there?"

I turn back to Ian. "I'm so sorry for whatever is about to hap-pen," I whisper, rubbing the skin between my brows.

Ian laughs. "I can go. I just wanted to check in. It was really nice talking with you." He reaches out and grabs my wrist for a fast two seconds before backing up.

"See ya around." I nod and then turn around to find Will mak-ing his way toward us.

Jesus Christ.

Quickly, I walk to Will so he doesn't get a chance to stop Ian. When I get to him, I grab his arm and turn him around toward the house.

"Who is that? Your new boyfriend? Are you hiding someone from us?" He raises his eyebrows at me.

"William, no," I growl. I don't know how far Ian got, but I hope to God he didn't hear that. When we get into the house, I shove him back. "Dude. I don't know if you're aware of this, but I'm not really announcing to the world that I'm…you know."

He shakes his head and shrugs. "Gay? You can say it, it's not going to hurt you." He laughs and then pats my arm. "I'm sorry, I didn't even think before I said anything."

"Clearly." I cross my arms and turn around. Yeah, it won't hurt me. But Dad might. Has anyone even seen him lately? I haven't heard anything about him or Mom in a while.

I shake the thought out of my head. The less I know the better.

Amused, he doesn't give up. "Is he, though?"

"What?"

"Your boyfriend."

"Oh, God no, Will! I have friends too. I can be friends with a guy without wanting to bone him."

"Alright, alright, don't get your panties in a bunch. I was just asking. I'm just saying, he looks like he would be a bottom." He winks at me.

My arms drop along with my jaw. "You did not just say that!"

"What, too soon?" His laughter fills the room. "*I would absolutely be a top, no doubt about it,*" he mocks.

"Are you using my letter to tease me right now? I knew I should have left that part out." I hate to admit it, but it is funny. Crazy how everything has come full circle. Will is one of my favorite people to talk to now because he's just as lighthearted about everything as I'm trying to be.

"Okay, no," he says, "but can I ask you a real question?" All signs of joking drain from his face. "Are you a virgin?"

I groan and throw my head back. What the hell, Will? Come on, man.

"No. I'm not."

I decide to answer like I'm ripping off a Band-Aid. I'm already in this awkward mess and he's just going to keep bugging me about it. Better to answer now when we don't have an audience.

"Cool. Cool." Will pulls his lips into his mouth and tries to act like he's satisfied with his answer, but I know he isn't.

I look around the room just to be sure no one is around. "Jessica Rosin. It was like eighth grade after my first time getting drunk."

"It was a girl?!" Will's whisper-yelling can't cover up his booming voice.

"Shhh! Yes, okay? I haven't ever done anything with a dude. I've never had time, I guess. Plus not telling anyone puts a damper on your options. After I saw what Dad did to Uncle Lennon, I swore I'd never do anything to put me in that position." I turn around again to check the hallway; I don't even know where anyone is. "Now shut the fuck up, and don't ask me any more stupid questions."

I've never been one to talk about personal experiences with my family. Will, on the other hand, asks some of the worst questions, and he'll tell you all his personal stuff, too. Even when you beg him not to. The only person I've ever felt remotely comfortable with telling personal stuff to is Katie, maybe because she isn't a family member.

"Hey, have you heard from Katie at all?" I ask. Since I'm thinking about her and all, I'd love to see her.

"Oh, yeah, she's doing alright. Some trouble at home or something, but she isn't doing too bad."

"Can I use your phone to call her?" My hand is already out. I know he won't say no.

He reaches into his pocket and drops the phone in my hand. "Worried she won't answer you?"

"Something like that." Actually, I was worried she'd answer the phone and immediately start yelling at me. I wouldn't blame her if she did yell at me. I can't help but feel responsible about her and Ian's relationship. Then again, I don't know anything about that. I guess I've been pretty selfish lately. I can't remember asking her anything about her life.

Chapter 24

"You were still getting pills, you dumbass! You were supposed to come to me when you were feeling weak. You should have told Ian you were sober earlier so he would stop giving them to you, dipshit! Although I guess you did tell him, and for some reason he just kept giving them to you. I mean, what the hell did he think you were doing with all those?"

Going to Katie's house isn't going quite as smoothly as I expected it would. I suppose it could be worse, so I'll take what I can get. I'll go ahead and spare you the breadth of the lecture. It was a back-and-forth, one-woman argument between Katie, Ian, and me. I'm not sure why she kept lecturing Ian; he wasn't even there. I even twisted around to check out the room a few times just to be completely sure he wasn't. But I wasn't going to stop her. I've never seen her mad and secretly, it's kind of scary.

All I can think about is how bubbly Ian is on drugs. I wonder what he's like when he's off them. We used to talk a lot, about our lives—well, my life, I guess. I talked a lot, and he mostly listened, believe it or not. Now you'd never guess that. But he's always been such an energetic person. He's forward, that's for sure, between constantly calling me out, following me outside after I bitched him out, that weird knee-touching thing he was doing, and showing up at my house. The kid isn't shy. It is odd, though, now that I think about it. I wonder what his motives are. Maybe he really does just need a friend.

I sit up more, remembering all the details of the conversations and moments we've had.

"As for my eyes…you tell me."

"I hear a lot about you from Ian."

All the times he made it a point to touch me. How excited he was when he saw me. The lingering knee touch and the way he held my wrist before leaving my house today.

There's no way. Ian wasn't…he wasn't flirting with me, was he?

Without pausing to listen to what Katie is saying, I interrupt her. "What's Ian like when he isn't on drugs?"

She stops talking and makes eye contact with me for the first time in the past hour or so. She thinks about answering, then decides she will. "He's fine, I guess. Kind of the same as he is now, but more full of life. He's funny, but in a sad way. Kind of like you."

"I'm funny in a sad way?"

She nods.

"Hmm, good to know. How do you come up with the 'sad but funny' trait for me?"

Katie folds her arms and looks up in thought. "You told me you were crazy depressed by quoting Harry Potter. You 'lightened up' your suicide letter by adding the fact that you were a top."

That will never not cause me to cringe. What was I thinking putting that in there?

"Ian now calls you Zombie and you answer to it. Do you need any other examples?"

When I got to her house, Ian used that dumb nickname again as he was leaving. I didn't answer to it, though.

"Alright, alright. I get it. Sorry I asked." Man, I was a little dark, wasn't I? "He told me he's stopping. Do you think he's going to survive that?"

"No. I don't know if he can do it. It's not as easy as he thinks it's going to be, but maybe if Aunt Grace can get him into rehab… Wait, when did he tell you he's getting clean?"

My hands find their way to my hair, and I brush it out of my face and behind my ear. "Today, he stopped by."

"He stopped by?" Surprise fills her voice.

"Yeah, he came by and asked how I was doing. He told me you guys got into it a lot, and that he's getting clean."

"Interesting."

"You think?"

"Well, no, I didn't mean to say interesting. It's just weird. I didn't know you guys were that close."

Neither did I. "I think he just wanted to apologize since he was the reason I had all the pills. He seemed pretty upset about it and everything that happened here with you two. Are you guys close?"

"Not really." The bed shifts with her weight as she sits beside me. "We used to be super close, but after our dad situation got worse, we started drifting away. And after Mom did what she did and left, we really distanced ourselves from each other. It's like living in a dorm. We acknowledge each other when we see each other but we don't go out of our way to talk."

"Damn, that's crazy. I don't know what I would do if I started losing my siblings." They were the only thing keeping me grounded half the time.

"When we first met, you told me you didn't want friends. I didn't imagine it was because you lived with four built-in ones! No wonder you never make any friends. You're so busy with everything and everyone at home."

"Okay, first of all, I never said I didn't want friends."

"You so did! You said something about 'I don't want friends, I'm a broody, depressed druggie, blah blah blah…' I remember it, that's exactly how it went."

She used a weird monster voice when quoting me, and I couldn't stop my offended laugh from escaping. "Yeah? Is that how I sounded? I did not say blah blah blah, either."

"So you admit you were broody, though?"

I click my tongue and push her shoulder. "I've missed you."

"I've missed you too." She pulls my hand to hers and holds it tight. "I'm really glad you're okay. I know you're probably tired of hearing that. But you scared the fuck out of me. You should have seen Suzie that day. Everything was moving so fast, and I was so scared. You're an ass." After shaking the brief spout of anger off, she continues. "You seem different, though… In a good way."

"Less broody?"

With a breathy laugh, she answers, "Definitely less broody."

A genuine smile fills my face. "I'm sorry. It's a really fucked-up situation. It's weird to grasp the way I feel about it all, so I can't imagine how you all feel."

"What do you mean?"

I lean my back against the wall with my arms behind my head and take a deep breath. "Like…I keep telling people I'm sorry, but I don't feel sorry for doing it. Just that I scared everyone, I guess."

"I'm not sure where the line is here, but are you upset that it didn't work?" Katie asks, leaning back and resting her head on the crook of my shoulder. She wraps her arm around my waist. More often than not, I'm not a fan of people touching or cuddling me. But I'm not mad about this. This feels nice, and I know it feels just as nice for her.

"I'm not necessarily *upset* that it didn't work. But…things are different because it didn't. I didn't expect to come back and face everyone after doing that, so I wasn't mentally prepared. But I'm not, like, mad to be here. It's a very different dynamic now. No one's talked about it or asked me anything. I don't know if it's because it's weird or uncomfortable or if they feel like bringing it up will magically trigger it to happen again. But it's like every time we're together, there's a huge elephant in the room, and it's just uncomfortable."

"I've never heard you talk so much in my life," Katie says. I feel her smile against me. "I get that, though. Maybe you should be the one to bring it up? They might be wanting to move at your pace. As for the fact that you're still here, you should make something out of it. Prove to yourself that it wasn't a mistake that it didn't work. Instead of having things happen and waiting for an explanation, you should make your own."

I haven't thought about that. It sounds simple but it's a lot harder to think simple logic when you are who I've been for so long. I've always just trusted fate or whatever.

I wrap my arm around Katie and pull her closer to me. "You're right. Thank you. I'm not really sure what I'm doing or how I'm supposed to change, but I do know I want to put in an honest effort this time."

We lay there silently, just holding each other and being in each other's presence before I break the silence. "Can I stay here tonight?"

Slowly, she sits up on her elbow to look at me. "Jace Carter, sleeping over at *my* house?!" She smiles and nods. "Of course you can."

*   *   *

After a night of talking and hanging out, Katie brings me home the next day. When we walk in, everyone is already in the living room. I turn off the TV and stand in front of it. "I'm sure you're all wondering why I've gathered you here today," I announce.

"What?" Will says, the confusion clear on his face. "No, you didn't, we all came out here on our own."

"Also," Suzie throws in, "you just got here. All of us have been here for a while now."

"Yeah, well, whatever. Katie says I have to start taking accountabilities for all of my actions, past, present, and future. I wanted to say that I'm sorry for getting pills even after I decided to stop. It was a way for me to feel secure, like I had that blanket if I needed it. But I should have just talked to you guys about it."

No one speaks. They all just stare at me like I've grown a second head.

"Wait a second…did you just make a joke?" Tyson asks.

I contort my face and shake my head. "No, what part of that sounded like a joke to you?"

"The part about you gathering us here." He glances around to room at everyone else. "Jace made a joke!"

If my eyes could get stuck in the back of my head as often as I roll them, they would. "You're all impossible. I'm trying to apologize for my past behavior, and you're worried about if I did or didn't make a joke?"

Will shakes his head. "No, no. You did. You *did* make a joke."

Katie gives me a shrug. "I told you they wouldn't give a shit about apologies. It's like you haven't met them."

I plop down onto the only empty chair and prop my legs up on the coffee table. This family is insane, but the more I think about it, the more grateful I am that they're mine. I don't know many people who could survive them, and lord knows I want to knock their teeth out most of the time. But they've turned out to be one hell of a support system.

"Okay, well, now that that's out of the way, what's next?" Suzie asks. "We've destroyed and cleaned Jace's room, confirmed he's now making jokes, Will caught him outside with a boy, things are moving great! But what's next?" She sits up on her knees, all business.

"You were outside with a boy?" Katie asks. "Oh, do tell!" Of course she turns right to Will, who's already leaning forward, excited to tell the story.

"It was Ian," I cut in before Will can make some elaborate story that isn't even close to what happened. "I already told you about it. Just when he came by to check in."

"You know that guy?" Will asks.

Katie seems less excited about the story now that she knows who it was. "Yeah, it's my shithead brother."

Will's eyes widen and he mouths "Oh!" before pulling his lips between his teeth to stop from smiling. I catch his gaze and slowly shake my head at him. He better not get any ideas or thoughts on the subject. I don't know what his colorful mind is capable of, but I don't want to be the center of one of his extravagant thoughts.

Tyson clears his throat. "I'd like to bring something up. Now that it's been some time and I've been able to do a bit of research on the subject, I think you should sign up for state-assisted therapy. The doctor at the hospital mentioned it, and you wouldn't have to pay for it, especially since you…attempted. I…we all think it would be good for you. There are a few different options. You could do in-facility therapy, group therapy, or one-on-one therapy. There's even an option for video therapy. We think you should strongly think about in-facility therapy or the one-on-one."

In-facility therapy? That sounds like a fancy way of saying rehab. I can consider that one for as long as I want. I'm not doing it.

Group therapy sounds interesting. A bunch of mentally ill people in a group triggering one another. No doubt a few of them will be druggies or alcoholics. One-on-one? I hate it. I hate all the options. I hate that this is a conversation we have to have.

I chew on the inside of my cheek and shake my leg. Everyone's eyes are on me like I'm supposed to make a choice right this second. I cross my arms over my chest and make lingering eye contact with everyone. All of them, they all talked about this. Are they always talking about me when I'm not around? I know they're trying to help, but this makes me feel more like an outcast. I wonder what else they've said about me or decided for me.

I pinch the bridge of my nose and close my eyes and attempt to hold back the bite in my tone. "Tys, that's a big thing, and it's something I'm just now hearing about. Do you expect me to make a choice right this second?"

"Oh! No, I guess not. Just think about it. Yeah?"

I nod, covering my eyes with my hand. I'm almost twenty-two and I'm still being treated like a child in this house. Maybe that's my problem. Maybe I've been babied too long. If they want to push me out of their plans and conversations, then I'll leave them to it. Two can play at that game. I'm going to start doing shit for myself, quietly.

"I'm going outside," I say, and without hesitation Tyson digs through his pockets and hands me the lighter.

Chapter 25

"Any fun plans today?" Tyson asks.

"Me?" Is he really asking me that? "Umm. No, Tys, I'm a recovering suicidal drug addict. I don't have friends, and I can't do what people my age do for 'fun.' So no, I don't have any fun plans today."

In fact, I've been sitting on the couch staring at the ceiling fan for the past thirty minutes. Life is so boring when you aren't destroying yourself.

"You're snappy." He looks down at his phone, probably not wanting to start something.

I'm not sure why, but I have been very snappy these past few days. I'm not sure what's getting into me. It's probably the whole "not on drugs" thing. The angry feelings I've been trying to push down are constantly resurfacing. I'm always able to manage it, but sometimes it slips out.

"I'm not snappy. That was just a dumb question." As true as that is, I probably should just stop talking.

"Hey, now, don't be rude. I was just trying to start a conversation." Tyson obviously doesn't want to talk to me anymore because he doesn't look up from his phone.

The front door opens and Will comes in, throwing his keys on the entryway table. "Fuck work, man." He falls onto the couch next to me, rubbing his face. "What are you guys doing?"

"Be careful, questions like that trigger Jacey-boy here now."

God, I'm so glad that nickname decided to stick around.

"It doesn't trigger me. It was a stupid question!" The annoyance is clear in my voice. Seriously, why is he so caught up on that?

"What, asking what you're doing?" Will asks, looking between Tyson and me.

Tyson drops his phone and looks up at Will. *Now* he wants to be present for a conversation. "Yeah, dude. You can't ask questions like that, isn't the answer obvious?"

He's mocking me, faking the same angry annoyance I'm feeling. Then he gets up and goes into the kitchen.

"Fuck you, Tys." After flipping him off through the wall, I go to my room and slam the door. I hate that being so upset feels good. I hate being easily irritable. But the anger, when it's not being drowned out by sadness, feels good. It feels like power. Which probably isn't a good thing, but I push it to the depths of my brain and lock it under the door labeled Things to Worry About Later.

Today is day one of working on myself. Step one is looking for a job. There aren't many places around our neighborhood, but honestly, I'm looking for anything within walking distance. Maybe I could work at a gym and use it to get out this pent-up frustration and anger.

I pull out the computer and start looking for anywhere that's hiring. I find a few places right away: a movie theater, a coffee shop, some clothing stores, and a gas station. Then there are more laborious jobs like house and school cleaning, an autobody shop, and a construction company. Currently, Will is working in construction, and I don't want to somehow manage to be in the same company as him. Plus, one look at my body will tell you I'm not made for heavy lifting. Hopefully, some other job will take me and I can put construction at the bottom of my list.

Under the desk, my leg is shaking, causing a clicking sound on either the desk itself or something on it. I don't mind it, though. It's a good sound to stay focused on. I can't help but think how much easier focusing and looking through jobs would be if I had a drink or something next to me.

My first craving since being back. Nice.

I know we cleaned and emptied out my room, but I can't help looking in all the places I used to hide bottles in hopes that one might reappear. When I decide it's getting to be too much for my head to handle, I grab a lighter from Tyson and head outside. I light a cigarette and decide to take a half-walk half-jog around the block. I'm not in shape, so even just a quick ten minutes wipes me out. But it does exactly what I needed to get the pestering thoughts out of my head.

Back at the house, Tyson and Will are involved in an intense game of who-knows-what on the TV. I debated going back in for a bit to hang out, but I was an ass earlier, so I figure I'll leave them to it.

The next thing I need to do is to sneak out of here to go to the places I've written down and ask about work. Fortunately, with the guys so into their game, it won't be hard to leave without being noticed.

*   *   *

My job hunt for today hasn't gone well at all. The local movie theater isn't hiring, and the grocery store isn't interested in adding another employee anywhere. No cleaning jobs, no food jobs. The last place I have in mind is an autobody shop. It's the last business I can get to on foot. If they're not hiring, I'm going to be forced to take a bus or have Will drive me to work, which will ruin my whole "take care of myself in silence" plan. The downfall? I don't know shit about cars. Not a goddamn thing.

I enter the autobody shop. It smells like oil and tires. It's not a smell I enjoy, but I guess it could grow on me.

"Hey there, have an appointment?" It's a man maybe in his 50s or late 40s behind the desk. He's covered in grease and his hair is a mess. You'd think he'd wear a hat or something when working on the cars.

"No… I saw you had an ad online for a job? Is that still available?" I tap the counter with my fingertips. I'm not sure why I'm so nervous about this. It's not like I've never talked to someone before. I just haven't talked to anyone in an adult type of way, especially when looking for a job.

He looks me over before meeting my eyes again. I look down at my shorts and gray T-shirt. I didn't think I looked too bad when I left the house, but now I'm starting to second guess myself.

"You know anything about cars?" he asks.

Shrugging, I reply, "Enough."

"How old are you?" His face is full of doubt. I'm not really sure what's making him assume I'm not the type of person who works on cars.

He somehow looks even less impressed when I reply, "Twenty-one. Twenty-two in a month, if that changes anything."

He thinks for a while. "What position are you looking for?"

"Any." It comes out faster and more eager than I had wanted. "I was hoping for an apprenticeship type of thing, but I can learn anything. I have a knack for answering phones and making appointments."

He chews his bottom lip and looks me up and down another time.

"What? Is there something wrong with me, my clothes not good enough to work here?" I joke.

The man erupts in laughter. "No, I'm just wondering why someone like you would want to work in a dirty run-down auto repair shop when you obviously don't know anything about cars."

"Left is the brake, right is the gas," I counter, showing him I do know *something* about cars. "Can't get much more complicated than that."

He doesn't look amused. A smile doesn't even flash across his face.

"What do you mean 'someone like me'?" I ask when he doesn't say anything else.

"You came asking for a job in exercise shorts, your hair is longer than my niece's, and you look like you haven't had a meal in months."

He isn't wrong, but damn. Whatever happened to "don't judge a book by its cover"?

"Please." Now I almost sound desperate.

He takes off his hat, scratches his head, then drops his arms to his side. "Joshua!" he yells to the back room before putting the hat back on.

A few moments later, a much younger man walks up to the desk. "Yeah?"

My jaw almost drops. Somehow, this Joshua character makes the grease and oil look…not disgusting. His shaggy black hair is pinned down behind a backwards baseball cap, and his eyes… I'm starting to see a pattern in my type. Those blue eyes are captivating. They aren't a sky blue with gold in the center like Ian's and Katie's. No, his are like ice. Bright blue, maybe even some stripes of white throughout them, with no other colors except the black ring that circles the cold blue. I have to tear my eyes away from him and pretend I'm looking at some tire article on the counter.

"Are you looking for an apprentice?" the older man asks Joshua.

From the corner of my eye, I see Joshua do as the older guy did and look me up and down with a confused look. He hesitates while I go back to looking anywhere else but him.

"I could be," he says.

I whip my head back to him. He *could* be? Wait, he would take me as an apprentice even though I'm sure he's noticing all the things the older guy mentioned?

"When could you start?" Joshua asks.

I look at my wrist before realizing I don't have a watch. *Why did I do that?!* I've never worn a watch. I try to play it off by patting my pockets looking for my phone before remembering I left it at home. Oh, my God, I look insane. Stop, Jace, just answer him.

When I look up, they're both looking at me, waiting for an answer.

I laugh. "Sorry, I don't get out much." Immediately, I mentally punch myself in the head. *What the fuck?* "Anytime!" I half-yell. "I can start whenever you need me."

At least the end of that helped clean up the mess I am. What's going on? I know I'm nervous about going into the real world and finding a job, but Jesus Christ. Get it together!

Joshua traces his bottom lip with his tongue before pulling it into his mouth, deep in thought. "Come back on Monday." He looks down at my shorts and then turns back toward the shop. Without turning around, he says, "Wear some jeans."

"Thank you!" I nearly shout as he walks away. "Thank you," I say again, this time more quietly, to the older man, who's still looking at me.

"Don't thank me. I wouldn't have taken you in." He huffs, turns, and follows Joshua into the shop.

I can't help but smile as I leave. I didn't expect it to be so easy, but on top of that… *he* is going to be my boss? I have no problem working with a view. I've never seen someone who looks nearly as good as Joshua does with his dark hair, blue eyes, and sharp jaw-line. He's maybe an inch taller than me and didn't tower over me like Ian. How have I never seen him before, working so close to where I live? I guess it comes down to the fact I never leave my room, but between making my own money and working with Joshua, I couldn't wait for Monday to come around so I could get there and spend my day drooling.

Chapter 26

I get home and plop down on the couch. I've been so busy running from place to place looking for a job that I haven't had time to think about drugs or liquor or even myself. It's kind of nice to not have to fight myself every second. I guess that's why they say the best way to fight a depressive episode is to get out and do something. In those depressed moments, though, it feels almost impossible to even get up off the floor.

I've been home and alone for thirteen minutes; I can already feel the emptiness threatening to pull me in again. Crazy how much being alone with your thoughts can take you under. I guess I'll have to add more to my list of things to do, keep myself busy. If I want to better myself, by myself, and for myself, I suppose I shouldn't fly at it blind.

Groaning, I push off the couch and head back to my room to get my phone. I Google "state-assisted therapy" and read through everything, all the information and hoops I'd have to jump through, reference numbers I'd need from the hospital I almost died in. I take a notebook from my shelf and start a checklist.

After I have my checklist for the therapy shit, I think about what else I'm going to need. Just so I can have some sense of accomplishment, I write down "get a job" and cross it off. It's small, but it's a good start.

My pen taps rhythmically against my thigh as I try to think of other new things I want to do. I look at myself in the mirror and for the first time I truly understand how underweight I am. I approach the mirror and pull off my shirt. If I saw any of my siblings like this, I'd be very worried.

I turn to the side and pull my arm up. I can see my ribs, and my collarbones stick out so much they looks like bowls. I used to weigh between 165 and 170 pounds and had a pretty good muscle mass. Nothing like Tyson, he's a beast. But back then, I at least looked healthy.

I drop my arms to my sides and stare at myself. I still hate me. This isn't the body I ever imagined myself having. It's embarrassing to see myself like this, and it's scary to think about how little I ate over the years. When I did eat, it was stuff like pizza or Will's Pop-Tarts. Never anything sustainable.

On my way to the bathroom, I think about the night I almost died. I had told Suzie not less than five hours earlier that I was trying, that I was getting better. How can she forgive me so easily? I shake my head and run my hand down my face. It's nothing I can change now. After searching every corner and cabinet in the bathroom, I find the scale up against the wall behind the toilet. Gross. With as few fingers as I can possibly use, I pull it out.

Without looking down, I step onto the scale. I'm not sure I want to know. Quickly, I look down. 133. Damn. Numbers really make everything real.

The scale slides easily back behind the toilet where it belongs. I wash my hands, put my shirt back on, go back to my room, and sit down at my desk. I write one more word on my list: *Eat.*

It seems simple, and for most people it probably is, but I have to write it down to remember. But more than simply eating, I have to have three sustainable meals per day, and probably snacks in between those. But until I get money to get real food, it's just "eat."

I need a mental break; I feel so exhausted. Is this how it feels to be normal? People are just running around exhausted all day? My warm bed welcomes me as I flop onto it, not bothering to aim my head toward the pillows. Immediately, all the thoughts I fight so hard to keep away come running right back to me. What makes me think I can get better? Why do I deserve to be better, and why now? I haven't let myself feel since being back. I don't want to know how I feel about failing at dying. I have a sense of happiness, I think. But I also still dread waking up every day for new reasons.

I don't want to disappoint anyone, or myself. Now the house is full of so many expectations, things I'm not sure I can meet. Suddenly, my cold dark room feels like a prison; one I used to take so much comfort in. This whole house feels like a cell. I have nowhere to go for comfort anymore. The old life I used to live is closing in on me. Every part of this house brings back a memory of why I became who I was.

"Give me a break!" I shout. The anger comes from nowhere. I wasn't expecting it at all, but yelling helps. I see my pack of cigarettes on the desk and suddenly, I need air.

Since Tyson isn't here, I resort to lighting it on the stove again. Outside, my butt finds its spot on the top step. The nicotine does its job quickly numbing my nerves, temporarily silencing the whirlwind of noise in my head. I let the sun warm my skin.

Just then, a car pulls to the curb, stops for three seconds to let someone out, and drives away. Once the face comes into focus, I fight the urge to run.

"What the fuck are you doing here?" Dad stops at the bottom of the steps to catch his breath. "Pardon my surprise, but I thought you were dead." The way his body sways makes him need all the support of the railing to climb the three small steps that lead to the front door. I scoot over to avoid him stepping on me, although I doubt that would stop him. "Wishful thinking on my part."

He pops the P in "part" and spits on me. Was that intentional? Who the hell knows?

My palm comes up to my cheek to swipe away his saliva. "A pleasure as always," I say, pulling my eyes away from him and over to the flowers in our neighbor's yard across the street.

My heart is racing. I'm still debating on whether or not I should run. I wish Tyson or Will were here right now. Hell, I'd take Katie at this point.

"Trying to kill yourself was the best thing you ever did for this family," he says. "It's a shame it didn't work. Seems you're a pussy even in that regard." He pushes the front door open but turns back around. "Nothing to say this time? You don't feel like getting your ass beat? Or is it because your bodyguards aren't here?"

Breathe. Just ignore him. He's drunk. He'll go away, just don't provoke him.

I remind myself of these things, but can't help letting his words hit me in a way they shouldn't. My hand curls into a fist at my side, and I close my eyes. Screw him. I take another drag then flick the cig out into the road.

"It is a shame, isn't it?" I agree.

My body decides before my brain does that were leaving. I stand up and make my way to Katie's house. If there's anyone that knows how to eat, it's her, and for the first time in a long time, I'm starving.

"Don't bother coming back, you fuck."

My laughter comes out louder than necessary just so I can be sure he hears it. "I hope you fall down those stairs, you lush," I yell back.

When I finally get to Katie's house, I knock on the door and lean over, putting my hands on my knees. When you don't have a body full of fake energy from drugs, going on a walk on an empty stomach is not ideal. I've never noticed how out of shape I am; I should probably add that to my list of things to do, as well.

"Hey, Jace, good to see you." The door opens and Katie's aunt, Grace, moves aside to let me in. She doesn't ask who I'm here for anymore; just lets me in and assumes I'll find my way to whoever I need.

"Good to see you too, just here to kidnap Katie," I call behind me as I run up the stairs to her room. I step lightly and open her bedroom door as slowly as I can before yelling, "KATIE!"

She jumps and screams and spins around in her desk chair. "Damn it, Jace! What is your problem? You scared the hell out of me!"

Smiling, I spin her desk chair in a circle. "I'm starving. I thought you could take me on a date."

"Is it only a date because you need me to pay?" she asks sarcastically.

"And choose the place!" It almost comes natural lately, to be in a good mood, to have a personality when I talk. I almost don't have to remind myself anymore. Almost.

"You're ridiculous." She gets up, picks up her bag, and walks past me down the stairs.

"It's a step up from broody," I joke, spinning around to catch up with her.

Once we've been driving a while, Katie turns down the car radio. "How has your day been going?"

"It's alright. Been thinking a lot, so that's…something." I lean my head back in the seat.

"I'm surprised you want to go eat, but I've never heard more beautiful words come out of your mouth." The smile on her face tells me she isn't kidding. I know Katie loves food. Not always good food, but she does love food.

"I've decided anytime I get a craving for pills or booze, I'm just going to eat instead." I put my feet up onto the dash and look out the window.

"Smart. Do you get those often? Because if you're always craving, that means you'll always be eating…that might be hard to keep up with." She turns her head to hide her smile. I know she's digging for extra information.

"Smooth, Katie, that was really smooth. No, not too often. Not yet, anyway. What's your excuse for all the eating you do?" I tease.

"Hey, shut up. I eat no more or less than the average American. If the food didn't want to be eaten, it wouldn't taste so good. And get your damn feet off my dash. Why do I have to tell you that every time we get in my car?"

I drop my feet and slide up the seat. "Jeez, sorry, Mom."

"Is it a crime to want to keep my car clean? Who knows where your nasty shoes have been."

"No, you're right. My bad." I hold my hands up in defeat.

She punches me playfully in the shoulder. "Tyson said you've been an ass lately. Have you?"

"You disguise your question about me craving things but straight-up ask me if I've been an ass? Interesting. No, I haven't been an ass. Will says you've been playing hard to get, is that true?" Will's been trying to get Katie to pay attention to him for…well, ever since I brought her home.

"No, I'm playing not interested. Now I'm starting to see where Tyson's getting his opinions of you."

"I'm not an ass, I'm just annoyed all the time. I can't believe he's so hung up on that. He asked me a stupid question, so I told him it was a stupid question. Why won't he drop it?"

"Because you've never fought back before."

I narrow my eyes at her. "What does that mean?"

She huffs. "He isn't used to you giving a shit about what he's saying. So when you shot back at him, it took him by surprise. I guess you don't normally have feelings when you guys get into your little brother spat things."

"We argue all the time. I don't understand why this was different."

"It's hard to explain. It's something that people who have family members in recovery notice. It's not really a good or a bad thing, just something he noticed."

"You guys talked about it?" Just as I thought, they're having weird meet-ups. Talking about me and discussing my actions without me like I'm some science experiment. She doesn't answer, but her eyes widen a tad like she wasn't supposed to mention anything. I change the subject. "Where are we going? You better not say Denny's."

The smile on her face tells me that's exactly where she's taking us.

Chapter 27

Finally, Monday comes around and I wake up to the sound of Sammy Davis Jr. singing out of my phone speaker. The weekend was too long. I didn't realize how much of a task remembering to eat would be. The whole weekend felt like my brain was on manual. Remembering to breathe, eat, clean, homework, breathe, eat, clean—I had to think about every task and movement to force them to happen.

The hot water fogs up the bathroom. Showering is still a thing that I dread for some reason. Once I'm in here, it's great. I feel amazing, like I have my whole life together. But convincing myself to get in is one of the worst parts of my life, for some reason.

After, I go to the kitchen to find something to eat. Something better than Pop-Tarts or cereal. Will and Tyson take turns getting groceries. Tyson's got a work-from-home job. I don't even know what he does. I guess I haven't really been present enough to find out. Will, of course, has his new part-time construction job and goes to school full-time. The only problem is that no one in this house cooks, so the food they buy is impractical. Stuff like frozen pizza, TV dinners, boxed noodles, cans of soup, and cereal. The closest things we have to "cookable" food are bacon and eggs, which I decide to make before everyone wakes up.

"Good morning." Tyson yawns and stretches as he walks into the kitchen. "I could get used to waking up to this smell. Now I know how Suzie feels every day."

"I figured I'd start pulling my weight around here. Starting with making breakfast before you get up. Coffee's done, too."

He gives me a skeptical look but grabs a mug and fills it up. "You going to school today?"

I nod and make myself a plate. "Yeah, I can't really afford to miss any more days." Tyson's eyes look at the plate in front of me. The smallest hint of surprise appears in his eyes before he shakes it off and acts casually. He sits down at the table across from me and opens his laptop.

Suzie comes in, serves herself some food, and sits down next to me. "Tys forcing you to eat today?" she laughs.

His head snaps up and his eyes widen at her. He shakes his head, probably worried Suzie's going to scare me off. Why does no one think I'm capable of making my own decisions?

"No." I force another bite of eggs and eat a strip of bacon. I still don't have much of an appetite, and eating almost nauseates me. But I do it anyway. I'm so tired of them looking at me like I'm broken. Internal battles will stay internal from now on. I just want them to feel like I'm a whole new person, like I don't have bad thoughts anymore.

"Dang, Tyson, you made breakfast for *everyone* today? What's the occasion?" Will practically lunges at the pan of bacon before anyone can tell him it's not for him.

I don't say anything. I just keep eating before I have a moment to change my mind. Out of the corner of my eye, I see Tyson point at me without looking away from his computer.

"You're welcome," I say. "I need to be at school a little early today. Mind if we leave in the next 20?" I ask Will.

"Oh…yeah, sure." He smiles, but the confusion is clear on his face.

"Thanks." I leave the kitchen and go to my room. I hear them whispering my name, but I don't care. Today is the day I change. Everything I do changes, and every motive I have changes. I can be depressed and hate myself and not want to live, but starting today, I'm also going to start being an adult. A depressed adult who is for once in their life giving this "fighting" thing a real chance. It's also my first day of working and spending who knows how long with Joshua. I wonder if we'll become friends or if he's going to be one of those ass-wipe bosses you can't stand.

I find a pair of jeans I don't think I've ever worn before and pull them on over my shorts; some habits will never die. I find a light-purple T-shirt in my closet. I'm sure someone got this for me, or maybe it used to be Will's or something, but I've never worn it. It feels different from the dark-colored shirts I usually wear. It looks nice against my olive skin and makes my green eyes stand out. It's a weird thing to see on me. I almost look like…I don't know. A normal person, maybe.

For the first time in my life, my eyes don't look sad or like they've seen too much. I almost smile at who I see looking back at me. I decide to go to school sans hoodie, which is going to be weird because I won't have my security cocoon of a hood, or the strings on the neckline to mess with. The first small step to reinventing myself is to put myself in positions I wouldn't normally be in. I need to get comfortable with being uncomfortable.

It's a weird thing to check out at such a young age. Now that I'm an adult, I don't know who I am. I don't know how to be anything but the 15-year-old I used to be. It's like I turned 15, went to sleep, and woke up at twenty-one with new expectations from everyone and a whole different way of living that I don't under-stand.

"Alright, I'm ready." Will pops into my room and his eyes

widen. "Holy shit, Jace." His mouth opens and falls shut a few times, like he wants to speak but doesn't know what to say. "Who are you? Breakfast and dressing like a proper young member of society? The neighbors are going to be thrilled that we got rid of the hobo who's been hanging around our house."

"Yeah…thanks, Will, 'ppreciate that," I say and pat his shoulder.

*   *   *

Will drops me off at school. I tell him not to bother picking me up because I have something to do after class, but I don't tell him what. Walking inside the building and through the halls, I don't miss people's glances. It must be because I look cleaner than usual, I'm not hiding behind a hoodie, or maybe everyone's heard about how I died and came back to life. I'll never know which. But something tells me it's a good mix of all the above.

Ian shows up next to me, matching my pace. "Zombie! You made it! Wow, you look…"

"Different?" I finish for him.

"Really good," he counters.

I stop walking and face him. "Thanks, man, I feel pretty good."

"You think you could share some of that feel-good with me?" Ian says. "I'm going through it right now. I've never felt so shitty in my life." His face falls with a sad laugh.

He's got purple bags under his eyes and the color is drained from his face. He's probably as sick as I was when I was quitting, if not more. I really hope I didn't look that bad when I was detoxing. There's no way you can hide that. I'm surprised he came to school.

"Well, I had to go through it too, so, I guess you can say you earn it," I tell him. His blue eyes are bloodshot. I wonder if he's been crying. "Why did you come to school today? You look rough."

He motions for us to start walking again. He isn't in my class, and I'm pretty sure the one he has starts a few minutes before mine. His eyes follow the floor, watching every step he takes.

"A way to stay busy." He shrugs. "Plus, a lot of my friends here are good support systems."

When he looks at me I could swear he glances briefly at my lips, but it's so fast I can't be sure. I quickly look away to my own feet.

"A distraction, I guess?" he finishes.

I can't tell if he's asking me to give him a distraction or if it's just a statement, but it throws me off, makes me feel weird inside. "Friends? Hmm, I think that was the one thing I was missing when I was putting myself through the hell of getting clean. Are these friends the type who don't do drugs?"

Ian smiles and nods. "Most of them. The ones that do are always supportive of sobriety. I mostly just keep to myself, but it's nice to be with those friends. They don't really get it."

"I guess that makes sense." We stop at the door to my class. "Well, hey, let me know if you need anything, alright?"

"Yeah, man, thanks! Have a good class." Ian smiles and adds, "I'm going to go puke before mine starts."

"Yeah…good luck with that." I look up briefly to smile at him before turning in to my class.

That was weird.

The classroom is pretty full. Fuller than it usually is, but I guess I'm only a few minutes early. I decide sitting in my usual spot is allowed, so I make my way to the back of the room, but before I sit, I hear Katie from behind me.

"no fucking way. JACE! Look at you, you're in jeans and color!

Wow, did you brush your hair?!" She runs up to me and wraps her arms around my neck.

I feel the heat rush up my neck and into my cheeks. The whole class has turned to see what she's going on about. Nice, thanks. I wish I had my hood right now so I could pull it over my head and hide.

My jaw drops when she pulls away. "Wow, Katie. You, my friend, are an asshole." My butt finds my chair quickly, desperate to get out of everyone's attention.

"You love me." Her grin spreads across her face.

"Well, now that we've discussed Jace and his jeans, let's get started with today's topic," the professor says from the front of the room.

I glare at Katie and shake my head. "Now you've done it."

"Have you heard?" she whispers. "The whole class thinks you and I are dating."

I glance around the room and then back to us. She's sitting right next to me, and we talk throughout every class. I don't doubt that's something being spread around.

"I could see that."

"Us dating? Gross."

"No, not…wait, why would that be gross? I'm the gay one, I should be saying 'gross' about dating *you*." Habitually, my hands come up to my neck in search of the hoodie strings I no longer have. Thank God, too, because with summer getting here, I'd be dying of the heat. Seriously, do they not invest in A/C anymore?

"Do you want to come over today?" Katie asks. "Aunt Grace is making some kind of fancy soup or something and said I should invite you over."

"As wonderful as mystery soup sounds, I actually have somewhere to be after school today. Tell her I'll take a rain check."

"You have plans after school?" Her head pulls back in surprise.

If I'm going to do this whole thing on my own, I better start coming up with better excuses as to why I'm busy. "Yeah, just something I have to do."

"…alright." She's skeptical, understandably. But, even with Katie, I want this to be just a small victory for myself. A part of my life that people aren't constantly asking questions about. It hasn't even started, and I'm already excited to just have something that's mine. *Excited.* That hasn't happened in so long. The thought of being excited about something gives me a genuine smile. I'm nervous but can't wait to get to the shop to work. It's the first thing that's making me feel like an adult, and I am so ready for that.

I'm also excited to get to know Joshua. I can't stop thinking about what he might be like. It would be nice to have a friend that isn't Katie, especially one that doesn't know everything about my past. I hope it goes as well as I want it to.

The class drags on, and somehow in the middle of it, Katie convinces me to do her work for her. She's ready to just give up on school. I'm not even sure why she's here or what she's going for. I'm not sure what Ian is here for, either. Will is here getting his engineering degree. What is he going to do with that, you ask? I don't fucking know. But he's very happy with his choice.

"I'm never going to pass the finals." Katie groans as we walk out of the class. She has four classes this semester. I decided on only two, so I don't have nearly as much to stress out about.

"I'm not doing your final for you."

"Damn it. Are you sure?" she asks, widening her eyes with a pout.

"Positive."

"What are you positive about?" Ian says, running to catch up with us. Was he waiting in the hall since his class got over?

"Jace won't do my finals for me," Katie says and shrugs politely, brushing him off.

"You want *Jace* to do your finals?" He laughs and then looks at me. "Oh, shit, no. I'm sorry, it's just that…I assumed your grades are kind of crap."

I open my mouth to tell him it's fine, but Katie starts talking before I'm able to. "They aren't. Jace is the smartest person I know. It's not very nice to assume things about people. Like when I assumed you'd be a better person and stop giving the recovering druggie pills." She storms ahead of us and leaves Ian and me baffled.

"That was very 'high school drama' of her, no?" he asks.

"Yeah. You must have pissed her off quite a bit." It was out of character for her to act that way, but it was a little dramatic, too, if I'm being honest.

"She'll get over it. Back to the grade thing. You really doing that well?"

We continue walking slowly toward the exit. I'm hoping Katie won't leave because I know she's Ian's ride home, and I'm not walking with him. I'm too excited to get to the shop.

"They aren't bad," I tell him. "I'm only taking two classes, though, so my chances of getting good grades are a bit higher. I mostly just have to show up." The way he stares at me when I'm talking, like he's hanging on every word, makes my stomach flutter. I feel a blush running up my neck to my cheeks, and I clear my throat. "Anyway, I'm gonna go. See you around!"

I turn and jog away—mostly to get away from that awkward moment, but also because I can't wait to start work.

Chapter 28

I forgot school is farther from the shop than the house. I'll have to pass my house and keep going to get to the shop. It's about a five-and-a-half-mile walk, so it shouldn't take too long, but the thought of it isn't a fun one.

I get to the autobody shop about forty minutes later—out of breath, nauseous, and a little dizzy. I was worried about being late since he never gave me a specific time, so I ran and jogged the whole way.

I guess I can add that to my daily workout. If I'm going to do this regularly, I'll need an actual meal plan because there's no way I ate enough to keep up with all the calories I just burned.

"You're here." Joshua checks the clock in the lobby and looks back at me, still panting and hunched over.

I'm sure on a normal day I'd be embarrassed about the way I'm acting right now, but Jesus Christ. My chest is tight and my legs feel like Jell-O. Somehow my arms are exhausted and are hardly holding me up against my knees. I put my arm on the doorframe, rest my head against it, and dry heave.

"God, what did you do, run here?" he says, backing away with disgust even though he's not standing anywhere near me.

I inhale deeply before looking up at his icy-blue eyes. They're just as stunning as they were the first time I saw them. On a breathy exhale, I answer, "Yeah." I cough again. After a few more deep breaths, I stand upright. "I didn't know what time you wanted me here."

He shrugs. "I didn't have a specific time. I wasn't sure you'd show up." He has on a dark-green baseball cap, backwards. His shaggy hair is sticking out around it, making my heart skip. This time he's wearing a gray button-up work shirt with the sleeves rolled up to right below his elbows. His arms are muscular. I don't doubt he works out. Everything about him is just…so hot.

Pulling myself out of my thoughts, I say, "Well, I did. So, where should I start?"

He regards my shirt and says, "First, I suggest changing. Wouldn't want to ruin your Hollister shirt." He chuckles and heads toward what I'm assuming is an office of sorts.

I look down at my clothes. What the hell is a Hollister shirt? I follow him anyway because I've grown to like this shirt quite a bit, so yes, it would be a shame to ruin it. When we get into the office, he throws me a shirt before I know it's coming. It lands on my head and I feel like an idiot. I rip it off and hold it in my arms. He laughs to himself and turns around to pull three more out of the box. Then he places them on the desk.

"When we're done here, I'll give you a few more so you can alternate them. Unfortunately, it's just the gray, but you're welcome to buy other colors. Just make sure they're Dickies. They hold up the best with the cars, grease, and tools and stuff." When he turns around, I'm still standing there holding the shirt. "You gonna change?"

I look around the room and then back at him. "In here? Now?"

He makes an amused face and smiles. "What, you got boobs under there?" He glances down at my chest and back up. The gesture causes tingles to spread through my body, and I feel heat creeping up to my face. I know it's just a joke, but I can't help letting my imagination tell me he was checking me out. He wasn't, but I can pretend.

I'm still uncomfortable about taking my shirt off because of how small I look, not to mention, taking it off in front of *him* makes my stomach flutter. Maybe if I throw in some small talk, he won't keep staring at me.

"So, what time should I be here regularly, and what days?" I ask. The moment he turns away to look at the calendar on the wall, I whip my shirt off and push my arms through the sleeves of the work shirt. The buttons are undone, but at least the majority of me is covered.

"Do you have things to do during the day?" he asks. "Ideally, we'd like you here between three and five. As for the days, as many as you're willing to give. We don't have a whole lot of staff, and with you being so…" He looks around the room like he's trying to think of the word "inexperienced." The word comes accompanied by a sly smirk. "You're going to need as many training hours as you can get. I'd like to think I can at least have you on things like spark plugs, oil changes, and tire duty in a week or two."

"I can be here between three and four. I have school until two every day. I'd just need the time to walk here."

"Feel free to walk, and not run. I'd rather you not show up at the door dry heaving every day." A soft laugh comes from him.

"Funny. What time do we leave?" I finish buttoning my shirt. If I had his build, or Tyson's, this shirt would look good. But I know for a fact I don't look anywhere near as good as Joshua does in it.

"When we're done."

That doesn't sound like any kind of job I've heard of. We don't have set hours? "And the pay?" As exciting as it is to be here, I'm not doing this for free.

"Since this is an apprentice position, you'll be paid hourly. It's $16.50 an hour."

Before I can stop myself, I ask, "Is that good?"

Regret. Immediate regret. What kind of dumbass question is that? This guy is going to think I'm stupid.

"It's...fair." His eyebrows furrow together "How old did you say you were?"

"I didn't. Twenty-two." I don't turn twenty-two for another month, but honestly, I think the extra year might help me out here.

"This your first job, kid?"

Kid. One of my least favorite words ever. I wish I could qualify as a kid. I've seen too much, been through too much. Besides, there's no way he's much older than me. I wouldn't even believe he was in his early thirties.

"Jace." I brush off my shirt and look back into his eyes. "That's my name, and you're Joshua?" I add that the last bit to sound less hostile.

He chews his cheek before deciding to drop the first question. "Call me Josh. Let's go get started, then."

We don't do much work at all. He takes me around the building and shows me different parts of the shop, how to log into the computer, what to say when answering the phone, and a brief description of all the tools and what they're called. To say this is all very overwhelming is an understatement. I'm worried I bit off more than I can chew. But Josh seems to understand how little I know about any of this stuff, which is probably why he's going into such detail on things and explaining them to me like I'm five.

When we get back into the office, he hands me the other shirts he promised me. "So that's the shop. I won't have you 'hands-on' for a while, just want you to learn your way around here first, understand the tools and stuff." He shoves his hands into his pockets.

"Any questions?"

"Why did you hire me?" I ask. "I mean, you could have hired anyone, someone who already knows all this stuff. I know this place is short on staff, so why waste time teaching me everything from the ground up?" While I wait for his answer, I put the clothes into my backpack and zip it up.

"You looked determined. Plus, no one else came. I figured if I took the time to train you, at least I'd have myself a mechanic that works the way I want them to. Sometimes inexperience is a strength, and I decided to trust that in this situation, it would be."

"Well, I'll try to meet your expectations." I give him a small half-smile.

"Cool. You can head out if you want. I don't have much in the way of things I can show you today. Tomorrow, we'll go through all the paperwork and get you officially hired and in the system."

"Thank you, again. I'll be back tomorrow right after school!" I throw my bag over my shoulder and leave.

I decide to keep up my theme for today of overwhelming myself, and jog home. The jog is much shorter than it was from school to the shop. The air is cooler, too, so I'm not sweating my ass off this time. When I get to the front door of my house, I pull my T-shirt out of my bag and quickly switch it with the work shirt. There was no way I was going to take my shirt off in front of Josh again to put on the T-shirt, but I also don't want everyone on my case about getting a job.

The front door opens as I'm pulling my bag shut. "Oh, shit! You fucking scared me." Tyson holds his chest as he pulls open the door. "Where have you been all day? It's almost eight."

"I just had some stuff to do after school. Nothing crazy. I'm going to bed, though. It's been a long day."

I kick my shoes off at the door; my legs and feet are killing me.

I can't wait to go to bed. Between all the running, walking around the shop, and standing for longer than I have in who knows how many years, I'm ready to dig myself a grave and take a nice long dirt nap. I'm also going to need some new shoes—something made for running if I'm going to make a habit of this.

"You want to eat first? Will made macaroni and hot dogs."

I have to hold back a laugh. "Macaroni and hot dogs?" I fold my lips between my teeth, but I'm sure the amusement in my face is apparent. I guess I should eat something, even if it's the worst thing I can think of eating right now.

Will's sitting at the table doing homework. "I'm going to eat your nasty-ass food," I tell him, "but I need to have a come-to-Jesus moment with the both of you. I'm making the grocery lists now. I don't know how you guys do it, but give me whatever budget you follow and I'll make the list of things you need to get. We'll have a cookbook or some shit in here that a four-year-old can follow so we can all start cooking *real* food. Because at this rate…" I gesture to the pan with noodles and chopped-up hot dogs. "…we're all going to have heart attacks before we're in our forties."

"Easy stuff only?" Tyson asks, unsure.

"Promise. I just…I need to start eating better. And it'll be a lot easier if you guys are doing it too. We can have assigned dinner nights."

"I'm in." Will smiles, pleased to hear I want to start eating again.

"I'll learn how to cook, especially if it's going to help your health," Tyson says. "Suzie has mentioned a few times wanting to cook more, so I already know she'll be down to have a day."

"Cool. Let's do it, then. I'll figure out all the details tomorrow. But tonight, I need to eat and go to bed. I've never been so exhausted." There's a big difference, I'm learning, between being mentally exhausted and physically exhausted. I'm not even sure I'll be able to keep my eyes open through this meal with how physically exhausted I am.

I don't even bother cleaning up or putting my bowl in the sink after I finish my childish meal. I head straight to my room, stripping down and crawling into my bed in my basketball shorts.

Like every other night, the darkness and silence creep into my brain. This is the one thing I wish could just fix itself and disappear—the time when I'm not busy and I question if anything I'm doing is worth it. The only reason I can think to try to get any better is to prove my family wrong about me. But motivation is motivation. Whatever works.

I still can't help wishing I could be exactly what I'm trying to convince them I am. The truth is, I think I feel worse than I did before I was in the hospital. Only this time, I've decided to fight back against myself by keeping so busy that I don't have time to ponder. I don't know if it's the right thing to do, but it keeps me alive…for now. Hopefully sometime soon I'll find out if I qualify for therapy. Maybe then I can figure out the method to my madness.

Chapter 29

Today I had my other class, the one Katie isn't in. It's incredible how much slower the time goes when you don't have an annoying-ass friend bugging you the whole time. My pen taps against the desk as I try my hardest to appear to give a shit. This is a math class of sorts, and by far my least favorite subject, but school is school, so I suppose I should still put in a solid effort.

The notes I take hardly make sense. I'm not even sure I'm doing them right, but I don't mind. There are only ten minutes left in class and all I can think about is leaving and heading over to Josh…I mean the shop.

Today, I made sure to bring an actual lunch. Now that I've been eating, it's weird that I get hungry throughout the day. I was surprised when an hour before lunch I was already contemplating breaking into the bag and eating everything. Somehow, I managed to hold off for a few hours. That way I'll have the energy for the run to shop but won't make myself sick by running.

The second the clock hits two, I'm out of my seat and rushing for the door. I get outside and find Will sitting on a bench.

"Shit," I whisper to myself. I forgot to tell him I wasn't going to need a ride today. Or any day, actually. Is that a red flag?

He stands up when he sees me walking toward him. "You ready?"

I could, in theory, have him drive me home and then walk to the shop. But I like the part where I force myself to exercise. Plus, it's a good way to work off some of the pent-up excitement and energy I have from being in school all day.

"I forgot to tell you. I don't need a ride today. I'm sorry, dude, I know you've been waiting. I can't believe I forgot!"

"No, it's cool, I haven't been here too long. I was hoping you would have Katie with you."

"You're still trying to get at her?"

"No! You brought her home, and now she's everyone's friend. It's not always about getting with people. Why, has she talked about me?"

I do love that at this moment, Will doesn't worry about why I don't need a ride. No questions are shot at me like I'd expected them to be, not when he's on a mission to see Katie. I don't want to lie to them, that's not what I'm trying to do here. I just want to do things on my own, so I'm withholding information.

"She has not, sorry, bro. Her class gets out in a few minutes." I pat his shoulder and walk past him, crossing the street.

He turns around. "Where are you going?"

"On a run, helps clear my head." Not a lie. I am going on a run, and it does help clear my head.

"You don't run," he laughs.

"I do now!" I smile back before picking up a light jog.

Jogging to the shop still wipes me out. When I get there, I stop just outside and do all my coughing and dying before going in. I should probably go easier on myself, but you don't grow from nothing. No pain, no gain, right? I'm sure after a week of this it should get easier, but for now, I'll die in secret, away from Josh's gaze. Luckily, I managed to steal a lighter from Tyson this morning before heading out, so I do the smart thing any athlete would do and get in a quick smoke break before heading in.

When I pull the door open, there's a trashcan right behind the door that I almost trip over. "What the fuck?" I pick it up and bring it over to the desk where it used to be.

"You're here. I left that over there for you just in case you decided to actually throw up today." Josh smirks as he gets to the computer and starts typing something into it.

Sarcastically, I shoot back, "You're hilarious, anyone ever tell you that?"

"All the time. You ready for mountains of paperwork?" He drops a small stack of papers in front of me. He clearly isn't in college if he considers this to be a mountain of papers. "After that, we'll do some hands-on stuff. I have three oil changes and one tire rotation. Both of those you can do."

I take the papers and go into the office so I can get them filled out and change my clothes. The paperwork is easy but annoying. I swear I filled out the same information repeatedly. When I was finished, I brought the stack of papers to Josh, who was leaning back in the desk chair with his feet up by the keyboard. I could get so used to seeing this every day. So far, he seems to have a pretty laid-back personality. He's made a few jokes and has been nice. I don't imagine he's a dick or anything, so he could be pretty cool to know, though I'm not good with small talk or getting to know people. With Katie, it was easy. We just hopped right into our deep dark secrets; there was no "warm up" phase or awkward moment between us.

After I drop the papers next to him, he stands up and leads me out the office door toward the garage. "Have you ever worked on a car before?" Josh asks, pushing up his sleeves.

I almost forget to answer his question. I'm too busy watching the way the muscle in his arm flexes as he rolls the sleeve up. "Uh, no. Not once in my life." I smile at him, then glance at the car in front of us.

"Alright," he says. "Points for honesty, I guess." He chuckles, then moves closer to the car. "Raise it up, grab this cart, it has a bucket on it for the oil. Drain the oil, change the filter, close it up, refill the oil. Not hard at all." He reaches into the car and grabs a manual out of the glove compartment. "In the back of this, it should tell you the amount you need and the viscosity, which is the type of oil it needs."

He throws the book back into the car and heads over to the table where all the equipment is, grabs the oil and the filter that's needed for this particular car, and walks back over to where we were originally. "I'll do this one, you watch, then you get the second one. It isn't rocket science, so if you don't grasp it, I may have to fire you before you even start."

"Noted. Check the book, get the shit, drain, filter, refill. I think I got it." I meet his eyes before quickly looking away again, acting interested in the car.

"Lift the car." He pushes a button that raises the car until it's above our heads, then without hesitating, he grabs the cart and pulls it under the car to show me what tools are needed, how to unscrew bolts, and where everything is. The process is quite easy to understand, and it feels weird that I didn't know this was how you did it before now.

That said, the information is incredibly hard to retain with the way he moves. When he stretches his arms above his head, his shirt pulls up, showing just a sliver of the skin above his waistband, and something about the black gloves he's wearing as he works does it for me too.

Somehow, I'm able to listen enough to surprise him when I do the second car completely on my own, only needing help figuring out how to work the buttons that move the car up and down.

I'm not a fan of being dirty. I got oil on my arms and my face from pushing my hair back so often. Next time, I either need to pull it back, wear a hat, or cut it off. I've never worn a hat before, and I'm not too sure I can pull it off. Tyson wears them quite a bit. Maybe I'll steal one of his.

"Not too bad, kid." Josh gives me an approving nod.

"Jace," I remind him, "and thanks. I told you I was a fast learner."

"Jace. Right, next is the tire rotation. Twenty times easier than the oil. I just wanted to make sure you were competent enough for that first." He points to the bucket of oil.

The tire rotation is on the same car. He walks me through everything needed to know. He's right about it being way easier. The only thing I need to really remember is to screw the bolts on in a star shape around the tire.

By the time we're done with two cars, my body already aches just from holding my arms above my head and carrying tires—which aren't heavy, by the way. Josh walks me back to the office. He sits in the chair behind the desk and I sit in front of it.

"Water?" he asks, opening a mini fridge behind the desk.

"Please, that would be great." He slides a bottle across the desk to me and looks through my paperwork. "Didn't you say you were twenty-two?" he asks, pointing to the date of birth.

I swallow and feign interest in the area he's pointing at. "Did I? I meant twenty-one."

That perfect smile appears on his face again. "Your age doesn't affect the way you're able to work on cars. I asked because you seemed…" He trails off, looking for the right word.

"Naive?" I offered. "Yeah, I haven't exactly had a job before. It's a long story, but school has been the focus for a while." A 100 percent lie; I won't even pretend it isn't.

"What changed?"

A loaded question if I ever heard one. "Circumstances, I guess."

"Well, for now, I can say you're doing pretty well. I don't think you'll have any problems here, so I guess it's official. Once you get going and I can trust you on things on your own, the speaker is communal. You can add any songs you want to the queue using the phone that's connected to the charging base on the desk. Breaks are all you. You decide when you need them and how long they are. Pay is every two weeks, you get benefits after your first ninety days. Do you have any questions?"

"Is there anyone else working here? I saw that guy at the front desk the day I came in, but I haven't seen anyone else."

"No. Not really. People come and go. I'm not really expecting you to stay either. I guess we'll see."

"Trust me, I'm not going anywhere."

"Each day you come in, there should be more for you to learn, so the days might get longer, but for now, that's all we have. I'll see you tomorrow, Jace."

The way he says my name makes my stomach flutter. I have to hold back a stupid grin, but I can't fight the blush. Instead, I pick up my bag and turn away. "See ya," I say and all but run out the door.

I get outside and smile as the door behind me closes. It felt oddly good to work on those cars, to feel like I had something to do, something that required my help.

Between that and the good company, I really enjoy being here. I can't wait until I know more about cars and I'm able to go off on my own.

I get home shortly after and quickly change my shirt, though not much can be done about the dirt and oil that's still all over me.

When I walk into the house, it's just Katie and Will on the couch playing one of Will's video games.

"Late night, huh?" Katie calls over her shoulder. I'm not sure she knows it's me who walked in. She's probably just making conversation with whoever.

"Yeah, I'm going to hop in the shower, then I'll make some dinner." No one acknowledges I said anything, so I go to my room. It never seems to stay clean. I'm hardly ever here and somehow within a few days, it's a disaster. I pick up all the clothes off the floor and my laundry chair and throw them into the washing machine. Then I pick up all the trash and stray objects I can find and clean off my desk. I even take the time to make my bed. I know when I come in here later it'll feel nice to have a bed that isn't a disaster.

After I feel satisfied with the cleanliness of the room, I take my shower, being sure to scrub my face and arms where I know the grease is. Dinner goes by quickly. I make a chicken parmesan of sorts with broccoli. It's easy to make, and I'm not in the mood to be jumping through hoops to make something out of this world. Still, it's better than frozen stuff.

Even though I'm exhausted, I make it a point to stay out in the living room with the siblings, watching Will kick everyone's ass in what looks like a racing game. I wouldn't know; I'm just a spectator.

"Do you like any games?" Katie asks me.

I scratch my head and push my hair back. "I used to like card games."

"Dude," Tyson laughs. "You and your old-man music and old-man games, I'm surprised you don't walk around all day with loafers on."

Will's laughter stops. "What's wrong with loafers?" He's a very classy guy; he does indeed wear loafers often. Not the lounging type, but the dressier kind. It's still funny.

"Nothing, nothing at all," I say and smile. "Do you guys know where Suz is?"

"Boyfriend's house, I guess," Tyson answers, not looking away from the TV. It's now him against Katie, and they're two of the most competitive people I know.

"When are we gonna meet this guy? We've just been letting her hang out at his house all the time without even knowing the dude?"

"I said the same thing!" Will yells, turning toward me. "She said something about us scaring him off or something. We'd be lucky to ever meet him."

I guess that makes sense. We aren't the quietest people, but if she's dating someone who's easily frightened, she's dating the wrong person.

I leave them to their game, clean the kitchen, and go to my room. This has been a long-ass day, and I've been waiting for the moment I could go to bed without being accused of acting weird.

Chapter 30

The week goes by insanely fast. I don't let myself stay unbusy for longer than the hour or so it takes to fall asleep. Most of the days are the same: wake up early to make breakfast, go to school, jog from school to work, then jog home. I've started eating lunch and being sure I have a snack of some sort at work.

I got approved for therapy and had my first session on Thursday. It wasn't bad. Nothing crazy happened. We just kind of talked about why I was there. We decided that I'll go in twice a week, on Tuesdays and Thursdays. It's on the same strip of road the shop is on, so I'll be going between school and work those days. I'll still make it to work by 5:30, so Josh was cool with it. Of course I didn't tell him why the time change was important, but he didn't pry, either.

Josh has been working my ass off. I'm now trained in oil changes, which is nice because it gives me a little freedom in the shop. I'm also fluent in tool talk now. Through all the teaching, we don't have much time to make small talk, although I find myself wishing I knew more about him.

I still end up dying from all the jogging, but I've learned to do all my coughing and dry heaving on the corner before walking calmly into the shop now.

Work ended early tonight. There were too many cars to get to and nothing I knew how to do or that Josh wanted to show me, I guess. Suzie asks if I want to watch *Supernatural* so I break out my homework, eat dinner, and watch at the same time.

"You been doing okay lately?" she asks. I can't tell if she's worried, curious, or asking because she feels like she's supposed to. She doesn't look away from the TV when she asks, probably attempting to make it seem casual.

"Doin' alright, yeah. You? You haven't been home much lately. I assume you've been out with Dean." I wink at her when she finally glares at me.

"Max. Yeah, we've been hanging out. But it doesn't distract me from the fact that you leave for school at eight and don't get back home until nine or ten sometimes. What are *you* out doing? Got a Dean of your own?"

A laugh escapes me. It's one I haven't heard before, somewhere between an embarrassed laugh and a "yeah right" laugh. Suzie's eyes widen and she looks back up at the TV. I can tell she wants to question me about something but holds back with a rather awkward face instead.

I guess another good thing about substance abuse is that it kills your libido. It straight-up demolishes your sex drive. I haven't ever worried about getting off or feeling worked up because it just didn't happen. Not often, anyway, and seldom enough that when it did happen, a quick shower and a bit of hand action held me over perfectly. But now…sexually frustrated might be a good word for how I've been feeling. That's not to say Josh has any impact on that, but Jesus fuck, that man. Between all the car talk, watching him reach up to grab things, and the way his forearms flex when he's working, or when he wears short-sleeved work shirts and his biceps move and strain under the sleeve…

Yesterday, when he was reaching up on the shelf to grab

something (I'll never remember what it was) his shirt pulled up to reveal a nicely outlined "V" shape right above the waistband of his jeans. Something about it has me feeling a way I haven't felt before, and it's safe to say that getting into the shower has become less of an activity now that I have…other motivations to get in. Don't judge me. Yes, it's totally unhealthy that I find myself jacking off to the thought of the hot mechanic with the dark hair, blue eyes, and seductive V-line. But it's not just him that has me all pent up. It's life in general now that I don't have drugs suppressing it.

I was so high all throughout puberty that it's just now hitting me, and hard. I should have gone through all these weird feelings when I was younger, but here I am, not in control of my body at all.

Suzie doesn't ask any more questions and doesn't think twice when I get up and leave. I check my phone messages in my room. I have a few missed calls and a text from Katie.

Jace, can you come over and maybe spend the night? I need a friend. I'm not doing too well.

Without thinking, I grab my gray hoodie and run out of my room. "Hey, Suz, I'm going to spend the night over at Katie's. Something's wrong. I'm not sure when I'll be home. Tell the boys, please." I don't wait for her response before I'm out the door and jogging down the road.

I've learned that knocking or ringing the doorbell only inconveniences people in this house, so when I get to Katie's, I walk right in and go straight to her room. She's lying on her bed in a ball with red eyes and wet cheeks.

"Katie, what's wrong? Are you okay?" I sit beside her and stroke her hair.

"I don't know," she says. "I'm just…not doing well. I didn't want to be alone. I can't fall asleep, but I'm so tired. Can you just hang out here and lay with me, at least until I fall asleep?"

Nodding, I climb under the blankets and wrap my arms around her. Cuddling is something we do often these days. Usually I'm the one covered in tears and being spooned. It's nice to be here for her, even if it's only in big spoon form.

"Do you want to talk about it?" I ask.

Her head shakes in response.

"Okay, we'll Harry Potter it." I kiss her head and pull her even closer to me.

I wish I knew how to help. That's the weirdest part about depression, the fact that you know exactly how they feel but you still have no idea how to help them.

Katie turns around and lays her head on my chest with her arm wrapped around my torso. "You smell bad," she whispers.

Again, Josh worked my ass off, and I haven't had time to shower since getting home. Of course I smell bad. "Then don't breathe," I joke.

She nuzzles her head against my shoulder and we lay there silently. Her room always smells so feminine, like peaches or vanilla, or some type of flower. Today, it's a coconut scent, probably one of my favorites. During these times, I like to just be here for her. I don't have any distractions or make her feel like I have anywhere else to be.

Her desk has become much like the chair in my room and is holding all her laundry, The pen and notebook on her desk are open when they're usually closed. There's soft music playing through her speakers, probably something Taylor Swift or Selena Gomez or whoever the popular artists are these days.

When I know she's asleep, I slide out from under her and cover her back up with her heavy fuzzy blanket. I take her clothes into the laundry room the way she once did for me.

I'm kneeling down shoving her clothes into the washer when someone runs into me. It's Ian.

"Jace? Are you…doing laundry at my house?"

I look down at my hands and stand up. "It's Katie's. She's asleep, so I figured I'd just…throw them in."

"I didn't realize you were in here. Usually people turn on the light in the room they're in," he smirks and flips the light switch.

I guess that's a habit for me. I rarely ever turn on the light in my room. I guess I've developed a special skill for seeing in the dark. "Hmm. Yeah, that could be helpful." Squinting, I turn around and shove the rest of the clothes into the washer.

"Hey," Ian says, "I've been meaning to talk to you about something, but I haven't been able to catch you at school." He leans against the doorway with his arms crossed.

I feel a flutter in my stomach. Something about the way he's looking at me, and that we're alone in the house at night. I wish he hadn't turned on the light because I know regardless of his question, my face is heating up.

"Yeah, ask away." I turn back to the washer nonchalantly and pour the soap in. I'm hoping he didn't see the blush on my face. I know he doesn't mean anything like *that*, but all this pent-up sexual tension has me looking into everything everyone says.

"Correct me if I'm wrong," he says, "and If I am, I apologize. But I assume you're a lot like me." He stops talking to give me a second to think it over.

I don't know if it's my current condition, but the meaning of the conversations has shifted and now I'm wondering if he does in fact mean what I think he means. I turn around slowly and catch his eye, mouth slightly open, laundry detergent still in my hand.

"I've been having a rough time with this detox thing," Ian continues, "and I think a distraction is something that would do me well. I'm tired of waiting on things in life, so I thought I'd just be straightforward with you. I was going to pull you aside at school on Monday, but since you're here at my house, what better time?" He laughs nervously.

"A distraction?" My voice catches in my throat, exposing the fact that I'm nervous or surprised by whatever it is that's going on right now.

"I guess there's no better way to say this." He bites his lower lip in thought. "I like you, Jace. I've been trying to figure out how to bring it up to you, or ask in a way that isn't weird…"

The news shocks me. Mentally, I have to pick my jaw up off the floor. So Ian really is gay…all the brief signals and signs weren't my imagination.

"I just…I've seen the way you look at me, and I pay attention. I know you haven't tried to do anything with my sister, which I've never seen any guy *not* do before." He stops talking as if whatever he had planned to say has run away.

"Ian…"

What do I do? When I told Will about losing my virginity, I didn't go into detail about how that was the only sexual experience I've ever had. That one time, with that one girl. I've never done anything with another guy, not kissed or touched or even held hands.

The butterflies in my stomach make their grand appearance. My heart feels like it's going to pound out of my head, or my neck, maybe my chest, everywhere all at once. I'm suddenly very aware of my hands. They get clammy, and I shift the container of soap a few times.

"I understand if I'm mistaken," he says. "I just don't want to miss an opportunity because I didn't ask." I don't miss how his eyes drop down my body.

"I… I'm not…" I struggle with my words. "Neither of us is

really in a place for a…relationship." Stupid brain. This is my chance to hop into bed with someone. A man. Something I've been waiting to happen for years. And I say some dumb shit like that?

"I'm not talking about a relationship," Ian says and chuckles. "But I'm glad to see I was correct in my assumption about your…preferences?"

Maybe I'm not the only gay man who can't say the word "gay" out loud. Or maybe he's doing it for my benefit because he knows about my dad. If Katie had told him about me, he definitely wouldn't have prolonged this conversation trying to figure me out.

Ian steps closer to me and softly runs his hand down my shoulder to my wrist. "Think about it. You know where to find me."

I watch as he drags his fingers down my hand and reaches for the laundry detergent. His fingers slide between mine before he takes the container from my hand and reaches behind my shoulder to put it back on top of the washer. The movement forces his chest against mine, our faces hardly an inch apart.

My breathing hitches immediately, and there's a tingling that follows exactly where his hand trailed down my arm. An instinct in me tells me to grab his hips and pull him closer, but the brain in me forces me to stay still.

Ian doesn't move. He leaves our chests pressed together as his eyes meet mine. My tongue darts out to wet my lips, which brings them to his attention. There's a smirk on his face before he leans in, slow enough to give me time to stop him. But I don't.

His lips press against mine softly. Against my will, my hands move up, one to his hip and one to the back of his head. He moves his mouth against mine, gently at first, then slowly picks up pace. His tongue slips past my lips, causing a small approving moan to escape his mouth. The small noise coming from him kicks me into some kind of overdrive controlled entirely by instinct.

I step forward between his legs, forcing him back against the wall, where I press up against him firmly. There's no hiding my hardening cock with how close we are together. His mouth continues moving swiftly against mine. His mouth tastes sweet, and his lips are softer than I'd imagined.

I push his hips up against the wall harder and grind my own into him. He lets out another soft moan. I pull my mouth away from him long enough to pull his bottom lip into my mouth and bite down lightly. Once I release him, I kiss down his jaw roughly, listening to every pant and heavy breath he has for me as I place each peck.

This time it's his hands on my hips as he pulls me into him and guides me to grind harder against him. There's no doubt in my mind this is better for me than it is for him, even though beneath his jeans I can feel he's hard for me too. There's no way in hell I'm about to tell him how long it's been for me, but at this rate, if he keeps doing that, I'm going to cum in my basketball shorts.

I latch onto his neck and try to steady my breathing. After repeating my kiss, bite, suck pattern a few more times, I pull my hips slightly away from him and push his chest to keep him where he is against the wall. I place one feathery light kiss on his lips and press my forehead to his.

I don't know what to expect next. I've never done…any of this. I don't know what we're supposed to do now, but I do know I'm about three seconds away from embarrassing myself. He hasn't even touched me, and I'm ready to explode all over for him.

Ian's panting grows heavier, but also more controlled. "I'm *very* glad my assumptions weren't wrong," he says and smiles, pulling his lips into his mouth. His hand runs down my stomach and slightly past the waistband of my shorts. "Next time, Carter."

With that, he lightly pushes me away and walks out of the room—leaving me confused, surprised, and all sorts of hot and bothered.

My breathing is still heavy. I can't control the pounding in my chest. Did that just happen? I turn around and lean back against the wall, my fingers grazing my lips, now swollen from the deep kisses. I stay against the wall, mouth halfway open and eyes wide for a good three minutes trying to figure out what just happened. Next time…? What did that mean? I don't know, but fuck, if I thought I was sexually pent up before this…

Chapter 31

I wake up in Katie's bed. She's still sleeping with her back toward me. Last night after that heated kiss with Ian, I stayed up to switch her clothes over to the laundry and contemplate my life. I have never felt like that. It took everything in me not to walk right into Ian's room and finish what we started. I'm honestly regretting my decision not to.

I blink at the ceiling a few times then trace my lips with my finger, remembering how everything felt last night. Now that the moment is over, I'm wondering if I should be embarrassed about taking control of that whole moment. I pinned him against a wall. How did I think to do that? I feel my cock twitch at the memory. It felt good to be in control of something…to be demanding and have him move the way I requested.

Fuck. I'm going to need to go home soon to take care of this. I'll go insane if I don't. But I also have more important things to do today, like be here for Katie. I wish I could tell her about everything. If it hadn't happened with her brother, I would.

When she takes a deep breath and snorts, I smile, knowing she's still out cold. I slide out of her bed, pick my hoodie up off the floor, and put it back on before deciding to make her some breakfast.

My hand hesitates at the doorknob. What if Ian is down there? Or worse, what if he's in the hallway? I didn't know how to act last night, there's no way I'm going to know what to do or say if I run into him.

Like an idiot, I press my ear against the door to see if I can hear any signs of life. It sounds empty, like the house is still sleeping. I swear the clock said 9 a.m. If this were my house, the chaos would have started an hour or two ago. You'd have to wake up at four in the morning to get silence like this. Sometimes even then if someone hears you up, it's fair game.

The door squeaks when I pull it open, causing me to stop and cringe. I look back at Katie, who doesn't seem bothered by it at all. The stairs squeak and croak with every step I take. This house has got to be the loudest house I've ever been in. The kitchen is much larger than ours. It has a rounded island with four barstools and counters that press up against three walls, and a huge window behind the sink overlooking the front yard.

It looks more like a kitchen than ours does, too. A spice rack, bread, fruit, and an organized coffee area are on the counters, along with some cooking appliances I don't recognize. The fridge is full of fresh foods, from meats, fruits, and veggies to things like fancy sparkling water and a crap-ton of condiments. This must be what it's like to have a responsible adult figure in the house when you're growing up. I wonder if Ian or Katie cook, or if it's all their aunt.

After being overwhelmed by the contents of the fridge, I look around some more. The spice rack contains things I haven't heard of before. I twist open a few of the jars and bring them to my nose. I make a mental note of the ones I like; it wouldn't hurt to get more creative in cooking when it comes to my nights. I wouldn't make anyone else in our house even think of anything other than salt and pepper right now.

"It's not cocaine hidden in those spices that you're sniffing, is it?" I jump and drop the dill seed jar onto the counter.

"Damn it, Katie." I chuckle and turn back to the seeds, which are now everywhere.

"It's okay, no one uses that one anyway. You want some breakfast?"

I put the jar back onto the rack and scoop the seeds into my hand before throwing them away. "Am I a shitty person if I make you cook? How are you feeling?"

"No, I enjoy cooking." She pulls the fridge open and takes out a few different things. "Better, I think. Thank you for staying with me. I don't think I would have been able to sleep if it weren't for you. I have no idea what happened. I was okay, and then I just…wasn't? I still feel foggy, but I'm willing to live now that I've had some sleep. I don't know."

"I'm glad I could help. Your bed is a lot more comfortable than mine is, so I'm always down to sleep here whenever you need me."

I round the island and take a seat in one of the chairs when I hear the stairs creaking. Immediately, my chest tightens and I feel my heart in my stomach. Katie's back is facing me, and she can't see the look on my face as I stare at the kitchen entrance.

"Morning!" Ian doesn't even glance at me as he enters and walks to the fridge.

"Yeah, yeah." Katie brushes him off. "Hey, Jace stayed the night last night…" She isn't done talking when she glances up at him. Then she stops.

I'm pretending to be busy on my phone, looking anywhere but them.

"Unless you already knew that," she finishes.

This brings my attention back up to them. Katie's eyes are wide, and she's pointing at Ian's neck with a spatula. Three fresh purple spots take up a good portion of his neck.

SHIT. Did I do that?! I didn't do that… I think I'd remember making marks like that. Either way, the surprise is no doubt evident in my face. I have to remind myself to close my mouth so I don't have guilt written all over me.

"Why would I have known that?" Ian doesn't miss a beat dismissing Katie. There's no suspicion in his voice. He covers his neck with his hand, one of those sparkling waters in his other. "I was out last night. Why would you have thought Jace had something to do with this?" He says it so casually that even I'm confused. So it wasn't me who left those marks on him. But why would he have asked me to be his distraction if he was already out with someone else?

Once he's behind Katie, he winks at me and walks out of the room. My heart melts and drops into my stomach. So I *was* the one who gave them to him. I didn't think I was that aggressive…but seeing my marks on him gets me going all over again, reminding me that last night actually happened. Everything in me is screaming to follow him, but I stay in my seat.

Katie looks questioningly at me. I shrug. She seems skeptical but slowly turns around to finish her cooking while I let out a deep breath. That would have been a really fucking weird conversation. "I know you were depressed and sad and stuff, but I totally sucked face with your brother."

*   *   *

After breakfast, I spend most of Saturday at Katie's house learning a lot about her, Ian, and Aunt Grace. It turns out that she pays *them* rent. She stays downstairs, which they've turned into a mother-in-law type thing. She has a kitchen, living room, bathroom, and bedroom down there, but I guess they usually have meals together up here. Everyone cooks; they all know how.

Katie's been working at the library in town, which doesn't surprise me since she's getting her degree in English—which I also just learned.

We don't see Ian all day, which I'm honestly happy about. Between Josh and now him… How am I ever going to survive? I'm a bit shocked to find out that Ian is gay, though. I wonder if I can use his little speech from last night as a way to ask Josh if he's interested in men. Something tells me I'd end up crying instead, though. Something about Josh is too damn intimidating.

"Do you want to stay another night?" Katie asks me. "I feel like I never get to see you anymore. It's been nice having you around. I'd love for you to stay longer."

Thinking about it, I glance at the clock, then back at her. "I'll stay another night. I agree, it's been nice getting to talk to you again. But I'm going to need a shower. Like you said last night, I smell bad."

"I think I can make that happen for you. As long as you're okay smelling like a girl, let's finish this movie up then we can go upstairs. I'm getting tired anyway." It's a little past 9 p.m. and we still have about forty-five minutes left of this dumb movie she's forcing me to watch.

She's the worst at watching movies. She talks through everything, asking questions or telling me something she did last week that she's suddenly just remembered. She doesn't even pause the movie to talk, just lets it continue going, not even paying attention.

"Hey, do you ever watch movies, or just talk through them?" I tease.

She shrugs. "I've seen it before."

"What? Then why are we watching it?"

"Because *you* haven't seen it!" Her laugh flows through the room.

"I haven't seen it now either," I counter, "because you keep talking to me. I don't even know what's going on. What's the plot of this thing?"

We laugh and she swats my arm. "Thank you again for being here for me. It means a lot."

"I'm always going to be here for you. Thanks for reaching out and not suffering alone." I pull her into me and lay my head on top of hers.

"I wish straight guys were like you," she sighs.

"No, you don't." Chuckling, I squeeze her tighter. "Drug-addicted, depressed, angry, and shitty straight men are the worst. You deserve someone better, someone so much better than I am, Katie." I push her slightly away from me to look into her eyes. "Please, never settle for anyone like me. Promise me?"

She makes a face. "There is no one else like you, Jace. I still don't understand you or know your motives. You're so mysterious. What have you been up to lately?"

I want to tell her. I want to let her know my plans and what I've been doing, but I don't want to be vulnerable. There's no risk of failing if I'm the only one who knows. Once everything starts going smoothly and I see a change in me or have something to vouch for myself, then I'll tell everyone. The look in her eye makes me want to be honest, though.

"Well, I…"

"Aww, this is precious." Ian walks into the room with his hand on his chest like he just witnessed the cutest thing imaginable. "I'm feeling bad. I was hoping I could get some advice from either of you. I can't stop thinking about leaving and getting some Oxy, but also, I feel sick as hell." He slouches into the oversized armchair and laughs before adding, "More so my sister. Sorry, Zombie, your methods are a little too masochistic for me."

I'm glad my attempt to unalive myself is something we can all openly joke about now. It doesn't feel bad or make me sad. I'm over that part of my life, and I don't want people to just ignore that it happened, either.

"Yeah, I wouldn't suggest it," I tell him. "I did spend a lot of my detox depression planning my own demise, so I was a little distracted."

Ian and Katie both laugh. "Plus," Katie adds, "your siblings wrangled you in pretty good there." Then she turns to Ian. "It was impossible to get time alone with him!"

"Yeah? I bet it was with a house full of guard dogs!" He lets out a soft chuckle and looks at me. "And how impossible is it now?"

I swallow and inhale deeply thinking about my answer. I can't help but assume this is a proposition of some sorts… My answer could decide a lot between me and Ian. Hell, it could decide a lot for me personally.

"Possible," I say without blinking. I'm not sure what else I could say! I also don't dare look in Katie's direction to see if she catches onto anything. My heart is racing as I realize what I may have just agreed to.

"You could try reading. Or drawing, or cooking," Katie says, switching the conversation back to the original reason Ian came to us.

"I started running," I offer.

He takes a deep breath before blowing out his nose. "I'll try those. My problem starts when I get bored, but I get bored so easily that I don't know how to counter it."

I almost laugh, mostly at myself. It's funny to see how upbeat Ian is, whereas I prefer being bored. Being not bored made me anxious and sent me spiraling. I know Ian would much rather be at a party or a group outing.

"Good luck with that," I smile at him then stand up. "I'm going to go shower. This movie sucks and I'm not interested in finishing it. So sorry!" I give Katie a fake apologetic smile before going to the upstairs bathroom.

It's a lot less weird than I thought it would be to be around Ian after last night. He has the type of personality that wouldn't make you feel awkward about anything, I guess, although I couldn't help noticing the shirt he chose clearly showed off the marks on his neck… my marks. I should have told him that the best way to get over drug cravings was to pen up your sexual frustrations. Takes your mind right off everything else.

I have no idea how to work Katie's shower, so the water is never right as it falls on me. It's either too hot or way too cold. I end up taking a shower that lasts maybe ten minutes just to get the smell of car off me. It's going to be a long night. I probably should have just gone home instead of putting myself through all this madness.

Chapter 32

The week goes by uneventful and calm, which is weird. Usually that means there's a shitload coming. The calm before the storm, or whatever. Tuesday was my second therapy session; it was good. We talked about me and who I was and what I wanted and stuff. I wasn't prepared for today's session, specifically how my therapist could change the direction so fast in just two days.

I walk out of my therapy session after discussing the last year of my life, my addiction, relapse, suicide attempt, and my current situation with my secret job, therapy sessions, and self-help mission. It seems Dr. Jewell doesn't agree with my choice to keep everything to myself and not confide in my support system. She says that by holding onto everything like this, I'm going to inevitably build a wall to keep people out of every aspect of my life. Besides that, she makes me think about things I don't want to think about, making me embrace the situations and feelings rather than hiding from them. I leave her office feeling angry and on edge.

The run to work helps cool off my brain a bit, but not enough. I get there and pull the door open to find Josh waiting for me at his usual spot behind the desk.

"Do you have a lighter?" I ask him. I gave the one I had back to Tyson, even though he didn't ask for it. I'm not sure why I did it, but I did.

"Good afternoon, I'm doing great, thanks for asking!" Josh jokes. He catches my expression, and concern spreads across his face. "You aren't going to light yourself on fire, are you?" He pulls a drawer open and digs around.

I huff out my nose and shake my head. "No, not this time." My fingers graze his as I take the lighter. The contact makes me sigh. I wish I had the energy to fanboy right now or even maybe flirt a little. Especially because he's wearing a black, unbuttoned short-sleeved shirt with a white tank top underneath that's hugging his muscles *very* nicely. Every aspect of it compliments him.

I groan out loud while briefly turning my head to the window. He had to look that fucking good today, of all days?

"You alright?" he asks.

I don't try to hide the fact I was just checking him out when I look back to him. "I'll survive." I hold up the lighter in a "thank you" gesture and turn toward the door. "I always do," I whisper to myself before walking back out the door and lighting a cigarette.

By the time I get the cigarette lit, I hear the door behind me open again. I don't turn around. Instead, I take another deep drag. I know therapy is supposed to do this, supposed to make you feel and question and realize, but who the fuck is paying for this type of stuff? "Here's seven million dollars, please make me hate myself more than I already do."

I shake my head at the thought. Dr. Jewell wants me to open up to everyone about everything. She wants me on antidepressants, wants me to remove half the stuff on my plate, and she told me that maybe I should ask for part-time work because working to avoid my emotions and thoughts is unhealthy and in the long run will make everything worse for me. Not to mention I should prob-ably tell Katie about my interaction and intention with Ian. Yeah, yeah, sure, fine. But the worst part is she wants me to forgive my dad. *Forgive* him. Like walk up to him and tell him that everything he's done in the past, everything he's doing *now*, is no big deal.

"Confront, do not deflect," her voice rings in my head.

Whatever good the nicotine's doing for me is immediately erased and I feel my body heat up again. It just makes me so mad. I hate being vulnerable and then having the person I'm trusting with my thoughts and feelings tell me some dumb shit like that.

Leaning my elbows onto the railing in front of me, I take two more drags back-to-back and blow out slowly, closing my eyes and imagining that the smoke leaving my body has encased all my rage as they fly away together.

"Do you want to talk about whatever's going on?" Josh comes up beside me and leans his back against the railing.

"If I had a dollar for every time I've heard or said that this year…I would have, like…" I look into the air and think about it. "Eighty dollars."

He smirks and crosses his arms. "This year as in…January until now? Or are you thinking more like last June to this June?"

An unwanted heat warms my face. That's the last thing I was expecting to come out of his mouth. I take a few more drags before flicking the butt into the parking lot along with the millions of others people have left there. I decide to make it part of my responsibilities to clean that up every week.

"My therapist says I have self-destructive tendencies." I pull out another cigarette and light it.

Josh makes a face at the second cigarette. "How dare she?" he says. "Clearly, she has no idea who she's talking to."

This pulls a laugh out of me. "I was thinking the same thing." I roll the lit end of the cig on the railing and drop it. "I'm sorry, I didn't mean to come in here and take up time throwing a fit out here. I just had a bad session today, and it's got me in a mood."

"Don't worry about it. I mean…you haven't clocked in yet, so no time wasted on my end."

I click my tongue and then lick my teeth behind a smile. "I miss our previous times together when you weren't so funny and just bossed me around."

"Yeah? Well, now that you know the basics, I figure I'd just point to things and you would do them. I need some way to fill in the gaps. Being funny just happens to be my specialty." He stands up straight and opens the door. "Now, get in here and change bay 2's oil."

I let out one more deep breath as I walk past him. "Yes, sir."

The hour flies by. The oil change should have taken fifteen minutes, but Josh played his music through the speaker of the shop and occasionally would stop his work to dance to something. It was a little distracting.

He isn't as upbeat as Ian but not quite as laid back as me. I imagine I'd have the same type of personality if I was a little happier with life. Josh seems grown up, but in the best way. He's the nicest person, too. When I mentioned therapy, he didn't even flinch or make fun of me. I admitted to someone I was in therapy, and as much as I hate to admit it, it felt good to get it off my chest.

He finishes his work on a truck and brushes his hands off. "Alright, we just need to test drive the Civic and the Focus, then we can head out of here for the night. Which one do you want?" He wipes his hands on the shop rag he keeps in his back pocket. I'm sure it used to be white, but now it's a mess of black and gray.

"Oh… Umm…" I look at the cars.

"Don't tell me." He tosses the rag onto the counter. "You don't drive, do you?"

"Not legally." I laugh, remembering a similar conversation between me and Katie when we first met. That seems so long ago.

"Do you know how to drive?" he asks.

I think Katie missed that question back then. I get how to drive, of course, but I haven't ever really needed to do it. I mean, I know the basics like red light, green light, gas, and brake. But I don't know any of the rules of the road, or what any of the buttons or levers in the car do.

"I'm sure I do," is all I can say.

Josh tilts his head and looks into my eyes, chewing on his cheek. "I feel like there's a lot to you I don't know about."

You have no idea.

"Alright." He claps his hands. "New job duty. Come in on Saturdays, we're adding driving lessons to your schedule."

My eyebrows pull in as my head pulls back. "You're going to teach me to drive?" It's more of a "Did I just hear that right?" rather than a question. "Will I be paid for this?"

"You need to know how to drive to be a mechanic, and you get paid to be a mechanic…however, it'll be less. Let's say $8 an hour. But really, kid—Jace. You can't work at an autobody shop when you can't even drive."

My heart fills when I hear how he changed "kid" to "Jace" without my having to make a big deal about it. I was going to let it slide this time. Being almost twenty-two and not knowing how to drive is embarrassing enough.

"So you want me here all week. And then also on Saturday? Are you sure you want to be around me that often every week? That's a lot of time."

"I mean, you aren't the worst company. You usually stay quiet and stick to yourself, so it can't be too bad."

At least it gives me another thing to do on a day I normally spend at home waiting for Monday anyway. "Okay, deal. I'll be here. What time?"

"Come in around 11. I go to the gym in the mornings, so that gives me some time to shower and clean up, then I can be here." His long stride pushes past me and into the office.

The gym? I've been thinking about adding that to my daily to-do list, but there isn't a gym close enough to walk to. I wonder where he goes. Before I know it, I'm following him out of the shop, and into the office.

"Could I go with you?" I ask before thinking.

Damn it, Jace, you can't just invite yourself into every part of some guy's life. I was just worried about being around him too much, and now I want to invite myself to yet another place with him? What is it about this guy that makes me so stupid?

"I'm sorry. I didn't mean to just ask you that. I've been thinking about going to the gym sometime, but without a car…"

He shrugs like it was a question he'd expect from anyone. "Sure. Text me your address. I can pick you up around 7:30." He finds a pen and paper and writes down his number. "You do own and know how to operate a cell phone, right?" His eyes look up at me from his lashes.

A nervous laugh escapes me. "Y-yeah, yeah I do." I'm nervous because I'm going to the gym. Not because the best-looking man I've ever seen in my life is about to give me his number. Not just for work either, but casually!

"Cool. See you tomorrow, then." Josh hands me his number, smacks my shoulder, and walks back to the shop, presumably to test drive the two cars on his own since I can't help.

My stomach flutters when I look down and see the winky face drawn above his number. I know it's an innocent gesture, and that's just his personality. But still, I'd like to imagine it means more. I quickly change my shirt, put the number in my pocket, and leave the shop to start my run home.

Chapter 33

"**H**ow have you been?" Will asks me the second we're alone in his car and on our way to school.

A tad suspicious, I lean away from him, closer to the door. "Fine…how have you been?"

"Good, good." His fingers tap the steering wheel. "Been hanging out with friends?" he asks with a sharpness in his voice.

"Making sure I'm not doing drugs?" I ask, mocking his tone.

He sighs. "It's just that you wake up so early, I drop you off at school, then I don't see you until nine, sometimes ten. When you come home, you go right to your room. I wanted to give you space and ignore it, but it's been almost a month of you just…never being home."

"I go to bed, Will. I go to bed when I get home, which is something people do when they wake up early."

"But what about all the in-between time? I'm not accusing you of anything, I'm just curious. You always say yourself that you don't have friends."

I shake my head and look out the front window. "Just curious… I used to be in trouble because I was in my room all day. Now I'm in trouble for being out of it? If Suzie or Tyson were gone all day, no one would think twice or even second guess it. No one would put them in a car and question them."

A breathy laugh breaks through my chest. I can feel the tension get thicker. I know Will is an angry guy and maybe some part of me wants him to be mad at me so he'll lay off. Or maybe he'll say something hurtful to me and I'll have an excuse not to talk to him for the next few days. Whatever it is I'm hoping for, I know it isn't healthy.

"Suzie and Tyson didn't just try and kill themselves, Jace. Suzie and Tyson aren't recovering from six years of drug use. I asked you a simple question and now you're getting all defensive, what am I supposed to think?"

"You don't need to think anything!" My arms are spread defensively. I hate feeling attacked every time one of them brings up anything about me. "Why are you required to have an opinion on what I've been doing? Why don't you just trust me?"

"Because I *have*, Jace! Because I have trusted you, I trusted you and then I had to call you an ambulance. I *trusted* you, and Suzie found you half dead on your bedroom floor. This isn't about trust, this is about the fact that I should be able to check in on my depressed addict of a little brother without him flipping his shit." He breathes heavily. "The only reason I know you're still there and still you is because of the old-man music that plays in your room at night. You know I can't sleep until I hear it?"

I hate that I can't be mad at him for this. That for once in his life he decided not to react like a dick and actually showed some vulnerability. He never opens up even just enough to mention he can't sleep until he knows I'm home safe.

"Fuck, Will. I'm sorry. I just wish the past could be erased. It sucks that I'm going to be questioned about everything I do or don't do for the rest of my life." I look out the car window at the people walking in and out of the school. We've been parked for a few minutes now.

"Only because we want to be sure you're good, not because we don't trust you."

"Alright." A few seconds go by, enough for me to calm down a bit. "I'm not doing anything you need to be worried about. Just going out and experiencing the world as an adult."

I look up and meet his eyes. He's nodding, but I'm sure he isn't entirely convinced. "Okay. Okay, I'll trust you on this, but could you try to be present more? It's not just me who's worried."

I force myself to stay awake two to four hours a night after work sometimes just to be more "present." He isn't the only one who's worried. Here it is again, their secret Jace circle that for some reason Jace isn't a part of.

"I'm not surprised," I say. "You probably all talk about me in the family group chat I'm not part of." I open the door and take out my pack of cigs along with the lighter I may have accidentally stolen from Josh. "I'm going to smoke. I'll see you tonight. Don't worry about driving me home."

The car door slams as I walk to the benches and sit down. I find myself rolling the lighter between my fingers. I notice a bright-green color on it and turn it to see what it is. It's a green car, the headlights as eyes and the grille a face with a tongue sticking out. The letters on it read "Peterson's Auto Shop." This looks nothing like anything else in the shop, but it makes me smile. It's cartoonish and a little goofy. It kind of reminds me of the Josh I got to know this week.

*   *   *

"Have you been studying?" Katie asks halfway through the lecture.

"For what?" I whisper back.

"Finals?" Disbelief spreads across her face. "You forgot about finals?! How? It's all anyone is talking about. Jace, finals are next Friday. You have exactly seven days to cram."

"Already?!" How did I miss that? I remember it coming up a few days ago…that *was* days ago, right? Fuck. I guess I'm not fully aware of anything these days. I kind of just show up and do my bare minimum.

"I hate that you haven't studied at all and you'll probably pass everything," she says. "Are you still sure you don't want to do mine for me?"

My phone buzzes. I pull it out and look at the screen on my lap. Ian: *Bathroom.*

My brows pull together. Did he mean to send that to me? I stare at it for a few more seconds, debating on responding. Unless…

I lock my phone and look up at the professor. Ian can't mean… not here, right? I glance in Katie's direction to see her slightly turn her head my way. I don't think she saw anything, but the look on my face could probably cause some worry.

"I'm not doing your finals." I shift in my seat and then add, "Hey, I'll be back." I stand up and walk faster than I'd like to admit. I'm sure this isn't a booty call in the middle of class, but something about the thought has me burning like a 17-year-old.

I crack the bathroom door open and slip inside.

"You came?" Ian asks from the sink.

"Yeah, I wasn't sure you meant to send that to me."

Briskly, he makes his way toward me and pushes my hair back. "I'm in desperate need of a distraction." He brings his face right to mine and presses his tongue into my mouth. The force of him pushes me back against the door, the taste of mint and nicotine mixing.

I hold his hips and shove my hands up under his shirt to his ribs. The feeling of his warm skin causes me to release a breath.

I've never known how in a cage I've felt. Everything about this moment feels right. It feels natural.

Ian's tongue continues to circle in my mouth while his hands explore my body. He feels me tense when he starts run them up my shirt. "You don't like that?" he asks between kisses.

It takes some mental force to break from his soft lips. "Umm…not really."

I kiss his neck down to his collarbone. He groans in response. Instead of bringing his hands back under my shirt, I feel him at the waistband of my jeans. It would ruin the mood if I was worried about my body the whole time we were doing whatever it is we're doing. I'd rather him not be touching or looking at any of the skin under my shirt.

His fingers slide into the waistband of my pants. My heart leaps…out of fear or excitement. Maybe both. I don't know what I'm expecting here, but I swear to God it better not stop. He unbuttons my pants and pulls them down. Then he slides his hand down on the outside of my boxers. I gasp when his hand glides down my hardening cock. He palms me while teasing my mouth with his tongue.

"Oh, shit," I pant. This feels so much better than when I'm doing it myself. I'm bound to last a whole three minutes before I come in my boxers. Before I even have time to think about that, he pushes my pants down my legs and drops to his knees.

My eyes dart around the bathroom. "Ian, what are you doing?"

"Is it not obvious?" He laughs and grabs the waist band of my boxers.

"Umm, I-I've never…"

His last tug pulls the cloth over my cock, releasing it right in front of his face. *Fuck.*

"Really?" He wraps his hand around my base and pumps twice.

My head falls backward against the door as I let out a deep moan. When I look down, he's smiling at the approving sounds coming from my chest. I can't answer his question, but I'm sure by now he doesn't think I'm lying.

Without warning, I feel his warm tongue slide from my base to my tip. His mouth wraps around the tip of me before he slowly pulls the rest of my length into him. The feeling is overwhelming. I see stars immediately as his saliva pools around me and he starts to bob his head. Without stopping, he grabs my hand and puts it in his soft blond hair. His movement becomes slow and torturous, encouraging me to take control. I wrap my hands in his hair and thrust twice, gauging how deep he's willing to let me go. The sight of him with me in his mouth is enough to pull me over the edge, but I hold it together and keep going.

It's so weird how natural this feels, like instinct took over and I'm now someone who's done this thirty times before. My hand tightens in his hair and my thrusts begin to quicken. I'm not sure who's in control here, but there's a lot less movement from him and a lot more from me.

"I can't even tell you how fucking good that feels." My thrusts push deep into his throat, harder and more confident. If someone would have told me how amazing this felt, I would have never picked up drugs. I'd be a sex addict instead. Drugs make you feel dead so you can pretend you aren't apart of the world. But this…this makes you feel alive, and it's a feeling I'm worried I won't get enough of, a feeling of power. A power better than the one when I'm fighting with my brothers or suppressing my anger.

I feel my stomach tighten and I know I'm about to come. Am I supposed to announce that? Should he have a warning? Does he even want it in his mouth? The overthinker in me takes over and almost ruins my orgasm, so instead I just grab both sides of his face and pull away from him without fully pulling out of his swollen lips.

"I'm about to come, so if you don't want it in your mouth, you better stop." Talking this way makes me feel so different, these words I've never said before, never even thought of before, flowing from me like it's a sentence I say every day.

He doesn't take his mouth off me or even answer. Instead, his tongue swirls around my tip again before sliding down my shaft and back up. I drop my head back against the door with my bottom lip between my teeth. My eyes roll back in my head as I grab onto his head with both my hands and shove myself as deep as I can down his throat.

"Fuck, Ian, holy shit."

As I spill into his mouth, I moan loudly. I look down in time to watch him swallow every drop of me. I lick my lips as he pulls me out of his mouth and wipes himself clean with the back of his hand.

"Damn, you're hot as fuck," Ian says. It comes out almost like a whine. "That lip-biting thing you did was…fuck." He runs his hands through his hair and then looks back to me. "You've never done *anything* before?"

Embarrassed, I shake my head. "Nothing." I reach down and pull up my pants. "Well, nothing with a guy."

"Whoever ends up with you is in trouble. The way you demand control is sexy. I'm into it."

"So, I wasn't…bad?

"Not at all. I wouldn't have guessed that was your first time."

"Are we planning on doing this again?" I don't want to sound too eager, but I could use that again sometime soon.

He smirks and checks me out from head to toe. "Are we?" His eyebrow lifts. "We should head back to class. Thanks for the distraction, Zombie."

He holds the bathroom door open for me, and I slide out and head back to my class without another word. I'm breathing heavy, blushed, and smiling like an idiot when I get back to class and sit back down next to Katie.

"You okay?" she asks.

I attempt to control my breath and wipe the smile off my face. "Yeah, why?"

She relaxes into her chair before talking again. "As odd as it is to say, you're smiling a lot and it's weird, so I wanted to make sure you weren't having a stroke or something." Finally, her expression matches mine when a smile grows across her face.

Chapter 34

I climb into the passenger seat of Josh's car and rub my eyes.

"Well, good morning, sunshine," he chuckles.

I wave him off while pulling the seatbelt across my chest. Usually, I wouldn't be so tired, but I was up all night attempting to study for those finals I somehow just learned about. I take the drive to wake up more, which is easy once the smell of Josh invades my senses.

I've never seen Josh in regular clothes. Today, he's wearing a loose black tank top and shorts that are higher up than I usually see men wearing. He's more muscled than I thought he was. His thighs are nice and large, and they make his shorts look tight even though I know they're supposed to be baggy. The armpit of his tank top is cut down to the bottom of his ribs, showing off the side of his toned chest.

Another reason I couldn't sleep last night was because I couldn't get over what happened at school. I'm still not a hundred percent sure I didn't imagine it. Ian didn't even ask for anything in return, just finished me off and went back to class. So now I'm stuck wondering when it can happen again, but I don't want to sound too weird and clingy by texting him.

"You like music?" Josh's voice pulls me out of my memory, probably for the best.

Confused, I respond, "Yeah...I like music."

"What do you listen to?"

Oh, God, I hate this question. "You'll laugh if I tell you."

"Well now I have to know. What is it, like girly-pop music? You have some Hannah Montana up your sleeve?"

"Not quite," I say. "It's old-man music, Frank Sinatra, Dean Martin, Sammy Davis Jr., I guess. Ella Fitzgerald, the Ink Spots, Ray Charles, stuff like that."

Josh's head shoots my way in surprise briefly before looking back to the road in front of him. "Hmm." He struggles to contain his smile. "So, the 1940s, then? Do you listen to anything current?"

I shake my head. "No. I haven't really had a social life. I grew up with family members who listened to older music and I guess I just never changed. I get laughed at a lot for it, but the stuff made today has nothing on older swing music." My grandpa used to listen to that music with us when we were younger before we moved here. He was my favorite; he always made me feel accepted and wanted. I was his favorite person. He passed away about two years after we moved here, so his music has always stuck with me. It makes me feel closer to him, in a way.

"Yeah, I'd have to agree with you there. But we're going to change that for you. I think you'll be mildly surprised."

So many people have tried to get me onto new music, mostly my siblings. I think they get tired of my swing music filling the house. "Hey now, don't go trying to change me. I can't be swayed, it's a proven fact."

When we get to the gym, Josh wastes no time getting on the treadmill for his warm-up. I follow behind him and pretend I know what I'm doing. He takes us through a few of the machines and teaches me how to use them, then pushes me much further than I'd like to finish what he calls "three reps of twenty." I hated it at first and regretted coming because I'm not in good enough shape to be doing this shit. But after a while, it felt nice, like a burst of energy and motivation pushing through me. By the end of the workout, Josh is smiling approvingly at me. After two hours, Josh leads us back to the treadmill for a cooldown.

My body has never felt so horrible but so good at the same time. My breathing is so rapid that I feel my chest getting sore. But I will absolutely be finding a way to add going to the gym to my schedule. Even if it means going with Will or Tyson.

"Did you bring any clothes?" he asks me.

I look down at my gray T-shirt and shorts. "What's wrong with these?"

"Well, for one, you smell disgusting, and two, you're covered in sweat. You aren't sitting in my car stewing in that while I teach you to drive. We'll swing by your house before we head out. I, on the other hand, did bring clothes, so let me hit the shower real fast. Then we'll leave."

I just nod and walk over to the drinking fountain so I can drown myself while he showers. I don't want to follow him in there, for obvious reasons, and I'm still dying from everything he had me do. I thought you were supposed to have leg day, arm day, upper body, lower body type of days or whatever. Why did this man force me to work out my entire body? I'll be lucky if I can walk and be alive tomorrow. Actually, I doubt I will be at all.

After a few minutes, Josh comes back out, his black hair wet and still dripping. He's wearing black skinny jeans and a tan short-sleeved shirt with four buttons at the neck. Fuck me, I wonder if *he's* opposed to quickies in public restrooms.

We drive back to my house, Josh telling me all about the music he listens to and everything he's excited to show me. I hardly listen. This is the first time I'm seeing him as him. He dresses nicer than I'd imagined, and he smells so fucking good. I watch the excitement in his face as he talks about music, or how good I did for my first gym session. We talk about a lot, but never about work. Something about that small fact feels intimate. Like maybe I have a new friend. I can't help the funny feeling I get listening to Josh talk about how good I did today. It's nice to have someone be proud of you for something.

He pulls into my driveway, and it makes my heart drop. I really don't want to have to explain this to anyone, but I try to stay calm and rush him away. "Alright, I'll shower, get dressed and eat, and then I'll meet you at the shop?"

"I can wait here. Go shower and get dressed. We can grab food."

I shake my head, "No, you don't have to wait, I can walk. It's not a big deal."

His head cocks to the side with a knowing smile. "Jace, why would we go to the shop if I'm taking you the opposite way to drive? Just run in. Oh, and leave your phone here so I can make you a playlist, it's going to be collaborative so I can add music to it from my phone."

Leave my phone here. With him. In my driveway. I glance up to the door and the bathroom window to see if there are any lights on. The only windows that face the driveway are mine and the bathroom. The kitchen is on the other side of the house, but you can't see the driveway through it. My only challenge will be getting in and out. As for my phone…would it be weird to delete text messages now, in front of him? Fuck it, whatever.

I toss my phone onto the seat after I get out and shut the door. "I'll be quick!" I yell and practically run at the speed of light into the house.

I don't hear or see anyone yet, so I waste no time running to the bathroom. I get in the shower, clean off, and get out, wrapping a towel around my waist. I comb my hair back over my head, which keeps it out of my face. I've never done that before, but it doesn't look bad. This way when it dries it'll part the right way and stay out of my eyes.

When I get to my room, I look at all my clothes on the floor and the clothes hanging up. Suddenly, nothing feels good enough. Against every bone in my body, I walk to Will's room. Maybe he isn't here. I knock softly before cracking the door open and leaning my ear in.

"Will," I whisper. No answer.

I sneak into his room and to his closet while he lies sleeping in his bed. I'm sure I can find some good stuff here. I find a pair of loose-fitting denim skinny jeans and a long-sleeved gray shirt that's a thin cotton fabric and looks like it'll be a little tight—not something I usually go for. I make an unsure face at it but grab it anyway along with his white Converse, because why not just keep the "Will's closet" theme going? I would have used Tyson's clothes, but I'd be drowning in them for sure.

Within minutes, I'm dressed and checking myself out in the mirror. I look so different. Human, almost. I've never dressed so intentionally, and I love the way the jeans fit on me, along with the style of shirt I'd never choose for myself.

I push the sleeves up to right under my elbows and…dare I say it, I'm happy with who I'm seeing in the mirror.

After our workout, my muscles feel strained and swollen, but it makes my body look not so sickly. Plus, the food I've been forcing myself to eat has absolutely been putting some weight back on me. Not much, but enough to see a slight change. I look like a whole new person, confident and excited. The fact that I see a difference in my body after eating make a huge difference motivates me to keep going and really work on the physical aspect of myself.

Before I get to the front door, I find Tyson sitting at the kitchen table with a bowl of cereal. He stops with his spoon halfway to his mouth. His eyes look me up and down but his expression doesn't change. I pull my lips awkwardly between my teeth then point to the door with both of my hands and leave the room.

Please don't look outside, please don't look outside, please don't look outside.

I get back into the car and shut the door quickly, buckling up just as fast. "Alright, let's go."

"Wait, wait, wait, I'm getting into a groove here." Josh is still scrolling through my phone, finding music on Spotify and adding it to a playlist.

I start bouncing my leg and tapping my hand on my thigh. The longer we sit here, the more likely it is that Tyson comes outside. "Josh, the car. Let's go."

His eyes widen in surprise as he takes me in. "Wow, you look good," he says. He follows my eyes to the front door and looks back with questionable amusement on his face. "Ah, who are we waiting for?" He puts my phone in the cup holder between us then puts his hands on his thighs.

"Please, just drive the car." I'm practically begging now.

He crosses his arms and smirks. "Who is it? Now I'm curious, should I introduce myself?" Playfully, he unbuckles his seatbelt and grabs the handle of the door.

"JOSH!" I grab his bicep in protest and to hold him in the car. "It's my brother. I just don't want him in my business, now *please* drive the car."

A fake, overly dramatic gasp escapes his mouth, and he covers it with a hand. "Oh, no, am I one of your self-destructive tendencies?!"

I can't hold back my smile at that one. I playfully punch his arm.

"Shut up, you know that's a sensitive subject." I laugh. The laugh that comes out of me shocks me. It wasn't forced, and it didn't sound fake. It was a real laugh…Josh made me laugh. This can't be good news for me, but it feels so good to be having emotions that come out without me manufacturing them.

Josh rubs his arm with a fake look of hurt on his face. "Clearly."

With a smile, he puts the car in reverse and pulls out of the driveway. With his theatrical act taking up more time than I'd have liked, I know that if Tyson was curious about why I looked like a normal person, he'd already found a way to snoop.

"I don't think I've ever heard you laugh," he says. "Should I be worried?"

I smile at him before answering. "Maybe. Your soul-splitting workout probably made me delusional."

"Oh, come on, I went easy on you." He gestures to my phone, still in the cup holder. "Now, I expect you to listen to that music, there'll be a quiz every Friday."

"Every Friday? You know school ends in a week. I expected to not have any more tests."

His eyes never leave the road. He looks relaxed. It's not very often I see anyone relaxed near me, so this is nice. It's just so easy to be here with him, to be an actual person.

"Perfect timing, then. You have to keep your brain sharp for next year, right?"

I drop my eyes to my lap. "I don't think I'm going back next year."

I haven't admitted it to anyone, but it's true. I don't want to go back. It's not doing anything for me, and I can't see myself in a job that's centered around a degree. It's just not who I am.

"Oh, shit. Really?" I can't tell if I hear surprise or disappointment in his voice.

"I guess we'll see how this summer goes. Where are you taking me?"

Josh respects the subject change and answers the question instead of pressing me on school. "A good place to drive. It's a small city fifteen minutes or so away. There aren't many people on the roads there, so we can go through street rules and stoplights without being worried that you're going to hit a person or animal. After that, we'll get food, as promised."

"Okay, that's reaching. I do know how to stop a car and watch out for people. Hell, I *even* know that red means stop."

"Wow, self-destructive and educated, who would have thought?" A playful smile appears on Josh's face, which brings a laugh out of me.

"I'll never live that down, will I?"

His smile widens. "Nope."

Chapter 35

Learning how to drive wasn't bad at all. Josh said he was expecting much worse. After driving around the city awhile, which was more of a town, we switched spots and he taught me all about road rules and signs and what to do at a four-way stop—everything you'd need to know to drive competently. He says I need to get a license as soon as possible because I can't test drive shop cars until I can do it legally. Which I guess is fair. I wonder what kind of license I'd need to test drive him.

Being around Josh absolutely put a certain type of strain back on me. He kept grazing my arm or my leg when he'd point to a pedal or reach across me to the blinker. His beautiful blue eyes were on me all day, and I wish my hands could have been on him all day. We stopped off at a burger joint, and despite my wonderful argument about how great a teacher he was, he wouldn't let me drive there.

Afterward, he drops me off at home and waits for me to get to the door before leaving. I watch him drive away and sit down on the porch for a cig. I pull out my phone. I'm not proud of it, but Josh isn't going to take care of the sexual frustration himself, so I text Ian.

Me: *Busy?*

I sigh and put my phone down next to me. Who the hell have I become? I feel like I'm having a damsel-in-distress-becomes-the-villain moment. I don't recognize who I am or how I'm feeling…but I like it. I feel in control, like I don't give a fuck that I don't give a fuck. Not to mention the newfound confidence in myself after seeing myself in real clothes. I'll have to go shopping when I'm able. I wouldn't mind feeling like that all the time. I think between the first real sexual experience I've had and being with Josh, I just feel normal. Josh makes me happy, giddy, excited to be around him. I really need to get the confidence to ask him about his sexuality. I just don't want to ruin whatever playful banter we have by making him uncomfortable.

Ian: *I knew you'd be back. (; Yours or mine?*

I take another drag then throw the cig into the road.

Me: *On my way.*

I open the front door quietly and sneak in just in case Katie's home. My steps are light up to Ian's room. When I open the door, he's shirtless on his bed, his gaze pointed at the TV on his dresser.

"Hey," I whisper.

"That was fast. Were you standing at the front door waiting for my response?" He smiles and stands up.

"No, I just got home, so I was outside."

"I'm kidding. I'm glad you texted."

I walk past him and sit on the edge of his bed. "I figured you shouldn't be the only one calling in favors." I look up at him.

"I didn't imagine I'd be the only one." He smiles and opens the door. "I need a shower, care to join?"

Hesitantly, I follow him to the bathroom across from Katie's room. Her door is open, but the room is empty.

"She's not here." Ian stands behind me and wraps an arm around my waist before pulling himself up slightly to plant a kiss on my neck. He guides me to the bathroom and the door shuts behind us.

He turns the shower on and finds his spot next to me again. My eyes move from the water to Ian. As ridiculous as it is to say, I still don't feel comfortable having my shirt off or being touched underneath it, so instead of stripping down and getting into the shower with him, I grab his hip with one hand and pull him into me, crashing my lips against his, my hand coming up to the back of his neck.

After the initial shock, his lips begin moving with mine. He doesn't hesitate, He tugs at my jeans, trying to unbutton them with one hand. Before he gets very far, I hold his wrist and pin it to his side.

"It's my turn," I say, and the words come out as almost a moan. I have no idea, but I've never heard a sound like that come from me.

My weight pushes up against him, causing him to lean into the bathroom counter as my lips move from his mouth to his jaw, then his neck. I'm nervous as fuck, but I'm not going to let it have an effect on anything. Just like Ian did the first day we were together, I drop to my knees in front of him.

"Are you sure?" he asks, surprised.

"Very."

I allow him to unbutton and pull down his jeans on his own. Although I'm worried I'm going to fuck this up, I'm also excited to do it. Getting all your firsts out of the way is the start of opening yourself up to lots of other opportunities. Plus, I've seen it before on porn, so I assume it's the same in real life…right?

"You can start with your hand if you want," I tell him.

His hands push under his underwear and those are removed as well. This is such an odd experience; I feel like I'm doing it backwards and the first time doing these things with someone should be when you're with them. The only thing that calms me down is that I trust Ian, and if I'm horrible at this, he won't hold it over me forever.

His cock is already hard. I've never seen someone else's in real life…especially so close to me. It's weird how similar it is yet also how different. The weirdest part to me is that I know exactly what I want to do with it.

Without letting myself second guess my actions, I lick my lips then glide him in past them. I decide to take all of him in just to see what it feels like before pulling away and using my hand for a moment. The skin is softer than I imagined it would be and doesn't make me gag or feel overwhelmed even when my mouth is at the base of him.

Pulling him back into my mouth, I roll my tongue to press up against the base of his shaft and then push him all the way into my throat. I have a controlling hand on the back of his thigh that I use to start a steady pace of pulling him in and out of my mouth, being sure I keep my lips tight and my tongue moving.

He lets out a hiss and his hand comes up into my hair in a fist, taking gentle control of the movements, pushing into me farther and faster. Every time he pulls me closer, his grip on my hair tightens, which feels insanely good. The pain causes sharp tingles down my spine, and I find myself wishing he was being rougher.

"Oh, fuck." He leans forward, looking down at me, but it's not my eyes he's watching. His gaze is fixed on himself, and my mouth. The next time I get to the tip, I stop and swirl my tongue around, which causes his grip to tighten, earning a deep moan from me, vibrating my mouth and him inside me. "Jesus. This can't be your first time," he pants between thrusts. My free hand comes up to join my mouth and help me move around him. This feels right, this is what I've been looking for my whole life.

Losing my virginity was a shit show. I couldn't keep it up.

Vaginas just didn't do it for me, and I didn't like the way she overdid the moaning. I knew it was fake. There was no way she was having *that* good of a time. Especially because I was trying to figure out how long it was supposed to go on before I could fake my own orgasm and be done. This is different. This I want to savor, I want him to lose control because of something I'm doing. It's not even over and I'm already thinking about when we can meet up again. This might be dangerous. Or, as Josh would say, "self-destructive."

I pick up my speed and my tongue movement. The look on Ian's face as I slide him in and out of my mouth almost causes me to change my whole "I'm not taking a shower" stance so I can also be getting off in this moment. I've never seen anyone in such bliss because of something I'm doing, which honestly gets me more excited, so of course, my mouth becomes even more eager to please him.

I suck my cheeks in and force myself to go all the way down, then all the way back up to the very tip. I feel him tense against my tongue, and I know he's close. Both of his hands are tangled in my hair now, pushing himself into me more forcefully before slamming into the back of my throat and stopping.

The sexiest sound I have ever heard comes out of his lips, his mouth wide open, and his eyes shut tight. That alone almost makes me come with him. Warm liquid hits my throat but never touches my tongue as I swallow it quickly.

"Fuck, Jace," he groans as I pull him out of my mouth and stand up. He leans onto his elbows on the counter behind him, still breathing heavily. "I didn't know what to expect, but it wasn't that." He pulls his shirt over his head and steps out of his jeans.

"So…I wasn't the worst?" I ask, my eyes dropping to his chest and stomach. Ian is pretty skinny too, but he still has a little muscle and isn't bad to look at.

"Fuck no! I'm still a little on edge from it. That was…I'll be thinking about it for a while."

That makes me smile. I also didn't know what to expect, but just those words of praise have me feeling a lot less stressed than I was when I came over.

"Did you want anything from me…or a quick platonic shower?" He smiles, pointing at the still running water. The bathroom is extra hot, and steam covers everything.

"As nice as a platonic shower sounds, I'm okay. Thanks for letting me come over, I should probably head out." How is he comfortable just hanging out completely naked in front of me?

"No problem. Call you later!" He places a soft kiss against my lips before pulling the curtain to the shower back and getting in.

*   *   *

I'm still in shock when I walk through my front door. I can't believe I just did that. And he said I was good. I smile and bite my lip at the memory, but I stop in my tracks when I look up to see everyone hanging out in the living room. I guess I should contribute here too. I'm not against them in any way. I just want to feel like an adult and take charge of my own future.

I walk over to the only available seat and sit down. "Are we having another family *Supernatural* watch party?" I ask, reaching across to take one of the cookies on the coffee table.

"Can we?!" Suzie shouts.

"Hell yeah, I'm in. You two?" I look over to Will and Tyson.

"Bro, are those my clothes?" Will asks, leaning in like he isn't seeing right.

"Yeah, man, he walked out of the house in them when I was eating," Tyson says. "I almost choked on my cereal!" He sits up and points at me like he's been waiting for someone to mention how weird it is.

"I felt like switching it up," I shrug.

Will keeps looking at me "My shoes, too?! Aw, man, I thought I got away with not having to share clothes when Tyson turned beast mode and you were moody and only wore baggy shirts and basketball shorts." He pouts and leans back onto the couch. "You look nice."

I laugh and look at Suzie. "Well, whatever you want, I'm yours for the rest of the night."

All of the events from today have me feeling like a badass. This must be the real version of "high on life" because I know for a fact I've never felt like this before. I can't even remember the last time I thought about taking pills or drinking. Well, yeah, I can. I think back to Thursday's therapy appointment and feel the anger creeping up almost immediately.

"You're staying here?" Suzie asks.

I mimic her wide-eyed surprised look. "*You're* staying here?!"

"This is weird," Tyson whispers to Will. "Does he seem happy to you?"

After a good two hours of hanging out with everyone and watching the show, I go to my room to study before I end up falling asleep. I connect my phone to my speakers and go to my playlists. Usually, there's one playlist of liked songs, and the only song there is "That's Life." But now there's another, one titled "Big Dick Joshua." I shake my head as a huffed laugh escapes my nose. When I click on it, there are so many different genres and artists. From things like Billy Joel to someone called Labrinth, and Bob Seger. I recognize a few of the older artists' names, and then of course the popular ones like Miley Cyrus and Harry Styles, but most of these are foreign to me.

I decide to give it a try, and I push play. The first song that comes on is called "False Confidence" by Noah Kahan. It doesn't sound too crazy, a good studying song. But when I sit down at my desk and pull out my pens, the song speeds up, distracting me from doing any type of studying.

I sit in my chair silently, unmoving, listening to the music. It's not what I normally listen to, nowhere near it, and it doesn't have the same effect on me that Frank does. But it's good, and it does something to me that is pleasant, and I know I'll listen to it again. I sit longer than I expected listening and experiencing. If people had shown me music like this instead of whatever rap type stuff, I would have branched out sooner!

Another couple of songs play as I stare at my wall with my arms crossed, just being here in the moment: "Movement" by Hozier and "Goodbye Yellow Brick Road" by Elton John. Then everything is disturbed when I hear Eminem's "The Real Slim Shady."

I smile in disbelief. Josh had to have added some songs as a joke. Who doesn't know Eminem? I let it play anyway while I try to force some studying. The songs continue playing, but I manage to keep it behind me and pay attention to what I'm doing. Luckily, it looks like I understand enough so that my current classes aren't going to murder me with their finals.

Chapter 36

Yesterday must have been a manic episode. Or maybe even the natural highs of life have a wicked comedown. Honestly, you'd be asking too much to always be happy, so I don't know why I expected this pleasant new turn of circumstance to be permanent.

I roll onto my back and put my hands over my eyes. I had so much planned for today, but I can't even move. I can't convince myself to get up. Just the thought of picking up my room is paralyzing. Not allowing my mental health take total control, I decide I need to at least get up and eat breakfast. It looks like it's going to be one of those days where you put one simple task on your to-do list and hope you get it done, then add another simple thing like "brush your hair" or "put on pants" to the list.

I pull a hoodie over my T-shirt and walk into the kitchen. Everyone is already in there talking and laughing. I don't engage with anyone I'm worried that if I do, I'll get distracted, forget what I'm trying to accomplish, and end up going back to bed hungry. Luckily, Suzie made some type of sausage and veggie egg bake, so I fill my plate and turn back to my room. As much as I love my mornings with the fam, I just don't have the energy today. I wouldn't be very fun company anyway, and don't want to ruin their day by bringing my rain cloud to theirs.

"You're not eating in here?" Tyson calls after me.

I twist my head back and answer, "No, not feeling great."

My room is dark like it's always been, only now I don't even have my LED lights because Suzie had the idea to hang them on my hospital room wall. I think they're still on the floor of Will's car.

"Hey." Speak of the devil, Will pops his head into my room. "I'm having some problems with my car, so we'll have to walk or get Tyson to drive us tomorrow."

I know he's just coming up with an excuse to come check on me. He could have told me that at any time, but he chooses right now. I'm in a very irritable mood as I always am when I get like this, so I try to keep my attitude coiled up.

"Alright." I sit on my bed and put the plate next to me. I really don't want to eat this. The thought of eating anything is nauseating, and I'd much rather just go back to bed. I look down at the food and have to hold back a gag, but I know when Will leaves, I'll force myself to eat every bite.

"You sure you're alright? You've been acting weird lately, and I can't believe I'm going to say this, but this isn't like you. To lock yourself in your room and only answer with one-word replies."

"Yeah. I told you I just don't feel good."

"Mentally or physically?"

My brows furrow together, and I shake my head. "I don't know. Both?" Why does it matter?

"Should we be worried? Did something happen?" He steps farther into my room and crosses his arms.

I rub my fingers on the bridge of my nose, trying to contain my outburst. I can't do anything right around here. Can't be happy, or sad, or upset, or tired. Can't be home all the time, can't leave, can't be out of my room with them, can't be in my room. I don't know what they want. I wish they would just *tell* me what they want.

"I can't have an off day?!" My hands slam down onto my legs as I glare at him. "I'm not allowed a day where I can just be alone and sad, and manage my shit and get over it? I need to be happy every second of every day? You said it, Will, you were the one who told me I'm the one who just almost died, I'm the one who's getting over an addiction. That isn't easy on me. I have so much shit going on in my head, and I don't get a day to just…be?"

I hear Katie's voice in the other room and wonder how long she's been here. I always hate being this person when she's near; she rarely sees it. Not since that day with Dad, and I hate thinking I may end up changing her opinion of me.

"What shit, Jace? You don't tell us *anything*. I'm not the only one thinking you've been acting weird, and not a normal weird, not something we'd expect to see after everything. But a whole new weird!"

"So there *are* expectations?" I laugh. "I'm glad you've all had a chance to discuss my actions. Then tell me how I'm supposed to act. What would you like to see from me?" I stand up. Will is taller than me, but I'm not going to let him feel that way by arguing while sitting.

Tyson comes in and pulls Will behind him. "Woah, hey, what's going on?"

"Jace is being a fucking dick." I feel the spit in his words. I pushed his buttons, and as much as I wish it didn't, it causes a mischievous smile to appear on my face. I can see the mix of surprise and concern flash across both of my older brothers at the way I'm reacting.

"Biggest dick you've ever seen." I open my arms wide and shrug. Something about making them mad makes me feel good. I think Dr. Jewell mentioned that it was just the act of feeling in control of something in my life. She said I'm more likely to be drawn to strong emotions; they are a bigger distraction from the rest of my thoughts. I should probably figure out what to do about that, but right now…it's been a long time coming.

"Jace…" Tyson's voice is nothing but horrified surprise. Sober fighting has given me a leg up for some reason. Maybe it's the years of pent-up sarcasm rushing back to me, or like Katie said a while ago, maybe it's because without drugs I actually have feelings and care about how others are making me feel.

I look over and see Katie and Suzie at the door. I make eye contact with Suzie and find them filled with disappointment. I know I've been losing her. I've been trying to push them all away, and I seem to be succeeding with her. I know she's tired of my shit, and I'm not sure how much more she's willing to take.

"You disappear, you sleep when you're home, you're even gone on weekends," Will says. "You talked to us and spent time with us a lot when you got home from the hospital, now you do anything to avoid us. You go to school and get cryptic texts from your ex-drug dealers to meet in the bathroom."

Kate looks away as Will reveals that piece of information. That fucking does it. She's been reporting back to them about me—what the fuck? She didn't even think to ask me about it, either, just assumed I was going for drugs.

"We saw you leaving Katie's house yesterday afternoon while she was gone," Will says, "then you came here all happy and energetic just to disappear into your room again."

Tyson picks up from there. "Not to mention, you had suspicious cars picking you up early on yesterday, bringing you back, then leaving again. Also, the music you played last night…that wasn't you. I almost broke into your room expecting to see you doing something you weren't supposed to or finding you've been replaced with someone else."

"So, what, you think I'm doing drugs again? I don't know if you remember, seeing as you didn't even notice I was doing them for seven years, but drugs make me tired, not energetic."

"The drugs you used to do would make you tired. Other kinds do the opposite." The words come from Katie. I stare at her with as much hate in my eyes as I can summon.

Holy shit. Why is everyone attacking me right now? I know they don't know what's going on with me because I don't tell them. But do they not understand how accusing me of being on drugs again makes me feel? I've been working my *ass* off to stay away from them. I get no fucking credit, no support. It creates a hollow feeling in my stomach, and right now that hole is filling with anger—and not the kind I can contain.

I tune out for half the stuff they're are saying before Tyson's voice brings my head back into focus. "Then today, you're back to being sluggish and not talking to anyone. You didn't even notice Katie in the living room. We want the truth. If it isn't drugs, then it has to be something else."

"Oh, *yeah*, it *has* to be," I mock, my breaths coming out fast and heavy. I cross my arms to add to the sarcasm. If they weren't so quick to accuse me of shit, I'd consider coming clean and letting them know about everything I've been doing to better myself. But not like this, not when they're forcing me to do it.

I wanted to be proud of myself when I told them. Have some proof to back me up, not have it yanked out of me because I'm trying to prove I'm not on drugs. The worst part is that I'm telling them I'm not doing drugs and they don't believe me. They assume I'd lie to them about it when in the past I've done nothing but come clean every time I slipped up or thought about slipping up.

"Hmm, what else could it possibly be? Come on, guys, put your brains together. I'm sure you can come up with something really good!" I clap my hands together and look around the room. Tyson's mouth opens, ready to say something, but I cut him off. "Oh, shit, I'm sorry. You guys prefer to do that when I'm not in the room, right? Do you need me to step out for a while? I'm happy to do so, then later we can get back together and you can tell me what my problem is, and what I'm doing then." I muster up the fakest smile, which reaches my eyes, but there's no amusement behind it.

Will walks around Tyson and shoves me in the chest "You have a smartass mouth now? Quit that shit, we want to help. No one is attacking you."

I shove him back. "Everyone is attacking me. I'm not *doing* anything," I shout.

"We wouldn't be attacking you if you weren't so defensive," Suzie adds.

"So you admit this is an attack? Or do you not see anything wrong with having meetings about me behind my back? You're all accusing me of doing something I'm not doing. Of course I'm defensive! What the fuck am I supposed to do, lie and agree with you so I can avoid an argument? Fuck all of you, seriously." I laugh and turn to face the wall before I get brave and deck Tyson or Will in their smug fucking faces.

It feels like my heart is breaking. I know I'm about to start crying. Why don't they believe me? Is that really all they see me as? Is this all they're going to see me as? Questioning every motive I have? I'm sure the neighbors can hear every word between us. Katie has a permanent look of disbelief on her face. I'm sure she knew I was capable of things like this, but she's never seen it. Welcome to the family, Katie. The bullshit she's pulled on me proves she belongs here.

Trying to rile me up, Will takes another step toward me. "What, you getting mad?" he asks, grabbing my shoulder and turning me to face him. "It's a little weird for you to be this upset about something you 'aren't doing.' And don't you *ever* talk to her like that again."

"Suzie? She's a grown-ass adult, and if she wants to act like you two," I point between Will and Tyson, "then she can get treated that way, too." I move around the room for a moment, trying to calm down, but it's no use. I can't concentrate on anything other than how shaken up I am. "As for you, Katie, congratu-fucking-lations. I'm glad you found somewhere you fit in, because you're no different than my condescending bitch of a family." I take a deep breath and smack my hands on my sides. "I'm so glad we all trust each other around here."

"That's enough!" Tyson yells. "We want you to take a drug test." Finally, it comes out. I was waiting for that.

I laugh. "You want me to piss in a cup? You really trust me so little."

"No, the mouth swab kind," Will says. He wants to hit me, it's so clear on his face he's waiting for it. I really wish he would.

I look at Tyson, then Suzie and Katie. Both the girls have stepped farther into my room, making it an obvious four-against-one battle.

I lick my teeth and laugh, shaking my head while I take three steps right up to Tyson's face. He has the swab in his hand already, of course. "Swab my mouth, Tyson," I say through my teeth in a deep whisper. The next thing that comes out of my mouth haunts me forever. "But don't be surprised when the only thing you find is another man's cum."

Everyone's eyes widen. Will looks like he's going to explode. I can't tell if they all feel bad, are shocked that such words left my mouth, or if my sudden disappearances finally make sense and they all feel like shit about this not-needed "intervention."

So the damsel-in-distress-turned-villain kicks off in full. I'll never come back from this, but maybe now when I'm acting weird they won't immediately think drugs.

I pull the swab out of his hand, swirl it around my cheeks, tongue, teeth, and the roof of my mouth a few times before handing it back. I get my phone, cigs, and lighter from my dresser and shove past everyone. No one says anything. They're all sharing the same uncomfortable expression, the same stance, and they have the right mind to get the fuck out of my way.

I get outside and pull out my phone just to stare at the screen. I have no one. I don't have anyone to call, no one to cry to or calm me down. There's no way I'm going to Katie's right now for Ian, and believe it or not, I'm not in the mood for a physical kind of distraction.

My finger hovers over Dr. Jewell's name but I decide to push the power button instead. "FUCK!" I yell, throwing the box of cigarettes and lighter across the lawn. I pull my hoodie over my head and throw it on the steps. Then I start running.

Chapter 37: Will

We all stay silent, the front door slams, and then Jace yells. I see Suzie wince. I wonder if she feels as bad as I do. In a normal situation, I'd break the silence, but now it feels wrong. I think we broke him—Jace, the boy who a few weeks ago wasn't even comfortable telling me he'd lost his virginity, practically spat the word "cum" in Tyson's face. I'd laugh if it were under different circumstances.

The longer the silence goes on, the more awkward this gets. Please, someone, say something—anything, at this point. I look at Tyson, who's having an internal battle with himself. He wants to believe Jace, I know he does. He wants to be able to throw away the test and not even doubt his baby brother is telling the truth. But he can't, we can't, too much has happened, and we just need to be sure we're worried for nothing.

"Test it, Tyson," Suzie speaks first. Her eyes are full of tears that haven't yet broken.

"I know," he sighs and twists the swab back onto the tube.

I've never wanted to punch Jace in the face more in my life. It wouldn't feel like we were all against him if he wasn't lying to us and always acting so defensively. I came in here to be supportive, and he went off on me. I look at Katie, who's leaning against the doorframe chewing her nails.

"So…Ian?" I ask, hoping she understands that I'm asking if he, too, is gay. Her eyes meet mine and she gives me a small nod. I'm not sure why we all just decided together that Jace was getting drugs from Ian. Katie told us he was getting clean. I guess none of us thought that maybe they were just getting their rocks off together. Of course no one thought to mention that Ian's also gay, or bi, or whatever he is. But it does explain the weird bathroom text and the oddly perky mood Jace has been in. Good for him. I knew him getting laid would fix the attitude problem. Well, subjectively.

"Does Ian drive?" Tyson asks Katie.

She keeps her eyes on me but replies, "No."

"Hmm." Tyson turns back to the test and looks to see if there's a result yet.

"Why?" I ask.

"The car on Saturday, there was a dude driving it. I thought maybe it was him. The Ian thing only explains a fraction of what's been going on. I feel like we're still missing a lot."

"Was he blond?" Katie asks. "Ian is blond, like me."

"No, he had black hair." He stops to think for a bit. "When I saw him leave the house wearing Will's clothes, it actually put me in shock. I ran to his room to look out the window and see what he was doing." He looks up at me with sadness in his eyes. "He was smiling and laughing…a *real* smile that I haven't seen in a long time. It was almost like instead of forcing it, he was trying to hold it back but couldn't, and the laugh was genuine, one from the stomach. He just looked so happy and in the moment instead of in his head like I always see him."

My brows furrow and I purse my lips. "So he's right, then? We decided to drug test him because he's…happy?"

That doesn't sit right with me. I'm starting to see things from Jace's perspective. "Just going out and experiencing the world as an adult." He told me that. He wasn't lying. It's a small truth, but now I understand he wasn't trying to hide anything.

"Well," I say, "I feel like shit."

Katie drops her head into her hands. "He hates me. Did you see that look he gave me? He hates me. I didn't even ask him about the text on his phone from Ian. I should have fucking known. When he stayed at my house last weekend, the next morning Ian came downstairs with hickeys. I should have fucking known."

"Damn, for real?" I ask. "I'm not sure I'm enjoying the sexually active Jace…" I see tears in Katie's eyes so I reach for her arm and pull her into me. "You did the right thing. And trust me, he's hated all of us. He always comes back around. But honestly, I think this is the first time he has a right to hate us."

Everyone nods in approval. We've been so worried about what he's been hiding from us that we didn't realize we were hiding things from him too. He's mentioned a few times that he feels pushed out of the group, that he feels like it's us against him. It sounded silly, but now I see it.

"What's it say?" Susie points to the test. She wants it to be positive, just so she can feel like she didn't just screw her favorite person in the world over for nothing. She wants to have a cause. It's easier to come back that way.

Tyson picks it up and holds it to his face. "…It's negative."

It's amazing news, it really is. But none of us look relieved. We're shitty people. If he relapses today or gets hurt, it's going to be because of us.

I take a deep breath. "What do we do?"

"Where did he go?" Suzie asks, sounding panicked. "What is he doing? Tyson, he left! He hates us all. He thinks we hate him. He's going to hurt himself. I can't do that again. I can't go through that again. And what if this time…"

"He's going to be fine, Suz! This test proves he's fine. He's right, we just need to trust him." Tyson runs his hand down her arm.

"I need to talk to him," Suzie cries.

"He'll be back," Tyson says in an assured voice.

I've held off being me for as long as I can before some dumbass remark slips through. "But come on. Two dudes at a time? Good for him!" Everyone looks at me, but not in a humored way. "Too soon?"

Katie breaks into a small smile "He's playing my brother?"

I laugh. "Who would have guessed Jace was a player. But seriously, I can't believe he said that before he left. That was insanely out of character for him." I wish I would have been recording.

Tyson nods. "I think it was part of him trying to push us away. I can't say it didn't work, though. I never expected him to say anything like that."

"Maybe we should let him live his life and just be here for him," Suzie says. "It's exhausting reading into everything he does. Why don't we just…live our own lives for a bit. Maybe stop talking about him behind his back like he needs to be fixed. We need to stop being scared of him."

"Speaking of being scared of him, have you guys noticed he's gaining weight?" I ask. "Maybe muscle, too. I don't know, Suz, if we continue letting him live his life, he might be able to kick our asses in a few months. Hell, I'd pay to see him kick Dad's ass right now."

Katie's head shoots toward me. "I have noticed that! I was lying down with him the other day and it felt quite a bit more padded than usual. I was going to bring it up but didn't know if that was weird."

"He forced us to start cooking real food and following recipes, and we accused him of being on drugs," Tyson says. "He really is trying. He's bettering himself on his own. Maybe we bring up therapy again and then drop it completely?" He rubs his face in frustration. He's never been the bad brother. *Welcome to the club, friend.*

"Maybe we should focus on an apology before anything else," Katie suggests.

The longer we wait, the more I expect that Jace has wandered off to find a new home and a new family. Okay, that's dramatic, but it's been a few hours, and he still isn't back. The thing that worries me the most is that we found his cigarettes in the grass. There's no way he's going to survive much longer without those.

The front door opens and my eyes jump to the door where I see Jace standing. Well, I think its him… "You got a haircut?" What a weird way to work off your anger. His hair was getting past his shoulders, now it's cut to above his ears and looks like an early-season Joey Tribbiani from *Friends*. "Very 90s of you." I turn back to the TV.

"Your car wasn't broken," Jace says, and I look back at him, confused "That grinding noise you were hearing was because you haven't changed your brake pads since you got the car, and you drive like a freak. You wore out your pads so bad that the metal was grinding into the rotor. I replaced them for you. You owe me $200."

What the fuck? I notice his hands are dirty before he walks into the kitchen and turns on the sink. He replaced my what? What the hell is he talking about? I stay stunned on the couch, not sure if I should follow him or wait for him to come to me. Did he say he fixed my car? That couldn't be what he was talking about. Maybe he meant he took my car to get fixed. Tyson comes out of his room and sits on the chair with a huff.

I lean over to him. "Does Jace know how to fix cars?"

He makes a face like that's the dumbest question I've ever asked. "No."

I nod. "Yeah, that's what I thought, but he said he just fixed my Rolos or something," I whisper.

"He's here?" Tyson sits up before slouching back down and giving me that same dumb look. "Your Rolos? Isn't that a candy?"

I shrug. "I have no idea! He just told me he fixed my car and I owe him $200."

"Hmm. Where is he?"

"Kitchen."

"It's my night for dinner. I'm making chicken alfredo," Jace announces when we go into the kitchen.

"Where have you been?" Tyson asks. "Are you okay?"

"Yeah! And how did you know to replace my rolo?" I add.

Jace turns toward me with a confused face. "Isn't that a candy?"

"That's what I said!" Tyson exclaims.

Jace just shakes me off and continues talking to Tyson, his face still full of anger. "So, what's the verdict? Clean or dirty? And this time, do you want to put a lock on the outside of my door so I can't get out of my room without your permission, or on the inside so I can't get in?"

"I'm sorry. We were way out of line, and I see that now. I won't ever be able to apologize to you enough about this. I just wish you could see it from our side as much as you want us to see it from yours. I think both of us hiding things from each other is going to create that separation, though. I can't see how you're doing if I don't know what you're doing, and the same goes for us. I didn't mean to make you feel like you were being singled out. We had our last group talk about you, without you, and decided that we're done. Anytime we need to talk about you, you're there too. Any concern or worry we have goes to you and not each other. All of us are going to live our lives and let you live yours, but we're here for you whenever you need any of us."

"Thank you." Jace's tone is harsh. "Glad that you all decided I'm grown up enough to handle myself. But I'm sure it wasn't decided until after the test came back clean." He clicks his tongue. "Yeah…see, I don't care what you guys do anymore. Talk about me, don't talk about me, do whatever you're going to do. I promise I'll keep my emotions as neutral as possible and stay in communal areas with my hands where they're able to be seen at all times when I'm home." He looks at me. "As for you, I still see the way you look at Katie. Have her. I'm not interested in being friends with someone who's going to sell me out and embarrass me in front of my family when she could have just asked. Now, are we done here? I'd like to finish cooking so I can go to my room. After I receive your approval, of course."

Flabbergasted. It's not a word I've ever used, nor is it a word I'd ever us again, but right now there's no other word for how I feel. As much as this Jace is a total dick, I can't help but feel a little proud of him. He's always let people push him around and take advantage. It's refreshing to see him fighting back. Not against us, but for himself. I can't even be mad because he isn't being rude, just very matter of fact.

"Don't you start on this again!" Tys shoves his finger toward Jace, but I grab his wrist and pull him back.

"You're right," I shrug. "Again, we can't apologize enough for how we've acted and treated you. But your actions have spoken loudly, we just haven't been watching enough. Look at you, gaining weight, doing homework, laughing and smiling with friends, leaving the house, waking up early, and cooking. I'm sorry, Jace, and I understand anything you decide that you feel you have to do."

He's frozen and has nothing to say. I don't think anyone

expected words like that to come from me—words so accepting of his feelings and thoughts.

"I love you, and I'm proud of you, little brother." I give him a small smile before grabbing Tys and leading him out of the room with me. Before I leave, I turn around again and say, "And thanks again for the Rolos, however you did that."

Once I'm out of the room, I hear Jace say one word under his breath: "Rotors."

Chapter 38

School on Monday is awkward as hell. I sit in my usual seat, but Katie sits on the opposite side of the classroom. She isn't mad at me, but she knows I'm pissed off at her. I can't help but look over at her every once in a while. She's been faking a frown the entire class, probably trying to make me feel like I did something wrong—or like *I'm* the reason there's no more trust between us. I look over and see her looking at me with a stupid puppy-dog face. It pisses me off so bad. I should be the one who's broken up right now, not her. I should be upset that my only friend turned on me without a second thought, over something stupid, too. The anger builds up until I feel like I need to get up and run or scream. I stand up, pushing my chair back and heading for the door. She's watching me, fake concern painted on her face.

Just to be an ass, I turn to the professor and announce, "I have to take a piss. Didn't want anyone getting any weird ideas." The professor waves me off, ignoring me almost completely. I hope Katie got that the message was for her, and I hope it made her uncomfortable.

I get into the hallway and pull out my phone to call Ian. He isn't at school today, but I need someone to talk to and currently, he's all I have.

"Miss me already?" Ian says. I can hear his smile through the phone.

Honestly, I wouldn't mind a quick session right now. Maybe that's been my problem. I shouldn't have left his house on Saturday without also getting off. "Kind of," I admit. "Your sister's pissing me off. I can't sit in that fucking class any longer."

His laughter is loud on the other end of the phone. "Welcome to my world. There's a reason we aren't close. You doing okay?"

"Yeah," I lie. "…No. I don't know. I'm sorry I called. I know we never agreed to emotional support, just physical, but I don't really have anyone, and I just need someone who understands."

"Hey, don't apologize for that. Talking to you is better than sitting with myself contemplating everything I've ever known. Plus, again, I know how my sister is."

I groan. "Ugh, I don't think I can go back in there."

"If you make that sound again, you're going to have to come here."

I felt my face heat up. I've never had someone who talked this way to me. I have no idea how I'm supposed to react or what I'm supposed to say. But I do know my body reacts to the way he says those words.

I look around, then hide my mouth with my face just in case anyone is within earshot. "I may have to come there anyway."

"Oh, you would come, for sure."

That one hits me. Fuck, I'm going to have a bigger problem on my hands than I already do. "Damn it, Ian." I drop my head back and look up at the celling, trying to contain this boner I absolutely should not have at school.

I hear him chuckle on the other end, then shift in his bed. "Go to class, Zombie. I'll be here in my room alone thinking of your mouth wrapped around me…"

Frustrated. That's all I can say. Sexually, mentally, physically frustrated. "Fuck you." I laugh before hanging up on him and walking back to class. Fuck, and I have to see Josh after school. Ugh, this is going to end up being a very romantic night with my hand.

*   *   *

Therapy today was annoying. Dr. Jewell just continued her whole "you need to forgive him" rant. She better forgive me when I end up punching a hole in her wall. The jog to the shop from her building calms me down a bit, but it's not nearly as long as I need. I stop to smoke, trying to clear my head before going inside.

We have a few cars, most of which I'm able to work on by myself, so Josh and I both busy ourselves with separate projects. As I'm pulling on the black gloves, my phone vibrates in my pocket. I pull it out to see Tyson's name.

Tyson: *Dad's home. Just wanted to warn you.*

Great. I curse under my breath but decide not to let it get to me right now. The last thing I need is to get worked up over that when I'm already worked up in so many other ways. I put my phone back in my pocket and finish pulling on the gloves.

"You want to tell me why I have Tenacious D songs stuck in my head?" I ask Josh.

"Wow, an odd group to listen to casually, but to each their own."

He knows he added them to my playlist on purpose. I find myself listening to good music, then the song switches and it's something from a musical or some Irish fighting song. He's a comedian, I'll give him that.

"How was therapy today?" he asks.

I hate when he does that. I wish I'd never told him about therapy.

"Thought-provoking," I answer in a bored tone.

"You don't want to talk about it, got it." His tone isn't sarcastic or rude, but more understanding.

"No, it's not that. I'm sorry. It's just, last weekend was a shit show and I'm kind of over explaining myself to people who don't want to listen. Not that you don't want to listen…"

Josh nods in understanding "You've just pled your case so many times with no reciprocation. I get it."

He seems to be the only person who does get it. It's nice having him around, someone who doesn't know the past me. Someone who doesn't look at me like I'm broken. I'm glad he became a good friend of mine. I think some fresh faces in my life is exactly what I need.

"Exactly." I step out of the bay and light a cigarette. I've been craving hardcore for the first time in a while. The cigs do little to hold it back, but I've been chain smoking all day and I know Josh has noticed.

"You shouldn't smoke," he says from under the F-150 he's working on. "It's not good for you."

I glance down at the lit cigarette in my hand, imagining a time when it was a bottle of pills or booze, and smile. "Yeah. I know." This is a much healthier poison. I take another drag and lean up against the building. "I fixed a car on my own," I offer casually.

"Yeah? How'd it go?" He stands up and brushes his hands off on his pants.

"Good. Nothing crazy, just a Civic with worn-out brake pads. Blew my brother's mind when I told him I replaced them and the rotors." I laugh.

He walks out of the bay and leans on the wall next to me. "Nice. I'm going to have to graduate you and throw you into the salary position." He gestures to the cigarette, and I hand it to him hesitantly. His finger brushes mine when he grabs it. I hate that a small thing like that causes my face to burn red.

Quickly, I change the subject. "Why didn't you hire anyone else? I mean…it's just you and me? You could have hired someone with experience, or even hired me *and* someone with experience."

He takes a drag and blows out the smoke with a disgusted look on his face. "My dad was forcing me to get some help. Didn't want me to be overwhelmed with projects when he retired. We had a listing out for a while but anyone who applied didn't stay long. I saw you show up and hoped the same would happen, honestly. I thought if I hired an apprentice, my dad would get pissed and just forget about it. I didn't expect you to be so headstrong about working here." He laughs, takes another drag, and hands the cigarette back to me. "I knew I was fucked when you showed up here dry heaving all over the place."

"Yeah, not my strongest moment. I just wanted to be out of my house, to feel like an adult." I take a deep breath, wondering how much I want to tell him. "Life at home is shitty. I'm supposed to be forgiving my dad for something that I don't think is possible, my siblings are…something else. I've just been so alone and confused, I guess. Jogging here from school felt nice, and was a way to get my stamina up. Once I felt how good it felt—after the dry heaving, of course—I didn't want to stop."

"Do you want some advice, or just an ear?" Josh asks. It shocks me. No one has ever asked me that before. I shrug and shake my head in a way to tell him I'm open to either. "I had to forgive my dad for something once. It was impossible. I didn't think I'd ever do it. Instead, I decided to forgive myself for the way he made me feel. I forgave myself for his actions. Once you break the bond between you two, it feels almost as freeing as forgiving him."

I let that sink in. It makes so much sense, but how would you do something like that? "Hmm."

"*If* that applies to you. If not, then forget I said anything." He pushes off the wall and walks back around to the F-150.

"What did you have to forgive him about?" I ask before realizing how personal that is.

"What do you need to forgive yours about?" He asks with a slight smirk.

"Right. I didn't mean… Sorry." I take another long drag then pat it out on the ashtray Josh added outside.

"Come to the gym with me more," he demands.

"Me?" I ask, following him to the front of the truck.

"No, the other person in the shop. Yes you. You can let out a lot of that pent-up anger, it'll do you better than running all over the place. Plus, not in a weird way or anything, but you're putting on some weight. It's a really good look on you. I can pick you up three times a week or something before work now that school is out next week."

My eyes widen in surprise. "You want to deal with me for that long, that many times a week?" I ignore the way my heart leaps and my stomach flips at the comment about my weight. I've been feeling better about the way I look—a lot, actually. But not enough to be taking off my shirt and flaunting myself around yet.

"Hmm, you're right. Maybe I don't. You have been particularly whiney these days." He smiles. "Come on, we can alternate days with your therapy. Gym Monday, Wednesday, and Friday. Then you can have your weekends, after driving on Saturday, of course."

"Are you sure? Of course I would love that, but I don't want to impose." Holy shit, he basically wants to hang out with me all day every day. I don't know how to feel about this. What if he finds out I'm a shitty person?

"No imposition, I go almost every day anyway. I could use

someone to make me feel better about myself."

"Gee, thanks," I laugh. "That sounds fun. Let's plan on it."

After work, I walk home slowly, enjoying the warm air and thinking about Dr. Jewell, what Josh said, and the fact I'm going to go home to my dad. Just the thought of him is getting me heated. God, I fucking hate him.

Forgive him. I think of every single hateful thing he's ever said to me. Every time he hit me because I dropped something or laughed at a joke that wasn't for me. Every time I made a noise or looked at him wrong.

I put my headphones in. "All For Us" by Labrinth and Zendaya plays in my ears. I like this one, it pumps me up on my runs. But apparently it also helps feed into my anger. The anger feels good, really fucking good, so I keep the song on repeat as I run home and let my body fill up with memories of the past that heighten the anger more. At this point, I'm not sure I've ever felt the way I'm feeling right now.

The more the song plays and the faster I get, I just want to scream. I am not a problem. I am not a burden. I am not a mistake. And *I am not weak.*

I get to my front door and pull it open. I don't even bother changing my shirt or washing my hands. I walk past Will, then Tyson and Suzie. I can hear them talking to me, asking me what's wrong or what I'm doing, but I don't hear them. My face is hot and sweaty. I know for a fact I look as though I'm out for blood. I guess in a way, I am.

I walk straight into my piece of shit dads' room. It smells like piss, vomit, and booze. He walks out of the bathroom connected to his room and meets my eyes for one brief second before my fist connects with his face harder than I've ever punched anything in my life.

Fuck! Fuck, that hurt.

I mentally shake the pain off

He stumbles backward, trips over his nightstand, and falls on his ass in the corner. He looks up at me. Surprise, disgust, and fury fill his bloodshot, lifeless eyes.

"God didn't make me gay to punish me, like you say. He made me gay to punish *your* worthless ass." I spit at his face then kick him in the ribs. "You have no fucking power over me. I am so much more than you ever were, than you ever will be. You lay your hands on me or any one of us again, and you're going to fucking regret it. I will not hesitate to kill you. Prison sounds like a goddamn blast!"

I spit again and exit his room, leaving my siblings with their jaws on the floor as I go to my room and slam the door.

I'm done. I don't care what you call it. But I'm done taking shit and being scared of people. I pick up my phone and text Ian.

Come over.

I throw my phone onto my bed and look at myself in the mirror. I no longer see some frail, sad, scared boy. I don't even see me anymore. But the person I do see in the mirror…he's strong. He is confident. And he is powerful. He doesn't submit to drugs or sadness, just a solid brick wall of black. This Jace doesn't apologize for who he is. This Jace is not defined by his upbringing or his past. I am new and self-designed—and most of all, I answer to no one but myself.

Chapter 39

"For my benefit, and my benefit only, I'd like to tell you guys everything that's been going on."

I look at my siblings—Tyson, Will, Suzie—and Katie, who are all seated in the living room in front of me.

"Mostly because I'm done being petty, but also because Will saved everyone's ass when he told me he was proud of me. He showed me a vulnerability he hasn't ever shown before, and I appreciate you for that."

"Alright, so try and keep up, because I'm only saying it once, then we aren't talking about it again. A week after I got home from the hospital, I didn't want to be here under everyone's microscope, so I decided to take control of my life on my own. The first step was getting a job. Every day after school, I go to work. On Tuesdays and Thursdays, after school and before work, I go to therapy. Usually, I run from school to either therapy or work, then home. I work as a mechanic at a shop I found in town where I'm on my feet and lifting heavy shit all day. When I get home, between either running all over, standing all day, or being emotionally fucked at therapy, I'm tired. I eat, do some homework, and go to bed. Now that school is over, I'm not sure how my hours will change. But I'll still be working Monday through Friday. Are there any questions on my professional life?"

I pause and wait for an answer. No one says a word.

"Alright. As for my personal life, it isn't really anyone's business. But I feel like I need to tell everyone anyway. Yes, I'm sleeping with Ian. No drugs, no alcohol, purely physical. I do not want to hear anyone accusing either of us for using anything unless you see us popping pills yourselves. I have driving lessons every Saturday, because you need a specific number of driving hours before you can take the test. I'd like to spend my Saturday nights and Sundays here with you guys, but not if I'm going to continue to be treated like one small move might break me."

Everyone looks thoroughly surprised. This is the boost I need. I need to see people are shocked at how well I'm doing. They're family, and I can't give up on them when they've done so much for me growing up. But something inside me can't let go of what Katie did. She was the only person I *chose* to have in my life, the one person I trusted more than anything.

"Well, Fuck," Will says, "that's some character development if I've ever seen it. You didn't ask if we had any questions about your personal life."

Everyone looks at him like he's grown an extra head.

I sigh. "Are there any questions about my personal life?" I ask, regretting it immediately.

"Yes!" Will exclaims. "Who were you stealing my clothes for, you thief? Was it Ian? Because if I remember correctly, you weren't at Ian's until later that day. And who was it that picked you up that day? I heard he had black hair, not blond. Are you a player now that you're getting some action?" He stops, but not to wait for my answer. He's trying to think of more questions to ask. "So, when Ian messaged you about meeting him in the bathroom, you guys, like, totally did it in there, didn't you? At the school!"

"God, yuck, Will. That's my brother!" Katie groans.

"He said I could ask questions!" Will says.

I laugh at how ridiculous Will is, but I'm glad to see his personality hasn't changed just because mine has. "I was stealing your clothes for myself. I just wanted to try something different. It was my boss who picked me up that day. He took me to the gym, then back here so I could change, then out to some parking lot so I could practice driving. Don't worry about what Ian's message meant, you shit."

"That was your boss?" Tyson asks.

"Yeah, why?"

He shrugs. "I've just never seen you act that way around someone. It's weird that it would be your boss."

I think about it for a second. I knew he would have found some way to see us in the car that day. Thanks, Josh. "Tys, I just told you, Ian and I are diddling each other, and you think I'm lying about my boss?"

"I mean, Will has a point. Why would your boss pick you up from the house and take you to the gym? It's weird," Suzie asks.

"Okay, so he's my boss, and a friend."

"Oh!" Will nearly shouts. "So that's how you knew how to fix my car? You and your girly hands working on nasty, oily vehicles? I can't believe it."

Wow, Will's brain is a lot slower than I thought. "I know. But I actually like it a lot," I admit.

"Because of your hunky boss?" Suzie asks.

I smile at her. I knew she'd come around. I know how guilty she feels about everything, but I want her to grow as her own person as well, so I've been waiting for her to come back around on her own.

"Fine, alright! It might have something to do with my hunky boss." I avoid Katie's look. I know what she's thinking, but Ian and I both agreed it's just a physical relationship. I don't even take the time to mention that I doubt Josh is into men like that. "Cool, well, we're done with all that now. What are we doing for the rest of our Saturday?"

Talking about my personal life still makes me feel uncomfortable but I figured it would be best to just put it all out there and move on. My phone vibrates in my pocket, and I see it's a message from Ian. While everyone debates on what we should do tonight, I pull it out to respond.

Ian: *What are you doing tonight? There's a party for the end of the school year happening. No funny business, just need a chaperone.*

Finals were yesterday. I passed everything, but just barely. The school always does this end-of-year party. It's not for the school, though. I swear everyone in town gets invited. It's just another excuse for people to get super drunk.

Me: *Really?*

Ian: *It'll be fun, no pressure to drink or anything. Just don't want to be alone tonight, Katie is staying at your place.*

Me: *It's not very sex-buddy of you to invite me to a party.*

Ian: *I'll make it worth it for you. (;*

Katie is smiling at Will. I don't know if I should be suspicious or not about them. I also don't know if I should be upset about it. I guess I did tell Will he could have her. I just didn't think he'd jump on that so fast.

Me: *Fine. But I'm not walking.*

Ian: *I'll get us a ride!*

Oh, God, I already know I'm going to regret this. I figure I should probably go just to keep an eye on Ian and make sure he doesn't do anything stupid. I know how these parties can get, and I don't need him relapsing—heaven forbid I lose my only ticket to getting off.

"Will," I ask, "can I borrow some clothes?"

"Ugh, again?! I haven't even gotten the last ones back," he whines, but ultimately, he relents.

Will gives me a ride there since he was going anyway, but also so he can keep an eye on us, I'm sure. I wish I could explain to him how badly I don't want to be here. I hate people, especially a bunch of fucked-up people listening to music that's too loud in a house that smells like sweat. But I do like the idea of doing something new and being here for Ian.

Ian got a ride with a few of his friends. I wait out front for him, trying not to scowl at everyone who walks past me. I'm out of my comfort zone in so many ways. I'm wearing a dark-gray collared button-up shirt under a crème-colored sweatshirt, and my pants are some type of tight black slacks. I've never felt so…confined. Everyone said it looked great, and I'm starting to wonder if my style is a business casual type thing. I'm not sure, though. I hate how the clothes are touching me everywhere. I like my basketball shorts because they feel nonexistent. However, with my new short hair styled, the outfit, and my newfound confidence, I'd say I look devilishly handsome.

I laugh to myself and pull out a cigarette. Might as well get some nicotine into me while I wait. People glance at me as they walk by. I know almost everyone here knows me as either the druggie, the guy who tried to kill himself, or Will's little brother. I don't appreciate the way their stares make me feel. I want to sink into the ground and away from curious gazes. I take a deep inhale and run my hand through my hair.

"You know, if you keep dressing up like that, you're going to take my spot as the best-looking brother," Will jokes.

"Better than the drug-addicted brother." The smoke in my lungs does exactly what I hoped it would, burning and causing me to be numb for just a second.

"Well, you'll always be the drug-addicted brother." Will looks down, seemingly disappointed by that fact. Me too, Will. Me too. "I'm going to head in, will you be alright?"

"Yeah, I'm good. Thanks, man."

Will walks off behind me and I'm left standing on the front steps of the party house alone. I wonder if it's too late to decide I actually don't want to be here at all.

"Jace?" I hear the voice come from behind me. I turn around and see Ian's blond ass standing at the front door. "Holy shit, Jace, it is you! Damn." He checks me out slowly then bites his lip with a smile.

The small gesture makes me uncomfortable with so many people around to witness. I know that no one's watching or gives a shit. But still, the whole thing is new to me, and I don't think I'm ready for the whole world to know.

I make my way over to him. "I didn't see you come in."

"Yeah, I got here a bit ago. I just wanted to walk my friends in and grab a soda. You look hot as hell. We're going to have to find a bathroom somewhere later." He winks.

"We could find a bathroom now," I offer, half joking.

"Don't tempt me. I still get hard any time I think about our last night at your house."

Ah, yes. That was a good night. After I punched Dad in the face, Ian came over to help manage some of the stress. We didn't do much. I'm not ready to jump into bed and full-on fuck yet. He knows that, and he never pushes. But we did jack each other off while making out heavily. There are a few marks scattered around his neck still, but they're fading since it was a few days ago. Something about the way Ian shows off the marks I leave on him keeps me excited, it's a huge turn-on. We're the only people who know who they're from. I guess if Will happens to see it, he'll know too.

But to everybody else it just shows that Ian has someone, and that he's been busy.

I scratch the back of my head and meet his eyes. Fuck, is he sure he doesn't want to find somewhere to sneak off to right now? "Tell me about it. It'll be my new shower thought for quite a while."

A smirk fills his face, and he looks around before leaning into me. "Do you often think about me…while you touch yourself?"

Oh, fuck, seriously…these pants don't conceal much. This is dangerous territory. I'll grab him and take him to the first room I find.

I narrow my eyes at him then nod toward the door. "We should go in before I do something I won't be able to take back."

"Fine. But I'll expect some fun later." He claps my shoulder and walks inside with me right behind him.

Chapter 40

This party sucks. I've been sitting on a couch with a cup of warm water, watching Ian run all over the place saying hi to people I don't recognize. I'm sure they used to be drug friends or whatever. He comes back and sits down closer than I'd like him to, but at the same time, the butterflies arrive in my stomach. As much as it throws me off to be closer to him in public, I have to admit it's nice to feel wanted.

His leg is brushing up against mine; I can't pull my eyes away from it. I keep trying to think of excuses to stand up or scoot over. Ian is oblivious, talking and laughing loudly with his friends. I look around the room for Will, but just as I'd assumed, he's nowhere to be seen. Some part of me wishes he would have hovered so I can use him to break away.

As Ian talks, he leg pushes harder into mine. A few times he leans back almost onto me, but I dodge it every time. I feel bad. I probably look uncomfortable, but I just don't know how to react.

I lean into Ian so I can talk to him over the music and all the talking. "Hey, you okay if I run outside real fast?" I ask.

Am I an asshole if I admit I miss it when we just suck each other off and leave? I'm not a fan of this hanging out thing, and he isn't who he normally is with me.

"Yeah, you good?" he asks, turning back a bit so that the back of his shoulder is leaning against my chest. I pull my head back so our faces aren't so close together.

"Just need some air." I move around him to get off the couch and walk to the door. I don't stop on the stairs this time. I walk all the way down to the curb and into the road. There's an old Chevy Impala to the right of me that reminds me of Suzie's dumb show. I choose that car to lean against. The pack of cigs makes a slapping sound each time I tap it against my palm. I'm going to need at least seven of these back-to-back to stall for as long as I'm wanting.

The quiet out here is calming; the birds are chirping but there's no one yelling over music or the pounding bass. You can hear the music from inside still, but it's not too much. The sun is going down, but for now it casts gold shadows over everything, I close my eyes and embrace the warmth that floods over me.

I wonder if Ian would notice if I left. This is all too much; too overwhelming. I already don't like people, but when you throw them all in a room drunk…I can't stand it. I'm about to pull out my phone and let both Will and Ian know I'm leaving when I hear a shuffle and a voice behind me.

"You know, you shouldn't smoke."

I turn and see Josh standing there. Josh? What the hell? Genuine confusion flashes across my face. "Hey, what are you doing here?"

This is a very unexpected turn of events. Why would Josh be here? To be fair, I don't even know how old he is, but I do know he doesn't go to my school. Either way, I'm happy to see him.

"Some friends convinced me to meet them here, they go to the school. I'm not a party person, but it beats being home alone." He shrugs. "Why are you here?" He takes a few sips of his beer.

I turn and look to the door and then back at him. I take another drag before answering—for the dramatics, obviously. "It's a party. I never miss a party."

"You don't say." He laughs and joins me leaning against this stranger's car. He knows me well enough to note the sarcasm. "Well, then, Mr. Party, tell me, why are you hiding outside by yourself?"

Is he drunk? I click my tongue. "I thought I'd give someone else the chance to bring the life in there. I feel bad stealing all the attention."

He smiles and holds out his beer as if to share. I stare at it for a few seconds. I mean, one beer wouldn't hurt. Hell, one sip wouldn't hurt. I can't resist the excitement of putting my lips anywhere his have been. I've done so good, though. I shouldn't even be debating this. I know myself better than that. I can have a sip and be fine. I can do it. This is the new Jace we're talking about.

I reach for his beer and he pulls it away. "Ahh...I've learned not to give people who hesitate beers. You did it. You hesitated."

I give him a narrow-eyed look. "Were you testing me, Josh?"

"No" He shrugs. "It was a hypothesis. I was experimenting."

Does this mean he assumed I have some type of substance abuse problems? What kind of "hypothesis" could he possibly have about me?

"So...a test, then," I state.

He smiles. "Yeah, yeah. Schrodinger's cat or whatever."

"Are you drunk?" I laugh. "I think I'm hearing more about quantum physics coming from you right now than I've heard from anyone, ever. Do you usually get all...whatever this is when you're drunk?"

"You knew that one? Smart guy." He finishes the rest of his beer and shoves the bottle into his pocket. "I don't know what you're talking about. I'm always like this. I'm pretty and smart. It's rare, but it does exist."

I chuckle and shake my head. "Does it, now?"

"You get it, though."

My mind stops. Did…did he just call me pretty? I toss my cig and light another. After it's lit, he grabs my wrist with one hand and uses his other to take the cigarette out of my hand and brings it to his lips. The way his hand feels wrapped around my wrist causes my cock to twitch. His grasp is firm, demanding. I know he's being playful, or whatever, but I'm already on edge. He can't be doing shit like this. All I can imagine is how his hands would feel wrapped around my wrists while he holds them above my head.

"These taste and feel so much better after some booze," he says. He lets my wrist go, and the comment pulls me right out of my perverted fantasy and throws me, crash landing, back into this world.

"Yeah? Hmm. I wouldn't know." I don't know how he expects me to keep my cool after that. He knows what he did. I can see it on his face. I wonder if I've been overthinking everything. Maybe I don't need to ask him what his sexuality is. Maybe I just need to step back and watch for a bit. Who knows? I'm just surprised he expects me to respond to his cigarette and booze comment. Thinking about it now, I never really smoked at all until after I tried to stop doing drugs. I have no clue how they feel after a few beers.

"Who did you come with?" Josh asks.

"Oh…umm. My brother, and a friend of mine."

He nods, takes another deep inhale, and hands the cig back. "Was that your brother with you on the couch in there?"

He saw that? I didn't even know he was here, and he'd already seen me? Does that mean he followed me out here?

I look up to find his eyes already staring back at me. Oh, God. What do I say?! This could be my chance to tell him I like guys and see if he's on the same page. Or it could be my chance to chase him away forever by telling him I like guys. The third option is to say yes and start our friendship off fresh with lies.

"The friend, then?" he asks after yet another hesitation on my part.

I look down at my feet. "Something like that." It's nearly a whisper.

He looks surprised. "Oh? Do tell."

Damn, I really wish I had that beer right now. I don't know if this is exactly how I want to have this conversation. Not while he's drunk, and not at some stupid party.

"Some other time?" I take a few steps away from him. "Hey, I'm going to head in and find my brother. I'm ready to go home. You aren't driving, are you?"

Josh looks around at the cars surrounding him then shrugs.

"Josh. You can't drive."

He smiles. "Give me a ride, then."

There's another meaning to what he says. I'm not imagining it. I can tell because of the look on his face when his eyes drop to my lips, then to my neck.

Swallowing hard, my breath picks up. I clear my throat. "You know I don't drive."

Josh pulls his keys out of his pocket and tosses them to me. "I know you *can* drive, though."

"I still have to go find my brother. To let him know I'm leaving."

Josh nods and stands up straight. "And your friend, right?"

"Yeah, and Ian." It comes out a little more questioning than I was expecting, but seriously. What is he getting at?

He gestures to the house as if telling me to lead the way. Josh's personality is completely different from what anyone might expect. He's funny, silly, caring—nothing you'd expect from someone who looks like that. Not that you have to look a certain way to be nice, but I've read a lot of books, and he isn't the gray character I was expecting him to be.

Josh follows me into the house. Ian is still exactly where I left him, but something about the way Josh is looking at him tells me to find my brother first.

Will is a very social person; he's probably in the kitchen or out back. We move through the house, weaving through people until I find Will standing next to a plant with a few other guys.

"Will!" I yell. I finally get to him and pat him on the shoulder. "Hey, I'm going to go home. Can you keep an eye on Ian?"

He nods. "You okay? Is the alcohol too much? Did someone pressure you to do dru—"

I slap my hand over his mouth and widen my eyes. "No, Will."

Will's eyes look behind me, and his whole attitude changes. He pushes my hand from his mouth and smiles at me. "Black hair. You must be the boss-friend?" Will asks, looking at Josh.

I drop my head into my hand, creating an audible slap.

"Boss-friend?" Josh laughs. "Josh." He holds his hand out to shake. Then he nudges me in the shoulder. "Aww, you talk about me."

I mentally punch myself in the head.

"Oh, he talks about you, alright," Will winks.

"How sweet. All good things, I hope?" Josh smirks at me before looking back to Will.

"Dude, your eyes are killer! Those things are so fucking blue." Will's comment sends a tinge of jealousy down my spine. It's a feeling I'm not familiar with, and I'm honestly shocked to feel it.

"Thank you," Josh says. "I do find them to be my best quality. What do you think, Jace?"

Will smiles deviously. "Yes, Jace. What *do* you think?"

If he didn't know I was gay before, I'm almost positive Josh does now, thanks to Will's bitch ass.

I give will a look that says, "What I *think* is that I'm going to kick your ass," but instead I go with, "I'm driving him home. Then I'll be home. Don't do anything stupid."

"Hopefully your driving lessons worked," Will says, shaking Josh's hand again. "Good luck getting home alive."

"Cool," I say. "And now that were done with that, I'm going to let Ian know I'm headed out. *Please* keep an eye on him."

Thanks, Will. I'm glad out of all the siblings, it was his dumb ass who came here.

I make my way back to Ian and he smiles at me before his eyes drift to Josh. I make a judgment call and ignore it. "Hey, I'm going home. It's…hard being here." It's an excuse, but I think it works.

Ian stands and takes a few steps toward me. "How are you leaving? Is Will going with you?"

"No, I'm going to drive his car and take him home first," I say and point to Josh. His eyes are daggers. I've never seen him in this mood before, and it makes me wonder how different I looked to people when I was on drugs—or how different I look to people now. Although drunk Josh is very alluring and charming, this personality isn't one I'm a huge fan of.

Ian looks Josh up and down. "And he is…?"

If I introduce him as my boss, it'll make our relationship seem professional. If I say he's a friend, it means we're casual.

I'm not sure what Josh's thoughts on us are, but I'm assuming after our conversation tonight, friend is a good way to go.

"He's a friend of mine," I tell Ian.

Josh holds his hand out to Ian, and the world's most uncomfortable handshake is brought to life.

"I'm ready to go too," Ian says, his eyes almost matching Josh's, but only for a moment before he looks back at me. "Mind if I come?"

Shit.

*　　　　　*　　　　　*

This is not how I expected the night to go. I hate it. I know there isn't anything between me and Josh, nor is there anything close to a relationship between me and Ian, but this is by far the most awkward car ride I've ever been in. I'm not sure who to talk to, or if I can even talk to anyone at all.

"You can drop your friend off, then take me home," Josh says from the passenger side of the front seat.

Quickly, Ian chimes in from the back seat. "Oh, no, that's okay. I live down the road from Jace, so I can walk with him."

Josh looks at me confused. "You were going to walk home from my house?"

"I don't know where you live. I assumed it would be close enough. If not, I would have called Will."

He doesn't answer as I stop at a red light. Instead, he laughs. "You were right, your driving is pretty good on the main road. I'm sorry I didn't let you drive to the burger store."

I take a deep breath, trying to choose my words. I'm not sure what Josh is trying to do, but it sounds like it's about to get even weirder in here. "Thank you…"

Yeah, sure, that was casual and not suspicious.

Ian watches our exchange closely.

"You in the mood for music?" Josh asks as he connects his phone to the car's Bluetooth.

"Oh, you don't want Zombie's music. He listens to old-ass music," Ian says mockingly.

If I could jump out of this car right now, I would. But unfortunately, the light turns green.

"He likes the new music *I* put on his phone," Josh says.

From the corner of my eye I can see Josh waiting for my answer. His icy-blue eyes are sharper than normal. God, he's so sexy, and after this insane car ride, I'm starting to come to the conclusion that maybe he's into me—although I can't imagine why someone as good-looking as him would. Ian is cute, don't get me wrong. But he's not my type, I guess. Still, this is the worst position I could have put myself in. What can I say to even the playing field right now?

"Billy Joel?" I ask.

Josh smirks but turns it on. I'm sure he knows exactly what I'm trying to do by choosing a song that's old, but not too old.

Ian's phone dings and he looks down, breaking us out of this conversation. Literally saved by the bell.

"Katie says you've been ignoring her but wanted me to tell you she's staying over and will be in your bed when you get home," Ian says.

Katie does this "funny" thing where she stays at my house, sleeps in my bed, and makes me either sleep on a corner of the mattress or out on the couch. She's the biggest bed hog in the world. I groan and drop my head back onto the head rest. "Tell her I'm not sleeping on the couch, so she better not be taking the whole bed up again." We haven't exactly made up after everything; I'm sure she wants to talk about it.

"Katie?" Josh asks, a surprised look in his eyes. "Is that your girlfriend?"

The sound that leaves Ian is not human. It's a mix of a laugh, a cough, a scoff, some type of bike revving, and maybe even part of a blender. Josh turns to face him for the first time with concern on his face. Making eye contact in the mirror with Ian, I shake my head. He seems to understand because he contains himself and clears his throat.

"My sister," is all Ian says before looking back down at his phone to message her back.

"She's a close friend, and a bed hog," I say and smile at Josh.

The look in Josh's eyes is different now. Not competitive or upset but soft and curious. If Ian wasn't in the car and we weren't driving, I wouldn't have had the self-control to not launch myself over to him.

Josh reaches his hand over the cup holders between us and lightly touches my leg with his finger before pulling away and leaning against the door with his head on the window. Tingles spread throughout my whole leg, and I want to grab his hand and pull it back to me.

"You can take me home first, then just take the car," he says. His voice is calmer than normal, and it throws me off.

"I can't drive by myself," I protest.

"You'll be fine. I don't live far from you, but I don't want you walking around this late at night." His eyes never leave the dashboard.

"I'm not taking your car, Josh." I know he's drunk, but seriously, what is it with him tonight? "How were you originally planning for me to get home?"

There's a slight frown on his face and his eyes meet mine, their icy blue reaching out and grabbing me. The disappointment on his face is clear. Holy shit, he wasn't...*he wasn't planning on me getting home tonight at all.*

There they are, those goddamn butterflies, back to haunt me again, along with the slowly growing boner in my pants. Only ever with him do I get that genuinely happy feeling no matter the situation, no matter what we're doing. In this moment, Ian doesn't even matter. I almost forget he's back there. Because here's my answer. The silent question I've been asking Josh since I met him. Here is his answer, right in front of me.

This feeling is so much better than any drug has ever made me feel. I can feel my cheeks heating up as our eyes remain locked. I'm actually a little worried about how good I feel right now, because if this were to ever for some crazy reason become something, I imagine it would feel so much better and I'd be giving him all the power to crush and tear me apart.

"The light's green." Ian's voice pushes through the little world I created for myself.

I pull my gaze away from Josh and look back at the road. My heart is racing, and even my breathing is picking up. I can't help but keep my eyes wide the whole time. He wanted me to spend the night. He was expecting me to stay at his house. My palms are sweaty enough to slide around the steering wheel.

I take Ian home first after Josh falls asleep. Ian thanks me but hesitates before getting out. I don't know if he expects some kind of affection from me or what, but it creates an odd feeling between us when I don't get out of the car. How could I after the revelation I just had about Josh?

Now, I know what the old Jace would do. The old Jace would take Josh home, drop him and his car off, and jog home. The old Jace would wake him up, get his address, and not think twice about heading right there. But I'm not the old Jace anymore.

I pull out of Ian's driveway and slowly drive down the street until my house comes into view. I stare at it for a second before fully committing and pulling into the driveway. I've never been this nervous in my life. My stomach is turning and fluttering so much I'm worried I might throw up.

I quietly open the door and run into the house, straight to my room to find Katie in my bed. I pick her up and carry her into Will's room since he's still gone.

"Sorry, Katie," I whisper then pull the blanket over her and shut the door. I'm not risking putting her on the couch. I'd like to make this an incognito mission.

Back at the car, I climb into the driver's seat and wake Josh up. I decide to use some of Ian's speech from that day in the laundry room.

"Josh, hey." He opens his eyes and looks at me, half awake. "Hey, I'm not sure your stance on things, but it's really late and you were asleep, so I didn't want to wake you up…"

He sits up and looks around. "Your house?" he asks, a smile slowly spreading across his face.

"Yeah…but if you want me to take you home, I'm more than happy to do that."

Without answering, Josh gets out of the car and walks toward the front door. I fumble as I turn the car off, pull out the keys, and pick up both our phones. There's no doubt in my mind Josh is going to walk right into my house, so I run after him and push the door quietly open. Once we're inside, I turn to him. "Umm…so my room is at the back of the hall, or you can have the couch. I planned on staying on the couch so you could…you know, have the bed."

Josh looks around the room, taking everything in and moving with small steps. The walls are dark wood panel, the rooms are too small, and we have furniture that looks like it's from the seventies. Things I've never even thought of before are suddenly all I can see.

"This way?" he asks, pointing down the hall.

A soft smile appears on my face when I nod.

"Show me," Josh says.

Lord, take me out right now.

I walk down the hall into my room and flip on the light. It's something I don't do very often, so I squint my eyes to try and get used to how bright it is. God, my room is a mess. My books are spread out all over the place again, but mostly on the floor. I've been reading any chance I have between my busy schedule. I forgot how amazing it is to disappear into a different world where you don't have any problems.

Josh steps past me and looks around. Why is showing people your house the most embarrassing thing? "Sorry for the mess," I say.

He turns around to face me and steps closer. His hand reaches up and pinches the collar of my undershirt between his fingers. After studying it for a moment, his fingers release it and move down my arm, brushing my fingertips.

"You look *really* good tonight, Jace."

I lick my lips, nervous about how close he is to me, and the words he's saying are for sure making me blush. He's drunk, I know that, and I know I won't let anything happen. But Josh is here, he's in my room with me telling me I look good. I wish I was a horrible person and I was willing to let whatever he wanted happen. I mean, this could be the only chance I have to be with and experience Josh.

He leans his head in, but right before his lips touch mine, I push my hand against his chest. "Josh…"

He lets out a sigh. "I know." Nodding, he steps back and sits on my bed, leaving me standing a few feet away. "Under different circumstances, though, would you have stopped me?" He's swaying slightly. I wonder exactly how much he's had to drink.

I sit down next to him and bring my knee to his. "No."

"Rain check, then. You can sleep in the bed with me…if you

want? Ill behave." He kicks his shoes off.

Laughter flows softly out of me. "You better. I don't know if I have the strength to tell you no again."

"Well when you put it that way…" He winks and lies back onto the pillow, scooting over to make room for me. I make the smart choice to keep my clothes on, but I switch into some basketball shorts and a T-shirt before getting into bed.

His scent engulfs me when I climb in next to him. I really hope it stays on my sheets because this man smells so fucking good. For the first time in a long time, I'm not worried about what happens next, or what I'm going to do, or how things will change. For the first time ever, I'm just here. I'm in the moment, and I am so over-whelmingly happy.

We're facing each other, and even though I've never had another man in my bed with me, this is exactly as I've always imagined it. His hand comes up and brushes my hair out of my face. His touch is soothing, warm, and immediately makes me want more. Before I can protest about the loss of contact, he grabs my hand and laces our fingers together before closing his eyes.

Hand-holding while the other party is intoxicated isn't frowned upon, is it? I assume not. Especially since his hand in mine is preventing me from running my fingers through his hair or exploring the softness of his skin.

Once his breathing pattern changes and I know he's asleep, I pull our interlocked hands up to my mouth and kiss the back of his hand. Even that small gesture…I wish I could have so much more with him. Why is it that this moment feels more intimate than any moment I've ever had with Ian?

"Goodnight, Josh," I whisper before closing my eyes.

Chapter 41

The sun shines through my window right into my eyes, pulling me out of the best sleep I've ever gotten. I look over and see Josh still in my bed, curled up against the wall, sleeping with his back to me. He is the sweetest sleeper. His soft and even breaths are the only sound filling up my room. I lie on my back and smile up at my ceiling, biting my lip as yesterday's memories fill my head. He likes me. He tried to kiss me. I've never felt this way about Ian. Never.

"Good morning." His voice comes out sleeping and rough when I stand up.

I kneel on the floor and lean into my elbows on the bed. His voice alone is enough to turn me on. I wonder if we had kissed last night if I'd be able to lean in and kiss him now. I have no idea how these things work.

"Morning." I smile back at him. His hair is a mess, and he has lines on his face from the pillow. If I slept well last night, I bet he slept amazingly. "I, um…I don't know how to do this part," I admit.

He laughs softly. "Does this house have any coffee? I have a wicked hangover, and I am not ready to be awake yet."

"Yeah, I'll go get you some. The bathroom is down the hall, second door on the left, if you need it."

He reaches out and runs his fingers along the outside of my

wrist. "Thanks for letting me stay here."

"Of course." I get up and head into the kitchen, where Tyson and Suzie are hanging out arguing over something I don't give a shit about. I try to remind myself to act natural. No doubt there will be questions if I walk in there smiling like a fool. I drop the smile, but nothing can be done about the way I'm blushing. Knowing I'm blushing puts that dumb smile right back on my face.

"How was last night?" Tyson asks.

Josh appears in my head, and I have to fake rubbing my nose to hide the smile. "Not too bad. I had a bad moment for maybe ten seconds, but overall, it just solidified my hate for other people."

"That's fair, I'm glad it wasn't too hard for you. But did you have fun?" he asks as Suzie places some coffee in front of me.

"It was alright." I take a few sips "Not really my scene, I guess."

"Will came back early this morning, how did you get home?" Suzie asks.

I assume both she and Tyson haven't seen the car in the driveway yet. Which means Will got home and kept his mouth shut. Very unlike him.

"I got a ride from a friend." The image of Josh looking at me in the car with those sexy eyes hits, and another smile breaks out on my face without me noticing.

"You came in so quietly," Tyson says. "You didn't even have your music on last night. I only knew you were home because I heard you laughing."

Suzie shakes her head in disbelief. "You heard him *laughing*? You were laughing? In your room, by yourself, in the middle of the night?"

I give up trying to take the smile off my face and stand up instead. "What? A guy can't laugh?"

"Yeah, just not you," she jokes. "Is Katie in your room?"

"Nope." I pop the "p" as I pour coffee into a second mug.

"I told you!" Tyson exclaims.

"Do I even want to know?" Suzie says.

"I'm 98 percent sure she slept in Will's room last night," Tyson says. "Is that not strange to anyone else?"

In perfect time, the sound of my bedroom door opening and closing pulls their attention from the Katie and Will argument. Suzie and Tyson lean their heads around the wall to look down the hall. I remain with my back to the hall and close my eyes tightly like it's going to lower the volume of the real world.

When I open one eye, they're both looking at me with shocked expressions.

"Alright, well, I'm going to take my coffee back to my room," I say through an embarrassed and dismissing smile.

"Jace! Is there someone in your room!?" Suzie asks, amused.

"Umm…no. It sounds like there's someone in the bathroom, so my room would be empty currently." I scratch my head then turn and leave before anyone can ask me anything else.

Once in my room, I put the coffees on the desk and figure I should probably clean up this mess. A few moments later, Josh walks back in and leans against the closed door, watching me pick up my books. "You read a lot?" he asks.

"Yeah, I used to. I'm trying to get back into it."

He looks around at the shelf, my arms, and the floor "It usually helps to read one at a time."

I pull my lips into my mouth and nod my head sarcastically. "Ah, that's what I've been doing wrong. Thanks for the advice."

He takes a few steps toward me and touches my fingertips with his. "Any time." His hand tightens around mine and he softly pulls me to him. With his left hand still holding mine, he brings his right hand up to my jaw and traces a line from my ear to the back of my neck. He pulls my head closer, letting his bottom lip barley touch mine. "Any objections?" he whispers.

"No," I breathe.

His lips meet mine, softly at first. I feel the butterflies that live in my stomach for him burst and spread across every inch of my body. I can feel his hand on the back of my neck, his other now firmly on my hip. The one on the back of my neck tightens enough to cause me to moan softly, which apparently was the approval he was looking for. His kiss gets rougher. He's kissing me like he's feeling all the spark and electricity that I am. His tongue grazes hungrily across my bottom lip before he pulls it into his mouth.

He pulls away and looks into my eyes. His eyes are *really* making me melt now. I have never experienced a kiss like that. So full of emotion and want and need. Not a need for just anyone, though. A need specific for each other.

"I'd lay you down on your bed and take this further, but there were, like, four people out there that watched me leave the bathroom and walk in here."

I rest my head on his and laugh. "Well, I'll need a second before I can walk out there."

"Think it's too late for me to jump out the window?" he asks, his laughter filling the room.

*   *   *

The best course of action here is to pretend like nothing weird is happening. We'll leave the room and act like Josh has always been here. Like there hasn't been a good amount of face-sucking and grinding. I guess the good news is that I kept my neck-sucking to myself. I don't know what it is about that, but now that I think about it…is it weird that I'm here with Josh while Ian still has my marks on him? I'm overthinking it. I didn't know Josh was into me like that.

"Are you heading out after this?" I ask him.

"Do you want me to?" he shrugs.

"No…I just wasn't sure what you were interested in doing. I'm just trying to find a plan of action here. You hungry?"

He grins then plants a small peck on my lips. "Starving."

I look away so he can't see my face. Without the heat of the moment, even the smallest things like that make my face heat up and get the butterflies in my stomach moving. I can't believe how happy he makes me. Even before now when we were just at the shop together hanging out as friends, he's always had a way of making me feel as if I belong somewhere.

My hand hovers over the doorknob. Okay, this is fine. This isn't weird, this is fine. We didn't even do anything! I don't know why I'm so worked up about it.

Josh reaches around me and grabs the door. "I'm assuming I'm the first man you've brought home?" he asks, his lips brushing my ear.

"First person ever, aside from Katie. I don't have friends or relationships or…people interested enough to come over."

"That Ian kid seemed interested enough."

With Ian, I was able to sneak him in and out through my window, just like the non-classy gents we are. I never felt like answering twenty questions after, especially since Ian and I weren't romantically interested in each other. Josh, though…I actually like him.

"Another time," I answer dismissively.

I don't want to ruin the mood we have going on here with talk about Ian. Josh pulls the door open and steps aside so I can lead the way. I walk too slowly to the kitchen and accidentally make eye contact with every single person in the living room. Nice.

Looking through the cabinets, I find out that no one has gone grocery shopping this week, so we're down to Will's favorite. "I'm so sorry, my brother is a child, this is all we have," I say, holding out a package of brown sugar Pop-Tarts.

"Not a child," Will says. "Boss-friend, nice to see you again, in my kitchen. Early in the morning." He raises his eyebrows and smirks as he makes his way into the kitchen.

"Ahh, yeah! Will, right?" Josh says, absentmindedly taking the Pop-Tarts and opening them up.

Will only smiles and then sits down. Everyone else files into the kitchen as well, acting like they had a reason to come in.

I clear my throat. "Yeah, that's Will." I point to everyone behind him. "Tyson, Katie, and my sister, Suzie."

"Josh, nice to meet you all." His dazzling smile is welcoming, and he seems genuinely happy to be meeting these psychopaths. He points at Katie and then looks at me. "Wasn't she supposed to be in your bed last night?"

I rub the back of my neck and bite my lips. "Was she?"

Katie crosses her arms. "Yeah, wasn't I? I guess that explains how I woke up in Will's."

I shrug and make a "who knows" face.

"I wasn't complaining," Will says with a smirk.

Katie punches him in the arm. "Don't act like anything happened. Your ass decided to sleep on the floor because you were scared."

"I wasn't scared, I was being respectful!" Will shoots back.

"So, Josh, who are you to Jace?" Suzie asks, leaving Will and Katie to argue in the background. "How do you know him?"

Josh looks at me. "Uh…"

What am I supposed to say? I don't know the answer to that

question. We haven't talked about it ourselves.

"Ah, I see," she giggles.

"I'm sorry," Tyson says, "we just aren't used to Jace bringing people home. I'm surprised he's gotten out enough to find someone to bring home. Friends! I mean, he doesn't bring friends over…or other…people."

Nodding in amusement, I slap Tyson's bicep. "Nice. And I had the highest hopes for you." I shoot Josh an apologetic smile and lead him a few steps away from everyone. "I'm not going to make you eat Pop-Tarts. Let me take you to breakfast or something."

"I didn't even put out, and you want to buy me breakfast? That's so sweet," Josh says loudly enough for everyone to hear.

Will chokes on a Pop-Tart of his own behind us while trying to conceal a laugh.

"Thanks," I mouth.

"Well, I'd love to go to breakfast," Josh announces to the kitchen. "I'm going to go out to the car, and you can pretend you need to grab something, that way you all can talk about me for a second." He turns to me. "Walk me out?"

We go outside and stand beside his car. "I'm glad you were at that party. But I had no idea you were such a lush," I joke.

"Shut up, I am not," Josh snickers. "I never even told my friends I was leaving. I've just never been around you in a setting like that. It was so casual, and I was so nervous. I can't believe the way I behaved in the car, either. Oh, my God, I'm so sorry about that." He shakes his head. "I had a feeling that Ian kid knew you better than me, and I wasn't sure if you two were…anything."

"They call it liquid courage for a reason. But I'm glad. I don't think I ever would have made a move if it weren't for last night. Since the first time I saw you, I've been trying to figure out how to ask if there was a chance you might be into me."

"I knew you were into me since you saw me for the first time. I just needed to feel you out, see past your dry heaving. If your personality sucked, I would have left you in the dust."

"Alright, alright. Let me go get my pretend-thing I lost so we can all talk about you. And no more talking about my dry heaving. It was a dark moment."

He cups my face in his hands and kisses me deeply, so much so that I almost say "fuck it" and take him back to my room. When he pulls away, he smiles.

"How old are you?" I ask.

"You probably should have asked sooner, now it's too late to matter." He kisses me softly again and gets into his car. "Twenty-six. So you're officially into older men. You're welcome. Now go talk about me so we can get breakfast."

I run into the house to catch everyone shuffling out of the bathroom. They were watching us from the window.

"You two are much more friendly than you were last night," Will says. "Did you finally tell him what you thought about his eyes?" He winks.

"Shut up, you don't know anything." I can't hold back my smile, so instead I rock back on my heels. "Oh, yeah, thanks for not making that awkward for me. Really appreciate it," I add sarcastically.

"Hey, our baby brother brings home a dude for the first time, and you expect us to just act cool about it?" Tyson jumps over the couch and lands on his butt, twisting to face us. "What about the older brother privilege we have? We're supposed to be able to embarrass you."

"Those were some pretty…intense kisses out there." Suzie smiles. "I'm so glad you're happy. I haven't seen you this happy in…well, ever."

"Thank you. I'd be happier if you guys weren't so fucking

awkward." I turn to my room to change my clothes before leaving. Of course, Will follows me, and so does everyone else.

Will sits down on my bed and leans back, watching me run around looking for something to wear. "So what did you do last night? Anything exciting happen? Oh, my God, should I be sitting on this?!" He jumps up and away from the bed.

"Nothing happened. He was drunk. I didn't even let him kiss me."

"Wow, so you guys had your first kiss this morning, then he kissed you like that at the car? You two are in trouble if I know anything," Suzie says.

"It's just so easy with him. It always has been. He's so much like me, he reminds me of who I would have been if it weren't for…everything. Anyway, I'm heading out."

"What about Ian?" It's the first time Katie has spoken.

"What *about* Ian?" It comes out colder than I expect.

"What are you going to tell him? Are you going to keep seeing him?"

Shit, I didn't really think about that. What do I tell him? Do I have to stop with stuff between us? Josh and I haven't really talked about the rules, or labels, or whatever. But to be completely honest with myself, do I even *want* to be with Ian anymore? I mean, I started with Ian as a way to get my pent-up shit about Josh out of my system, but now I have Josh, so… Wait, is Josh interested in any of that type of stuff?

"Fuck. I don't know." I brush her off and walk out of my room and into Will's to look through his clothes.

Tyson's voice carries down the hall. "Don't kill his mood, he's having a good morning. Just let him be in the moment."

"But that's my brother."

I roll my eyes as I find a nice hot-pink short-sleeved shirt. It has a few buttons on the collar, and the sleeves are rolled a little. I steal it and a pair of dark jeans that are probably going to be too big on me. As I'm pulling everything on, I yell out the door to Katie, "Don't act like you two are close. I'll talk to him, but honestly, it doesn't concern you." I push my hair back and make sure it's parted in the right spot. "Thanks for the clothes, Will! I'm headed out."

I get back to Josh's car and climb in. Is what I said to Katie rude? Yes. Do I really give a shit? No.

"Wow, you bring a guy home, make out a little, and now you're ready to announce your sexuality to the world?"

My brows furrow in confusion. "What?"

"That is a very loud shirt." He puts the car in reverse. "I'm not complaining, it's a good color on you, a really good color."

"I've been trying to branch out. Get out of my comfort zone."

"Oh, I've noticed. Anyway, have you been to Angela's?" he asks, referring to a small, cute family-owned diner nearby. He must live closer than I thought if he knows it.

"Of course I've been to Angela's."

I don't want to ruin the mood with a "what are we" conversation, but I don't want to know just for my own sake. I want to know so I don't end up hurting Josh or hurting Ian for no reason. This feels like more than a platonic friendship thing, but I don't want to make assumptions.

I guess I can start with something light. "Hey, so…my birthday is next weekend. I think my family is throwing together something small and dumb. Do you maybe want to come? Of course, you don't have to. It's not, like, intimate or anything."

"Oh, yeah, July 26th, right?"

"Yeah…but we're doing it the Saturday after."

Josh nods. "Your family seems nice and supportive. Katie, too."

"I guess so."

"I'll be there. Also, again, thank you for dealing with me yesterday. I don't usually drink that much, and I know I was probably a lot."

"No, don't worry about it. I was trying to figure out how to stop being friends with Ian anyway. Turns out a manic drunk was the way to do it."

We both laugh and then Josh scratches his head. "Seriously, apologize to him for me, please. Or let me go apologize. I have no idea where all of that came from. I was such a dick!"

"You don't know where it came from?" I press. "That's literally just your personality."

"Hey, now, every good relationship needs a dick, and a self-destructive prick." He laughs, but my heart stops.

Relationship. Holy fuck, what does it mean? Obviously "relationship" doesn't mean "romantic relationship." But how do I know? Ugh. This is even more stressful than when it was just *Does Josh like me?* I have a lot to learn about this.

"No, come back, really? Wow, should I be worried?" he asks me.

After blinking a few times and remembering to exist, I look back into his face. "Huh?" *Wow. Yes, good job, me.* Honestly, I stopped listening after he said relationship, so I have no idea.

The amusement leaves his face and is replaced with genuine concern. "You...okay?"

"Oh, yeah, I'm good. Sorry." I'm trying not to be weird, but I don't know how to do this.

Chapter 42

"**A**re you excited?" Suzie asks me.

"For what?" I ask through a mouthful of chips.

"Eww, dude. Your party, obviously."

I swallow and push my hand through my hair. "I guess?" When she and Will continue looking at me, it tells me that wasn't a good enough answer. "What, do you want me to get on my knees and thank you? This is literally going to be the same as any other day that I hang out with you, but this time I'm 22."

"Dude, Josh has to do a better job. You're somehow grumpier than you normally are."

"What does he have to do with…" Oh. "Jesus, thanks, Will."

He assumes Josh and I have been fucking. We haven't done anything, and I haven't met up with Ian again, either. In fact, I've kind of been avoiding him altogether. This week has been busy with work and the gym and my constant mind battles. Between really wanting a drink and questioning my own worth, it's been a long week.

I haven't had much time to actually talk to Josh privately, and when we've had the time, nothing has really happened. Sometimes it's back to the way it was before everything, and I actually really enjoy it. Any time spent with Josh is a good time. I just have one tiny problem, and that's that I'm back to solo hand stuff. Now that I know how other things feel, that's not good enough anymore. So yes, I may be a bit on edge and grumpier than normal. Sue me.

"Is he coming over?" Will asks.

"I think so. He mentioned he was going to."

"Okay, well, we kind of figured we'd just hang out, drink some beers, and watch a movie or play a video game. We got some Capri-Sun for you." He ruffles my hair.

I only have one thing to say about the hair rubbing and the drinking comment: "Fuck off."

My birthday isn't a huge thing for me. I've never really been too interested in it. So of course, I've always told everyone I just want to do whatever they want to do. Which has carried on until now—hence the video games and movies. We don't really do parties around here. We do hang-outs, but with more food and a healthy amount of harassment toward whoever's birthday it is.

"Okay," Suzie announces, "I have some news, but I want us all to remember how awkward and new Jace's…thing…with Josh is. Okay?"

"Suzie, if you're pregnant, I'm going to personally kick your ass." Will stands up and takes a few steps toward her.

"God, no. But Max is going to come over. I figured since it's Jace's birthday and all, the least I can give him is the chance to meet the guy I'm seeing, plus taking a little stress off his back about inviting Josh over. Besides, Max has been an ass, so he deserves to be trapped in a room with you three."

"Max is coming?" I ask. "Fuck yeah, this is a treat." I've been waiting for this moment.

"Only if you change your attitude, though," Suzie said. "I don't want to be sitting around here while you whine like a bitch."

I glare at her in place of a response.

"He won't whine," Will says. "The second Josh gets here, he's going to be like 'Oh, I'm so happy you came, I've missed you so much.' And then we're going to hear the laugh we haven't heard in years, and an hour later we'll be wondering where they went and what those noises in the bedroom are."

"Jesus, Will, that was funny at first, but you took it *too* far." Suzie plugs her ears and turns back to me. "If I can't have Max in my room tonight, no Josh in yours."

"Fine," I groan. She has a point. I don't want Suzie and Max behind closed doors when I'm right here, knowing exactly what's going on.

"And everyone's hands above any blankets!" Tyson adds. He's been in the kitchen making food and snacks, which was nice to see, but very different. "How did it end up being you two with the re- lationships and the oldest people with no one?"

"Uh, mine's not a relationship," I say, even though I'm not 100 percent sure. But I think it would be better for everyone if that was their opinion from the get-go.

"Situationship, then?" Tyson asks.

"I don't think that's what it is either," I say, mostly to myself, but Suzie chimes in: "Friends with benefits? Don't you have, like, a huge crush on him?"

"Shut up. I don't have a *crush*. Twelve-year-olds have crushes."

"Well, relationship, situationship, friends with benefits, crush, whatever it is. He's walking up to the door now," Will says, stand- ing up.

Josh's frame is clearly visible through the frosted window on the door. "Oh shit. Now?!" I jump up and run to my room. I wasn't expecting him until later. I told him six, and it's only three! I throw on a purple hoodie but keep the basketball shorts on. He's only ever seen me like this on the first day we met, the first time we woke up together, and, well…now. We aren't going anywhere, so I want to be comfortable without looking like I'm trying too hard.

I fix my hair in the bathroom mirror, put some deodorant on, and a tiny amount of Tyson's cologne. My hand hesitates on the bathroom doorknob. Fuck! Basketball shorts and cologne?! *Now* I look like I'm trying too hard.

Whatever. I leave the bathroom and find Josh already sitting on the couch talking with Tyson and Suzie.

"Hey, you're early." I walk in and sit on the chair farthest from the couch. As usual, I'm not really sure how I'm supposed to act. That dumb smile I always seem to have around him fills my face and I look away, trying to figure out the moment and what the fuck I'm doing right now. I don't ever get nervous around him, but with him here, around my family, it creates a whole different situation. I've never felt more self-conscious.

"Yeah," Josh says, "I had nothing to do and figured we'd get this weird family part out of the way sooner rather than later." He smiles, then looks at Tyson and Suzie. I'm not sure where Will ran off to, but I don't really care right now.

I shift in my spot and rub my palms on my shorts. "That's probably a good idea. I'm glad you came early. It's keeping me from kicking both Suzie and Will's ass."

I glare at Suzie, who has a smile on her face that tells me it's game on. I can't wait until Max gets here. These poor boys have no idea the family they decided to walk into.

"I'm so happy you came, I missed you so much," Suzie whispers, mocking Will's earlier comment. She whispers it loudly enough so that everyone in the room hears it. I kick her in the shin, hard enough for her to be surprised. At the same time, I hear Tyson snicker as he walks back into the kitchen.

"Hey, do you wanna go in my room?" I ask, resisting the urge to kick Suzie's ass right here.

Josh laughs and stands up. "Yeah, we can do that."

"Umm…" Suzie stands and moves between us.

"Really?" I ask, folding my arms. "Max isn't even here yet! You expect us to stay out here with you crazy assholes the whole time?"

"You did make a deal," Tyson yells from the kitchen.

"Hey Tys, stick to your room. We don't need your added comments in here." Suzie's face hasn't changed; she's serious about this. "Fuck. Fine."

"I feel like I'm missing something here?" Josh asks.

Shrugging, Suzie replies, "Bedrooms are off-limits, no matter the relationship status."

Ah, damn. That's fucking awkward. I wince almost like it physically hurts. I don't even know where I'm supposed to look. Now Josh knows we were talking about our relationship status, or title, or whatever.

"Man, so I can't be in Will's room with him alone? There goes my shot," Josh jokes but sits down on the couch next to Suzie.

Just to prove a point—even though I don't know who I'm proving it to—I move to sit on the other side of him. Even this feels more natural than when I was at that party with Ian on the couch. "Will would be the best choice, too. Tyson is too stuck up, and Suzie…well, you'd have to go through us first."

"Who's Max?" Josh asks. "Did he go through you guys?"

"Ah, sweet, sweet Max." Tyson hands Josh a beer and sits down across from the couch. "This will be our first time meeting him. So you will get the honor of watching us three work him out."

Josh takes a sip of beer and sets it down on the coffee table. "Oh, no, no. I want in on this. I'm the youngest, so I never get to have any fun."

I make a mental note to ask him about his family. I remember his dad from the shop, but that's the only family I'm aware of. I can believe I haven't asked yet.

My thoughts get cut off when Josh places his hand on my bare thigh. My heart pounds against my ribs, and his skin against mine causes my breathing to hitch. He's still talking to Tyson about what they're going to do to Max, but I can't hear. He's touching me like it's a habit, like he's always just laid a reassuring hand on me to remind me he's here. It's probably weird for me to be looking at his hand on my leg for that long, and I'm sure I look as shocked as I feel, but…*he's touching me*, and in front of people!

I realize my mouth is open and my eyes are wide. I look at Suzie, who seems almost as excited as I am. We share a silent moment together with our eyes. There's no judgment from her, no sign that she's going to tease me about this. Just genuine excitement for me. Oh, shit, what do I do now?

I pull myself together and am about to rejoin the world and hop into their conversation when Josh's thumb starts rubbing soothing circles against my skin. *I am about to explode.* I've never understood the term "fan girl," but now I think I understand. It's the smallest things, like his hand brushing mine or touching my leg, or hovering over my back while we stand talking about cars that really does it for me. The kissing and stuff is nice, yes, but something about the small pieces of affection mean so much more. It's as if even when we aren't being intimate, he still wants to be with me. With Ian, it was purely sexual. We didn't hold hands or hug or brush against each other unless we were already planning on doing more.

I hear a question behind me coming from Tyson, I think. But I don't register it. Suzie reaches behind Josh and smacks my arm, pulling me out of whatever freakout was just happening. I look up to find both Tyson and Josh looking at me, waiting for an answer. "Huh?"

"I said Will's competitiveness when it comes to video games can get dangerous," Tyson says.

That doesn't sound like a question. "…Okay?"

Josh gives me a knowing smirk, then glances down at his hand on my leg before slowly moving it up higher, making sure no one but me notices. Maybe his hand wouldn't be causing so much emotion if I was getting more like that when we're alone.

"What is your deal? You didn't hear any of that? I was standing right next to you!" Disbelief is written all over Tyson's face, almost like he's wondering if he should be concerned that I didn't hear him.

"Sorry. I was, uh…" I'm trying to figure out an excuse that doesn't *sound* like an excuse.

"Distracted?" Josh asks, the smirk still plastered on his face.

What an ass. He doesn't give me any type of sexual anything, and when he decides to do it for the first time, it's both teasing *and* in front of my family? On top of all that, he announces it…brings attention to it.

Tyson's eyes drop to Josh's hand on my leg, and then he quickly looks up and away. The hand itself is innocent enough. He's about mid-thigh, so nothing bad. But the way it makes me feel is the embarrassing part.

"Josh, I like you," Tyson laughs. "That was actually pretty funny."

"Please get Max here. Now." I glare at Suzie with a pleading look.

Josh kisses the top of my head before slinging his arm over my shoulder. "I'm sorry, happy birthday."

Chapter 43

I don't want to say it too loudly, because saying it out loud seems to change things. But life has been pretty okay this past month. Josh and I have been hanging out more away from work and have had some heavy make-out sessions, but he never takes it any further. I wonder why.

I guess we still aren't officially together, but I'm starting to wonder if maybe he's seeing someone else and that's why nothing more has happened. Honestly, I wouldn't mind. I love being around him, and my family is starting to really enjoy having him around as well. I like the nights when he has a beer or a drink during a movie. His kisses taste like booze and keep me craving him. He's literally becoming my new addiction.

Therapy is going well. Dr. Jewell is proud of where I'm headed, though she wasn't thrilled to hear about the way I "forgave" Dad. She's also worried about Ian. I'm not sure why; Ian knew what we were. She says I should have a heart-to-heart with him about my choices or whatever, but we laid down pretty specific rules. I mean, sure I should probably let him know why I've been gone. But I don't think it warrants a huge conversation.

Katie and I are still rocky. I'm wondering if the relationship is salvageable. Between how betrayed I feel, what I'm doing to her brother, and just being busy with Josh and work, I'm not really sure I have time to work on the relationship. She's been trying to talk to me, but I haven't had the energy. I told her I'd meet her today for lunch.

Dad decided to leave. I don't know where he went, and I don't care. He mumbled some shit about living in a house with a "faggot" and walked out with a backpack full of clothes. I give him a month until he's back again. Mom hasn't been back either. She's another person I don't care to see again. But she isn't usually gone this long.

Josh forced me to get my license, so now I can drive legally. Which in turn has mostly just made me Will and Tyson's bitch.

"What you thinkin' about?" Josh asks from under the car he's working on. His shirt has rolled up enough to see from the waistband of the jeans to his belly button.

"Fuck, Josh. At least try and keep yourself innocent around here." I force myself to look away and take a big drink out of my water bottle.

"What, this?" He pulls his shirt up even more and flexes. "This doin' it for you over there?" With an annoyingly sexy laugh, he pulls his shirt back down and slides out from under the car.

I swear, I'm drooling. I just want to lick him everywhere. I lick my lips to keep my smile at bay. "Yeah. Actually, it is. You better watch yourself."

That dumb smirk of his appears as he walks toward me and wraps his hand around the back of my neck before pulling me so that my ear is next to his mouth. "Or what?" he breathes. He pulls back and glances down at my lips before licking his own. "You're going to take me into the office and show me exactly what I'm doing to you?"

What? What is happening?! I can't help the immediate response that happens in my pants. He's kidding, right? Does he expect me to respond? What do I say? I don't know any sexy words.

His fingers wrap tightly around my wrist and he pushes my hand up under his shirt, onto his stomach where he's slightly sweaty from working, but also very, *very* fit. I almost melt. His back and stomach are two things I find quite attractive. Clearly, he knows it.

"What *am* I doing to you, Jace?" With my hand still on his stomach, Josh leans in and flicks his tongue over my lips, then kisses me once before pulling my bottom lip between his teeth. His hand has moved to the front of my neck, which is something I haven't experienced before, but *fuck*. The self-control I have to not strip him down right now is astonishing. He kisses me softly again before running his thumb down the lip he just bit. He pulls away, walking back to the car.

My breathing is as heavy as it would be if we'd just fucked. I can feel my heartbeat everywhere. The points of my skin where he touched are on fire. I'm planted on the ground, my head tilted and eyes shut, trying to bring myself down from whatever the hell this is.

"You okay?" He's pretending to be concerned, but even with my eyes shut, I know this is amusing to him.

I take a deep breath and then drop my head back, trying to allow myself to get even more air. "Yup." I blow out a breath and open my eyes. "I need a smoke."

Holy *shit*. I have no idea what he's doing with all the teasing and kissing and grinding, but nothing more. Never anything more. If I even try to push us further, he stops us and changes the subject. This better not be an edging kink, because I have no idea how much longer I can deal with this. Soon, people are going to start wondering why my right arm is so much bigger than my left. I take a long, deep drag of the cigarette when I hear him coming up behind me.

"I admit, that was rude," Josh says, his amusement still present.

I huff and look into his beautiful, wonderful eyes…will I ever get tired of looking at them? "Yes, I can tell you're very broken up about your behavior."

"Hey, you came in here all whiney and huffy. I was just trying to take your mind off it. Seriously, though, is everything okay?"

He did just do me dirty, so I guess now is the best time to ask. "What did you have to forgive your dad about?" Since I've had his tongue in my mouth more than a few times, I figure I can pull out the big questions.

Surprise flashes across his face. "Ah. I think you owe me a previously promised conversation before we hop into my daddy issues."

"Hmm." After flicking the ash from the cig, I realize what he's talking about. "The Ian conversation?"

"I usually don't give a shit, but he had some weird possessive energy about him that night."

"*He* did? What about you? 'Jace *loovveess* my music.' And the second you heard there was a girl in my bed, you were so concerned."

Smiling, he nudges me. "Alright, alright. Enough, I get it. But I was drunk. What's his excuse?" He drops to his elbows on the railing and looks at me. "He had hickeys on his neck that night. Was that from…" His fingers tap on the metal. I'm sure he's trying not to ask questions he doesn't want the answers to. "Were they from you?"

I rub my mouth with the side of my hand, trying to figure out how to answer. I don't want to lie, but I'm worried about the questions that'll follow. Do I really want to have this conversation right now? I'd really much rather take him to the office and stick his dick in my mouth.

"Uh…" Another deep breath. "Yeah, those were mine."

Quietly, he thinks, no trace of anger on his face. "So, you two were, like… fucking?"

My head tilts in thought. "Eh…we weren't fucking."

Why is the conversation so much less awkward with Josh? Usually, I get this horrible feeling in my stomach when I'm talking about my sex life with anyone—my siblings, Katie, even myself. "But we were doing other things."

"How often?" He shakes his head and rubs his eyes. "Oh, my God. Don't answer that. I'm sorry. I guess what I'm wondering is…the last time, I guess? I know we didn't put a label on anything or make any rules, so…"

"No, no, there's nothing." I turn so my body is facing him and place my hand on his hip, twisting his shirt between my fingers. "It's just you. The last time was the Thursday before that party. After that, it's always been just you. Well…just you and the things I do to myself because your ass…" I lean in to kiss him and slowly open my eyes again. "…likes to tease."

For the first time ever, a blush creeps up Josh's face, and he pulls his lips into his mouth as an embarrassed smile appears. "Jace Carter, are you jacking off to me?" He stands up tall and shoves his hands into his pockets. "I'm also not seeing anyone else, in case you were wondering. There's just one more thing I can't shake about the kid. He called you Zombie. What kind of pet name is that?"

My smile fades and I look down at the pavement. I'd almost forgotten that time in my life existed. I never thought I'd be at a point where I forgot how I felt and acted back then.

Apparently, I was quiet for too long, because Josh said, "I'm sorry. If it's really that bad, we don't have to talk about it."

"No, no, you've dealt with my moody ass for months now. I

think that's cause enough for you to know me a little better." I let out a nervous laugh. "I…I guess I'll start with the Zombie thing. It's exactly what it sounds like. I died and came back to life. Wow, when I put it that way, it sounds like some beautiful miracle. But that's not how it was at all…"

I haven't ever had to tell anyone the story outside of Dr. Jewell. What if he thinks differently of me after? He's the one person in my life who doesn't know that part of me. Who didn't look at me and immediately see a broken guy. I'm going to tell him, and he's going to leave me. I guess we aren't *official* official, but still.

I take a deep breath and keep going. "I attempted suicide a while back. I was found on time and taken to the hospital, but I guess I died a few times on the way there."

Josh takes a few steps to the bench outside the garage and sits down. "Oh, my God, I had no idea. When was that?"

I smile slightly. "Exactly a week before I showed up at your doorstep begging for a job."

"Oh, shit. I…I'm sorry to hear that. But what an insensitive dick, calling you Zombie and constantly reminding you of that day."

I shrug. "I deserved it. There's a lot you're going to learn about me that won't be pretty. And if you decide to leave me after you find out, that's okay."

"Leave you? Am I your *boyfriend*? Do I have 'leaving you' power?"

"I didn't mean it like that! I just…I meant…you know what I meant!"

Josh drops the smile and his face grows serious. "Jace."

"What?" I say stubbornly, which honestly comes out kind of silly.

"I'm not going to leave because of something you did or felt in the past. I'll be honest. It's scary knowing you did that, especially so recently. Of course it took me off guard. But I'm not going to judge you for it or leave because you have feelings."

"You don't even know the worst of it."

He caresses my cheek, his hand stopping under my chin and pulling my head toward him. "We'll get there. You don't know the worst of my worsts either. I'm not worried about it. You shouldn't be either." He pulls his rag out of his back pocket and wipes off his hands. "Besides, you learn a lot about people just by paying attention. I'm sure I already know more than you think." Absent-mindedly, he brings the rag to my chin and wipes at it. In the moment, I'm not even worried about what it was he accidentally put on me.

I feel my phone buzz in my pocket. I pull it out to find a text from Ian.

Ian: *Are you busy? I really need someone. Please, I'm not doing very good.*

I look at the car in the bay and put my phone back in my pocket. I'll text him back as soon as I wash my hands. I have to finish this car before I can get into a whole thing anyway.

"You think?" I ask.

Josh smirks. "I wasn't *that* drunk that night. And I wasn't lying when I told you I've learned not to give alcohol to people who hesitate." He kisses me before standing up and walking over to the wall of tools.

"I forgot about that," I huff, looking at the ground.

"Are you okay now? Do you think about drinking, or…dying, I guess?"

He thinks I was an alcoholic. Interesting. Do I correct him, or just answer the question? I'm not really sure I want to get into it right now, but his eyes are full of concern. I look down at my feet.

"Umm…I'm okay. I think about it sometimes. Not in the same

way, though. I don't know how to explain it. I'm just…I'm an angry person. Sometimes that anger overwhelms me to the point where I just want to break my teeth or claw out of myself. During those moments, I think about how easy it would be to calm myself down with something."

I almost forget he's standing there; it's like I'm talking to myself.

"Shit. I'm sorry. I didn't mean to get into that. I've been much better. Especially now that I'm not hiding myself. I've come a long way. You should have seen me a few months ago. Actually, you shouldn't have, but you know what I mean." When I look at him, he's still looking at me with concern and care. "Okay, enough about me. I told you *way* more than you asked for."

He gives me a gentle smile before replying. "He didn't like my life choices."

My jaw drops in disbelief "That's it? I expose myself as a piece of shit and you've been hiding that?"

He laughs and playfully tosses his rag at me. "There's more to it. He basically chased my mom away with his alcoholism and drug addiction. She left, and he fought really hard to keep me just to get back at her. After he got custody of me, he basically acted like I didn't exist and continuously told me it was my fault my mother left. He had me convinced I'd killed her at one point. I was making my own food, cleaning the house, putting myself to bed, and showering myself at the age of five or six. He didn't get me into school, so I was held back a lot and ended up having to do online school and graduated four years later than I should have. The first time I brought home a boy, he embarrassed the hell out of me for being gay. Then he put his hands on me for the first time ever. It never happened again, and he started working on himself after that. But some things you just don't forgive."

"Damn, that's a lot. I'm sorry. That's horrible. Have you seen your mom since?"

He shoves his hands into his pockets and shrugs. "I was too young to get any contact information. We moved around a lot after that."

My face drops into a frown.

"It's fine, though. You hungry? Let's get some food or something."

I'm grateful for the subject change, but I wish I could be better for him—be better at comforting and talking. I've been so caught up in myself that I don't know anything about him. I hate that we aren't so different.

Chapter 44

Another month with Josh flies by. It's September now, and the year is going by quickly. But you know what *isn't* going by quickly? My sexual frustration. We never get any time alone. And when we do? *Nothing.* He doesn't make any moves. We've had more than enough heated make-out sessions, but then he just stops. My hand is getting more action than ever before.

I rub my face and groan before sitting up in bed. If I have one more dream like that, I swear to God I'm going to jump Josh's bones. I sit in bed for a few more minutes to calm down before climbing out and entering the world. I'm as bad as a teenager, waking up with a boner almost every day. I just can't get rid of the images of Josh's hands grabbing my wrists and neck. The way he bites my lip... *Fuck.* Guess I'm taking a shower this morning.

I get up, turned on about the prospect of going to the bathroom. What? It's the closest thing to any Josh action I can get. But before I'm even able to get down to business, my phone rings and Ian's name lights up my screen.

"Shit," I whisper to myself before answering. "Ian, hey!"

"I'm outside."

What the hell? I turn and look out the window and see him standing in the driveway.

"Are you okay?" I ask, grabbing my shoes and walking to the front door.

"I don't know," he answers honestly. "I'm sorry for showing up. I know you've been avoiding me, and I'm assuming it's because of that Josh guy, and I have no business showing up here, but I just needed someone."

Shaking my head, I walk out of my house and hit the end button. "I'm not avoiding you," I call to him. "I'm sorry, I've been so busy working and I completely forgot to answer your texts. I'm a shit person, I'm so sorry." I waste no time throwing my arms around him and pulling him into a hug.

I know what it takes to practically beg for help, and Ian doesn't look good. I wish someone was around to just hold me when I need it. I didn't mean to ignore his texts the other week; I completely forgot after Josh and I got into that deep conversation.

"I relapsed," Ian whispers into my shoulder.

I furrow my brows and hold him tighter. "I'm so sorry. When?"

"The party. I made you go with me because I knew you'd go outside, and I was waiting for it. I didn't mean to use you like that. I just can't do this anymore." I feel him sob against me.

I push him back and look into his eyes. "Hey, I know it feels that way. I know it feels impossible, but it isn't. I'm so mad I didn't try harder before I ended up almost killing myself. Because once you get onto a path away from drugs, it gets easier. What happened to the rehab your aunt was sending you to?"

"I just didn't go. I have no motivation, and I didn't want her paying for something I knew I wasn't serious about. I don't have anything for me, Jace. I have no one, nowhere, no nothing. Nothing to be sober for."

"I got sober for the dad who beat the fuck out of me. I got sober for the family that didn't even know I was on drugs for seven years. I know how it feels to have nothing. But you have to create something. Because now…now I have me. And no matter how hard those cravings hit, no matter how badly I need to feel nothing and escape my brain, I don't let it win because I have me. You just have to get there."

He takes a deep breath. "You still have cravings?"

Nodding, I answer, "All the fucking time."

"See, I can't live like that. I'm just not made to endure things like that. Anyway, I just needed to get that off my chest. This isn't a depression thing, or anything to be worried about. It's just…not who I am anymore. I'm not me. The main thing I'm here for is to ask if you hate me. And are you and Josh together?"

"I don't hate you! And I don't know what's up with Josh and me."

It's truth. We still aren't official, and we haven't made any rules or anything. Plus, we haven't done anything physical, so I mean…how together could we *actually* be?

"So…you're free, then?"

The confusion must be clear on my face. "You came here to tell me you relapsed, cry…and now you want to fuck?" I laugh.

"I'm done for, Jace. I've already made my decision about what I'm doing. I just wanted to be honest with you. That doesn't mean I want to stop what we had, though."

Did I sound this insane when I was on drugs? What the hell is he talking about? I bring my hand up and rub my eyebrows. I don't know what's worse—this shitty situation he's putting me in or the fact that I'm considering it. Josh has been leaving me dry, and again, we don't have any ground rules set up. But since being with Josh, I don't have those types of feelings for Ian anymore. Most of all, I absolutely shouldn't be hanging around someone who's using drugs. It's too much of a liability. Plus, the confession between me and Josh about there not being any other people is much too meaningful to me.

"Ian, I can't. You know I can't. You're very…persuasive, and I don't want to be caught up in all of this. Have you told Katie? Maybe you should talk to her about it. Also, we didn't have anything. We messed around a few times, that's it."

"I don't believe that."

"You don't *believe* that? I think we both made it pretty clear that whatever was going on was just a distraction. And again, I don't think I should be hanging out with people who are using. I don't know if you know this, but it's been seven months for me. That's both a long time and *not* a long time. I'm not risking my sobriety for some cock."

Ian grabs my arm and pulls me into him, pressing his lips against mine. He is rough, and his mouth doesn't feel good. He's nipping and licking all while holding me tightly against him.

After the shock of having him attack me, I'm easily able to push him off. "Ian, what the *fuck*!" I wipe my mouth with the back of my hand and see blood. He fucking bit me.

"I love you, Jace!" he yells. "I've always loved you. And I can't stand you avoiding me and acting like I don't exist. I made you. I showed you that it's okay to be gay, and you took it and found someone else. You left me in the dust for some guy who doesn't even know you."

"*You* don't know me! You don't love me. And you sure as fuck didn't *make* me. I made me. I put myself through hell to recreate myself. You were my first blow job. That doesn't warrant you anything."

"Hey…I wasn't going to interrupt, but this sounds like it's getting heated." I turn and see Suzie stepping out of the back of a car that's parked in our driveway.

"What the hell are you doing?" I see Max in the backseat as well, buttoning up his shirt. "Oh, for God's sake." I drop my head back and turn back to Ian. "Ian, get the fuck out of here, and don't fucking come back. I'm not here to fix or fuck you anymore. I did my shit on my own, and I'm done cleaning up everyone else's. Get help, dude. Grow up." I turn around and stomp back into the house, wiping my bloody lip on my arm again. "Morning, Max," I mumble as I walk past the car, not bothering to look at him.

I pull out my phone and press Josh's name.

"Jace! I was just thinking about you." I hope this isn't another teasing concept of his, because I can hear the shower running in the background. Within seconds, the anger cools down and I smile.

"In the shower?" I say teasingly. "I thought I was the only one who embarrassingly admitted things like that."

"Yeah, well. When you're always out here teasing me, what am I supposed to do?" I can hear the smile in his voice.

"Sounds sexy. I know a few other things I could do to tease you, or…not tease you."

"Is borderline shower sex one of those things?" I can hear in his voice that he's also getting riled up by the conversation.

I shrug even though he can't see me. "It could be."

"Well, it's much better than the mental spank bank material I have of you."

I'm not sure why he decided to completely ruin the moment by saying spank bank, but he did.

"Wait, so were you really about to get in there and get all hot and heavy thinking about me?" I bite my lip, imagining what Josh might look like stroking himself.

"I might have been."

Suzie's voice carries down the hall. "*Please* close your door. You're much louder than you think you are."

Her voice is followed by Max's. "I'm rooting for you, man, get some."

I stand up, walk to my door, slam it shut, and plop back down onto my bed.

My breath comes out a with a little moan. "Why don't you come over instead?"

"Yeah? I can be over in 10."

My heart skips, and the heat of anger turns into a heat of lust. "That sounds good." It comes out low and raspy. If I don't get laid right now, I'm going to lose my mind.

*   *   *

Josh's tongue traces the inside of my mouth. His fingers twist into the belt loop of my pants to pull me closer to him.

"Are you sure your lip is okay? I don't want to hurt you," he whispers between gentle kisses, his hips grinding against mine. He asked about my lip the minute he saw it. I told him what happened, leaving out the parts about drugs. He seemed less than impressed with Ian but wasn't upset at me in any way. It was kind of nice, especially since I'd been freaking out about how he might react. I didn't know if I was a shit person for letting it happen.

"Josh, I'm fine. Less talking." I push him back against the couch and lean into him so almost all my weight is on him. I take his lip back into my mouth before thrusting my own tongue into his mouth. His hip lifts, causing some much-needed friction against my hardening cock. "Fuck…" I moan. It's been a long time. A long, torturous, agonizing time. And if this doesn't happen today… I'll probably keep living like normal. But I'll be much more of a dick than people already say I am.

"Jace, you can't make those noises while we're on your couch." His hip meets mine again, forcing that same noise out of me. I can feel he's just as hard as I am.

"Then let's go to my room." I kiss down his neck, determined to get at least some kind of action. He doesn't make any attempt to move, and I know this part all too well. The part where he pulls away and changes the subject. "Is there something wrong with me?" I ask.

"What? No, of course not! Why would you ask that?" He pulls up so I'm not fully laying on him.

"I don't know. We just never…get any further. I want to make sure I'm not doing or saying something wrong because *fuck*, Josh. You're giving me problems I didn't know I could have. I just want to jump on top of you all the time, but it seems like you aren't interested."

"I'm so sorry! Of course I'm interested. Very interested." He gestures to the bulge in his pants. "I'm just not sure of you, or what you want or how fast you want to move. I'm the first person you've brought home. I didn't want to move too fast or make you feel like I only wanted you for that. Now that I know you're up for it, let's go. Let's go right to your room, or the bathroom. Fuck, take 'em off right here." He grabs my ribs and squeezes, causing girlish laughs to come out of me.

"Okay! Okay, I get it! I'll try to be more open with my want for this." I push into him again, showing him exactly what it is I want.

"Gross!" Will grunts, slamming the front door closed. "Get a room, you two. You look like you just got tickets to Fuckfest. It's disgusting."

"Aww, Katie still not putting out?" Josh jokes.

"No! She isn't, and I can't even bring myself to find anyone else to take care of the frustration. I got it bad." He plops onto the chair next to us and kicks his legs up onto the coffee table.

"Well…good luck with that," Josh shoots back. "You need a good lay, you're crabby as hell these days."

Watching my brother and my…*guy*…bicker like this fills my heart. I never thought I'd find someone who would put up with me, let alone my family. He fits in so well, we need to protect this one with all our being. God, now I sound as dramatic as Will. But seriously, I'm so scared of the way he makes me feel. I know he has me falling, and I'm scared of what that means for the future. But right now, watching him fit in and being comfortable in my house, with me still laying on his lap, I need him to get to my room.

"Okay!" I shout, making them both jump. "If you don't mind, my man and I are going to find a room." I stand, grab Josh's hand, and practically drag him to my room.

"Excited?" he smirks.

"Be my boyfriend?" I ask once we're alone in my room.

Oh, shit, that came out of nowhere. Was that bad? Should I have said that? Oh, God. Why isn't he saying anything? Please say something.

"I don't know, you have a lot of baggage…" He pretends to think about it. "Of course. I thought you'd never ask." He pulls me in for a softer, more sensual kiss. I melt into him.

He wraps a hand around me as the other pulls at the button on my jeans. Oh, shit, this is happening, this is finally happening.

I push my hands up his shirt until he lifts his arms, allowing me to pull it over his head and off. Before I'm able to get my lips on his, he pulls away from me and grabs the bottom of my shirt. Habitually, I tense and grab his wrist.

"You don't have to take it off." He kisses my lips, then down to my collar bone. "But I'd love to put my hands and mouth all over you."

My grip on his wrist loosens. I can do this. "Okay, go ahead."

He grabs the hem of the shirt, avoiding touching my skin, and slowly pulls it off.

"Damn, Jace." He admires my body and runs his hand down my chest. "When did you get so buff?" He turns me around so I'm facing the mirror with him behind me. "You came to the shop that first day, skinny and scared. I remember the first day when you tried distracting me so you could change without me looking. Now look at you."

I haven't looked at myself in forever. I'm much bigger now. Both in fat and muscle. I'll never be like Tyson, but I have formed abs and that V-line above my jeans. My biceps are thick, and I fill out all my clothes to a point where I should probably buy new ones.

"You look amazing," Josh tells me. "You've come a long way from when you first showed up at the shop. I'm so fucking proud of you." He kisses my neck and trails his hand down my abs to the top of my jeans. Then he pushes his hand down into them and holds me in his palm.

I let out a gasp and bite my lip, my arms still to my side. Watching him run his hands all over me and seeing his hand in my pants is doing all sorts of things to me, making me feel ways I haven't felt before.

"I love the sounds that come out of your mouth." He pulls my earlobe between his teeth and squeezes me in my jeans. My cock twitches, causing a mischievous smile to form on his face. "One of the best parts of teasing you for so long is that I've had time to explore, and I already know what you like. Even if you don't."

All the dreams, all the fantasies I had about Josh never prepared me for the way I would react to the way he talks. He doesn't even have to touch me. I can get off from just the way he's talking to me.

I look back at the mirror, to his hand moving against me, and his mouth on my neck. I push my ass back against him and he pushes his hand against my cock harder, causing me to grind into him.

"Josh…" I breathe.

His fingers wrap around me, and he starts sliding up and down at a steadier pace. His other hand trails up my stomach to my chest, then lightly up my neck before he softly wraps it around the front of my throat.

"You like watching that? Watching me with my hand down your pants in the mirror? I bet you didn't know this," he says as his hand tightens slightly around my neck, "would turn you on so much. You were almost begging for me."

I can't speak; he's right. I wouldn't have guessed that would be my thing. And his hand in my jeans stroking my cock is an out-of-this-world feeling.

"Tell me, Carter." He pulls his hand out to undo my zipper before shoving the jeans down my legs, leaving me in just my boxers. "Exactly how experienced are you?"

I step out of my jeans and turn toward him, moving my mouth to his teasingly slow. I run my tongue against his lower lip then move to his collarbone, placing a rough kiss before licking up his neck to his ear.

"Not very," I admit, "but it seems like you're going to be a great teacher." My fingers slide up the outside of his leg, then to the front of him. He doesn't give me an instant to think before he's thrusting himself against my hand. His tongue flicks out against my upper lip before finding its home in my mouth. Once I feel him in my mouth, I suck on his tongue while wrapping my own against him, similar to how Ian taught me to do with a dick.

Josh pulls away from me, surprise in his eyes. "Shit. You're going to be the death of me." He smiles when I grab his pants and unbutton them. I yank them off and drop to my knees to help him out of them. Once they're off, he steps backward up until the backs of his knees hit my bed and he falls into it.

"I've only done this a handful of times," I say as I follow him to the bed and sit down beside him.

He pulls me toward him and places a reassuring kiss on my lips. "Well, let's see how well you've learned, shall we?"

His lips meet my cheek and he pulls me over, straddling him. His hands grab my ass and guide my hips as they grind against him. I feel his back muscles strain as he sits up higher to reach my mouth with his. He kisses me deeply, then flips us over so he's hovering over me. Rough sucking and kissing trails down my chest. The fears of having my body seen leaving with every hungry touch of his mouth. He takes his time on my stomach, pressing soft kisses across the top of my waistband.

With Ian, it was always right to the point, never just being with each other and enjoying the moment. If Josh decided right now he didn't want to do anything else and just wanted to kiss me all over, I wouldn't be upset.

"Your body is so perfect," he says. "Your chest." Three kisses on each side and a playful flick of his tongue on my nipple causes a feeling to shoot down from my stomach to my dick, causing it to twitch against his leg. "Your stomach."

His tongue trails down the center of my muscle. Looking down and watching him, I see it now. I have abs; abs that you can see. And my body looks good. I don't know if it's my body or seeing my body as Josh worships me, but either way, I'm not the frail, skinny boy I was seven months ago. And unlike Ian, Josh did create this for me.

"But this…this is my favorite part," he says pulls my boxers down just to the very top of my cock, which is now screaming to get out. Below my belly button, his tongue traces the top of the waistband first to my right hip, kissing on the inside of the bone, then swirling his tongue around the area, letting it slip into my boxers, then trailing it all the way to the other side, doing the same.

I moan again and arch my back, pushing up into him. "That feels so good."

Leaving me dry, he leaves the lower half of me and follows the same path back up to my neck. He places a kiss right under my ear, then on my lips. As he's kissing me, I feel my boxers slip past my hips, and his hand finds its place wrapped around me.

I groan into his mouth, wrap a hand into his hair, and find the other a home on his ribs. His skin against mine is such a soothing and comforting feeling. The smell of him engulfs me, and the way our stomachs and chests move against each other makes me squirm. I take my hand off his ribs and build up the courage to push it into the front of his pants.

"God fuck, Jace. Why haven't we been doing this the past few months?" His hips buck, thrusting into my hand. His tongue finds its way back into my mouth and swirls around mine once more. The feel of him all over me is captivating. I'm not sure I'll ever be able to think of anything else.

He kisses down my jaw and neck to my chest, where he leaves a few rough kisses before trailing back down my stomach to the top of my boxers. His hands slide up my thighs and loop under the waistband, pulling them down quickly and taking me into his mouth without a second thought.

A gasp escapes me, and I sit up onto my elbows to look down at him. "Holy shit." He is perfect. The way he looks right now…the way he's making me feel. I guess it's true that this type of stuff is so much better when there are feelings involved. His mouth is moving against me while his hands explore my body. Truly, he's everywhere, all over me, even his scent is filling my room. Singlehandedly, Josh is recreating the safe space I lost a while ago.

My hand travels up into his hair, tangling my fingers into it and guiding him to the pace that feels the best. I can't help my heavy pants or the way my tongue continues wetting my lips because I just want to taste him. I pick up the speed, wrapping my hands more tightly into his hair. I can hear and feel him moaning now. I glance down farther and see he's stroking himself as well.

This is the most perfect view. I don't think I've ever been so turned on. I have no idea how I didn't come just from him kissing my stomach. My head drops back, and a groan that's a bit louder pushes through me just as I push farther into him and release myself into his mouth.

"Fuck, Josh," I pant, covering my eyes with my arm. His mouth doesn't move off me until he's sure he's gotten every drop.

He sits up, still stroking himself but hovering over my stomach. I lock eyes with his hand and that perfect cock. I want my mouth on it, on him, but the way his arms flex as he moves in and out of his hand has me unmoving. Every fantasy I had from the shop while watching his arms move has nothing on what's happening now. Our eyes meet, and in that moment, he bites his lip and tenses up, meeting his own release on my stomach.

"Fuck," he breathes. "That would have been so much better if you were the one who finished me off. But watching you watch me was a very close second." He drops his head back and rolls onto his back beside me.

"It was just as good for me to watch," I say. "I had no clue that would be so…*fuck*. That was hot as fuck."

We're both out of breath, chests heaving and naked on my bed. He turns his head to face me and kisses my nose. "Now that we've opened that gate, I'm not sure I'm going to get enough of you."

His next kiss is against my lips before he stands up. "Am I okay to shower?"

"Oh, yeah! Yes, of course. Help yourself. I'd get up, but I'm sure you've killed me." My arms and thighs are throbbing from holding myself up over him. "Maybe I'll meet you in there." I wink.

"Aww, my sweet little bottom." He bends down and kisses me again before pulling his pants up and wiping my stomach with a handful of tissues from my desk.

"Not a bottom," I state.

"We'll see about that." He winks and leaves my room.

After our shower together, I go into the kitchen in my shorts to get us some water. Everyone is gone, so I don't bother putting on my shirt. I still can't believe that just happened. It was so much better than I ever could have imagined. All the pent-up teasing and waiting was kind of worth it. That was the best fucking orgasm I've ever had. Even just thinking about it has my dick growing.

"Jace!! My man!" Max slaps me on the back as he walks into the kitchen.

"Umm. You're supposed to be gone." I look over my shoulder and see him opening the fridge.

He shakes his head. "No, dude, we decided to stay here and watch a movie."

"Ah. Okay, then." I turn, ready to make my escape, when Suzie walks into the kitchen.

"Holy shit, Jace. What is it with you and your vampire kinks?! Jesus Christ. Put a shirt on, I don't even want to know where those lead."

It's exactly what I was trying to avoid. While Josh was making a very well-made point about how amazing my body is, he was leaving marks all over. I mean *all over.* There are at least three on each side of my chest, then a line of them down my stomach, and even some scattered across the lower half of my stomach.

When I asked him about it in the shower, he told me he did it so that for the next few days, whenever I looked in the mirror, I wouldn't hate what I saw. Instead, I'd remember the way he worshipped every part of me. Honestly, so far, it's worked fantastically. When I see those marks all over me, I just remember how it felt to look down and see him devouring my body.

Chapter 45

"**D**o you really think you're ready to stop sessions?" Dr. Jewell asks.

"I mean…yeah?" I didn't expect her to question me about it. Am I wrong? I feel pretty okay and in control of things. I've gained a lot of tools and thought processes from her that I use every day.

"Jace, this is how people are. They feel okay, and they stop talking and get bad again. I'd love to continue to see you. What if we did once a week, or even every other week?"

"You don't think I'm ready?" I ask, leaning forward.

"I don't think anyone is ever ready. I'd refer the world's most mentally healthy person to see a therapist as well. It helps to have someone to talk to, about anything. I'd hate for something to happen and you not have anywhere to go. The highs are really high, and you're doing some great stuff right now! But those lows are going to be low, and it's still so early, so soon from the hospital visit. Once you leave and it's on paper, the state can refuse to pay for future sessions if you decide you want to come back."

With a nod, I reply, "Alright. Let's do once a week for now."

"Sounds good. I'm proud of where you are. I haven't seen any of those self-destructive tendencies, and it looks like you've learned to stand up for yourself, which is exactly what I want to see. Do you have anything else you want to talk about today?"

"Umm…yeah." I think about the last time Ian came by. "Ian relapsed. He came to my house acting really weird and told me he'd given up on himself and made his own decisions. Then he tried to sleep with me." I pause for a moment. "He told me that he loved me, and that he had always loved me, and it's kind of been on replay in my head."

"Why do you think that's bothering you so much?" she asks, adjusting her glasses.

"I don't know. Because I went through so much. I did *everything* on my own. Not even just after the drugs. Before drugs, while on drugs, after drugs, through the suicide, the recovery, and the rebuilding. I didn't have friends or people around me who got it. His sister was who was there for me. I just… He has so much. He has people around him, and he's choosing to fuck himself over again. It's frustrating to know how hard I worked to get where I am now, and now he feels like he has some ownership over me? That, and the fact that he came to my house high, told me he didn't care. Then he tried to sleep with me. It felt like he was trying to drag me back down with him."

"Even though you don't understand, his struggles are still struggles," Dr. Jewell says. "Even if they seem smaller than yours. Maybe his home life isn't the way you imagine it is. Ian is an adult, and he's allowed to make his own choices. How did you handle him coming over?'

"It made me so mad. I told him to fuck off and not to come back."

Dr. Jewell tilts her head as if to say, "Told you. You still need me."

"But I didn't hit him," I go on, "even though I really wanted to. I just turned around and went inside. Josh came over later that day, and it was like the anger immediately disappeared."

"I'm glad Josh was able to help. Without him around, what would you have done to help yourself?"

Why does that matter? He was there, he calmed me down, and I got over it. I don't know what I would have done if it hadn't been for him. I probably would have gotten pissed and taken it out on one of my brothers. "I'm not sure."

We talk for a while longer before the session ends and I leave for the shop. I'm still pissed at Ian, and I don't give a shit about what Dr. Jewell says. He knew what he was doing, and I know for a fact he assumed it would end in us both getting high and getting off.

I open the shop door and find Josh at the desk. "Slow day today," he says, watching whatever he's watching on the computer screen. "We don't have any drop offs until around seven."

"Can I tell you every shitty thing I've done this year?" I ask. "Just so I can get it out there and stop worrying about it? I'm always so on edge that you're going to find something out and leave me for it or hold it against me."

"Oh, wow. I suppose therapy went well today. You can tell me whatever you want, but you don't have to. I'm not going to leave you or hold anything against you." He pauses the show he's watching and leans forward on the desk.

I don't wait for anything else; I just start talking. I tell him everything: the drugs, detox, how close Katie and I got, my screaming matches with Will and Tyson, my fights with Dad, the drug test Tyson made me take, how angry I feel all the time. I even tell him about the first time I tried drugs and when Dad first started beating on me. By the time I'm done, tears are falling down my face. Now he knows everything.

"I just can't get over why everyone is out to get me. I can never do anything right, and I don't want to fuck us up because of it.

Everyone has so many expectations from me. They all want me to be something I'm not, or someone else, or fuck…I don't know. I'm sorry, I'm on a roll now. I just don't know what to do anymore, and I feel like I'm fucking drowning. The Ian thing just set it off because if I'd allowed him in that day, do you know how easy it would have been for him to turn me into someone completely different from who I am now?" I take a deep breath. "It would have been so easy for him to convince me that 'it's just one pill' or 'just this one time.' And all because he told me he loved me. He knew that. He told me that to break my guard."

Josh stands and practically runs to me to pull me into a tight hug. "You are not weak, Jace. You are not weak at all, and you didn't let him in that day. Thank you for telling me all of that. I can't say I'm not shocked. I wouldn't have guessed you were the type to have so many anger problems. I mean, yeah, you're angry, but I didn't know it got that bad. I'm so sorry. You've been through so much. I had no idea. How are you still you?" He pulls away and places his hands on the sides of my face. "How are you still my sweet, shy little Jace after seeing so much ugly in the world?"

The sincerity in his eyes pools into me. Josh doesn't see me as a bad person, just as me. He sees me as Jace, even after everything I told him. Between the realization and his beautiful eyes looking into mine, I feel grounded. My heartbeat slows, the shaking in my hands stops, and I can almost feel the anger and anxiety flow out of me.

"Josh…you." I lift my head up and rest my forehead on his. "You helped save me before you even knew me. I don't know where I'd be right now if I wasn't busy running from school to work every day because I was so excited to be next to you." I see him open his mouth to speak so I quickly cut him off. "I swear to God, if you're about to mention anything about dry heaving, I take back everything I just said."

His smile grows, but he says nothing.

"There's been so much growth within me. But I feel more lost than ever. I've gained myself, but in that, I lost so much. I managed to push Katie away, and Ian. I know you aren't the biggest fan of his, but he was there for years, and we got close over the last half year. I just…I can't help but feel like I'm the reason they both aren't with me anymore."

"I could do without Ian," Josh says. "But if it means that much to you, try talking to him. But know that when you grow, so does the world around you. Sometimes you grow out of your friends to make room for the things that are in your path. Ian won't give up the drugs, and you did. Maybe it's the world paving you a new path, and unfortunately, he isn't in it. It sucks, but you have to make sure you're allowing yourself to change. Get comfortable with being un-comfortable."

*   *   *

"Reading smut?" Tyson asks as he sits beside me on the couch.

"Always." I don't look up from my book. I finally got a moment to get into it, and of course someone has to come and disturb me.

"It's weird to see you here alone. Talk to Katie lately?"

"Yeah." I close my book. Obviously, I'm not going to be read-ing right now. "We had lunch a few days ago. It was nice. A little weird, though. I don't think we're in a great space still." Which is inconvenient because I'd love to tell her about how big of a dick her brother is. But I won't stick my head in other people's shit anymore. "I feel like were different now that I'm with Josh and she's doing whatever with Will. It's like were each other's back-ground characters all of a sudden."

"I get that. Well, keep trying. You guys were great together. She helped you out through so much shit that we couldn't. Don't push her out just because she ratted on you about Ian."

It's not just that. "Yeah, I know." I wish he could understand. I'm not mad that she told them about my conversation with Ian. I'm mad that she was the first person I had ever trusted, someone I wasn't forced to live with, and without a second thought, she turned on me.

My phone rings on the coffee table. Ian's name lights up the screen. I ignore it.

"Doing anything fun tonight?" Tyson asks.

"Besides dodging Ian's calls? Nope. Josh has a thing, but he'll be here in a few hours. I wanted to stay home and hang out with everyone, but no one's here. Now, I'd love to read my book."

Tyson smiles and pats my leg. "Good ol' Jacey-poo is back." My phone rings again, and he looks at it. This *has* to be the sixth time Ian's called me today. "Is he alright?"

I shrug. "Don't really give a shit." I open my book back up.

"Alright…"

That's not true. Of course I care. He was my friend. I just still can't get over how he came at me like that. And honestly, I'm pissed he relapsed. I get it, but the way he told me was kind of fucked. If we tried, we could have been really good friends, I think. With or without the benefits. But I'm going to need time before I talk to him again.

Tyson finally leaves me alone to read my non-smutty book. A few hours later, Josh walks in and plops on the couch without even a "hello."

"Come to my house with me," he says.

I furrow my brows and lean back. "What, now?"

"Yeah. I have a few friends there. I want you to meet them."

I've never been to Josh's house. I've been outside it, and I know he rents a house with two other people, but we don't ever go over there. It's for my benefit, of course. I'm not sure how ready I am to be openly gay. I know his roommates and friends don't give a shit, but it's just another piece of control I give up when I allow everyone to know that part of me. We've been talking about it a bit. He brought it up one day when we were in public and his hand brushed against mine. I guess I tensed up and pulled it away. But when we got back to the car, he brought it up and asked me how much I was comfortable with, or what my expectations were.

The worst part was that I had no idea. I didn't know what I wanted, or how much I wanted to put out there to strangers. But I told him I'd be willing to explore and see what felt comfortable. I said I didn't give a shit what people thought and agreed to start taking it further in public, which in turn made us feel like a real couple. It's always felt real to me, but having it out there makes me feel that other people take us seriously as a couple too.

"Okay."

His eyebrows raise. "Okay? Alright! Let's go." He grabs my hand and pulls me up and toward the door.

Meeting his friends, huh? I forgot about that part of a relationship. Luckily, I don't have any friends for him to meet. I know these are the friends who were at the party the first night Josh and I expressed ourselves. But I haven't met them, not even in passing.

Chapter 46

"So, Jace, what do you do for fun?"

There are four people here. Two roommates, and two friends. The roommates are sitting on the floor and leaning against the wall. A guy and a girl, Levi and Presley, I think. The other two friends are also a guy and a girl, Dustin and…Linda, maybe? Lacey? I don't remember. So far, I'm not a huge fan of that one.

I look at Levi trying to figure out what he expects me to say but also because I don't really do anything (besides Josh) for fun. "Uh…I read, I guess, and I like the gym?"

Presley sits up excitedly. "What do you read?! I read! Do you read good books? Oh, my God, Josh, if he reads good books, this is the best person you could have brought home."

"Well, damn, let him answer," Dustin says. "Also, please remember he's Josh's boyfriend. Not someone you can just invite to your bed because you find out you have something in common."

"Presley's kind of a hoe, flavor of the day type of person," Levi adds, looking at me like I really give a crap about what Presley does.

She darts her eyes at him then turns back toward me, still waiting for an answer. I don't get self-conscious about many things, but this…this is such an odd question. You get judged pretty roughly if you answer this question wrong.

"He reads a lot of romance fantasy stuff. You know, like beast porn, books about fairies or something, and pirates," Josh casually throws out there.

Confusion fills my face, but Presley's brown eyes light up. "We're going to be great friends!"

"Okay, I don't think I've read anything with pirates in it," I say. "But the rest… Yeah, I guess."

"That's all you do for fun?" maybe-Linda says with a scoff. "I like to hike, bike, swim, sing, and write."

Everyone gives her the same annoyed look. If they don't enjoy her, why is she part of the group?

I nod my head and smile at her. "Good for you. That explains why you're sitting here with a bunch of college kids playing video games on a Saturday."

"*Daaammmmnn*. Jace brings some heat!" Levi stands up and high-fives me. If he thinks that's "heat," he'd die if he witnessed an argument between me and my brothers. "You can come here any time. Usually, these fuckheads aren't here" He leans forward, studying my face. "You go to my school, right?"

I don't make a huge impact on anyone at that school, so the only reason anyone would notice me would be the drugs, Ian, or the whole suicide thing. Great. "Yeah, I did. I think I'm a year or two behind you." I've seen him before. He's one of the guys Katie accused me of checking out when we first became friends.

"Right. Carter, isn't it? Will's in one of my classes."

He's going to leave out the real reason he knows me? Looking at him, I see a slightly apologetic smile. He didn't want to bring up all the crap with these people here—but I'm sure if he catches me here without them around, he'll have no problem bringing it up.

After nodding in appreciation for not embarrassing me, I decide to keep the subject on Will. "Yup. That would be my brother."

"Funny guy."

That's usually people's opinion of Will. "He's funny" or "he's cute."

Josh and I are on the floor leaning against the couch. It seems normal for them to have furniture but not use it. Not that I'm complaining. I've always been a floor type of guy.

Once Josh feels like I'm comfortable here, he lies on his stomach with his head in my lap and his arm around my waist. My heart is practically not beating…or beating too much. I don't know. But this is the cutest fucking thing I've ever seen. Forgetting that everyone is here, I push my hands through his hair, earning myself a rewarding moan.

"So how long have you two been together?" Dustin asks. "How did you meet?"

The way Josh looks right now tells me the question is all mine to answer. "Umm…it's been two months together now, I think. I showed up to the shop begging for a job."

"Two months?" Lucy asks. I'm sure her name starts with an L… "That's not what Josh said."

"No, no. You're confused. They weren't together, but Josh was already crushing hard. You just think it's been longer than two months because we've been hearing about him forever," Dustin says after thinking about it for a moment.

I smile and look down at Josh still in my lap, but now his eyes are wide open. Cringing, he yells, "Hey, shut up!"

"Say, what month *did* we learn about Jace?" Presley teases.

"Ah, I know!" Levi says, raising his hand.

"Seriously, shut up." Josh sits up and lunges at Levi, pushing him over.

I do like these friends; they're funny and easy to get along with. I also like seeing who Josh is around them. He's different, but not in a bad way like Ian was. I also like that he isn't afraid to be affectionate toward me with them around. He really is the most perfect person.

"Something about the second day he came in?" Dustin says. "No…not that. Was it his first oil change, maybe? 'He was all dirty and clueless and listened to everything I said.' "

That familiar heat runs up my neck to my face. He was already talking about me then? Why do I like that so goddamn much? I'm so glad it wasn't completely one-sided.

"Josh has a control kink. So you listening to him and following his rules right away really turned him on," Larissa says, casually picking at her nails.

A control kink? I think back to every time he's told me what to do or grabbed my wrists, or my neck. I thought I was the one who had a control kink… Maybe that's why he called me a bottom. What if he wasn't joking about that? But mostly, how does she know about his kinks?

"Okay! Okay, we are done with all of that. Jace, do you want to go to my room? I just wanted you to meet everyone, not get emotional trauma from them." He laughs, then grabs my hand and stands up.

"It was nice meeting…most of you." I'm not going to lie.

Levi grins and claps my shoulder. "You too. I hope to see you around more. Also, Dustin is right, it was your first oil change."

After shoving Levi's face back, Josh leads me to his room. It's much bigger than mine. Cleaner and brighter. "I'm so sorry about that. I should have introduced you to them one at a time. I just figured we could get it out of the way." The door closes behind him, and he moves to the loveseat on the other side of the room.

"No, it's fine, I liked them. You just…you know me. I'm not much for conversation." I follow him to the couch and sit next to him. "What was that redhead's name?"

"Lexa. She isn't really my friend. I think she and Dustin are doing it or something. So wherever he goes, so does she."

I nod in understanding. "What is your sexuality?" I ask. I don't mean to. I'm just worried there was something between him and her. I know there must be better ways to ask, but I just…I want to know.

He pushes his hand through my hair and swiftly leans in to kiss me. "I like men. Just men. I've never been with a woman and don't want to try it. You?"

I tap my leg and chew on my cheek before answering. "I'm the same, but… I did lose my virginity to a girl. Worst time of my life, so I won't be trying that again."

Absentmindedly, he plays with my fingers. "I have been meaning to ask since you mentioned it the other day. You think you're a top?" The way he asks is so casual. Like he assumes I was wrong, or that I was kidding.

"I *am* a top."

"Hmm…" His hands drop from mine into his lap. "Are you sure? I mean…you haven't tried anything, right?"

"I'm *pretty* sure." Sometimes there are just things you know, things you're sure of. This is one of them. He should know it's one of the things you're sure of.

He pulls me closer and presses me back onto the loveseat, hovering over me. "If you're so sure, why do you always end up under me when we're making out?"

He pushes his tongue into my mouth before connecting our lips. The way his teeth graze my lip has me already pushing up into him. He grabs my wrists and pins them above my head with one hand, squeezing slightly, causing my mouth to fall open with a groan.

"You like that, don't you? I saw the way you reacted that day at the shop when I grabbed your wrist. I almost took you back to the office then and there." His grip tightens even more, his hips grinding into mine. "You can't tell me this doesn't excite you." With my hands still pinned above my head, he presses his other hand against my hip as his body moves rhythmically against me.

Okay, it's hot. Really fucking hot. Having my hands pinned and watching him rock himself into me. The only thing that could possibly make it better would be if his other hand was around my neck and his shirt was off. But if I say yes, that I do like it, he'll assume I just gave him the power. I'm competitive, and I'm not backing down from this. Besides, I know I'm a top. I said so in my goodbye note.

"You can bite your tongue all you want. I can feel how much you like this." With a thrust that's rougher than the last few, he pushes against me harder. Without my consent, another moan mixes in with my breathing.

He kisses me again and his hand wraps around my neck, squeezing the sides tightly. He sits up over me and looks into my eyes. "On your knees."

Uh…fuck. Seriously, anything for him. Without thinking, I drop to my knees on the floor in front of him, already tugging at his pants. He sits down on the loveseat with me between his legs and grabs my chin between his thumb and forefinger.

"You may claim to be a top, Jace." It comes out as a whisper, the most sensual, heavenly whisper I've ever heard, and I'm ready to just melt for him. "But you will *always* submit for me."

There's a dark look in his eyes. Those icy-blue eyes have never looked so stormy. Unfortunately, the way my body reacts and my mouth pools with saliva, I think he's right. Fuck me. He's going to destroy me.

Chapter 47

The months have been amazing. Josh has been wonderful, and life… It hasn't been too bad. I've been in such a constant loop of Josh, gym, and work that I don't have time to think of other things like Dad, life, or drugs. Work has been busy, so the gym trips have slowed down somewhat, which is fine. Josh and I find ways to work out between cars in the office, if you catch my drift. Both of us are still fighting for the "top" position, so nothing big has happened between us, but I'm so close to giving in just so I can have that with him.

It's been quiet at home. Max is over a lot, but the boys are out quite a bit. I think both have picked up extra shifts now that school is over, and Tyson isn't worried about me dying every second of the day.

I've still been dodging Ian's calls. I know I need to talk to him, and I want to. I want to let him know I'm still here if he needs me, but I'm not going to be the guy he can go to for a quick nut.

Max and I have been sitting on the couch for the last two hours going through all the music in my Josh playlist. He's been adding more, and now that we're actually getting at each other, the songs have escalated, and some really get you going.

"Damn…this one is really good," Max says, clicking on a song called "Bad Things" by Nation Haven. He's made me listen to it twenty times, and honestly, it is really fucking good.

My phone rings with Katie's name, but I quickly click the end button and keep scrolling through the music.

"She's called you a lot," Max says. "Do you think you should answer?"

I rub my face and drop my phone into my lap. "No." He looks at me as though he's waiting for me to change my answer. "What? I don't have anything to say to her, or Ian right now. And if she's calling me, it's because she either wants to argue with me about us or Ian."

"Alright, man. Sorry, she's called a lot. It's just a little weird."

The past few times she's called have felt different, like I have a pit in my stomach. I admit, it is a little weird. But things have been going good, life hasn't been shitty, and I don't want to know if she has some kind of bad news. But he's right. I should probably talk to her.

"Fuck. Thanks, Max." I stand up, already dialing Katie's number.

"Not that you fucking care," she tells me when she answers, "but Ian's dead. I thought you would want to know, though now I know I should have left it alone."

My heart drops, along with the world. Everything has been moving so fast, moving forward at lightning speed, and now it's come to a screeching halt. Everything around me fades out as her words repeat in my head. *Ian's dead.* He can't be, she has to be fucking with me. Whatever this is, it's a sick fucking joke.

With a tear falling down my face, I cover my mouth. "No he isn't."

"Fuck you, Jace. Go fuck yourself. If it wasn't for you… Fuck you!"

The line dies, but I can't remove the phone from my ear.

How could he be dead? He isn't dead. It's Ian, my longest

friend. The outgoing, funny, annoying blond boy who never seemed to leave me alone. He isn't…he isn't gone.

I can't think or talk. I drop the phone on the floor and run to their house. I get there and push the door open, stopping when I see Katie on the stairs with her head in her hands.

She looks at me with anger in her eyes. "Get the fuck out."

The hostility throws me off, but I'm more worried about why she thinks Ian is dead, or where he is, or if she's okay. Then I see it. Ian's phone is in her hands.

"Katie…"

"*NO!*" she yells. "You like yelling and fighting? Don't get it enough at home, so you had to come here? Get the fuck out. Now, Jace." Before I have a chance to speak, she stands up and slams her fists against my chest. "You knew. You fucking *knew*, and you didn't do anything, didn't even tell me. He called you and texted you asking for help. You ignored him! You're so fucking full of yourself, Jace. I don't want to see you. You could have stopped this, you could have gotten him help."

She has every right to hate me. I did know; I did ignore him. "What does my home life have to do with anything? I'm here. I'm here to help." I shake my head, still not believing Ian's gone.

"I don't want your help. There's nothing you can do."

"….What happened?"

She sighs. "They found him in a bedroom at a party. Overdose." She lifts his phone and shows me the screen. "He called you. He called you before it happened, but you're so stuck in your little world of punishing anyone who isn't as good as you are now. You are *not* better than everyone else, quit fucking acting like it. What…we weren't good enough for you, so you had to go off and find yourself a new man? Someone who doesn't know the fucked-up you, am I right? He probably has no clue who you really are.

My brother wasn't good enough for you, so you left him behind like you did me. If you're so worried about becoming a new you, do me and your family a favor and leave. Disappear like your mom and dad do. You guys are always so much happier when they're gone, so I'm sure you know how much it would help everyone around you if you did the same."

My head falls to the side. I feel the anger creep in, more than I ever have before. I can't figure out if I'm supposed to be upset about Ian or pissed about whatever the hell it is that's coming out of Katie's mouth. How the fuck is this my fault? How is this all of a sudden turned on me? I think about leaving everyone every day. How everyone's lives would be so much better if I just went away. I've been saving my money to do it. Fuck, I'm going to start saying some shit that's going to hurt her. I can't do that. I can't be that guy right now. But my mouth has other ideas.

"I'm glad to know you cared enough to help a friend through detox but not your own brother. If anything, it was a joint effort between you and me to cause this." I inhale slowly. "Call Will if you need anything," I say through my teeth as I turn around and leave.

I get to my front yard and take three deep breaths. I want to punch something; I want to punch something so bad. He's gone. Ian's gone, and it's my fault. I'm a shit person, and Katie had no problem laying that out there.

I turn around and punch Will's car, right on the trunk. "Oww! FUCK!" I'm so mad and confused that I hardly notice Josh's car pulling up to the house.

I never got to talk to Ian, to apologize for being such a dick. I left him. I fucking ghosted him at a time I knew he needed me most. For what? To get my dick sucked by someone new? The tears flow down my face as memories of Ian pop into my head.

The night in the laundry room, the morning after when he winked at me about the hickeys, the way he taught me how to feel good… All the talks in the hallway at school. All of it is fucking gone. I called him for mental support, and he picked up and talked me through it like he'd done it his whole life. Yet he calls me twenty times and I'm nowhere to be found.

He was at a party? He knew he'd accidentally overdosed and called me? Why didn't call a fucking paramedic? Fuck, Ian… I died, though. I died and they got me back. They can get him back too.

The tears fall faster and harder along with the anger building right back up. I kick the tire and get ready to swing again, but someone stops me.

"Woah, woah, woah!" Will says. "What the hell did my car do to you? Easy, I just had the rolo replaced!" He grabs my arm and turns me toward him. "Jace, you're crying. Are you okay?" He pulls my fist down and pins it to my side.

I almost punch him in the face. Not because he did anything, but because I don't know what to do. My anger is overflowing and I can't stop myself. I have no idea how to manage it, I have no escape right now. I just…want to explode. I want to find Ian and hug him, tell him I'm sorry and that I don't hate him. I want to rip out my own hair. All the noise I've left behind, the sounds in my head and the buzzing. That fucking buzzing, all of it rising back up to my head until finally I let out a loud sob and fall to the ground, taking Will with me.

"Ian's dead," I whisper before falling into his shoulder.

"Oh, my God. Are you okay? Is Katie okay?" He wraps his arm around my waist and squeezes. "Is he really gone? Oh, my God…"

Tyson walks up slowly, probably gauging how mad I am given my previous track record. I see Josh right behind him, running up to me.

"Hey…are you okay?" Josh says. "I saw you punch the car…" I can tell he's worried, maybe even scared. Fuck. My own boyfriend is scared of me.

I really am a shit person. Tyson's literally walking on eggshells right now, my own boyfriend is scared of me, and my friend… Ian's *dead*. All of it, everything, is my fault. I caused this. Dr. Jewell was wrong about me having self-destructive tendencies. Turns out I destroy everyone and everything around me.

I hear Will tell them about Ian, and then Josh takes my arm, pulling me into him.

"You're scared of me," I say. "Everyone hates me. I'm the reason Ian's dead and why Suzie is always gone. I even drove my dad to fucking abuse us and leave the house, and I told my mom to get out and never come back. I've said some of the worst things to Tyson and Will, and I'm such a piece of shit. I don't know what I'm doing. I can't stand it anymore."

"No one is scared of you," Josh insists. "I saw the way you were feeling and I was worried *about* you. Not scared of you. You did *not* kill Ian. Don't think like that, please. There's nothing you could have done."

I look up and meet his eyes. Always so understanding and forgiving. I don't deserve him. If anything, I'm just tearing him down along with everyone else in my life, and he doesn't deserve that.

"What does that mean, you can't stand it anymore?" Tyson says. "You've been doing amazing. Please don't let this drag you back, it wasn't your fault. There's no possible way you could have caused that. You aren't a piece of shit."

He says that, but all I keep imagining is the shit I've done to people since coming back from the dead. I always thought everyone was out to get me, that I was an inconvenience in everyone's lives, but it turns out I'm actually just a dick. No one is out to get me; I do this shit to myself. I'm out to get everyone, not the other way around. Katie was right. I do think I'm better than everyone. And why? Because I *stopped* doing drugs? More sobs fall from me and I clench onto Josh's shirt, holding on like if I don't, he might disappear.

"I've never seen him like this…" Tyson whispers to Josh. "Once, I guess. But it was different."

"I'm going to call Katie," Will says and disappears into the house, leaving me with Tys and Josh.

"I've never *felt* like this," I say. "I feel like I want to call him. I want to be there for him, but I'm too late. I hate myself. Not only for this, but for everything. I've been such a prick. I should have just fucking died that day. Everything would be normal by now, no one would be in this position, and…it's too much. It's too much, I can't do it." I look at Josh. His face falls, and sadness fills his eyes. "What do I do?"

Tyson gets up and walks away, probably trying to hold himself together. I know how scared this makes him, but I can't help it.

"I am so sorry," Josh says. "I don't know…I don't think you're in a place to listen to advice. Let us just be here for you. You're wonderful, you're not a piece of shit, and you deserve to live." He pulls me into his chest and kisses the top of my head, his hand in my hair.

Nodding, I drop my head and take a few deep breaths. I thought I was doing so well. I thought I was creating a new me who's stronger and better, but I don't know who I am. How do you re-build yourself as a 22-year-old when you stopped living at the age of 15? I'm a child. I don't know how to be an adult. I don't have the mentality. I have no goals. I may think I'm fixing myself, but is that really true when I still have no idea where I'm going? How long can you really take it one day at a time before you miss your whole life? What do I want? I don't even know what I'm doing with Josh. What do I expect out of that? I'm saving up money to leave, but where am I going to go? I killed my friend.

I push away from Josh and stand up, wiping my eyes with the bottom of my shirt. He takes a few steps back, giving me some space to calm down. Within a few seconds of me finally pulling myself together, Will comes storming out of the house, his face red and his fists clenched tightly at his sides. He's walking right toward me, and I already know what's coming. I brace myself for the impact. No point in blocking it.

Before I know it, his fist hits me right on my cheekbone, sending me stumbling back against his car. My hand comes up, cupping my cheek. He's never hit me. All the times that he's ever looked like he was going to, or wanted to, he never has.

"Who gave you the right to talk to Katie like that?" he shouts. "Us, fine. Fight us, yell at us, blame us for everything. But do not *fuck* with people outside of this house!"

"Will, what the fuck, dude?" Josh says, stepping between us.

"Fuck no," Tyson yells at Will. "We do *not* get physical with each other! Will, go cool off!"

"He told Katie it was her fault Ian died," Will says, shoving his finger at me.

Tyson's face drops. "You didn't…"

I mean, I didn't… Not really, anyway. I *know* this is my fault. Katie was right when she told me that. But there's no point in fighting, so instead of explaining, I shrug.

"You told her that?" Josh asks.

Ah, this is familiar. *This* is what I've missed. Three against one. I know that anything I say right now won't be heard. They're waiting for me to fight back. Will absolutely wants to fight, and I'm considering it just to get it out of my system. But the way Josh is looking at me is grounding. He's waiting for an answer, actually listening. Plus, I'm worried that if I start a fight with Will, I won't stop.

Still holding his gaze, I shake my head, answering just him. "No. I didn't." I can't tell if it's a lie when it comes out of my mouth. I didn't tell her that…did I?

Josh nods, and the fact that he believes me shocks me. I was not expecting that.

"You prick. Yes, you fucking did." Will moves past Josh to stand in front of me again.

"No. I didn't." I push his shoulders back softly, just to get some space between us. "You should have heard the hateful shit she said to me, Will." My voice cracks. The tears are starting up again, I know they are. "You should have heard what she was saying to me. I went there to help. She called *me* and no one else. I showed up, and she attacked me. I said some stuff I shouldn't have, sure. But I never said it was her fault Ian's dead."

Those words again…

"What did you say to her?" Tyson asks me.

"Okay. No. I'm sorry, a good friend of mine just died. We're not going to make this one of those moments where I'm the guy everyone's gaining up on. I'm not having this conversation. Believe me or don't. I don't fucking care anymore. I'm used to it. You've never believed me in the past, and I don't expect that now. But either way, I need some space. Will, I hope you feel better after that." I gesture to my face. "I know Dad and I always do. Welcome to the club."

I walk past them into the house, slamming the front door behind me.

Looks like we've reentered phase one of healing.

Chapter 48

Three days. I haven't left my room for three days. Everyone is at the funeral, but I couldn't bring myself to go. I didn't want to ruin the day for Katie. So instead, I've been in my room listening to "I Lost a Friend" by FINNEAS on repeat. Dramatic, I know. But now that I've been branching out with music, I love finding things that understand how I'm feeling. It helps me feel not so alone.

I can hear the world outside moving, people talking, cars driving, everyone just living their lives. How have I gotten back to this? Back to the me that's self-loathing, not wanting to exist, hating myself. I don't even care when I see the next human. In times like these, I find myself melting into my bed. It physically hurts to think about moving.

I still can't wrap my head around the fact that my idea of "doing good" was being a dick to everyone. Katie was right. I did push everyone away because I thought I was better than them. Now I know I'm no better than anyone. I just exist.

My bedroom door opens and Josh peeks in. He comes in and crawls under the blanket with me. "Hi." I force a smile.

"How are you?"

"Not great," I answer with a sigh.

"I know. I tried giving you space, but that was as long as I could handle."

"No, I love having you around. I'm glad you came."

"I'm sorry about the situation the other day. I can't believe Will hit you."

I huff. "It's been a long time coming. I'm sorry you had to see that, Is he okay? I hate that we keep using our dad against each other. It's just the easiest way to hurt each other, I guess. I didn't want to be that person anymore, but I can't handle everyone being after me and against me. It feels like everyone just wants me to hate them, so I'll leave."

He sits up and touches my cheek to get me to look at him. "The world isn't out to get you, Jace. No one is out to get you. I know this isn't something you want to hear, but everyone's 'actions' around you are actually 'reactions' to the situation or the way you behave. It's been a rough life for you and them. A *really* rough life, and this has caused all of you to not have any communication skills. You all just act on impulse, and that impulse seems to always be anger."

My brows pull together, but I stay silent, letting his words sink in.

"I'm not saying that to be mean," he continues. "I'm sorry if it came out that way. I think you just deserve some honesty." He pulls me closer to him and kisses my chin.

I never thought of it like that. Now when I think about it, I can't remember us ever just sitting down to work out our problems. We are all reactive. When we argue, we don't listen and consider. We wait for our turn to yell, to try and force each other to hurt enough to break our guards down in hopes our point will make it across.

I softly smile and press my lips against his. "Thank you."

"Also, Will is fine. But I do think that what you said hurt him pretty bad. You should probably talk to him when you feel ready."

I nod. "Will used to be the angriest person in this house. I think he's grown more than I have. Or maybe I was just on drugs for so long that I wasn't worried about other feelings. These days, I get so mad so fast that I can't focus on anything else. I had the power stripped from me for so long. It feels good now to know I have it. I have the power to hurt people or make them feel as bad as I do."

"That sounds self-destructive." For the first time, his use of those words is no joke.

"Yeah, I guess so."

"You know, you don't have to use that power to make people feel bad. You can use that power to make people feel good. Make them feel better than other people make them feel. You're a great guy, you just don't know how to…be a human, for lack of better words. You're learning." He takes a breath and sits all the way up. "But…"

My eyes shoot to his. "But…?" My stomach drops; I have a feeling I know exactly where this is headed.

"I think you're in a bad place," Josh says. "Everything is so new to you, and you're learning how to live, and how to be… Ian's gone, and I know that's fucking you up, along with all these new feelings you have about who you are. You need time to grow, time for yourself. I asked you a while ago, as a joke, if I was one of your self-destructive efforts. But now I know I am. You can't keep hiding from yourself behind everything else."

"Wait. So you're breaking up with me? You said you weren't going to leave me because of these things. I told you everything with one fear. One fear that you were going to leave!"

"Hey." He pulls my hands to his lips. "I'm not leaving you because of who you are, or who you were. I'm leaving so you can become who you're supposed to be. You can't grow on your own if you can't even be happy or calm down without me. We haven't been together long. Let's stop now so it doesn't get complicated."

"Complicated?" I stand up from the bed and meet his eyes with mine. "Josh, it already is complicated. I *work* with you. I've told you things no one knows. I've trusted you. I…fuck. I love you, Josh."

I do. I love him. I knew I loved him after that party, in the car when I saw the way he was looking at me. I fucking love him, and it's a love I've never felt before. He can't be doing this. He told me he wasn't going to do this.

"I can't be with you knowing I'm holding you back. I can't and I won't be that guy. You need to find yourself on your own. You can't love me without loving yourself. And you have no idea who you are."

I sit back down on the bed with my head in my hands. "You couldn't have done this on a different day?"

His hand rubs a circle on my back. "What, let you mourn and then break you again? That hardly sounds fair."

"I should have known this would happen. This always happens to me. I'm so over being vulnerable to people. It used to be so much better when…" I cut myself off before I say anything stupid.

"When what?" he asks, but the tone in his voice tells me he already knows what I was going to say. "When you were high? When you were hardly even a person?"

I don't answer, which is answer enough. It's true, though. It was better when my only worry was when I'd get more pills or alcohol.

"Okay, the world is *not* out to get you," Josh says. "I don't know how many times I can tell you that. Cause and effect, Jace. You're a smart guy, and I know deep down this is exactly what you want. You live for the fire and the anger, you live by forcing big emotions to surface, you just choose hate to be the emotion."

"You think I enjoy this? You think I like watching everyone around me tiptoe around their words because they're worried I'm going to explode? You think I like the constant burning inside of me? I *don't* want this!" My words come loudly, but I'm not yelling; I'm holding back.

If Josh is going to leave me for the exact same thing he said he wouldn't leave me for, I want him to go on good terms, at least. I mean, I think I do. It would be easier to make him hate me. It would make more sense if he just hated me and that's why he left.

"You're the morally gray character in your own story, Jace! Look at yourself. This isn't how normal people act. You think everyone's out to get you when in fact *you* are out to get everyone. You can't keep holding people's pasts against them. You just straight-up hate everyone. I love you, Jace, I do. But you missed a lot growing up, and I don't think you're quite ready to give me what I want from you."

"Normal people. Nice. What does that make me, then, my own morally gray character? And what exactly is it that you want from me?"

"A future."

I inhale deeply because he's right. I can't give anyone a future when I'm so stuck on my day-to-day living. I realized it the other day. You can't go anywhere when you aren't trying to. "Fuck," I breathe.

"I wish it were different. But you're going to be great. You're going to do amazing things, and maybe sometime down the line, our paths will cross again."

"I understand. I do, really. Thank you for being so open. You're right, it's much better to have conversations like this rather than screaming at each other. Thank you for everything. I promise next time we meet, I'll be a whole new guy. You gave me a lot to think about. I suppose you should also consider this my official resignation."

"Stay in therapy, kid," Josh says with a laugh. "I've really enjoyed getting to know you and working with you. Are you going to be okay?"

It's the first time that question has meant something to me. Because it means he's leaving. He's actually leaving me.

"No. But I'll survive. I gotta, right?" I don't even try to stop myself from crying.

He pulls me up to stand in front of him. "Right." He smiles. "I do love you, Jace, and I swear this is hurting me just as much as it is you." He leans in and kisses me, lingering longer than normal. When he pulls away, he brushes his thumb against my cheek and walks out, leaving me standing in my room alone.

Back to square one. Back to January. Only this time, I don't even have the pills to keep me company. No friends, no siblings constantly bugging me, no boyfriend, no plans, no ambition. Nothing. Nothing but me and these thoughts, and that goddamn fucking buzzing.

I pull my window open, light a cigarette, and lean against the window frame. From here, I can see Josh walk to his car. He gets to the driver's side and looks back at me. We don't wave or smile. Nothing. I pull the cig up to my mouth again and inhale deeply.

He gets in, closes the door, and drives away. Taking with my entire heart, leaving me empty and numb. For the first time in my life, the numbness isn't a pleasant feeling. It makes me realize all that I've had and taken advantage of. I wish I was someone else, someone more deserving of this life. Someone more deserving of him who could give him everything he wants. That's not me, though. I've always known it wasn't me, but...

"Hour by hour, day by day," I whisper to myself. If it was only an hour I had with him, I'd take it. Selfishly, I'd take anything he was willing to give. I'm never going to forget him or the way he made me feel. I hate it, but I know I'll always love him.

Chapter 49

It's the weekend after the funeral, and apparently, we're hosting a lunch in memory of Ian. Why are we doing it? I don't fucking know. It's not our responsibility, but you know how we are: the most considerate people you'll ever meet. The house is chaotic. People I don't know fill the rooms, siblings are everywhere, Katie is still avoiding me, and some of Ian's friends are here too. It's really a wonderful time. I don't know whose idea it was, but we have cocktails—yes, cocktails are being offered at a memorial for an addict. There are drinks sitting all over the place, and I've never had a harder time convincing myself to not take one.

Suzie's voice comes from behind me. "Hey, brother."

"Hey." I smile and take a sip of my Coke.

"You know, Dean dies," she says matter-of-factly.

I turn toward her my brows pulled together. "Should I know what that means?"

She nods and smiles. "In our show we never finished. Dean dies at the end."

What the hell is she going on about? "Does he, now?" I ask skeptically.

"There's a whole speech thing he does with Sam before it happens. I just wanted to tell you that you should watch it sometime. Because everything he says, word for word, is how I feel about you. I know you've been going through a lot these past few weeks, even your first heartbreak. And I heard about what happened outside with the boys. I just wanted to tell you that I don't think you're a dick. I'm so proud of you and everything you're becoming. I've never seen you so strong. I love you. You'll always be the Dean to my Sam."

My mouth falls open. I'm at a loss for words. She always knows exactly what to say, and I've been so scared that she's hated me since all this shit started happening. She has no idea what these words mean to me.

"So I'm still the favorite brother?" I ask.

"Always."

"Are you telling me I'm going to die before you?"

"No, I just mean in the show, they're all each of them has. Dean dies, and Sam continues living his life just being human. You're going to get through everything bad that's happening, especially if your boy Sam can get through it."

"Come here." I pull her into me and give her the biggest hug I've ever given her. I got so lucky having her as my sister. "Thank you. I really needed that."

"I know. I haven't seen you come out of your room in almost a week. I'm trying not to worry about you, because you're allowed to be sad. But I figured I'd just let you know how I feel."

"You can worry about me. I'm sorry, I understand why all of you have been so up my ass. But I'm here. I'm here to stay. I've been through worse my whole life."

I'm not going to lie; I've been slipping back into depression again. Hard. But not in the same way.

I haven't thought about dying or disappearing. The one thing that's getting unbearable is the craving to be high, to the point where I've almost told Tyson about it so we could figure out what to do, even if it means going to rehab or the psych ward. I decided against it. It's already a hard time for all of us.

"Like I said," Suzie continues, "I've never seen you so strong. I can still see life and hope in your eyes. But I've missed you." She looks across the room to where Max is standing. "I'm going to head back over to him. I love you, Jace."

"Love you, Suz."

It's becoming weird how often my family is throwing around the L word these days. Not a bad weird, but it's weird for sure. I walk past a table decorated with a few bottles of liquor that make my mouth water. It's been a year. I could say I deserve just one drink…

I spot Katie by the fridge. Leaning against the counter next to her, I nudge her. "Hey…"

She doesn't look at me. "Hi."

"Listen, I'm sorry for what I said. I didn't mean it. I'm not sure why it came out of my mouth. You hurt me, and I just…"

"Wanted to hurt me back? That's not very healthy."

"Me, not healthy? You said some fucked-up shit to me first. I was there to help. Do you want to know why I was ignoring him when he called that day? I was ignoring him because—"

"You know, Jace, I don't really care. You used to be my best friend, but I got kicked from that position with no warning and no forgiveness. So, no. I don't really give a shit about your excuses. I'm over it, and I'm done with you. Okay?" She sips her water and pushes past me.

I'm done with you. She may as well have told me I was dead to her. I wonder how different everyone's lives would be if I actually had died that day. Less fucked up, I'm sure.

"Jace, could you grab some towels out of Dad's bathroom? Some dipshit spilled everywhere," Tyson says, pulling me out of my thoughts as he runs into the kitchen.

"I'm not a dipshit! I said I was sorry!" some kid next to Will yells back. They're sitting around the coffee table in the living room looking like they're in an intense game of cards.

"Yeah, sure." After glancing at the bottles one more time, I go to Dad's still-empty room. Everything around me is in a sort of tunnel vision. People blur past, and I hear the faded voices from conversations nearby.

I'm not doing well at all. I don't doubt this is an anxiety attack about to surface. I miss Josh and Katie; I miss Ian. I had a group of people around me, and I pushed them all away in the span of a few months. I don't even know what to do next or where to go after today. It's been so long since I've been alone, and now I truly am alone.

The door to Dad's bathroom creaks as it opens. I reach in, take the towels from the rack, and turn to leave. But just as I do, I see a bottle of prescription pills on the counter next to the sink. A quick peek around the door tells me no one's around. I don't know why I do it, but I pick up the bottle and read it. Lorazepam. It has my mom's name on it.

"Jace! The towels!" Tyson yells from the living room.

"Yeah! Coming." I shove the bottle into my pocket.

Out in the living room, everything is normal. People are standing, sitting, talking, eating. There are drinks all around, and I can tell some people have had more than enough. It's crazy how the world keeps going even when you don't.

"Here. Sorry, I didn't mean to take so long."

"You're good, thanks. If there weren't twenty people showering in this house, there would have been some in our bathroom. I just don't want this red shit to stain!"

I look down at the white rug and chuckle. I'm not sure why he thinks towels are going to help that. It looks pretty done for.

"Hey, I'm going to go to my room for a bit," I tell him. "I'm not really feeling up to a party."

"You sure?" he asks, scrubbing the red deeper into the rug.

"Yeah, I just need a bit."

He nods and waves me off. On my way to my room, I stop in the kitchen. God knows I could use some food. I palm two premade sandwiches Will probably bought from the store earlier. They don't look great, but they'll do. As I'm walking out, I see a bottle of Jameson on the table that hasn't been opened. I close my eyes, snatch it, and speed walk out of the kitchen.

As I turn toward my room, I feel someone looking at me. I look over my shoulder and my eyes meet Josh's.

They invited him here? What the fuck…and he came? His gaze drops down to my hand. The bottle is hidden behind my leg, but I'm sure he didn't miss it. When his eyes look back at mine, they're filled with an emotion I don't understand. Disappointment, maybe? If not, it's something similar. I blink a few times, turn away, and continue rushing back to my room.

Why would they have him here? It feels like my heart is breaking all over again, the memories of everything between us flowing back to me: in the driveway of my house the first time, every passing glance at work, the first time we kissed, watching him at the gym, telling him about therapy. The car ride with Ian.

Ian. His memories flow in just as hard. The park bench where we had our first conversation. He didn't even have a favorite color. He didn't know himself just as much as I didn't. He was my first kiss, my first experience with anything natural for me.

Lately, I haven't been me. I haven't been the old Jace or the new Jace, I've just…been. Anxiety attacks have replaced the anger, attacks that I keep to myself, crying in my room just wishing it would end.

I put the bottle on my desk and set the pill bottle next to it. A slight smile finds my face. What a nostalgic feeling. If Josh came in here right now, or Will, I'd probably have my ass handed to me.

I sigh and sit down at my desk with the two bottles before me, one whose amber contents are calling to me like an old friend, the other promising the numb, thoughtless feelings I crave. My mind swirls in a whirlpool of despair, and the choice is simple.

One voice whispers, "Just one sip to numb the pain," while another counters, "You've come so far, don't let it all slip away."

Both the loss of Ian, and Josh leaving, punched a fiery hole through me, forcing old wounds to resurface, and the pain is unbearable. My hands tremble as my fingers inch closer to the bottles, and in that fragile moment, I feel as though I'm wrestling with the past and the present, with hope and despair, with a story that could still be written or forever rewritten. The decision hangs heavy in the air, as uncertain as my future. A choice left to me and only me. The power consumes me, overwhelms me, and brings that same sense of control back, rushing over me.

I knew what I was going to do before I came in here. I lean back in the chair and close my eyes.

Fuck.

About the Author

Anzley Lukehart is Utah native who recently made the leap to Oklahoma to fulfill her family's dream of starting a micro farm. With the support of her wonderful husband and two amazing kids, she is finally jumping into that exciting adventure while also pursuing her passion for writing. Getting an English degree has been a dream of hers, and she's thrilled to be on that journey while also creating her own stories. When not locked into reading, working, or writing, Anzley loves to be outside soaking in the sun. While she used to enjoy hiking, camping and lake swimming in the beautiful Utah mountains, she is now creating garden blueprints, finding bugs with the kids, and playing with her chickens. Growing up, she had an amazing example set by her mom, who did everything on her own—including going to school, working a full-time job, and having a baby—with a smile on her face. Her example inspires Anzley to create and explore, both in the pages of books and in the way she lives.